Rim

New Beginnings for the Surplus Girls

Polly Heron has worked as a librarian specialising in work with schools and children, an infant teacher, a carer and a cook. She lives in Llandudno in North Wales with her husband and two rescue cats, but her writing is inspired by her Mancunian roots. She enjoys reading, gardening, needlework and cooking and she loves living by the sea. Polly also writes as Susanna Bavin and Maisie Thomas.

Also by Polly Heron

POLLY HERON

New Beginnings for the Surplus Girls

CORVUS

Published in paperback in Great Britain in 2023 by Corvus,
an imprint of Atlantic Books Ltd.

10 9 8 7 6 5 4 3 2

A CIP catalogue record for this book is available from
the British Library.

Paperback ISBN: 978 1 83895 237 2
E-book ISBN: 978 1 83895 238 9

Printed in Great Britain by CPI Group (UK) Ltd,
Croydon CR0 4YY

Corvus
An imprint of Atlantic Books Ltd
Ormond House
26–27 Boswell Street
London
WC1N 3JZ

www.corvus-books.co.uk

To the memory of
Gladys Edith Hope Cook
(*née* Wilmore, 1929–1994)

And to Gary, Kevin and Des

Chapter One

New Year's Day 1923

'MISS MASON, COOK says can you come, only the grocer's lad and the chap from the dairy have arrived both at the same time and she needs a hand unpacking and checking.'

Jess looked at Ivy, a well-meaning, awkward girl who, according to Cook, was good for peeling veg and washing up and not much else. Certainly not for checking deliveries.

'Thank you, Ivy. I'll be there directly.' Jess glanced round the hotel foyer, with its wood panelling and parlour palms. It was empty of guests at present. She turned to Angela, smiling at the fifteen-year-old. 'Will you be all right on your own for a few minutes, Miss Hitchcock?'

'Yes, Miss Mason,' Angela replied with warmth. 'Happy to.'

That was no surprise. Angela loved nothing more than to be behind the reception desk. Not that she was ever given any responsibility as such, but when the boss's daughter asked and the boss didn't say no... Jess headed for the kitchen at the back of the building, where crisp winter sunshine poured through the windows, striking the donkey-brown floor-tiles and transforming them into rich bronze. The big wooden table on which Cook prepared food was covered with boxes of foodstuff.

'There you are, Miss Mason.' Cook looked relieved. 'Can you help me tick everything off?'

Jess smiled to herself as she set to, deducing from the various items what Cook would soon be making. Oranges and walnuts meant orange tea bread; lemons and cooking apples meant taffety tart; while the extra eggs and dried apricots were for Cook's special twelfth night pie, which would be served this coming Saturday and all the diners would be warned to watch out for the coins buried inside for luck.

'Folk come from miles around for my twelfth night pie,' Cook was fond of saying and it wasn't much of an exaggeration.

Jess finished checking her list and left Cook putting everything away at the same time as she scolded Ivy for making eyes at the grocer's boy. As she opened the door to return to the foyer, Jess saw Mr and Mrs Gulliver at the reception desk, their suitcases at their feet. They were a well-dressed couple, pleasant and appreciative. Everyone liked them. Everyone! That made it sound as if the Sea View Hotel employed dozens of staff instead of being a small concern that had been in the hands of the Hitchcocks for twenty years.

Angela was behind the polished desk, beaming at the guests. Normally Jess would have come forward at that point to take Mr Gulliver's payment, but this morning she hung back, giving Angela a chance to prove herself. As a rule, all Angela did was give guests directions using the street-map or take bookings for the dining room, but she had watched guests settling up on many occasions and Jess had explained the process to her several times, preparing her for the day when she would be permitted, under Jess's watchful eye, to take a payment herself.

'Thank you for everything,' Mrs Gulliver said as her husband wrote a cheque. 'We've enjoyed our stay with you very much.'

Angela smiled back. 'I hope you'll stay with us again the next time you treat yourselves to a seaside holiday.'

Jess smiled. Angela had picked up that line from her.

'I'm sure we shall,' said Mrs Gulliver.

Mr Gulliver replaced the cap on his fountain pen and glanced at the front door. Mr Tenby, the old chap who in these post-war days acted as doorman, porter and boot-boy, picked up the Gullivers' handsome leather suitcases, standing aside for the guests to lead the way. Jess pushed open the door and hurried to the desk. Angela had been so busy smiling and enjoying her role that she hadn't looked at the cheque. Jess twitched it from her fingers and examined it, her heart delivering a thump.

The front door had already shut behind the departing couple. Jess hastened after them.

From the top of the steps, she called, 'Mr Gulliver! Excuse me.'

At the foot of the steps, the Gullivers looked round. Their Morris Oxford was parked in front, ready for them to leave. Jess walked down the steps. She mustn't cause embarrassment by seeming to chase them, even if that was what she was doing.

'I'm sorry, Mr Gulliver,' she said quietly, 'but you've made an error on your cheque. You've written the wrong year.'

'Have I? Oh, so I have. A slip of the pen – easily done.'

'If you wouldn't mind popping back inside,' Jess murmured, waving him ahead of her while smiling apologetically at his wife. Courtesy at all times was the first rule of the hotel trade, no matter how trying certain times might be.

Mr Gulliver didn't return to the desk but stopped by a side-table, unfastening his overcoat and producing his pen from the inside pocket of his jacket. Jess handed him the cheque. 'If you'd kindly alter the year, then sign where you've made the change, sir. Thank you.'

Mr Gulliver did as she asked before returning the cheque with a smile and an apology. Jess looked at what he had written.

'Thank you, sir.'

He raised his trilby, said goodbye and left. Jess sighed. Now she had to give Angela a talking-to, but in such a way that the girl would neither sulk nor fly in floods of tears to her parents. After all, though the fault was Angela's, the responsibility lay with Jess because, when Mr Hitchcock wasn't there, she was in charge of the reception desk. Mr Hitchcock was a decent old stick and Jess knew he valued her because she was hard-working, capable and willing. Mrs Hitchcock valued her for the same reasons, but also for the additional reason that Jess was female and could therefore be taken advantage of. Jess resented that, but it was the way of the world, so she had to put up with it. At least she was accorded more freedom and responsibility here than in her previous jobs. There was a lot to be said for that.

Angela's chin wobbled. 'I'm sorry.'

'Ninety-nine times out of a hundred, it wouldn't matter that you hadn't checked.' Jess judged a bracing tone was needed rather than a scolding one. 'It so happens this was the hundredth time.'

'Lots of people carry on writing the old year at the beginning of the new year.'

'Yes, they do, and often the banks will honour those cheques,' said Jess, 'but Mr Gulliver didn't put 1922. He put 1921 and no bank would accept that. If your father had presented the cheque to the bank, it would have been refused. At that point, we would have written to the Gullivers... and found out if they had signed the register with their genuine address.'

Angela gulped. 'You mean they were confidence tricksters. But they seemed so *nice*.'

'I don't know whether they were tricksters or not. They may have been perfectly honest. Since the error was rectified, let's give them the benefit of the doubt. Cheer up. Consider this an important lesson.'

'Yes, Miss Mason. I promise I won't make the same mistake again.'

Dead right you won't. Angela wasn't the only one who had learned something. Jess had too. After all the instruction Angela had received from her, Jess would have expected her to have the sense to ask the Gullivers to wait a few moments while she fetched Jess from the kitchen.

'Miss Mason, can I have a word, love?'

It was Elsie Tippett. Elsie had worked at the Sea View as a cleaner ever since her parents had hoicked her out of school at the age of ten to start contributing to the family coffers. How long ago that was Jess didn't know. Suffice it to say that Elsie, stick-thin and stooped, was now a grandmother, but she could give the young chambermaids a run for their money when it came to elbow grease.

'What is it, Elsie?' Jess asked.

'I've been sent for, urgent, miss. Our Bert, that's our Betty's oldest, has broke his leg and the bone's sticking out so he's been carted off to hospital.'

'Goodness, what a start to the year for him,' said Jess.

'So I'm needed to watch over the little 'uns and the babby. Can I go, miss? You can see how it is.'

'Of course you must go. I hope Bert will be all right.'

'I've done everything but polish the front stairs and the foyer.'

'Don't give it a thought. Go and see to your family.'

Elsie disappeared. Jess glanced at Angela. Had the girl been a proper member of staff, Jess could have asked her to muck in and finish the polishing, but Angela only 'helped out', as her father put it, even though she longed to be part of the family business. Helping out, as Jess had learned in no uncertain terms from Angela's mother, did not include cleaning.

'Will you remain on reception, please, Miss Hitchcock? If anyone wishes to purchase a street-map for tuppence, you may sell them one, but anything that involves a larger financial transaction must be referred to me.'

Angela blushed. 'Yes, Miss Mason.'

Jess put on an apron and folded back the sleeves on the dark-blue dress she wore for work. Its waist was a little on the high side for the new fashion, but although Jess was competent enough with a needle, she lacked the skill for what would have been for her an ambitious alteration. Besides, there seemed to be an expectation that women in the workplace should be dowdy, as if they were meant to blend into the background and not attract attention. Talking of dowdy, she couldn't help raising a hand to her hair. She had wanted to have it cut into one of these new bobs, but Mrs Hitchcock had refused to let her. Shorter hair on a woman gave the wrong impression, apparently, and judging by the way Mrs Hitchcock sucked in her cheeks when she said it, the wrong impression involved dark desires and inappropriate availability. So Jess had been stuck with keeping her hair long. She had taken to wearing it smooth against her head, with the back tucked up into a bun while the sides were plaited and coiled around to be woven – or more likely, stuffed – inside the bun. She had, however, had a fringe cut into her hair, as bare foreheads seemed very old-fashioned.

Jess set to work on the smooth banister rails, enjoying the scent of the lavender polish. She never minded helping out in whatever way was needed. It was something she found pride in, even though she knew the Hitchcocks sometimes took advantage.

Mrs Hitchcock hadn't been best pleased when her husband had chosen Jess for this job, but she had soon changed her mind, as Jess had discovered to her chagrin when she overheard Mrs Hitchcock discussing her with a friend.

'My dear, the beauty of employing a girl is that she has to work twice as hard as a man to prove she's worth her salt. Plus, you don't have to pay her anything like as much.'

Jess rubbed away at the spiral-twisted spindles beneath the banister-rail with renewed vigour, imagining she was rubbing the complacent expression off Mrs Hitchcock's face.

'Miss Mason.'

Jess hastily rearranged her thoughts. 'Yes, Mr Hitchcock?'

'Could I see you in my office, please?'

'Of course, sir. I'll be there in a minute.'

She removed the apron and put away the polish and cloth in the cleaning-box before rolling down her sleeves and fastening her cuffs. She took a moment to check her hair. She had the same colouring as her late mother; dark hair, dark eyes. Poor Mum, dying like that. The influenza after the war had been so cruel.

Jess went to the office. Mr Hitchcock hadn't left the door open for her. She knocked.

'Come.'

'Ah – Miss Mason.' Mr Hitchcock made it sound as if he had sent for her hours ago.

Jess waited to be offered a seat, but the invitation wasn't given. Was she in trouble? Mr Hitchcock glanced at her and half-smiled, then changed his mind and frowned. What was going on?

'Miss Mason, you've heard me speak of my son, Rodney.' Mr Hitchcock stopped.

'Yes.' Jess tried to ease things along. 'And his family.' Talk about breeding like rabbits.

'Quite so. His family. The thing is,' and now Mr Hitchcock looked directly at her, talking in a rush, 'Rodney has lost his job and needs a new one. He has a family to support.'

Jess started to say, 'I'm sorry to hear that,' but Mr Hitchcock bowled on as if she hadn't spoken.

'So he'll be coming here to work at the Sea View.'

'I see.' Jess was taken aback. 'In what capacity, if I might ask?'

'In – well, to be blunt, in your capacity. I'm sorry, Miss Mason, but your services will no longer be required.'

Chapter Two

JESS GAZED OUT of the window at the snowy landscape as the train approached Annerby, but she didn't really see anything. She still felt cold and fluttery with shock. She hadn't merely lost her job; she had lost it on the spot. The Hitchcocks hadn't even wanted her to stay on until their son was in residence, let alone until he had been trained up. That smacked of a guilty conscience, thought Jess. They felt rotten for dumping her – well, Mr Hitchcock did, but Jess didn't kid herself that his wife felt bad on her behalf.

'It's a proper shame, that's what it is,' Cook had said when Jess went to say goodbye. 'You deserve better, Miss Mason. I hope you find another position soon. Will you look for hotel work again?'

For a moment, Jess couldn't speak. Look for hotel work? She would be looking for *any* work. 'I'll see what's available.' She forced herself to use an airy voice. 'Mr Hitchcock has promised me a good reference.'

'And so he should after everything you've done here.'

Mr Hitchcock had also made up her wages not just to the end of this week, but to the end of next week.

'To give you a bit of breathing space,' he told her. 'But not a word to anyone, mind,' which meant he didn't want Mrs Hitchcock to find out.

At the promise of extra money, Jess had felt tears of gratitude rising and she'd felt ashamed of herself for that. She didn't want to be beholden to the man who had just sacked her, but she couldn't afford to refuse. She needed to find a new job as soon as possible, before she was forced to dip into her precious savings.

Now she was arriving back in her hometown. The train coasted alongside the platform. The rhythmic chuffing sound ceased and the brakes shrieked as the mighty machine slowed. Even before it halted, doors were flung open and people started alighting. This was the end of the line and everyone had to get off, but Jess stayed put for a minute, letting other passengers disappear, reluctant to risk bumping into anybody she knew on the platform. Was she being daft?

Standing up, she fastened her coat and reached up to take her carpetbag from the net luggage rack, then picked up her handbag. Stepping down onto the platform, she walked along to the guard's van, where the porter was unloading boxes onto his wooden sack-trolley.

'My trunk is in the corner over there.' Jess pointed. 'It says "Miss J. Mason" on the label. If you put it in the luggage room, I'll arrange for it to be collected.'

She tipped him a sixpence and made her way to the ticket-barrier where the collector, in his smart uniform and polished buttons, took her ticket.

Outside the station, Jess paused. The air was bright and fresh with snow, but she missed the sea air. She had loved living by the sea. People thought that when you worked in a seaside hotel, it must be like being on holiday all the time, but actually it was jolly hard graft. Not that she minded hard work. She liked to be busy and the more varied the work, the better.

On the same side of the road as the station stood the grand Station Hotel. Maybe she could get a job there. She didn't really want to live here in Annerby, but it wasn't easy for a woman to get a good job. Surely, though, with the experience she had under her belt, she stood a reasonable chance.

Wrapping her fingers securely around the handle of her carpetbag, she headed along the road. A sandwich-board on the pavement outside a newsagent's declared in black capitals:

ANCIENT
EGYPTIAN
KING –
LATEST

Presumably the board wasn't wide enough for TUTANKHAMUN. And was Jess alone in finding it amusing there should be 'latest' news about someone who had died all those hundreds of years ago?

How long would it be before her own 'latest' was spread around? The neighbours would be pleased. Although one or two of them had secretly told her they admired her for leaving home to earn a living, the overriding attitude was that her duty lay very much in the home, and she had no business abandoning her poor, widowed father.

Talk of the devil. There were Mrs Clothall and Mrs Bennett across the road. Jess pinned on a smile and called a greeting, but didn't stop walking and certainly didn't cross the road. She picked up her pace, keeping to the narrow path that had been trodden through the snow. If she walked through the market, she'd get home quicker – oh no. She groaned silently. Here was Mrs Bryce coming towards her – and in full view of the two across the street. That meant she would have to stop and exchange a few words – either that, or walk away weighed down by the certainty of the old gossip that would be gleefully resurrected.

'Good afternoon, Mrs Bryce.' Jess stopped, gripping the handle of her carpetbag. 'How are you?'

'Hello, Jess.' Mrs Bryce's hair, which Jess always thought of as salt-and-pepper, was now grey. She still wore the same wispy fringe and bun under her hat. Mind you, the same could be said for Jess's hairstyle. 'Fair to middling, thank you. Here to visit your dad, are you?'

Jess grasped the handle even tighter. The truth behind her ignominious return would get around soon enough, but Drew's mother wasn't going to be the first to know. 'Yes,' was all she said.

'He'll be pleased to see you. Give him my best.'

'Thank you. I will.'

There was an awkward moment. It was all right for Mrs Bryce to mention Dad, but Jess couldn't reciprocate by mentioning Drew.

'Well, I'd best get on,' said Mrs Bryce and they parted.

Jess entered the cobbled market square, where the savoury aroma of freshly made pasties mingled with the tang of dried herbs and the full-bodied scent of the soil that clung to the potatoes on the vegetable stalls. It was said hereabouts that you could buy anything in the Annerby market. Having lived away from here, Jess wasn't so sure about that, but it was still a pleasure to glimpse the many different goods for sale – everything from books and second-hand clothes to cough-drops and old musical instruments, not to mention the vast array of foods. Some of the stallholders, after years of crying their wares, had damaged their voice-boxes and employed young lads to do the calling for them.

Jess walked through the market and out the other side in the direction of the hill. Annerby sat in a valley floor. Steep hills stood to either side, with moorland at the top. The oldest houses were in rows at the foot of the hill and the higher you went, the newer the houses became. Not that any of them were particularly new. At the bottom were mean little lanes of cottages. Then came larger dwellings in roads named after flowers; and above these were streets named after birds. Above all of these roads was a gap and then came the biggest houses, where the posh folk lived, looking down on the plebs.

Jess had grown up in one of the flower streets – Clover Lane, which might sound pretty and countrified, but the flower and bird streets had been built when the factories came to Annerby. Had the bosses thought that fancy road names would make the workers think they lived somewhere appealing?

Jess made her way along Clover Lane and opened the door to her childhood home, a narrow house with the tiniest of lobbies inside the front door. Walking through into the parlour, she set down her carpetbag, feeling the echoes of the past settle around her. The shock of losing her job had taken her breath away. Now, back in the house that so many folk believed was the right and proper place for the unmarried daughter of a widowed father, she felt defeated. The pressure to conform, to be a good daughter, would bombard her from all sides when word got round that she was unemployed. It had been bad enough when she had come here on visits, disapproval hanging heavily in the air, so thick she could almost taste its sourness. Now – now everyone would expect her to stay put.

And she didn't want to. She loved Dad and she loved Annerby, but her life had moved on. She had different expectations now. She had – and she didn't care if it sounded unwomanly – ambition. She wanted a good job, a responsible job, and she knew she was capable of it. It wasn't just ambition either. It was necessity.

Here in Clover Lane, a husband, a fiancé and two sweethearts hadn't come home from the war – four men from Clover Lane alone. And Clover Lane was just one of the flower streets, the flower streets just one section of the town. If every road in the kingdom was similar to Clover Lane, how many widows were there now? How many girls wore their engagement rings on chains around their necks, tucked away beneath their blouses instead of on their ring fingers? And that was just the women in official relationships. How many bereaved were there altogether? If two lasses in Clover Lane had lost their potential husbands, how many girls must there be countrywide in the same position? And it wasn't just the girls who had been walking out with a fellow. It was all the girls who hadn't yet met the right chap – and now never would because he had copped it in Flanders.

Too many girls and not enough men.

It was a scary thought – well, it was if you wanted to get wed, which Jess didn't after the way she had been let down. But she couldn't help thinking of all those girls from time to time. Surplus girls – that was what they were called. What was going to happen to them? Were they supposed to rely on their fathers and brothers to support them? Or would they, like her, decide to be independent and work for their living? If they did, they'd soon find, as she had, that the world of work didn't always look kindly upon women.

Just what did she imagine she was up to, standing here, lost in thought? Dad wouldn't be impressed if he could see her.

'Run out of steam, have you?' he would say, not troubling to hide the sneer that had become common once she had decided to earn her daily bread. 'Too full of fancy ways to soil your hands with housework?'

Jess took off her hat and unfastened her coat, hanging it up before going to the fireplace. Dad had banked up the fire before going to work at the furniture factory and she quickly got it going again, taking a couple of lumps of coal from the scuttle to help get the room warm. Should she start with some dusting or should she polish the brass pieces that had been Mum's pride and joy? But as she looked round, she realised the parlour was spick and span. She hadn't seen it looking like this since Mum died. Was Mrs Douglas spending more time here? She was the neighbour from over the road whom Dad paid to do his washing and keep the house ticking over, but Dad's idea of ticking over was very different to Jess's. On previous visits home, it had grieved her as well as making her feel guilty to see the house looking a little less cared for each time. Mum would have played merry heck, but Dad wasn't fussed about the looking-glass not sparkling or the oak dresser not smelling of polish.

'Your dad pays me to do the weekly wash,' Mrs Douglas had told her, 'and he pays me for one hour of housework, which includes the time spent ironing. He's a man, love. Dust is invisible to him.'

Now, Jess looked admiringly around the parlour, taking in the golden glow on the horse-brasses and the sheen on the tiles in the fire-surround, which had clearly been washed and buffed up with velvet. Even the silver-plated rose-bowl, which had been dull on every previous visit and which she had herself polished each time, winked at her in the firelight.

Jess felt warm inside. What a lovely homecoming, and so unexpected. She smiled. Mum must have come back and haunted Dad until he dug deeper in his pocket and paid Mrs Douglas to do a proper job.

There was a knock at the door. Jess was still smiling as she answered it. Her smile widened when she saw who it was.

'Mrs Douglas, come in. How nice to see you. I was going to pop over and thank you.'

'Thank me?'

'All this.' As they entered the parlour, Jess waved a hand. 'It hasn't looked this good since… well, since Mum. I'm very grateful. I'm glad Dad has finally—' She stopped. She didn't want to suggest Dad had previously been mean.

'Oh – you know, then?'

'I can see it.' Jess sniffed, inhaling the scent of polish and remembering her beloved mum. 'I can smell it too. He's obviously coughing up for a proper amount of housework, and not before time.'

'Nay, lass. This weren't me.'

'Has he taken on a different cleaner?'

Mrs Douglas drew in her chin, making her fleshy neck swell. 'Well, he's taken on a new summat.'

'What d'you mean?'

'Your dad's got himself a new lady-friend. Didn't you know? She's the one what's bringing the house up to scratch. Making herself indispensable, I reckon.'

'You might have told me.' Try as she might, Jess couldn't keep the note of accusation out of her voice.

'Oh aye?' Dad wasn't about to give an inch. 'And how was I supposed to do that when you're never here? You didn't visit as Christmas.'

'It's a busy time in the hotel trade,' said Jess. 'I've explained that before. And you could have written.'

'To the daughter that never writes to me?'

'I used to write, Dad, every single week, but you never answered.'

'Letter-writing is women's work.'

Jess sighed. It was an old argument. Dad just didn't understand how dispiriting it was to write letters and never receive a reply. After a few months of feeling fed up and unappreciated, Jess's letter-writing had tailed off.

They were in the parlour in front of the fire. Dad was sitting in his armchair with Jess sitting on the hearthrug, where she had knelt down to pull off his boots, like she had when she was a child. She hoisted a smile into position.

'Anyway, I know now. Mrs Douglas says it's a Mrs Nolan from the bird streets.'

'Well, if you've heard it all from Mrs Douglas…'

'Come on, Dad.' Jess swivelled to kneel beside his chair and slide an arm around his shoulders. 'All Mrs Douglas said was that she's a widow with no children. Why don't you tell me about her?'

'Are you?' Dad's expression softened and he looked vulnerable. Was he remembering Mum?

'Of course I am. You need looking after.'

'Says the daughter who refused to stop at home and do it.'

The dig was vexing; it made her feel guilty too. He was never going to let her forget. Jess got to her feet and sat in the other chair. Mum's chair. Did Mrs Nolan sit here now?

'Dad, please don't let's go over that again. You know what made me leave Annerby. I needed work – and not the factory job I'd have got if I'd stopped here. I'm a surplus girl and that means it's down to me to support myself for the rest of my life. I'll never earn what a man gets, but I need to work somewhere that doesn't pay rock-bottom wages to women; and if I'm to work until I'm old, I want a job that's interesting and worthwhile.'

Dad shook his head and cast his gaze up to the ceiling. 'Get off your soap-box, Jess. I've heard it all before.'

Aye, heard – but never truly listened.

The mouth-watering aroma of onion gravy drifted through from their dark little kitchen. Jess got up to see to the meal.

Maybe Dad would be more amenable afterwards. Mum always said he was grumpy until he'd eaten.

Jess placed the table felt on top of their old drop-leaf table and laid the cloth over the top, smoothing it and taking a moment to lift one of the corners to run her fingertips over the flowers. As a bride, Mum had embroidered her tablecloth with marigolds. Jess glanced across at the rose-bowl and at the figurine on the mantelpiece, of a cat playing the fiddle. What would become of Mum's pretty things if Dad married Mrs Nolan? It wasn't a question the daughter who had upped and left was entitled to ask.

There had only been one chop in the meat-safe, but Jess had popped out earlier to buy a second one for herself, extra vegetables, and mutton to make into a stew tomorrow.

As he tucked in, Dad nodded approvingly. 'You've got your mother's touch.'

Jess smiled to herself. The secret ingredient in Mum's gravy had always been a drop of Lea & Perrins. No matter how lovely Mrs Nolan was, Dad would never forget Mum's gravy.

'When am I going to meet Mrs Nolan?' Jess asked.

Dad shrugged. 'Soon. More to the point, what brings you here? It's not like you to fetch up out of the blue. The one time you do put pen to paper is to tell me to expect you.'

Jess's mouth dried up. She put down her knife and fork. 'I've lost my job.'

Dad's head jerked up. 'What? Another one? I don't know how you have the nerve to talk about supporting yourself into your old age. You can't hang onto any position for more than five minutes.'

'That's not true. I had to give up my first job to a returning soldier and I've lost this job for a similar reason. And the job in between – I didn't tell you at the time, but there was a man who couldn't keep his hands to himself. I complained, but he denied it and I ended up having to leave.'

'You should have said. I'd have gone along and given him a good hiding.'

'Dad, I worked fifty miles away in those days.'

'I'd still have done it.'

'Thanks, Dad.'

'But you can't blame him, can you? Not when you think about it. A girl who ups sticks and leaves home to live all that way away: what does that say about her, eh? He probably thought you were flighty, and if he did, you've only yourself to blame.'

Chapter Three

TOM WOKE EARLY, as he usually did. 'It's because I'm a builder,' he would say in a jokey way if it came up in conversation. 'We always have an early start.' The bit about the early start was true, but it wasn't the reason he woke up before the rest of the world. It was down to the war. On winter mornings like this, he would lie in the darkness, imagining thousands upon thousands of men all over the country, and all over other countries too, lying awake because... it was safer than sleeping.

He had heard of men who, in the depths of sleep, would yell their heads off as they dreamed of the horrors they had witnessed. He had never done that, never shouted in his sleep, but he did dream, he knew he did. He never remembered the dreams afterwards, but he knew he'd had them. Sometimes they made him weep in his sleep. He pictured it as his dreams hiding behind a long black curtain that, awake, he was unable to draw aside... but then, why would he want to? At the same time, not looking at his dreams, not showing that courage, left him feeling ashamed.

But he was lucky, better off than most. He lived in a comfortable home, with Mum spoiling him rotten, and he had a loving family – Dad, Mum and three sisters, all married, a whole platoon of nieces and one nephew. Tom adored his nieces, but Danny, Molly's lad, was extra special, being the only boy. He was eleven. Molly and Aaron had adopted him when they got married last summer and Tom reckoned that young Danny was the best present the Watson family had even received. He smiled in the darkness. There was to be another 'present' from Molly this coming summer. She would be twenty-eight by the time the child was born. Tom had overheard the tail-end of a whispered conversation between his other two sisters, Tilda and Christabel, about how twenty-eight was ever so old for having a first baby and Molly would need to have a special eye kept on her. But Tom knew this wasn't Molly's first baby. She'd borne a love-child during the war, a little boy she had been obliged to hand over to be adopted, because she was unwed and the baby's father had been killed in action. Not that Tom would ever tell anybody. It was Molly's secret, not his.

He had a big enough secret of his own.

Now then, now then, he chided himself. That was the trouble with trains of thought. They often led where you didn't want them to go. He had always been an optimistic person. It had been easy to be an optimist, growing up in the Watson family, where there was plenty of love and enough money to get by comfortably. That optimism, that cheerful acceptance of the good in life, had been hammered out of him during the war. Now he was trying to grow it back.

It was a straightforward enough thing to do on the surface. On the surface, there was his family and his job. On the surface, there was the gratitude for himself and his brothers-in-law having come home complete with the requisite number of arms, legs, eyes and lungs.

Underneath he still struggled with knowing that Billy and Joe, his mates ever since school, were gone for ever. He struggled with the sight of disabled ex-soldiers standing on street corners, selling matches; with seeing fatherless families in church; and with hearing war widows and elderly bereaved mothers asking shopkeepers for yesterday's loaves and fruit that had gone over, because they couldn't afford the fresh stuff. By the stars, war was a cruel business. It wasn't just the killing and maiming that happened on the battlefield. It was the difficulties and despair that dragged on afterwards. It was knowing there was never going to be any let-up.

Perkins and Watson, the family building company, did a bit to help. They didn't charge war widows for small jobs, repairs and such, replacing a missing roof-tile, re-hanging a dropped door, mending broken steps. The women were grateful, but that made Tom feel guilty. The least their country owed these women was a pension sufficient to cover basic repairs on top of the week's housekeeping.

Tom sat up and swung himself out of bed, pushing his feet into his slippers before padding across to light the gas-lamp on the wall. There was a soft *pop* and inside the tulip-shaped glass shade, the flame glowed. Tom turned the little winder underneath to adjust it.

He'd had this bedroom since coming home from the war. The Watsons lived in a semi with two double bedrooms and a decent-sized boxroom and, as the only lad, he'd been given the boxroom as his bedroom when they were all children. But when he and Molly returned home after the war, with Chrissie and Tilda both married by then, Mum had put Molly in the boxroom and awarded Tom the big bedroom. Nothing had ever been said and Molly hadn't objected. It was just what happened when you had a son and a daughter both at home. The son got the best.

Now Molly was married and living with her Aaron and Danny in Soapsuds House. Tom grinned: he loved that name. The house was so called because it was in a road known locally as Soapsuds Lane, because of the laundry. Aaron had started off living in Soapsuds Cottage, but when the old lady next door had gone to live with her daughter, Tom and Dad had knocked the two cottages into one as a wedding present. Tom could never go there without feeling a glow of pride at knowing how happy this had made his sister. She deserved it.

He dressed and went downstairs, shaking the kettle to see how much water it contained before putting it on the gas. While it boiled, he raked out the ashes from the kitchen and parlour fireplaces. Plenty of men wouldn't have bothered, because it was housework – women's work – but Tom didn't see it that way. Since he was up early, it made sense to get the house warm. Besides, it made it nicer for Mum to come downstairs to.

Kneeling in front of the parlour fireplace, he arranged some kindling, adding a few sheets of screwed-up newspaper, and struck a match. As the flame caught, he took the brass shovel from the companion set and dug several lumps of coal from the scuttle. Then he did the same job in the kitchen before taking the full ash-pan through the scullery to the back door, the sharp winter air cutting into him as he went to the dustbin. He removed the metal lid, holding the pan right inside before he upended it, so the ashes didn't fly up in a cloud.

When he returned to the kitchen, Mum was there, tying her apron behind her back. She looked bleary; she didn't care for dark mornings, but come the spring, what she called her morning face would be clear-eyed and smiling from the moment she rose from her bed. She was in her fifties now and her hair, which had once been the same strawberry-blonde as Molly's, had faded to a pale fairness that was tipping over towards grey.

He gave her a hug. 'Morning, Mum.'

She pretended to rub her cheek. 'Get yourself shaved before you come near me. You're up early.'

'You should have stayed in bed a few more minutes and I'd have brought you a cup of tea.'

'It's enough that you do that on a Sunday. Other mornings, I've got work to do. I've never yet sent your dad out without a proper breakfast inside him and I'm not starting now.'

Mum took pride in lining the stomachs of her menfolk and it was a good thing she did. Working long hours outside in all weathers was a hungry business and Mum's hot breakfasts made a good start to the day.

Tom poured boiling water into his shaving-mug and went into the scullery, shutting the door behind him, not so much for privacy as to stop warmth leaking out of the kitchen. They had three sinks in their scullery. Three! Very posh. Most houses, especially the smallest, had one. Better places had two, one for crockery and one for linen. But as Mum would say, one of the perks of being married to a builder was that you got all sorts of improvements done to your house – and one of these had been a third sink for personal washing.

Above it, a looking-glass hung on the wall. Tom wetted his shaving-brush and lathered his cheeks and chin, paying his reflection only as much attention as was needed not to slash himself to pieces with his razor. He couldn't be doing with looking at himself these days. He had gone to war with hair as brown as Tilda's and had come home with hair as white as Gran's. It shocked folk, the first time they saw him. A young man, early thirties, with white hair. His eyebrows were still brown and that made the white hair all the more obvious, because you could see brown was his natural colour.

Tom was always aware of the thought, the question, in people's eyes. How had the war done this to him? What had he seen – what had he been forced to do – that had troubled him to the extent that his innermost self had rebelled to the point of turning his hair white?

Oh, how he despised himself.

Chapter Four

JESS CAST A professional eye over the foyer as she walked into the Station Hotel. It was much smarter than the entrance to the Sea View had been, but that was only to be expected. The Sea View had catered for couples and families enjoying a holiday, whereas the Station Hotel's clientele... well, just who were they likely to be? Annerby wasn't a holiday destination. Commercial travellers? Businessmen, here to talk to the factory-owners? The place felt better than that, more upper-crust.

A chintz-covered sofa was positioned beneath an oil painting and there was a sizeable parlour palm next to the foot of the staircase. A pair of guests stood at the reception desk, asking questions of a tall, thin man whose immaculate suit and serious air made him appear every inch the gentleman. Jess waited for the guests to depart before she approached.

'Good morning, madam. May I be of assistance?'

Although the man's manner was faultless, Jess was aware of his swift, assessing glance – a glance she had herself delivered many a time when an unexpected person walked through the Sea View's front doors.

'Good morning. My name is Jess Mason and I'm looking for hotel work.'

'We don't require any chambermaids at present, miss.'

'I'm an experienced receptionist. I have a reference from the owner of the Sea View in Morecambe.'

'Indeed? The Station Hotel doesn't employ ladies behind the desk.'

She hadn't expected that. Of all the things she had prepared in advance to say, that wasn't among them.

'Maybe you should,' was all she could think of.

'I'll be sure to mention your suggestion to the hotel manager.' The man waved a fountain pen in the air as if about to write with a flourish in the register.

'I didn't just work in reception,' said Jess. 'I took bookings for the dining room, ordered the provisions and oversaw the work of the chambermaids.'

'At the Station Hotel, we have different members of staff for each of those tasks, but then, this isn't a little seaside boarding-house.'

'Neither was the Sea View. It wasn't a grand establishment like this, but it was a proper hotel.'

'And you were its Jill of all trades.'

'Aye – and I was jolly good at it,' Jess retorted. 'Good morning.'

She swung away, feeling hot and cross. As she hurried through the front door, she almost bumped into someone. She caught a brief glimpse of a costly blue wool coat and a fur stole and matching muff as she stepped quickly out of the way.

'I beg your pardon,' she said.

'Jess! Miss Mason, how nice to see you.'

Jess shed her disappointment on the spot as the warmth of happy recognition flowed through her. Leonora Minford was an old friend – or at least, she might have been had it been possible for women from their two different classes to mix socially. Mrs Minford was the second oldest of five sisters who were still known locally as the Henderson girls, even though four of them were married. She and the oldest sister, Vicky Rodwell, had set up and run a hospital for soldiers during the war in a grand house up the hill, which was how Jess had met them. She had trained as a VAD nursing assistant. The Hendersons were a law family and not just middle class but decidedly upper-middle, way beyond the reach of folk from the flower and bird streets.

But the war had brought them together, especially when Jess had proved to be an efficient organiser. Another of the important ladies at the hospital, Mrs Thornley, had put Jess firmly in her place, but that was Mrs Thornley for you. If you'd cut her in two, she would have had 'snob' written all the way through her, like a stick of rock.

But Vicky Rodwell had had other ideas.

'As valuable as you are to us as a nursing assistant, we also need girls who are competent in other ways. There's a lot of organising goes into a place like this if it's to function at its best.'

So Jess had divided her time between the wards and doing some basic clerical tasks.

Some of the other girls had been jealous.

'I trust nobody is making you uncomfortable,' said Mrs Minford.

Jess sighed. 'They'd soon stop envying me if they had to spend a whole morning counting bandages and splints and marking new sheets with the laundry pen.'

After the war, when Jess had been anxious to find herself a job, she had dared to approach Mrs Rodwell for a reference.

'I'll do that for you with pleasure.' Mrs Rodwell's light-green eyes, which could be cool and assessing, had warmed.

Jess's first job had lasted a matter of months, then she'd had to give it up in favour of a returning soldier.

'Men need work,' said her boss.

'So do I.'

'You'll get wed. Women do.'

'Not these days. Besides, I like my job – I love it. It's satisfying to feel I'm making a difference to the lives of people in need of assistance.'

'You're very good at it, I'll give you that.'

'Then let me stay.' The niggle of anxiety grew all at once and her hands went clammy as real fear took hold.

'Miss Mason, make no mistake. Your job is to be given to a returning soldier. Now, either you are gracious about it, in which case I will write in your reference that you surrendered your post willingly and generously. Or – well, I'm sure you don't wish to be unpatriotic.'

Dismayed, Jess had trailed home to Annerby.

'Back for keeps, are you?' asked the neighbours. 'Here to take care of your dad?'

'So much for your fancy ideas,' said Dad. 'Couldn't hack it in a proper job, could you?'

Uncomfortably aware of her boss's hint about her lack of patriotism, Jess kept quiet about what had happened. Let folk think what they liked. But she didn't want a mangled version getting back to Mrs Rodwell and Mrs Minford after they had been so good to her, so she wrote a short letter to Mrs Rodwell. The letter was merely a courtesy and she'd never intended anything to come of it, so she was deeply embarrassed when Mrs Rodwell sent for her and told her of a post she'd heard of.

'I never meant...' Jess began.

'I know you didn't. Now please allow me to help you.'

That job had been the one with the man who thought female colleagues were fair game. When Jess left, she didn't tell Mrs Rodwell because she didn't want to seem to be angling for more help. Besides, she was ashamed – which was stupid, because she hadn't done anything wrong; but that was how being pawed had left her feeling.

Now here she was, face to face with Mrs Rodwell's sister, Mrs Minford.

'How are you?' Mrs Minford asked.

'I'm fine, thank you. I hope you are as well.'

'Yes, indeed, as are Marcus and the children. Maximilian is eight now, if you can believe it. Listen, I'm meeting Vicky – Mrs Rodwell – and I'd love you to join us. Please say yes. We haven't seen you for such a long time.'

Mrs Minford slipped her hand into the crook of Jess's arm and bore her inside, turning right and entering a room with diamond-paned windows. As well as a fireplace with several over-mantel shelves, the walls were furnished with paintings and bookcases. In a corner was a pleasant nook with three armchairs grouped around a low table.

'We'll sit here.' Mrs Minford dropped her fur stole and muff onto the arm of the chair and hooked one ankle behind the other as she sat. She smiled as a waiter approached. 'We're waiting for another lady. When she arrives, please bring tea and a selection of your lovely little cakes.'

Jess deliberately avoided the waiter's gaze, well aware of how she must appear, sitting here in her well-worn cavalry-twill coat, felt hat and stout shoes, with Leonora Minford looking utterly gorgeous in her expensive coat complete with rose-bedecked hat. Even the colour of her coat spoke of money. Only the wealthy could countenance wearing mid-blue in winter. The less well-off made do with colours that didn't show the dirt. Jess wasn't the sort to envy the better-born, but she knew she and Mrs Minford looked like a lady interviewing a prospective nanny or personal maid.

Then Vicky Rodwell arrived and her pleasure at seeing Jess was so warm that Jess's reservations faded and she began to enjoy herself.

'We want to know what happened to you – don't we, Vicky?' said Mrs Minford. 'You went off to that position my sister found for you and the next thing we heard, you'd moved to a hotel by the sea. Didn't the position suit you?'

'Yes, very much. Even if it hadn't, I'd have stayed because it was a good job for a woman and jobs aren't easy for anybody to come by these days.'

'Then why did you give it up?' asked Mrs Rodwell.

Jess pressed her lips together. *He probably thought you were flighty and, if he did, you've only yourself to blame.* But she couldn't lie to these two. In as few words as possible, she explained about the male colleague with the wandering hands and then, before her listeners had time to exclaim over it, she told them about the Sea View.

'So I landed on my feet in the end – well, until the owner's son came back.' Heat swept up the back of her neck and across her face. Had it sounded like a hint for help? She got to her feet. 'I'm sorry, but I really can't stay. I – I have an appointment.'

It was true in a way, she thought wryly as she left the hotel. She had an important appointment with the Situations Vacant column in the local newspaper. To her relief, there were two positions with nearby local corporations that looked suitable and she wrote letters of application that same day.

Some days passed while she waited for replies. In that time, Dad introduced her to Mrs Nolan, who was a pleasant, middle-aged woman. Jess could almost hear Mum's voice inside her head, saying, 'She seems a good sort of body,' which was what Mum always said about women she approved of.

'I've heard about you.' Mrs Nolan's tone was friendly enough, but Jess sensed she was being tested. 'The daughter who piked off to find work instead of staying put and looking after her dad.'

'That's me.' Jess couldn't suppress a touch of flippancy.

'And now here you are, back again.'

'Not for long,' said Jess. 'Only until I find another post.'

'Well, that's all right, then.'

For a moment, Jess thought battle-lines had been drawn, but then Mrs Nolan surprised her with a hug and a kiss. Holding Jess's chin, she looked into her face. 'I wish you well. And don't feel you need to rush off on my account.'

Jess soon found that Mrs Nolan had her own door-key and had no qualms about using it. Jess was taken aback at first, but this was clearly what Dad wanted, so she had to take it on the chin.

Mrs Nolan was there one afternoon when the post arrived, bringing with it a reply to one of Jess's applications.

'Any luck, love?' asked Mrs Nolan.

'No. In my letter, I said my three posts had given me varied experience, but it says here that three jobs makes me a fly-by-night.'

'They never said that, did they?'

'Not in so many words, but that's what they mean.'

The following morning brought a second disappointment.

This post has attracted a number of applications of high quality, stated the letter, *and we shall be interviewing the gentleman candidates.*

It was no use being upset, no use thinking that it was now a week since she had been sacked; no use thinking that she'd been paid until the end of this week and needed to eke out her wages as far as possible. She'd given Dad some money, of course. That was their unspoken rule. If she came for a proper visit, she didn't pay, because she was a guest, she was family; but if she stayed here between jobs, she had to tip up her share.

Jess took the cleaning-box upstairs to do the bedrooms. Mrs Nolan might have got downstairs shining like a new pin, but it was clear she had never set foot upstairs. Jess made the beds, wiped the skirting-boards, dusted the picture-rails and was washing the windows with vinegar-water when the mid-morning post arrived. It was an invitation from Mrs Rodwell, asking her to come to tea the next day. Jess wasn't sure how she felt about going, but it would be churlish to refuse.

The next afternoon, she donned her Sunday best and walked to the Rodwells' attractive villa. To her surprise, the Henderson sisters were all there – Vicky, Leonora, Madeline, Anastasia and Bonnie. No wonder folk admired them. They were good-looking and well dressed and four of them were married to prosperous men. Only the youngest, Miss Bonnie, was still single. Jess much preferred to think of unmarried girls and women as single. She loathed the word 'spinster'. Such an ugly word. It made you sound old and desperate even if you were as young as Bonnie Henderson, and she wasn't yet twenty.

Although Vicky Rodwell and Leonora Minford were the ones who had influenced the course of her life, it had been Madeline and Anastasia whom Jess had known best during the war. She had barely set eyes on them since. She knew they each had a young child and now they were both well advanced in pregnancy. The Jess who had helped the two of them change beds and serve meals longed to offer congratulations, but the Jess who knew her place was well aware it wouldn't be appropriate. The war had changed a lot of things at the time, but afterwards they had changed back again.

'You may well look alarmed at the sight of all of us,' Miss Bonnie declared. She had the same dark hair and dark eyes as Madeline Howard, the middle sister, but there was a lively gleam in her eyes that had never appeared in Mrs Howard's. 'We've turned out in force, I'm afraid, but don't worry. It's because we're determined to help you. It's all thanks to Daddy, really.'

'That'll do, Bonnie,' said Mrs Minford and Jess wondered if Miss Bonnie had been on the verge of spilling some very interesting beans.

'We need to ask you a question,' said Mrs Howard. 'We know your jobs have taken you away from Annerby, but would you be prepared to go somewhere even further afield?'

Mrs Rodwell spoke up. 'Our father, Mr Niall Henderson, has a special friend in a place called Chorlton-cum-Hardy, which is on the south side of Manchester. All five of us are looking forward to going there on a visit in February, when Madeline and Anastasia are both able to travel again. In the meantime, I have subscribed to the *Manchester Evening News*, so that we can get a feel for the place, as it were.'

'We've found a job for you,' said Miss Bonnie, 'if you like the sound of it.'

'It's in an old soldiers' home,' said Mrs Minford. 'A manager is needed to run it and we thought that with your experience in both local corporations and hotel work, it's something you could do.'

'There's an advertisement,' said Mrs Rodwell, 'and there's also an article about it. Here – I cut it out for you.'

'The man who is setting up the place already has one home for old soldiers,' said Miss Bonnie. 'Now he's found a suitable house for his new establishment, but it needs to have work done on it to make it ready, so the new manager would have to keep an eye on all that. What do you think,

Jess – I mean, Miss Mason? I bet you could do it standing on your head.'

Jess was startled into laughing. 'How wonderfully kind you all are to go to this trouble for me.'

'We want to help you.' Mrs Langley smiled at her. 'I'll never forget folding sheets with you and writing letters for the wounded men.' The smile fell from her face as her blue eyes clouded. 'I'll never forget how you and I sat up all night with that poor boy whose face had been burned off.'

Jess shook her head, barely able to acknowledge the memory, because it was so distressing, but it meant there would always be a connection between her and Miss Anastasia – she might be Mrs Langley now, but to Jess she would always be Miss Anastasia, even if only in her thoughts. Jess fell in between Madeline and Anastasia in age, the three of them having been born in the final years of the old century. For a time, the war had brought them close together, but look at them now, their VAD aprons long discarded, Madeline and Anastasia comfortably married, Madeline with a three-year-old and Anastasia with an eighteen-month-old, and both of them with babies on the way, while plenty would see Jess as an unwanted spinster.

That wasn't how she perceived herself. It wasn't the way she felt inside. On the inside, where it mattered, she was a surplus girl and proud of it, because it spoke of her independence. She had discovered a drive within herself to work outside the home in a position that would make her feel useful and satisfied. That was what she sought in life: a good job.

She smiled at the Henderson sisters. 'I'll certainly give this post serious consideration.'

'I'm afraid there isn't time for that.' Mrs Rodwell looked apologetic. 'It's my fault, I'm afraid. If I'd realised, I'd have asked you to call sooner.'

'Realised what?' asked Jess.

'The article about the old soldiers' home and the advertisement for the position were both published in the paper at the beginning of last week,' said Mrs Howard.

'So if you intend to apply,' added Mrs Minford, 'you shall have to write your letter and post it this evening.'

'I see.'

Jess's heart thumped. Her local corporation jobs had both been in welfare, and then there was her hotel experience, so she reckoned her background would be as good as anybody's. But Manchester was a long way from here, right in the south of Lancashire, much further from home than she had previously gone. Then again, Dad and Mrs Nolan were certain to get hitched and how would she feel being a gooseberry? What if no other suitable jobs came up? Or what if they did but applications were invited only from men?

It would be foolish not to apply for this. It might be a long way away, but it looked like a worthwhile, interesting position.

'Forgive the question,' said Mrs Rodwell, 'but do you have suitable stationery at home? I should be happy to—'

'I have my own, thank you,' Jess said quickly. She didn't want to be offered stationery. It would feel like charity.

But later, at home, she wondered if her pride had been misplaced. She hadn't realised she was down to her final two sheets of writing paper, but that should be enough. She wrote her letter carefully, detailing her experience and explaining why she believed it would be relevant to this post. She ended with *Yours sincerely* and underneath signed *Jess*— Drat. There was a small blot at the end of her name, but she didn't have another piece of paper, so it would have to stay. Lifting her pen away, she gently dabbed with blotting paper, waiting for the ink to dry before she added her surname.

Most girls would have signed themselves *J Mason (Miss)*, but not Jess. Signing her name the way she did was a deliberate choice that was to do with the way she had embraced her future in the workplace. Jess Mason – surplus girl. Jess Mason – career woman.

Chapter Five

THE WORKING DAY always ended with Tom, Dad and Uncle Bill in the office of Perkins and Watson, though 'office' might be a bit of a grand word for it. It was just a small building in their yard. It was a time of day Tom had always liked. The lads had gone home and there was the paperwork to catch up on and the diary to check so that the necessary materials could be ordered in good time for forthcoming jobs. It was also the time for mugs of tea and a chinwag.

Dad and Uncle Bill were arguing good-naturedly about a job that was lined up for next week. Bill Perkins wasn't Tom's real uncle, any more than Grandad Perkins had been his real grandfather, but the honorary relationships were a sign of the closeness and trust that had existed within the business ever since Thomas Watson and Obediah Perkins had first set up in business together some seventy years ago.

'I tell you, we'll be doing more of those over the years,' Uncle Bill was saying to Dad. 'Well, you and I won't, because it won't get to be an ordinary thing for years yet and we'll have retired long before then, but young Tom will still be here. What do you think of it, Tom?'

Tom laughed and shook his head. 'Don't drag me into it.'

'Well, I don't care for it,' said Dad. 'It'll spoil the look of any house when it's done.'

'That's your opinion,' said Uncle Bill, 'but these folk with a few bob in their pockets won't see it that way. They'll see it as something that makes them better than their neighbours.'

'It'll still ruin the look of a street,' Dad maintained. 'And what makes you think landlords will let their front gardens be dug up that way?'

Uncle Bill shrugged. 'Some will, some won't. But the ones that allow it will take it as a sign that their tenants are happy to invest in the property. They'll see it as a well-heeled tenant who wants to stay long term instead of moving somewhere bigger.'

'Just as well,' Dad retorted, 'because the way I see it, the landlords will have a devil of a job letting those houses to new people afterwards. Not everyone wants an eyesore outside their front door.'

Uncle Bill lifted his mug, raising his eyebrows at Tom over the rim. 'You mark my words, lad. By the time you're an old man, it'll be normal for properties to be like that.'

Tom tried to picture it. It was difficult to imagine that one day it would be ordinary for folk to give up their front gate and part of their garden wall, not to mention a sizeable chunk of lawn, in order to park a motor car right outside their house. Dad was right: it didn't sound at all attractive. But – would that many folk own motor-cars in years to come? That was hard to picture as well.

He got to his feet. 'I'll leave you to it. I've got an appointment to see Gabriel Linkworth before I go home.'

'Oh aye, the bookshop fellow,' said Dad.

'That's the one,' said Tom.

He disappeared into the back room to get changed. It was one of the firm's rules. You didn't go to price up a new job dressed in your building-site clobber. Tom exchanged his faithful old waistcoat for a smart one, his collarless shirt for a collared shirt and tie, his dust-encrusted trousers for lightweight wool, and his sturdy work-boots for a pair of lace-ups. Then, patting his jacket pockets to make sure he had his notebook, pencil and tape measure, he set off.

It wasn't far to go. The Perkins and Watson yard was just along from Chorlton's little railway station. The main post and telegraph office was over the road, then came all the shops on both sides of the street, and the banks stood at the crossroads. Tom went over the road and walked along for a couple of minutes and there, waiting outside the vacant premises, stood Gabriel Linkworth. Tom had first met him coming up for a year ago, when Linkworth had inherited his uncle's bookshop on Beech Road, a short distance from here. Although Linkworth had loved bookselling, he hadn't been able to keep the shop on, because he couldn't afford the rent. Since then, he and his fiancée Belinda had both been working hard as clerks as they saved up for their future with the ambition of setting up in another bookshop, this time with living accommodation above.

Tom had liked Gabriel Linkworth from the start, and he was glad to see him now, shaking hands warmly. 'Thanks for coming out in the evening,' said Linkworth. 'It wouldn't have been possible for me to get time out of work to meet you.'

'Pleasure,' said Tom. He wondered how Linkworth had managed to get together the necessary funds after just a few months, but he wasn't going to ask. He had never been nosy.

The empty premises had housed a couple of different shops over the years. It had been a grocer's when Tom was a lad. There was a tobacconist's next door, which had been there for years, and the two shared an inset porch, their doors set at angles within. Between the shop doors was another door.

'Before we go inside,' said Linkworth, 'there's another job I'd like Perkins and Watson to do as well as improving this property for me. You remember the land in Limits Lane?'

Oh aye, Tom remembered. As well as inheriting the book-shop from old Mr Tyrell, Gabriel Linkworth had inherited the old boy's cottage at the bottom of Limits Lane. The cottage had been burned down one night, though fortunately Belinda's family, who had been staying in it at the time, had all escaped, thanks to Gabriel's courage. The fire hadn't been an accident. Someone had set the place alight on purpose, though no one had any idea who. Afterwards, Gabriel had used what money he had left to pay for the land to be cleared so that no eyesore remained. That had been last spring.

'The land belongs to me,' Linkworth said now. 'It's not a huge plot, just the space of the old garden. I'd like to do something with it.'

'Build another cottage?' Tom frowned. If that was the plan, why were they here?

'No, nothing like that. Belinda and I have talked it over and we'd like to provide an allotment for the benefit of the other cottage-dwellers. I'd like Perkins and Watson to prepare the ground and lay it out properly and build a shed, which I'll kit out with tools. It'll be a good way of using that land. Belinda suggested calling it Mr Tyrell's Garden. The cottagers were kindness itself to me after I lost my cottage.'

'We can do that for you,' said Tom.

'Good.' Linkworth indicated the door in front of them in between the two shop-doors. 'That leads upstairs to the flat. But first, let's take a look round the shop, shall we?'

He produced a key and let them in, their footsteps loud on the wooden floorboards. There were counters on three sides with floor-to-ceiling shelves behind.

'The shelves will be useful,' said Tom, 'but you won't want all these counters.'

'I thought I'd keep one, cut down to half its length. Other than that, I want plenty of bookcases in the body of the shop.'

'I'll measure up,' said Tom, 'and we'll decide on the best layout. I reckon you'll need at least a yard in between bookcases to allow sufficient space or else your customers will feel cramped.'

'Come and see the back rooms. There's a storeroom and a little office and the old living quarters.'

Tom frowned. 'What about the flat upstairs?'

'Until now, upstairs and downstairs have been separate. Upstairs used to be an employment agency at one point, but it's been empty for some time.' Linkworth lifted his arm and indicated the ceiling from above the large front window to the rear of the shop. 'Upstairs, all that space, plus more behind it, is one vast room. You'll see when we go up. I want you to think about dividing the space and putting in stud-walls.'

'It sounds like it's going to cost a pretty penny.'

'I had a windfall.'

Tom looked round approvingly. 'It looks like you've found yourself a splendid place. Plenty of room.'

Linkworth's serious face softened into an expression of warm satisfaction. 'I promised Belinda I'd do my best for her family, so we might well have her younger brothers to live with us when the time comes, though it isn't definite yet. And we want room for our own family, of course.' He shook his head, as if he couldn't believe his luck. 'It's everything I could possibly ask for – the girl of my dreams, the work of my dreams and space for a family.'

Tom's heartbeat quickened, a sudden tug of envy taking him by surprise. Gabriel Linkworth wasn't the only one with dreams. Tom had them too – a wife, children – but unlike Linkworth, he had to keep his dreams locked away in the most secret corner of his heart.

Chapter Six

ARMED WITH THE directions that the boarding-house landlady had gladly provided, Jess put on her coat and hat and went downstairs. The dining room door was open, and the landlady and her maid were inside, clearing the tables. The smell of bacon still hung in the air.

'You off already?' Mrs McEvoy came to the doorway. 'You don't need to go yet. It won't take you five minutes to get there.'

'I'd rather be early.' Jess kept moving. Mrs McEvoy had already shown herself to be a talker.

'Well – good luck,' Mrs McEvoy called after her, following her to the front door.

Jess raised a hand in thanks as she set off. It had rained all night on top of the snow and the pavements were slushy, but the privet hedges smelled bright and fresh. The houses round here had small gardens at the front and Jess glimpsed clumps of snowdrops and glory of the snow, its starry flowers pale bluey-violet with white centres. She turned a corner and entered a different sort of road, wider, with smarter houses and bigger gardens. The road-name said Whalley Road and her heart gave a little bump. During her time at the Sea View, she had built up a lot of confidence and it wasn't like her to be nervous – but that had been before she had lost her job to the Hitchcocks' son.

She soon found Oak Lodge. A pair of gates was set into a wall over which scrambled long, curving stems of winter jasmine, dotted with tiny yellow flowers. Resisting the temptation to peer over the gates, Jess carried on slowly down the road. She was way too early, but she hadn't wanted to risk not finding her way. Rightly or wrongly, she had a sense of urgency about this interview, which had started when she'd had to apply immediately without having time to think it over. She had sent her letter by the Tuesday evening post, so Mr Peters at Oak Lodge had received it the following morning and she had then received a telegram on Wednesday afternoon, bidding her to attend an interview this morning – *this* morning – Thursday. Yesterday afternoon had been a terrific scramble – packing a bag, racing to the station and throwing herself onto a train. When she reached Manchester Victoria, she had shown Oak Lodge's address in Seymour Grove to a taxi driver and asked him to take her to a nearby guesthouse – and now here she was, feeling all of a flutter as she walked round the block to kill time before presenting herself at Oak Lodge. This wasn't the new home that Mr Peters was setting up. This was the old soldiers' home he already ran. Thank goodness Mrs Rodwell had torn the article out of the newspaper for her. By this time, she knew it by heart.

It was time to go to Oak Lodge. She returned to the gates and let herself in. In front of the large bay-windowed house was a short driveway wide enough for a horse and cart. Aside from a tall yew clipped into a spiral, and a huge clump of tall, feathery grasses, the garden looked bare, but that was probably the time of year.

Jess walked up the front steps and took a moment to straighten her shoulders and smooth the anxiety from her face before she rang the bell. The door was opened by a maid in a black dress and white apron with a frilled edge.

Jess smiled at her. 'Good morning. I'm here for an interview.'

'You need to go round the back,' said the maid.

'Round the back?' How bizarre.

'Aye. You shouldn't have come to the front door. You should know better. You won't get the job at this rate.'

'Is there a problem, Rose?' A plump middle-aged woman came across the hall behind the maid.

'It's a person for the cleaning job, missis. I've told her to go round the back.'

Cleaning job!

'I'm here to be interviewed for the post of manager of the new home,' Jess said.

The woman's eyes widened. 'I don't think so. I mean...'

'I assure you I am. Mr Peters himself sent for me. I can show you the telegram. Perhaps you would kindly tell him I'm here.'

The woman bridled, but then her face took on a kindly expression. 'I'm sure there's been a mistake. You'd better come in, Miss...?'

'Mason.'

'Miss Mason – and I am Mrs Peters. If you'll wait here in the hall, I'll fetch my husband.'

Wait in the hall? That wasn't a good sign. Being invited into an office or a sitting room would have been a good sign. Being abandoned in the entrance hall was more or less a guarantee that she wasn't expected to stay more than a few minutes. Jess's throat closed up. What was going on? Had she mis-read the telegram? No, of course she hadn't. She had been asked to come here. Even so, she couldn't quell a rising agitation and had to force herself to stand still and not bounce on her toes or crush her handbag to her.

A man appeared. He was smartly dressed in a suit and he probably had a genial sort of expression as a rule, but just now his mouth was tight with annoyance. He marched ahead of his wife and then stopped dead at the sight of Jess. 'This is Miss Mason,' said Mrs Peters.

'You're a woman,' said Mr Peters. 'I was expecting a man. You signed your letter as if you were a man.'

'No, I didn't.'

'Yes, you did. Jesse Mason. Jesse – that's a man's name. Like Jesse James, the outlaw.'

'Not Jesse – Jess.'

'It was definitely Jesse.'

This was ridiculous. Jess spoke in the firm voice she saved for chambermaids who sneaked outside for a roll-up. 'My name is Jess, short for Jessica.'

Mr Peters turned to his wife. 'Would you fetch the letter, please? It's on my blotter.'

Mrs Peters disappeared for a few moments, returning with Jess's letter in her hand. She gave it to her husband, who practically waved it under Jess's nose.

'Look – there. Jesse. You've got this interview under false pretences.'

Ah. Yes. Now she understood. 'That isn't an "e" on the end of Jess. It's a blot.'

'A blot?'

'Yes. I didn't pretend to be a man to get this interview. What would be the point of that? And why does it matter anyway?'

'It matters because this is a job for a man.'

Jess spoke in her pleasantest voice. 'Surely it's a job for whoever is the best qualified.'

'I'll take no lip from you, young lady.'

'I mean no disrespect, sir. What I mean to say is that my application was clearly good enough to warrant your offering me an interview. I obviously have appropriate experience.'

'That's beside the point.'

The point being that this was a job for a man. It wasn't the first time Jess had found herself up against this sort of attitude. She kept a polite smile on her face even though she felt more like tying Mr Peters to a chair and explaining to him all the reasons why women were every bit as capable as men.

Then she had an idea. 'If you had sent me a letter instead of a telegram, you'd have addressed me as Mr Mason and I'd have known I wasn't wanted. I could have written back and apologised for wasting your time. But the telegram came to J Mason and here I am.' She hated trying to wheedle round him, but it was her only chance. Could she make him feel guilty about the trouble she had been put to? 'I realise you aren't keen to employ a woman, but I've travelled a long way, and at very short notice.'

'Maybe she deserves an interview,' Mrs Peters murmured. 'You did say her letter was the best one.'

'Well – well – all right. You can have your interview, Miss Mason – but not now. When I received your application after all the other interviews had been arranged, I put you at the top of the list for this morning, but now I don't want to waste my time seeing you first. You can come back later, after I've interviewed all the real— that is, all the other candidates. I'll see you at the end.'

Oh, her face would crack in half if she kept this smile in place much longer. 'Thank you, Mr Peters. I appreciate the courtesy.'

'Save your appreciation for something that warrants it,' Mr Peters replied. 'This is a post for a suitable man.'

'You never know. Perhaps you'll end up with a suitable woman.'

'There's no such thing,' said Mr Peters.

*

Vivienne Atwood walked up the staircase in the town hall, heading for the office used by the Board of Health. She enjoyed her job. It was a big improvement on her previous posts, one of which had been with a charity whose patronising attitude to the poor had made her blood boil and the other of which had been with a local corporation that was run by stuffed-shirt types who gave the most interesting tasks to the men. It was different at the Board of Health, though that wasn't necessarily because women were valued for their brains and their potential, but rather because of the work itself, which was largely centred around families, which meant it was often seen as appropriate work for women.

That attitude was annoying, but Vivienne didn't let it worry her too much, preferring to concentrate on the importance of her role and the freedom it gave her to use her initiative. As a childless war widow, she had a duty to herself to make the most of what life had left her with and it was important to have a job that enabled her to make a difference to the lives of others. That gave her a sense of fulfilment – not like the happiness she had enjoyed so briefly in her marriage before it had been torn from her, but still – fulfilment.

In the corridor of the town hall where the Board of Health had its rooms, the boss, Mr Taylor, had his own office, where he spent a considerable part of his time behind a closed door, avoiding Mrs Wardle. She wasn't an official member of staff, but with her connections to a couple of the old Boards of Guardians that had run the workhouses, she had been able to wangle her way into the local Board of Health – or rather, she had elbowed her way in and dear Mr Taylor hadn't been able to stand up to her. By rights, Mrs Wardle shouldn't have any authority at all, but her years of being one of the top dogs in the charity sector had given her a toe-hold and it would take dynamite to shift her. In the main office, there were four desks all facing the front, and a fifth one that faced the rest, like a teacher's desk. That was where Mrs Wardle sat, in a position that made her look as if she had authority over the four paid members of staff. She behaved as if she had authority too, and, since Mr Taylor had never put her in her place, she got away with it.

Vivienne entered the office, exchanging good mornings with her colleagues, Miss Cadman and Miss Byrne. She removed her coat and hat and slipped her gloves into her handbag before sitting at her desk and opening her top drawer to take out a file of notes. Her dear friend Molly had worked alongside her here for a short spell last year and she missed her. They would have made a good team, but now Molly was happily married to Aaron Abrams and adopting Danny had provided them with an instant family.

Molly's replacement in the office was Miss Boodle and Vivienne hadn't taken to her at all. Neither had her colleagues. They called her Boodle the Poodle behind her back, because she was in thrall to Mrs Wardle. Miss Boodle had earned the post on her own merits, but then it had turned out that her parents were chums of the Wardles and it had been Mrs Wardle's idea for Miss Boodle to apply. Miss Boodle was in her thirties and Vivienne didn't like to be catty, but she was pretty sure the Poodle's glossy black locks came out of a bottle. She had a dainty, up-tilted nose and rather a luscious mouth. She wore her hair in a very short bob, with a dead-straight fringe cut well above her eyebrows and dark eyes. A curl lay on each side of her face, high on her cheeks, just beneath her eyes, cleverly creating the illusion that her face was narrower than it was.

The door opened and Vivienne looked up, sighing inwardly as Mr Taylor hesitated before walking in. He was a dear man and good at his job, but his fear of Mrs Wardle did him no favours – did none of them any favours. He had waves of white hair at the sides of his head and a neatly trimmed beard over a prominent chin, though anyone who associated a jutting chin with a determined character had clearly never seen Mr Taylor scuttle for safety when Mrs Wardle swanned into view. Vivienne wanted to jump to her feet and assure him it was safe to enter the office, because You-Know-Who wasn't here.

'Mrs Atwood, might I ask a favour? You're going to visit Mrs Hunt in Chorlton this morning, aren't you? Might I ask you to drop into St Anthony's Orphanage and deliver this document for me?'

'Of course.' Vivienne took the thick envelope from him and placed it beside her blotter. The orphanage was one of her favourite places.

Mr Taylor departed. The next time the door opened, in came Mrs Wardle. She was a plump lady who was always superbly well dressed. She removed a wool overcoat to reveal a costume of pale-blue silk dress beneath a matching light-weight coat. Tiny silken forget-me-nots floated in a cloud of net around her pillbox hat. She had so many fine clothes you'd think she was a duchess rather than the wife of a solicitor.

Vivienne got up to leave.

'Where are you going?' demanded Mrs Wardle.

'Chorlton.' Vivienne kept her voice polite and cool. It was the only way.

'Really?' Mrs Wardle seized the office diary. 'Ah yes – the widow with the tearaway boys. You don't need to leave yet. You've got plenty of time... unless you intend to do your shopping on the way,' she finished sarcastically.

Vivienne didn't respond to that final barb, though she did feel obliged to say, 'I'm also calling in at St Anthony's.'

'To do what?' asked Mrs Wardle. 'I'm the official visitor there, so I'm entitled to know.'

'Mr Taylor has asked me to deliver something.'

'What? This?' Mrs Wardle seized the bulky envelope from Vivienne's desk. 'There's no need. I'll take it. Mrs Rostron will wish to discuss its contents with me.'

No, she won't, you old bag, Vivienne wanted to say. It took all her willpower to do no more than smile sweetly and reach out to take hold of the envelope. Mrs Wardle didn't let go.

'Mr Taylor particularly asked me to deliver it,' said Vivienne. 'Besides, we all know how extremely busy you are, Mrs Wardle.'

Busy? Busybody, more like. Vivienne wrenched the envelope from Mrs Wardle's podgy fingers and stuffed it into her handbag. Mrs Wardle tossed her head, sending the little forget-me-nots dancing, and marched from the room.

'Where's she gone?' said Vivienne.

'Probably to put the kettle on, ready to steam open your envelope,' said Miss Cadman. 'I'd make tracks if I were you.'

'Good idea.'

At least she left the office on a laugh – but really there wasn't anything very funny about having to work with Mrs Wardle.

Chapter Seven

JESS PACED THE streets of Seymour Grove, marking time until she could return to Oak Lodge. The nerves that had assaulted her earlier had increased, but she felt vexed too. Why should being female make her unsuitable for a responsible position? Especially when, on paper, she was the strongest candidate. She would have to get rid of her annoyance before her interview. She must transform it into determination. After all, it wasn't as though this was her first experience of being looked down on for being female.

She kept having to undo the top buttons of her coat to look at the dainty timepiece she wore attached to her blouse, so in the end she unfastened it and popped it in her coat pocket. It was interesting to walk around Seymour Grove, but not exactly useful since the new home for old soldiers wasn't going to be here. The place for that was Chorlton-cum-Hardy – what a mouthful!

At last it was time to return to Oak Lodge.

Rose admitted her. 'Would you sit here, miss. Mr Peters is with someone at the moment.'

Jess sat down. The hall smelled of polish. That was a good sign. It showed the place was looked after.

Two elderly gentlemen came downstairs, one thin with wispy hair and sunken cheeks, the other with a pot-belly and a spot of dried blood on his chin where he'd cut himself shaving. The thin one missed his footing on the bottom stair. Jess jumped up to help, but the old boy caught hold of the newel-post and steadied himself.

'Are you all right?' Jess asked. 'Take a moment to get your breath.'

The two men looked at her in surprise.

'Well,' said the one who had stumbled, 'I'd have flung myself on the floor if I'd known there was a pretty girl to rescue me.'

'Don't listen to him,' said the other. 'He's always had an eye for the ladies.'

'Has he indeed?' Jess smiled.

'Oh aye. Love 'em and leave 'em, that's him.'

'Thanks for the warning.' Jess was enchanted.

The one who had stumbled had bright-blue eyes that now twinkled at her. 'Chance would be a fine thing these days.'

On the other side of the hall, a door opened and Mr Peters appeared with a middle-aged man in tweeds, sporting the sort of moustache from the Lord Kitchener poster.

Mr Peters stopped to speak to the old men. 'This is Mr Painter, who is here about the Holly Lodge position. Painter, these are two of our residents, Captain Wingate and Captain Styles.'

The men shook hands.

Mr Peters hesitated before completing the introductions. 'This is Miss Mason.'

'Visiting the old chaps, are you?' asked Mr Painter. 'Good show. I'm sure they enjoy seeing a pretty face.'

Jess seethed inwardly. Being called pretty by Captain Styles was one thing, a piece of gallantry from a man old enough to be her grandfather. Coming from Mr Painter, it was patronising.

'As a matter of fact—' she began.

'Rose, will you show Mr Painter out, please?' said Mr Peters.

He couldn't get Jess into his office quickly enough. Was he ashamed of interviewing a woman? Jess's spirits dipped. Honestly, what was the point? He obviously wasn't going to employ her. Then she stiffened her spine. It had cost her good money to travel down from Annerby and she was determined to do her best in this interview.

Mr Peters shut the door, waving her into a seat before settling himself behind his desk.

Before he could speak, Jess said, 'I enjoyed meeting the two captains. Will they carry on living here or will they move into the new house when it's ready?'

Mr Peters didn't look pleased to be forestalled, but he answered civilly. 'There is no reason to suppose they'll wish to move.'

'If all the old soldiers are as charming as they are, it would be a pleasure to take care of them.'

'Quite so.' Mr Peters cleared his throat. 'Now then, your letter.' He picked it up.

'I was delighted to hear that mine was the strongest application.' And thank heaven for that blot or he would never have considered her.

'On paper, maybe, but I've had time to think since seeing you earlier on. Obviously the experience you listed must all have been underpinned by support and guidance.'

Jess trod carefully. 'Everyone requires guidance in a new post.'

'And some continue to require it. Let us be frank, Miss Mason. Women just aren't cut out for responsible positions. They need someone to lean on.'

'I disagree, sir. If you would care to see it, I have a reference in my bag from Mr Hitchcock, who owns the Sea View Hotel. He says I showed initiative and imagination in the way I tackled problems that arose and also that he had full confidence in me to run the hotel on a day-to-day basis when he had to be away.'

'Hm, yes, well.' Mr Peters cleared his throat.

'I could do that for your old soldiers' home, Mr Peters. I could run it competently, following all your rules. My experience in the hotel means that I know how an establishment of that size needs to be organised. I know the routines of ordering provisions, dealing with the laundry and getting the cleaning done.'

'That would be useful, I must admit. My wife sees to that side of things here at Oak Lodge.' Mr Peters lifted his face and looked squarely at her. 'It was my intention to employ a housekeeper in Holly Lodge in due course. Perhaps you would be suitable for that when the time comes.'

Oh yes, get the woman to handle all the domestic duties!

'Were I the manager, I would naturally oversee the domestic side as well as taking care of all other matters. My hotel work has given me experience of handling money and dealing pleasantly yet firmly with all manner of folk. And I've worked for two local corporations, so I have recent knowledge of services that are available and also of the standards that are required of institutions that take care of groups of people. I would foster links with the local community – women are so good at that sort of thing, don't you think?' She smiled innocently. 'For example, a nearby school might send children to sing carols at Christmas or members of an amateur dramatics group might provide an evening of readings.'

'You've thought it through, I'll say that for you.'

'Thank you. Yes, I have, because I'm very interested in the position.'

Mr Peters pressed his lips together, forming a line that went downwards at each end. 'But it wouldn't do, you see.

There's still the other matter. Holly Lodge isn't ready yet. It needs some building work, then there'll be the decorating and so forth, and I'll need a man to oversee all that. A woman wouldn't be able to.'

'Why not?' Jess asked bluntly.

'I beg your pardon?'

'I asked why not. Why shouldn't a woman oversee building work and decorating?'

'Because she's a woman, that's why. You can't expect men to let a woman check up on them.'

Jess thought for a moment. 'The men you interviewed – were they builders?'

'What? No. Of course not.'

'So how would you expect one of them to oversee the work? They wouldn't have any special knowledge of it. How would your builders feel about that?'

Mr Peters huffed out a sharp breath. 'Your point, Miss Mason?'

'That I'm as capable as a man of keeping an eye on work of which I have no specialist knowledge. An honest tradesman would soon recognise my ability to watch work unfold.'

'Through feminine wiles, you mean?'

'Through observation and asking questions. Naturally I would refer any concerns to you. The workmen at Holly Lodge would, of course, be aware that they were ultimately responsible to you.' Jess held her breath. Would that be enough?

Mr Peters thought for some moments, his eyebrows drawing together in what looked like fierce thought.

At last he said, 'I'll think about it.'

Vivienne alighted from the tram in Chorlton. She liked it when her work brought her here, because it was where she lived and the orphanage in particular held a special place in her heart. It had been established in the last century as St Anthony's, but now the Orphanage Committee was going through the legal process of changing its name to St Nicholas's – and it had been Vivienne's idea. She wasn't the big-headed type, but she couldn't help lifting her chin with pride when she thought of it. St Anthony's had always struck her as being an inappropriate name. Whoever had imagined that it was right to name an orphanage after the patron saint of lost things? Children weren't things! The new name – St Nicholas's – was much better, because St Nicholas was the patron saint of children. Vivienne smiled to herself. Best of all, as far as the children were concerned, was that St Nicholas was Father Christmas, so they would grow up in the Christmas Orphanage.

First of all, she had to call on Mrs Hunt, a worn-down widow with next to no money, who was struggling to cope with her boisterous lads. Unfortunately, Mrs Hunt didn't seem to have been blessed with much backbone and however much support Vivienne provided, somehow Mrs Hunt always needed more.

'I've made the arrangements for the boys to have free school meals, Mrs Hunt,' Vivienne told the woman, 'and I've made it clear to the dinner ladies that they must eat everything on their plates and aren't allowed to save anything to bring home.'

'Oh, but I rely on that, a bit of summat to have for tea.'

'That isn't what school dinners are for. I have found a local office that needs an early morning cleaner and I've also arranged for you to have an interview with the greengrocer about an afternoon job.'

Mrs Hunt perked up. 'Would I be able to get my veg cut-price if I worked there?'

'I really couldn't say and I suggest you don't ask in the interview, because it would create a poor impression. Here are the details.' Vivienne held out a piece of paper, keeping her arm extended until Mrs Hunt gave up waiting for her to put it on the table and took it. 'It's up to you now, Mrs Hunt.' In a kind voice, she added, 'I know how difficult life is for you, but this is your chance to improve things.'

'Easy for you to say,' Mrs Hunt muttered. Oh, but she was a difficult woman to deal with! Mrs Wardle would eat her for breakfast, but Vivienne had always done her best to empathise with the people she helped, knowing that sometimes life's difficulties could be overwhelming and could drag people down and make it nigh on impossible for them to cope.

As she left the crummy little upstairs rooms, a woman appeared at the foot of the staircase. She stopped in the shabby hallway, so that Vivienne could come down.

'Are you the Board of Health lady?' she asked. 'You've just been to see Florrie Hunt – my sister.'

'That's right.'

'I'm Mrs Page. You'd best tell me what you've sorted for her, because left to herself she'll do nowt about it. She's a leaner, is our Florrie. She leans on anyone who'll let her. That's what our mam, God rest her soul, always said about her. "She's a leaner and she'd sink through the crack in the floorboards if she had nobody to lean on." Aye, and she's been worse since her Ernie never came back from the war. So you tell me what's what and I'll gee her up.'

It wasn't the done thing to hand out information about cases – that was what the people were called whom the Board of Health helped. Cases.

'Come with me,' said Vivienne and led the way back upstairs.

Mrs Page barged straight in without knocking. 'Aye, I might have known you'd be sat there drooping all over the table. You may well look surprised, our Florrie. I'll have you know I'm back from Urmston now, cos I'm moving in with my Lorna and that means I'll be giving you a kick up the whatsit if you think you can get away with sighing your way through the days. Right.' She turned to Vivienne. 'What have you got sorted for her?'

'May I say?' Vivienne asked Mrs Hunt.

'Aye, if you must.'

'Aye,' said her bossy sister, 'she must.' She pounced on the piece of paper with the details Vivienne had written – printed, because Mrs Hunt couldn't read joined-up writing. 'This it, is it? Right, you can get off now, miss. I'll sort our Florrie out. You come back in a fortnight and she'll be a different person. Well, no, she'll be as droopy as ever, but she'll be droopy with a bit of money behind her, if I have owt to do with it.'

Vivienne went on her way, hoping that Mrs Page could work the wonders that she had herself failed to do. It was a relief to know that Mrs Hunt would be watched over. Now came the enjoyable part of her visit to Chorlton, calling in at St Anthony's.

As she walked along High Lane, she passed Holly Lodge, which was over the road from the orphanage. The old house had stood empty for a while, but this morning a man was clipping the hedge, which was good to see. Maybe the landlord had found a tenant.

Vivienne crossed over and walked a short way down Church Road, alongside the orphanage's brick wall, heading for the gates. Coming towards her was Nancy Pike – or Nurse Nancy, as she must remember to call her these days. Nancy had lodged in the same house as Vivienne for a few weeks while she worked as a temporary clerical help in St Anthony's. Then, on Christmas Eve, Nancy had been given a new job for which she was perfect – in fact, the job had been created specially for her, and now she was Nurse Nancy, but as well as doing her share of the ordinary nursemaid tasks of taking care of the children and doing the housework, she had the additional responsibility of thinking up special activities to keep the children busy and happy.

Nancy had moved back home to live with her family when she wasn't required to stay overnight at the orphanage and she and her fiancé were saving up to get married. She was carrying a wicker basket, which she held out for Vivienne to see.

'Ribbons, braids and off-cuts for my crafts box,' she said proudly. 'The lady at the haberdashery said she'll keep odds and ends for me and I can go once a month to collect them.'

'That's good of her,' said Vivienne.

Nancy nodded over Vivienne's shoulder. 'Have you seen? They're going to do up Holly Lodge. It's going to be a home for old soldiers.'

Vivienne turned and looked at the property. 'How do you know?'

'Me and Zachary visit Oak Lodge in Seymour Grove. That's the old soldiers' home there. Mr Peters told us he's going to open Holly Lodge an' all.'

Vivienne laughed. 'You're not just imaginative and creative, Nurse Nancy, you're a fount of useful information too.'

A dab of colour touched Nancy's cheeks, her copper-coloured hair and fair skin making the blush all the more obvious. 'I'm not gossiping.'

'I know you well enough to know that.'

They entered the grounds. In many ways, the orphanage resembled a Victorian school, because the ground-floor windows were all set very high into the walls and were impossible to see out of. On a hot day, they could be opened for ventilation, using a long pole with a hook on the end. Inside the gates was the girls' playground, with what the children called the BB – the bog block – at the far end. The boys' playground was to the right, with a one-storey wing of the building sticking out and separating the two. The main door was reached via the boys' playground. Nancy and Vivienne mounted the stone steps and rang the bell to be let in.

With a cheerful goodbye, Nancy disappeared and Vivienne went upstairs to the gloomy corridor where Miss Allan, the secretary, occupied an alcove, which served as her office, where she was assisted by Miss Virginia, who until last summer had been one of the orphanage's children. Vivienne greeted Miss Allan politely and nodded to Ginny, knowing that Miss Allan wouldn't want her to engage the girl in conversation.

'Miss Virginia, please show Mrs Atwood to Mrs Rostron's office,' said Miss Allan and Ginny got up to obey.

Vivienne followed her down the corridor to the end, where Ginny knocked on the superintendent's door, waited for Mrs Rostron to call, 'Come,' and stepped inside to announce her, standing aside to let her by. Mrs Rostron look up from her desk, which was at all times so tidy that only the keenest eyes would realise quite how many papers and files were on it.

'Good morning,' Vivienne said. 'I'm playing postman today. This is for you from Mr Taylor.' She held out the envelope.

There was the tiniest pause before Mrs Rostron reached out and took it. 'Thank you. Have you time to stay for a cup of tea?'

'Actually, I have, thank you.'

Mrs Rostron looked across to where Ginny was waiting. She didn't say anything, but Ginny said, 'Yes, Mrs Rostron,' and disappeared.

Vivienne hung up her coat and sat down. She half-expected Mrs Rostron to excuse herself while she opened the letter from Mr Taylor, but she simply placed it on her blotter.

'How is Hannah getting on?' Vivienne asked.

Hannah was a little girl who had, at Vivienne's recommendation, been moved to St Anthony's towards the end of last year, because her previous placement in a huge orphanage had made her dreadfully unhappy.

'So-so.'

'Only so-so?' Vivienne was concerned. 'She seemed to be settling in well.'

'To begin with, yes, but that was because she was so relieved to be in a smaller orphanage. Don't forget she is a relatively recent orphan. It's now sinking in that this is the way her life is going be from now on. It's part of the process children go through when they enter an orphanage. We'll keep an eye on her.'

There was a pause as the tea tray was brought in and Mrs Rostron poured. Mrs Wilkes, the orphanage cook, had sent a plate of buttery-smelling shortbread as well.

Instead of picking up her teacup, Mrs Rostron picked up the envelope Mr Taylor had sent. 'Thank you for bringing this. Do you know what it contains?'

'No, only that Mrs Wardle was eager to get her hands on it.'

'I can't say I'm surprised. You and I know one another well enough to share a confidence, Mrs Atwood. I have been appointed to a new post as superintendent of an orphanage housing five hundred children.'

'Five hundred? That's a huge number. I had no idea you had applied for another position.'

'I didn't,' said Mrs Rostron in a dry voice. 'I was given it.'

'I see,' Vivienne said carefully. 'Are you happy about it?'

'It isn't a question of being happy or otherwise. I have been appointed. It was made clear to me that this is an acknowledgement of the good work I have achieved here at St Anthony's. So these will be my final weeks here.'

'It's sad to think of that, but it's exciting too.'

'You're still young enough to view a new position as cause for excitement. You're right, I am sad. I have become very attached to St Anthony's and I want only the best for it and the children. I hope the person who replaces me will maintain my high standards and enjoy great success.' Mrs Rostron looked closely at Vivienne. 'This is all highly confidential at present, you understand.'

'Naturally.'

'But I've chosen to share it with you, Mrs Atwood, so that you have ample time to consider whether you might wish to apply for the position of St Anthony's superintendent.'

Chapter Eight

SITTING IN THE firelight, his legs stretched out onto the hearth, Dad said, 'I hope you get a job soon, Jess, because I've asked Agnes if she wants to get wed, and she's said yes, but not until you've moved out.' He lifted his gaze from the flames to glance at her before looking into the fire again.

'Agnes? Mrs Nolan?'

'Of course Mrs Nolan. Who else? Don't cheek me.' But the gruffness was to hide the discomfort that showed in the colour touching his cheeks. He was embarrassed, as well he might be considering he had just asked his only daughter to leave home permanently. On the other hand, Jess was only here because she was between jobs, so she couldn't complain, though she couldn't help wondering what Mum would have made of it.

On Sunday after chapel, Jess took a few stems of wintersweet to the churchyard that nestled in the floor of the valley. It looked rather stark at this time of year, but once the spring unfolded and bright sunshine touched the dark-green leaves of the yews and cypress trees, a kinder, softer shade would be cast over the graves where families would once again place vases of flowers now that the danger of frost was over.

Jess placed the wintersweet in front of Mum's headstone. Mum's death was the great sorrow of her life, greater even than— She wouldn't dignify that event by letting it share this moment with Mum. Jess shook her head. How were you meant to come to terms with the loss of someone before their time? By, that Spanish flu had a lot to answer for.

As she was leaving, she spied Mrs Rodwell and Mrs Minford carrying flowers, and not pretty but inexpensive bunches, but costly bouquets, the blooms vivid against greenery so dark it gleamed. Jess didn't mean to intrude, but the two sisters glimpsed her and stopped as she came their way.

'Are you here visiting your mother?' asked Mrs Rodwell.

'Yes. Are you visiting yours?'

'We're visiting our father's grave,' said Mrs Rodwell. 'Today would have been his birthday.'

Jess nodded. Before their widowed mother had married Mr Niall Henderson, these two had been Vicky and Leonora Wildman. Not that anyone would have guessed it from the way Niall Henderson conducted himself. He was famous for treating all five daughters exactly the same, as if there was no such thing as a step-relationship in the mixture. That was good and generous of him, of course, and the late Mrs Henderson, mother of the five daughters, must have appreciated it, but Jess wondered what Mr Wildman would have made of it. Would he have been grateful that his successor had taken Vicky and Leonora to his heart, or would it have pushed his nose out of joint to find himself supplanted? What a mad thought. Mr Wildman was dead and gone long since and so were his opinions.

'Now isn't the time to discuss it,' said Mrs Minford, 'but we should so like to hear all about your interview in Chorlton. Are you free tomorrow morning, about eleven? That would suit you, wouldn't it, Vicky?'

'Just tell us one thing now,' said Mrs Rodwell. 'Did you get the job?'

'I honestly don't know, but I'm not holding my breath. The owner was looking for a man.'

'Honestly!' Mrs Minford exclaimed. 'Then why interview a woman? Some people!'

Jess was about to explain about the blot, but Mrs Rodwell brought their meeting to an end, and they parted company. Jess felt worried as she walked away. She hadn't seen anything else to apply for since she had been back.

While she was stirring the porridge on Monday, Dad appeared, holding out a letter.

'This just came for you.'

She left off stirring to take it from him. She would rather have been left alone to open it, especially if it should be a rejection, but Dad stood right beside her. Jess opened it. The words Oak Lodge at the top sent a nervous feeling skittering through her.

'*I am pleased to inform you...*' Dad read out loud.

But that needn't mean anything. Mr Peters might be pleased to inform her he had found a suitable man. Jess's gaze skimmed over the words.

'*... to inform you that I have selected you for the post of*— Oh!' She gave a little laugh of excitement. 'I've got it. For a trial period until Easter, it says – but I've got it. Oh, Dad.' She beamed at him. Then she straightened her face. This was the moment for him to say, 'You'll be off again, then? Leaving me in the lurch, as usual.'

But he said, 'Good for you, lass. When do you start?'

Was it silly to feel miffed that he would be glad to see the back of her? She ought to be pleased. It would be a relief to leave without having to feel guilty about it.

'I start next Monday.' She gave Dad a smile. 'You'll be able to get wed now.'

'Aye, I will. Watch that porridge. It'll catch if you're not careful.'

Jess hummed softly to herself as she finished preparing breakfast. The world felt a better place and she would have good news to share when she saw Mrs Rodwell and Mrs Minford.

'I don't think Mr Peters was exactly falling over himself to snap me up,' she told the two ladies later on after she had given them her news followed by a description of her interview. 'He kept me waiting before telling me, so he must have had to think hard about it.'

'But he made the right decision in the end,' said Mrs Minford, her blue eyes sparkling, 'and that's what counts.'

'Yes, it is,' Jess agreed, 'even if it is only a trial period. I'm sure a man wouldn't have had to do one of those.'

'It doesn't matter what a man might have had to do,' Mrs Rodwell answered, 'because a man wasn't good enough to be chosen. Don't do yourself down. This Mr Peters evidently didn't want to employ a woman, but when push came to shove, you were the best person. Never forget that.'

An uncomfortable weight seemed to evaporate inside Jess's chest. Mrs Rodwell was right. Mr Peters might have agonised over his decision, but he had appointed her in the end and that was the only thing that mattered.

Jess woke early on the day she was to start work in Chorlton. Pulling on her dressing gown, she drew one curtain aside and batted her way through the snowy net, sighing with satisfaction at the sight of dry pavements and skies of periwinkle blue. The fine day fitted in with her mood, though it wouldn't have mattered if it had been bucketing down. She would still have felt the same, a mixture of cheerfulness and resolve. She was determined to make a success of her new job and prove to Mr Peters that a woman could be as good as a man any day. She knew all about having to be better than a man in order to be considered as good as, but that was nothing new. She had met it all the time when she had worked in local corporations.

She was going to have to tread carefully with Mr Peters. Mrs Peters, on the other hand, seemed friendly and reasonable. Might she be an ally? She had written Jess a kind letter, explaining that she had booked her a room in a modest B and B in Chorlton. *Oak Lodge will bear the cost of your first week's accommodation and meals. Thereafter you need to make your own arrangements.* Jess had felt quite overwhelmed by such generosity and now that she was in Chorlton, she was eager to go to Oak Lodge and thank Mrs Peters personally.

But when she arrived at Oak Lodge and poured out her gratitude as she and Mrs Peters shook hands, Mrs Peters rather took the wind out of her sails by saying, 'Don't mention it, Miss Mason. I said to Mr Peters, "We can't possibly have a young lady come to work for us without sorting her out with somewhere to stay while she finds her feet." I would never have let my daughter go off to live somewhere all on her own.'

'It's very kind of you,' said Jess, but her spirits dipped. Mrs Peters wasn't an ally. She was a mother hen fussing over a chick – and not just a chick, but a girl-chick. Undoubtedly, a male employee would have been left to fend for himself.

A few minutes later, seated in Mr Peters' office, Jess thanked him politely for the week's accommodation.

'My wife insisted. Let's hope you're worth it.'

Jess was stung into replying, 'I can repay you, if you prefer.' Now she came to think of it, she would feel more comfortable that way.

'Mrs Peters wouldn't hear of it.' Then Mr Peters added, 'If I don't keep you on after the probationary period, you can repay the bill. That's fair, I think.'

Jess picked up her handbag from beside her chair and took out a piece of paper. 'I've taken the liberty of preparing a list of tasks for myself. Would you like to see it, sir? I'm sure you have your own list of jobs for me as well.'

Mr Peters looked surprised, but he reached out for the list, then put on a pair of reading glasses. '*Tell neighbours about building work*.' He removed his spectacles and looked at her.

'Yes,' she said stoutly. 'I don't know the extent of the work that will be required, but there'll be deliveries, workmen coming and going, maybe some noise. An apology in advance wouldn't go amiss.'

'Holly Lodge stands inside a large garden. The work shouldn't disturb the neighbours. But I take your point, Miss Mason. It would get us off on the right foot. As a matter of fact, Oak Lodge is very much a part of the local community around here and it is my intention that Holly Lodge should be the same in Chorlton, though I had imagined that sort of thing would commence after the place opens its doors.'

'It's never too soon to get on friendly terms with the neighbours.'

Mr Peters put his glasses on again. '*Talk to local butcher, grocer*, etc.' Off came the glasses. 'It's too soon for that and when the time comes, it will be for me to do. I'm considering using my current suppliers. I'm sure they'd be happy to deliver to Chorlton.'

'Pardon me, but wouldn't it be better to support local businesses? It would be good for Holly Lodge's place in the community. Also, it would make it easier to sort out any problems. What I intended – I mean, what I thought you might like me to do – is approach local greengrocers and so forth and ask for their terms and find out if they already supply other establishments, which would enable me to seek references. Then you would have all the necessary information at your fingertips when you require it.'

Mr Peters frowned. 'Miss Mason, are you going to be one of those pushy females?'

'Pushy?' Jess exclaimed before taking a breath and employing her pleasantest voice. 'Had you chosen a man for this post, and had he made these suggestions, would you think him pushy – or would you call him efficient?' She hesitated, then thought: Why not? In for a penny. 'Had I come here today armed with no ideas and just waiting to be given instructions, you would have wondered why you'd bothered appointing me.'

To her relief, Mr Peters smiled – not a wide smile that made his eyes crinkle, just enough of a smile to show approval. 'A valid point, Miss Mason. I can always appreciate a valid point, honestly made.' He handed back her list without further discussion. 'This morning I'll show you round Oak Lodge and explain how I run things. This afternoon, I'll take you to Holly Lodge and show you round. Holly Lodge is a big old place. There are rooms in the attics where the servants used to sleep when it was a family home, and there is a spacious basement flat, which used to be shared between the cook and the housekeeper, I believe. That will be the manager's accommodation. Please don't misunderstand; I'm not inviting you to move in. That wouldn't be appropriate, as you are merely the probationary manager. This week, Mr Thorpe, who is the landlord's agent, will show a builder round. It's a local company, highly reputable. They'll submit their quote. I've also been in touch with Mr Taylor at the Board of Health, so you can expect a visit from one of his people. And Mr Milner, who supplies fire extinguishers, will need to take a look round.'

'I'll have plenty to keep me busy,' said Jess.

'I am placing a great deal of trust in you, Miss Mason.'

'I understand that.'

'Do you? I have acquaintances in the business community here in Seymour Grove who are watching with interest. Some of them, I may say, are waiting with what amounts to glee for me to admit I made a mistake in appointing a woman to such a responsible position.'

'I won't let you down, sir,' said Jess.

'You better hadn't. If you do, you'll find yourself out on your ear, and never mind waiting for the end of the trial period.' Mr Peters looked pleased with himself. 'Chin up, Miss Mason. I have an advantage over my acquaintances. I have seen your letter of application and your references, all of which are of the highest quality. It now just remains to be seen if you are as good in real life as you are on paper.'

Chapter Nine

'WELL, WHAT DO you think?' Mr Peters asked when he had finished showing Jess round Holly Lodge.

She thought for a moment. As they'd gone round, she had jotted down the jobs that needed doing. As well as redecorating, there were repairs to be seen to, and Mr Peters wanted to add two bathrooms by converting the boxrooms on the first and second floors.

'It's tired and in need of attention,' said Jess, 'but once the work has been done, it's going to be splendid. That room with the bay windows will make the perfect sitting room. It has plenty of natural light and looks over the garden at the side as well as the front.'

'The landlord has paid a man to keep the garden in order while the house has been empty,' said Mr Peters. 'He would have had the house thoroughly cleaned before I took it over, but we agreed there was no need since I'm going to have workmen in.'

Jess could already feel herself taking an interest in the place, not just professionally but in a personal way as well. It would be a real pleasure to watch it being transformed and made ready for its new occupants.

'This is the manager's office.' Mr Peters opened a door onto a small room beside the staircase. 'Good: everything's arrived.'

Jess walked in. There was a desk and chair, with two extra seats for visitors. A typewriter sat on the desk and there were three large boxes on the floor. Two contained stationery, an accounts book, document boxes and so forth.

From an inside pocket, Mr Peters produced two bank notes and a little linen bag that clinked as he set it on the desk. 'Petty cash. You'll find a money-box in one of the drawers. Please keep it locked at all times and make sure you account for everything you spend. Not that there should be much to start with. What's in that other box? I didn't send it.'

Jess peeped inside and smiled. 'Some pieces of crockery and cutlery. Tea, sugar, a box of Huntley and Palmers.'

'My wife, no doubt,' said Mr Peters. 'Right, I'll leave you to get on. This book is the log book. At the end of every day, you must record all the significant things that happened that day. I'll drop in unannounced sometimes to see how you're getting on. If you encounter any problems, *any* problems,' he emphasised, 'please inform me immediately.'

'Of course,' said Jess.

When Mr Peters had gone, her first job was to write to the neighbours – no, her first job was to go and have another look around the building on her own. In particular, she wanted to have a good look at the basement flat. Would it be her home one day? Holly Lodge was built in such a way that the garden was at ground-floor level at the front and at basement level at the back. At the sides, the area around the basement had been hollowed out from the ground, so that outside the windows there were paths of about four feet wide. Jess immediately pictured them being full of tubs of herbs and shade-loving plants.

There was no kitchen in the basement. Apparently, the old housekeeper and cook had had the use of the main kitchen on the ground floor. Well, that would suit Jess. There were three large rooms – a bedroom for each of the women, plus a comfortable shared sitting room? It was more than ample space for Jess. There were several smaller rooms as well, where apparently goods had previously been stored, but Mr Peters had told her that the stores would now be kept on the ground floor and one of these rooms down here would be converted into a bathroom, though the work on the basement flat wouldn't be started until after the work in the main house was finished.

All in all, it would make jolly good accommodation for the new manager. Jess just hoped Mr Peters would see his way to employing her on a permanent basis.

She went upstairs to the office to write letters to the neighbours. Typed or by hand? Handwritten, definitely. It would look more personal and friendly. She wrote several letters, starting each one *Dear Neighbour*, put them in envelopes and dropped them through the letter-boxes of the houses on either side and two or three houses across the road. Next to those houses was the end of Church Road, on the opposite corner of which was a building which Mr Peters had pointed out to her as being the local orphanage.

She crossed over and walked to the gates. There was no obvious sign of a front door, so she walked around a single storey that jutted out and from there she spotted steps leading up to a big front door.

Soon she was introducing herself to the secretary, a prim-looking older lady, whose desk and cupboards occupied an alcove in a gloomy corridor with no natural light. Over to one side, seated at a table, where she was putting some papers in order, was a young girl aged about fourteen, dressed in a plain white blouse and dark-blue skirt. She had mousy-brown hair and a sweet face with a pointed chin.

'I hoped to speak to the orphanage manager, if he's available,' said Jess.

'Superintendent,' the secretary corrected her, 'and I'll see if *she* is available.'

Jess could have kicked herself. For her, a professional woman, to have made such a fundamental gaffe was unforgivable, but it showed how easy it was. Everybody assumed that the most responsible jobs were automatically given to men, because that was the way it had always been.

The secretary walked, straight-backed, along the corridor to the door at the end. She knocked and went in, reappearing a moment later. She walked all the way back to Jess before speaking.

'Mrs Rostron can spare you a few minutes. Miss Virginia will show you the way.'

Jess was about to say she could see herself into the office, but there was no sense in arousing this formidable secretary's disapproval. Instead she smiled at the girl, who got up from her work. Jess followed her along the corridor and thanked her for opening the door.

Mrs Rostron was a plainly dressed, serious-looking woman, who had never bothered with the new, shorter hairstyles and still wore a bun of considerable volume in which not a single pin was visible, though it must be crammed full of them. Jess put so many pins in her own hair that she thought it might be unwise to walk past a magnet.

'Miss Mason?' The superintendent shook hands. 'I am Mrs Rostron and I'm the superintendent here. Miss Allan tells me you'll be working at Holly Lodge.'

'That's right. I'm the new manager. Holly Lodge is going to be a home for old soldiers.'

'I'm aware of that.'

'Oh. I didn't know it was common knowledge.'

'I'm not sure that it is,' was the calm reply before a trace of humour appeared in Mrs Rostron's eyes. 'But I have my sources. To what do I owe the pleasure of your visit, Miss Mason?'

'Since we're to be neighbours, I wished to introduce myself,' said Jess, 'and to inform you that works needs to be done on the house, so there may be some disruption – noise and so forth.'

'I appreciate the courtesy, but I think you'll find we make quite enough noise of our own during the children's playtimes.'

'It's a lovely sound, isn't it?' said Jess. 'Children's voices. I hope that when Holly Lodge is up and running, there might be a relationship between our two institutions. The retired soldiers telling the children about life in the old days, that sort of thing.'

'I'm sure something of the kind would be of benefit to both places.' Mrs Rostron spoke in a measured way. She didn't show enthusiasm, but Jess sensed the superintendent meant every word and she was glad she'd come in person.

Not wanting to take up Mrs Rostron's time, she left soon afterwards and returned to Holly Lodge, where the first thing she noticed was the dust. It was no good. She couldn't leave the house in this state. There were some people – mostly men – who would claim it didn't matter if the place was neglected while it awaited the work that was to be done on it, but Jess wasn't one of them. The house might be bare and forlorn, but that was no excuse for it to be dusty.

Investigating the broom cupboard and the cupboard under the stairs, she found a pair of brooms, one soft-brushed for indoors, the other hard for outside, a mop and bucket and a box containing a banister brush and some cleaning rags. That was a start. Unlocking the money-box, Jess hesitated only a moment before taking out some cash. She made a note of it in the accounts book, then she donned her coat and hat and set off to find the shops.

She purchased soda crystals, a bar of carbolic and – yes, why not? – a tin of Brasso so she could buff up the door-knocker and letter box. Then, using her own money, she bought a long apron with a wide bib and a mob-cap. She spent the rest of the afternoon wet-dusting and floor-mopping. Before she returned to the B and B, she opened the log book and recorded that she had informed the neighbours of possible noise and that she had met Mrs Rostron at the orphanage. She didn't mention cleaning. Placing the book in a drawer, she locked up carefully before leaving. She was already looking forward to tomorrow.

The next morning saw her swathed in her new apron and with her hair tucked inside her mob-cap. She finished off the cleaning, saving the door furniture until last. As she rubbed the letter box to a high shine, a woman's voice boomed out behind her.

'Stand aside, if you please. I'm here to see the manager.'

Turning, Jess beheld a stout middle-aged lady in a woollen coat of the best quality. She wore a fox fur draped round her plump shoulders and her hat sported a mass of cherries.

'Actually, I'm the manager,' said Jess, smiling.

The lady looked her up and down. Jess had read stories in which a character looked someone up and down, but she hadn't realised it could happen in real life. But that was what this lady – she was every inch the lady – was doing to her now. With disapproval oozing out of her pudgy face, she lowered her gaze from Jess's face to her shoes and back up again all the way to her mob-cap. Drat! Talk about first impressions. Hating herself for feeling embarrassed, Jess fumbled behind her back to unfasten her apron, then more or less tore off her mob-cap, using her fingers to comb her hair.

'My name is Jess Mason. How do you do?'

'The new manager – and also the cleaner. How… adapt-able you must be.'

Jess summoned up all her experience of dealing with stroppy guests at the Sea View. 'I'll take that as a compliment. What may I do for you?'

'I am Mrs Wardle from the Board of Health.'

'Mr Peters told me to expect you. Come into the office and we can talk. May I offer you a cup of tea?'

'Are you also the parlourmaid?

'And the washer-up,' she said cheerfully. 'When Holly Lodge opens, there will naturally be a full complement of staff, but until then I am happy to turn my hand to whatever needs doing.'

Would the old bag sneer at that? No, actually she didn't. To Jess's surprise, she looked pleased.

'Then you must be very busy,' Mrs Wardle said sympa-thetically, 'and I'm sure you'll be glad of my assistance. Tell me. What is your background?'

'I have worked in two local corporations and a hotel.'

Mrs Wardle pulled in her chin and the cherries on her hat bobbed up and down. 'A hotel?'

'Which means I know all about running an establishment of this size.'

'A local hotel?'

'No. I'm from the north of Lancashire.'

'Ah – so you are new to Manchester. Then you shall require the benefit of my local knowledge. I believe there is work to be done on the building before it opens. I'll furnish you with the name of a reputable builder.'

'Mr Peters has already arranged for a building firm to look over the house.' Jess frowned. 'That isn't the sort of advice I would have expected from the Board of Health.'

'As I said, it is local knowledge. Regard me as your friend and adviser, Miss Mason, and you shan't go far wrong. I'll have a word with the butcher and grocer on your behalf and I'll help to conduct the interviews when you start to appoint staff.'

'We'll see,' Jess said diplomatically. Mr Peters had said nothing about the Board of Health adopting such an active role. 'The kind of support I would most appreciate is regarding the residents.'

'Yes indeed, Miss Mason. We shall work together to attract only the best.'

'They're all the best, in a way, don't you think, having served their country?'

'Yes, yes.' Mrs Wardle flicked her hand dismissively.

'Some will be paying guests with private means, but do you know of a local charity that might top up a man's expenses if he can't afford the fees in full?'

'Come now, Miss Mason. There's no call for that sort of thing,' Mrs Wardle declared. 'With Oak Lodge's excellent reputation, Holly Lodge need have no fear of being obliged to take charity cases, so put that out of your mind straight away. I will compose an advertisement for you to place in the northern edition of *The Times*.' She drew a deep breath, as if savouring the moment. It made her appear unbearably smug. 'We shall have no riff-raff in Holly Lodge.'

Jess got rid of the imperious Mrs Wardle by pretending to have an appointment, resisting the temptation to slam the front door behind her. Dreadful woman! And what sort of institution was the Board of Health if it didn't care about folk in need? Jess had wanted to tell her visitor that she could manage quite well without assistance – but she couldn't do that without speaking first to Mr Peters since he had specifically requested the Board of Health's involvement.

Needing to walk off her annoyance at Mrs Wardle, she decided to go out and look for butchers, grocers and greengrocers. Taking her comb from her handbag, she nipped upstairs to tidy herself in front of a looking-glass that had been left behind in one of the bedrooms, groaning inwardly at the sight of her messy hair. She did a quick repair, then fetched her hat and coat and set off. She introduced herself in some shops and made arrangements to come back another time to discuss the possibility of supplying the old soldiers' home. When she returned to Holly Lodge, the sun was glinting on the newly polished door-furniture and she smiled as satisfaction seeped through her. She opened the door and found an envelope on the floor. There was no stamp on it. It was addressed to *The Manager* and the words *By hand* appeared in the top left-hand corner. Inside was the business card of Mr J. Thorpe, Agent to Mr H. Benfleet, Property Owner, along with a piece of paper torn from a notebook. There was no greeting on it, just a tetchy message.

Brought builder to view premises. Expected you to be here. Please make yourself available tomorrow 2pm.

There was no signature, just *JT*. How rude. Yes, Mr Peters had told her the landlord's agent would bring the builder round, but did this Mr Thorpe take it for granted she would be here every minute, awaiting his convenience? Apparently so.

Jess was ready well before time the following day and the moment the door-knocker sounded, she went to answer it. On the top step under the porch was a tall, dark-eyed man with a moustache above a thin mouth. He wore a double-breasted overcoat with a grey homburg and he carried a cane. A cane! Not a walking stick for support, but a cane for show. Crikey. Being a landlord's agent must pay well. He held himself erect as if he were a man of importance.

Behind him, standing on the steps, was a man in a three-piece suit of brown wool, the single-breasted jacket declaring it to be several years old. The man had blue eyes and a rather earnest expression that suggested openness and a pleasant nature.

'Mr Thorpe?' Jess said to the first man.

Mr Thorpe walked straight past her, deftly switching his cane from one hand to the other as he removed his overcoat and hat, both of which he thrust at her at the same time as looking all around him, as if he were setting eyes on the grandest stately home in the kingdom. He turned round to include his companion in the moment.

'Here we are. Rather a good-looking place, don't you think? Spacious. If this young lady will kindly fetch the manager for me, we can make a start.' Mr Thorpe glanced Jess's way with a supercilious smile.

She smoothed his coat over one arm, dangling his hat from her fingers, so she looked less like a clothes-horse. 'I am the manager.' Was she going to be obliged to explain this to everyone who crossed the threshold?

Mr Thorpe's eyebrows climbed up his forehead. 'Then you aren't the secretary? A lady manager. Well, well.'

The builder politely removed his hat as he entered the hall. To Jess's surprise, his hair was white – and him probably only in his early thirties.

He held out his right hand to her. 'Tom Watson from Perkins and Watson. How do you do?'

Jess shook hands, hoping her surprise hadn't showed. 'Jess Mason. Pleased to meet you.'

She managed not to narrow her eyes as she replayed his words in her head, searching for a patronising note, but his manner was civil and professional. Good. She held out her hand to Mr Thorpe as well, then went to the office to dispose of Mr Thorpe's things and pick up her notebook.

She smiled at her visitors. 'I'm sorry I wasn't here yesterday, but I had to go round the shops.'

Mr Thorpe made a sound that fell somewhere between a snort and a laugh. 'That's naughty of you, Miss Mason, slipping out to do your shopping on Mr Peters' time.'

'I wasn't,' Jess started to say, but what was the point? The best she could do was ignore it and move on. 'I have my notes here of what Mr Peters wants you to look at, Mr Watson.'

'There's no need for that,' said Mr Thorpe. 'I have all the necessary information.' He looked at Tom Watson. 'Shall we start at the top and work down?'

'Actually, I'd prefer to start downstairs, if Miss Mason doesn't mind.' Mr Watson looked at her. 'Are there any alterations you'd like on the ground floor?'

'Yes. Let me show you the kitchen.'

She was grateful for his courtesy. Grateful! You shouldn't have to be grateful for courtesy. Or – horrid thought – maybe it wasn't real courtesy. Was Tom Watson patronising her in his own way? Not lofty-patronising like Mr Thorpe, but sympathetic-patronising, because he thought she couldn't hold her own. It was impossible to tell, and she should be concentrating on her task anyway.

The three of them went round the house. Mr Thorpe obviously had considerable knowledge of building structure in general and the specific work that was to be done here and Jess felt at a disadvantage until she realised that most folk, when they asked a builder round to talk about a job, wouldn't know much, if anything.

She made a point of saying to Mr Watson, 'Please could you explain that again, in laymen's terms.'

'There's no need for you to worry your head about it,' said Mr Thorpe.

Jess ignored him, fixing her gaze on Mr Watson, willing him not to dismiss her request. 'I want to be sure I understand.'

'Of course,' he said. 'I'll go through it again. If you stand here, you'll see better.'

Finally, they made their way downstairs once more.

'There's a lot of work that needs doing,' said Jess. 'Will it take a long time?'

Mr Watson smiled at her. 'You'll be surprised how quickly it all comes together, barring unforeseen problems, of course. Working in an empty building will make a significant difference.'

'Is Perkins and Watson interested in the job, then?' Mr Thorpe enquired.

'By all means,' said Mr Watson. 'I'll need to come back to take a closer look and do the measuring before I put together a quote.' He looked at Jess. 'Can we make an appointment for that?'

Mr Thorpe laughed. 'I'm sure she can fit you in between her shopping expeditions.'

Well! So far Jess had had two visitors and they'd both been obnoxious. Ah, but she was forgetting Tom Watson. He hadn't been snooty with her, but had his courtesy been genuine or had it been because he wanted to make up for Mr Thorpe's deplorable attitude? Jess couldn't tell, but she hoped it was the former, because Mr Watson had seemed likeable.

The door-knocker rat-tatted and Jess went to answer it. On the step was a good-looking woman with a heart-shaped face on which the faint lines under her eyes and at the sides of her mouth suggested she was past the first flush of youth. Thirty, perhaps. Her fawn edge-to-edge coat looked smart with its fancy top-stitching on the cuffs and collar. Under an over-sized beret, she wore her light-brown hair fashionably bobbed.

'You must be the new manager,' she said.

'Yes, I am.' In that moment, Jess could have dragged her over the threshold and hugged her. At last – someone who realised who she was! 'Jess Mason.'

'I apologise for appearing unexpectedly, but I had another appointment in Chorlton and thought I'd take a chance. I hope we can put something in the diary. I'm Mrs Atwood from the Board of Health – Vivienne Atwood.'

'I've already had a visitor from there.'

Mrs Atwood's face fell. 'It wasn't Mrs Wardle, was it?'

'Yes.'

'Dear me. This is rather difficult. May I come in? There's something I should explain.'

Jess stood aside to let Mrs Atwood enter. She waved one hand to indicate the bareness. 'Home sweet home, but there's a fire in the office. May I take your coat?'

Mrs Atwood was wearing a calf-length dress of olive green, with a sash that buckled at the hip. Either the Board of Health paid women above the going rate or else Mrs Vivienne Atwood had private means. She looked well dressed, though not over-dressed like Mrs Wardle with her furs and her bobbing cherries. Jess felt an instinctive liking for Mrs Atwood and didn't like to think of her heralding from the same place as Mrs Wardle.

As they sat down, Mrs Atwood said, 'I hope this doesn't sound impertinent, but would you mind telling me what Mrs Wardle said to you?'

It was impossible not to be intrigued by the question, but Jess knew better than to put her foot in it and she was careful how she answered. 'She offered to assist with various tasks, such as finding prospective residents.'

'I see.' Mrs Atwood pressed her lips together thoughtfully, then she sat forward. 'May I speak frankly? It's possible that

Mrs Wardle may have – how shall I put it? – expressed views that are not those of the Board of Health. When you say she offered to assist with finding residents—'

'She wanted to put an advertisement in *The Times*.'

Although Mrs Atwood's eyes widened, she spoke with calm politeness. 'That doesn't come as a surprise. I'm not going to put you on the spot by asking for other details. It's probably best if I simply explain that Mrs Wardle's involvement with the Board of Health is in a purely voluntary capacity. If I tell you the Board of Health's position, you can decide for yourself what to think.'

Jess listened carefully while Mrs Atwood described the type of support she could expect from the Board of Health. She mentioned a local doctor with a special interest in old war wounds and a charity that paid for the elderly to have well-fitting dentures, as well as an organisation that promoted physical therapy to help old people remain active.

'Thank you,' said Jess. 'That sounds ideal.'

'Good,' said Mrs Atwood. 'I'll be pleased to assist in any way I can, though I can't promise you won't be visited by Mrs Wardle again.'

Jess wanted to say, 'Over my dead body,' but settled for, 'Perhaps there should be a letter to the Board of Health to say thank you for the visits from two members of staff, but we mustn't keep so much professional support to ourselves, and please could we work solely with Mrs Atwood, as her ideas coincide with our own.'

'I'm sure that would do the trick.'

Honesty made Jess say, 'It's not up to me. I'll explain to Mr Peters and ask him if he'll write.'

She pictured his face when she dropped *The Times* and riff-raff into the conversation. Oh, he'd write the letter, she was sure of it.

Mrs Atwood looked as if she was about to get up. 'I'm sorry. I've barged in as if your time is mine to do with as I please. Perhaps I should return on another occasion. When would suit you?'

'Now suits me perfectly well,' said Jess. 'Even if it didn't, I would make the time for you, because you're the first person to come here who has assumed I'm the manager.'

'How annoying for you. I bet the others were men.'

'As a matter of fact, one of them was Mrs Wardle.' Jess stood up. 'Why don't I put the kettle on and make us some tea? I've got some nice biscuits too. Then you can tell me more about the Board of Health and we can look for ways in which you and I can work together for the good of Holly Lodge.'

Chapter Ten

'How did you get on at Holly Lodge?' Uncle Bill asked as he, Tom and Dad ended the day together in the office.

'It promises to be an interesting project. It's a handsome building and structurally sound. If we get the job, it'll be rewarding work.'

The amused glance that passed between Dad and Uncle Bill didn't escape Tom's notice and he knew what was coming next.

'Oh aye, it'll be most rewarding to watch the place grow, won't it?' said Uncle Bill.

Tom pretended to groan. 'I wish I'd never said that.'

But he was used to being teased about it and took it in good part and, yes, he did like to see a place grow. Yes, grow. He was aware how daft it sounded, but that was how he felt about his job. Sometimes Perkins and Watson built from the foundations up and then he really did watch the building take shape and grow, but repairs and improvements felt like a kind of growth as well. They represented the building coming into its own, preparing for the next phase of its life.

That wasn't the only reason why he looked forward to returning to Holly Lodge. He wasn't averse to seeing Miss Jess Mason again. Mr Thorpe's attitude towards her had irritated him. He hated it when men talked down to women. To try to belittle a working woman was especially inappropriate. Thorpe would never have spoken to a male manager in that condescending manner, and it had aroused Tom's protective instincts. To her credit, Miss Mason had taken it on the chin. He admired that – but how had she felt on the inside? There was never any excuse for a man to be disrespectful towards a lady – yes, a lady.

'Every woman you meet is a lady,' Dad had told him years ago. 'No matter who she is or what background she comes from, if you treat her as a lady, you won't go far wrong. No man can call himself a gentleman if he doesn't treat all women as ladies.'

Tom had never forgotten that. Not only was it one of the rules that governed his own life, it was also one of the standards by which he judged other men. It pleased him that his three brothers-in-law were all up to scratch in this respect. He liked all of them, especially Molly's Aaron.

'That's because he's provided you with a nephew,' Molly had joked.

Tom loved young Danny and wanted to play an important part in the boy's life. He was never going to have children of his own, so he wanted to be a loving and attentive uncle to his nieces and nephew. Much as he loved Chrissie and Tilda's girls, there was a special pleasure in kicking a ball about with Danny. Aaron was a carpenter and joiner and Danny was keen to learn from him, already showing signs of picking up the craft.

'Keep on like that, Danny,' Tom had told him, 'and I'll employ you in the family firm one of these days.'

Danny had grinned at him. He had a freckled, oval face with a dent in his pointy chin. It was a cheerful, eager face and that grin made his expression light up.

'Then you can be Danny Cropper Abrams Watson,' said

Tom. 'You have to be Watson if you're going to be in the family firm.'

'Danny Cropper Watson Abrams,' said Danny. 'Abrams has to come last, because that's Mum and Dad's name.'

'In fact,' said Aaron, joining in and ruffling his son's sandy hair, 'if you're going to join Uncle Tom's firm, you'll have to be Danny Cropper Perkins Watson Abrams. What d'you think of that?'

'With all those names,' said Molly, 'you sound like a football team.'

It never failed to touch Tom's heart when he saw how well Molly's ready-made family had moulded together. They deserved their happiness, all three of them.

He thought of them as he returned to Holly Lodge a couple of days later, because the house was over the road from the orphanage where young Danny had spent a desperate time during his real father's final illness; but it was also through being at the orphanage that he had met Aaron, and Aaron had met Molly. Life was like that sometimes. It brought the right people together.

Tom ran up the steps and knocked on Holly Lodge's door. When Miss Mason let him in, the sight of her caused an odd sensation in his chest, like a hand squeezing his heart. Miss Mason's brown eyes were bright, her complexion creamy. It made him realise the strain Mr Thorpe's unpleasant behaviour had placed on her. Now she looked confident and relaxed. Tom hoped Perkins and Watson would be offered the contract to work on Holly Lodge. He would like seeing Miss Jess Mason on a daily basis.

'Would you like me to come round the house with you?' she asked.

'I can find my own way, thanks. I'm sure you don't have a burning desire to watch me tap the walls and do the measuring.'

She smiled. 'Not really. I'll leave you to get on. If you'd like a cup of tea before you go, give me a shout before you finish, and I'll put the kettle on.'

Tom went round the house, making notes, careful not to miss anything out. No one wanted to employ the builder who couldn't get all the details right first time. He nodded his approval of the two boxrooms that were destined to become bathrooms. The existing plumbing was on this side of the house, so adding to it would be straightforward.

Just before he finished, Tom went downstairs in search of Miss Mason. He knocked on her office door, but she wasn't there. He went through to the kitchen and spotted her from the window. She was at the end of the garden, peering at the ground and various plants. With a smile, Tom filled the kettle and put it on the gas. He had to do some measuring in here and check the wall between this and the old breakfast room, so he might as well make himself useful while he did it.

Soon he had finished his notes and made a pot of tea. He opened the back door.

'Miss Mason,' he called.

She looked round and then hurried down the lawn towards him. 'That's a parade-ground voice if ever I heard one.'

He went cold inside. He had to remind himself that she didn't know. 'Actually, it's a builder's voice. When you work outdoors in all weathers, you have to be able to make yourself heard.'

'Are you done? Would you like some tea before you go?'

Standing back, Tom indicated the brown earthenware pot. 'Does that answer your question?'

Miss Mason— oh, what the heck. He knew her first name and he would use it, though only in his thoughts. Jess stepped into the kitchen and he shut the door behind her. It was a cool day but she hadn't bothered with a coat and the fresh air had put roses in her cheeks.

'Sugar?' he offered.

'I'm impressed. My father wouldn't make a pot of tea for a woman if his life depended on it.'

Tom couldn't help smiling. He started to relax again, feeling himself recover from the parade ground comment. 'Builders again. Making tea is a basic requirement of the job.'

Jess quickly assembled a tray and, before he could pick it up, she carried it through to her office, putting it on her desk before rubbing her hands together in front of the cheerful little fire. They took their places, she behind the desk, he in front of it, but in spite of the overt formality, there was an ease between them. Had making the tea got him off on the right foot with her? Or wasn't it ease at all? Was it a sort of scorn because she had dismissed him as unworthy, unmanly, because he had done what most folk would see as a woman's job?

But she seemed perfectly pleasant as she asked if he had got all the information he needed about the house.

'It's going to be splendid when it's finished,' said Tom, 'and I'm not saying that in the hope of my firm being chosen to do the job.'

'You're right. It will be splendid. I'm looking forward to running it.' Jess leaned forward and placed her elbows on the edge of her desk, leaning her chin on her clasped fingers. 'My previous job was in a seaside hotel, so I know all about how to keep a place like this ticking over.'

'I didn't realise this is going to be a hotel, but that would explain the bathrooms.'

'It isn't going to be a hotel. It'll be for a home for long-term residents, but running it will be almost the same as running a hotel – just without the huge change-over of guests every Saturday in the summer.'

'I think you'll be good at it,' said Tom.

Jess frowned and sat back in her seat, an obvious withdrawal. 'Don't say that if you don't mean it.'

'I do mean it. That is, I hardly know you, of course, but it's just the impression I've formed. I'm sorry if I spoke out of turn.'

'You didn't. I'm the one who should apologise. It's because of how Mr Thorpe spoke to me. I thought perhaps your courtesy was really you feeling sorry for me.'

'I would never talk down to a woman,' said Tom. 'For one thing, I have three sisters who would have my guts for garters. For another, all my sisters are married now, but one of them used to go out to work and I wouldn't want her to have been spoken to in the way Mr Thorpe addressed you.'

Jess smiled. She had a lovely smile. She must have to be on her guard the whole time at work, so as not to be caught out by a prejudiced man, but that smile showed the warmth that lay underneath.

'Do you always treat other women the way you treat your sisters?' she asked.

She was joking, but Tom answered seriously. 'Yes. It's one of the rules in our family. Years ago, my dad told my sisters that when they started courting, they had to watch the way the chap treated his mother and his sisters, because that was the way he would one day treat them.'

'It sounds like you come from a nice family,' said Jess.

'I do. The best. Do you have family?'

'There's just me and Dad, though I'll be getting a stepmother soon.'

'Do you mind?' Tom asked.

She thought for a moment. 'I don't know her that well. I haven't lived at home for quite some time. But I'll be glad to think of Dad being properly looked after.' It seemed she had finished, then she leaned forward slightly and added, 'Shall I tell you what I hope for about my new stepmother?'

'What?' Tom's interest was piqued.

'I hope she's a good letter-writer. That was how Dad and I drifted apart. He never answered my letters and in the end I stopped sending them.'

'That's a shame,' said Tom, quickly adding, 'for both of you,' so she would realise he wasn't passing judgement on her.

'Yes,' she agreed. 'Yes, it was. I wish now that I'd carried on writing. I stopped because I was annoyed with him for not replying.'

'If you're hoping for a correspondence with the new Mrs Mason, why wait for the wedding? You could start now. Write a letter to "Dear Dad and" – whatever you call her. I expect they'd both appreciate that. May I tell you something about my sister Christabel? Before she got married, she took her future mother-in-law to choose her wedding shoes. Mrs Evanson – that's the mother-in-law – told me how thrilled she was to be asked, because it showed Chrissie liked her. I know it's not quite the same thing, but your stepmother might appreciate some attention in advance of the wedding. Sorry,' he added, seeing a faint frown on Jess's brow. 'Have I spoken out of turn?'

She shook her head. 'It's not that. It's the thought of you chatting with your sister's mother-in-law. It's... friendly.'

'Oh, we rope everyone into our family, us Watsons.' Tom spoke in a breezy voice, but that didn't mean he wasn't serious.

When he left a short while later, he couldn't help feeling a tug of concern for Jess and the loss of closeness with her father. He couldn't imagine life without his own loving family. He was filled with a sort of stubborn warmth as his earlier wish to protect Jess Mason intensified. Was it mad of him to have a sudden wish to share his family with her?

Chapter Eleven

'AH, THERE YOU are, Mrs Atwood,' said Mrs Wardle as Vivienne entered the Board of Health office. She made it sound as if Vivienne was late, which she certainly wasn't. 'We've been waiting for you.' The violets on the front of her hat bobbed up and down.

Vivienne glanced round. Miss Cadman, Miss Byrne and Boodle the Poodle sat at their desks. Miss Cadman and Miss Byrne's faces were carefully blank, which wasn't unusual when Mrs Wardle was present, but the Poodle was sitting up straight, looking attentive and, unless Vivienne was mistaken, rather pleased with herself.

'I wasn't aware you had called a meeting,' Vivienne said calmly to Mrs Wardle. 'It's not in the diary.'

'Kindly take a seat, Mrs Atwood.'

Vivienne removed her wool coat and over-sized beret, hanging them on the coat-stand along with her silk scarf. She popped her gloves in her desk drawer and placed her handbag on the floor beside her chair. Was it wrong of her to spin everything out and take longer than usual? But, honestly, with Mrs Wardle watching her like a hawk and making a great play of not sighing in impatience, she couldn't help it.

'As you know,' said Mrs Wardle when Vivienne sat down, 'I take pride in bringing on those members of staff in whom I see potential. I was the person who placed the former Miss Watson in St Anthony's Orphanage.'

Vivienne's eyes widened as Mrs Wardle shamelessly rewrote history. The truth was that Vivienne and Molly had tied themselves in knots to get Molly into that position without Mrs Wardle's knowledge.

'I have been deeply impressed with Miss Boodle's performance since she joined us, and I believe she has a special aptitude for work involving children. Therefore, ladies, when you make any appointments concerning the welfare of children, please inform Miss Boodle so that she may accompany you. Kindly confer with one another so as to spread out the appointments in order that she may attend as many as possible.'

There was a shocked silence. Then Miss Byrne said, 'Yes, Mrs Wardle,' and Miss Cadman and Vivienne followed suit.

Mrs Wardle referred to the office diary. Vivienne's heart sank, but she also felt a surge of vexation at the knowledge of what was coming next.

'Mrs Atwood, you are due to see that foolish Mrs King woman, followed by a visit to St Anthony's.' Mrs Wardle turned to the Poodle with a beaming smile. 'You shall soon be an expert, Miss Boodle.'

'Thank you, Mrs Wardle,' said Miss Boodle. 'I'll do my best to repay your faith in me.'

The Poodle was the last person Vivienne wanted to have with her when she called on Mrs King. No, not the last. The last person would be Mrs Wardle, but the Poodle came a very close second-to-last.

As they set off on the tram, Vivienne told the Poodle what she needed to know.

'The Kings occupy a rundown cottage in Limits Lane on the border of Chorlton and Stretford. They lost one of their children in an horrific accident last year.'

'Oh yes, I know all about it,' the Poodle cut in. 'The boy ran out in front of a tram. His own fault.'

'That's a harsh view to take.'

The Poodle shrugged her shoulders inside her fuzzy crushed-velvet coat. 'The truth can be harsh. If he hadn't been larking around, he'd have paid more attention to the road. I've read the file. The mother is inadequate.'

'It doesn't say that in the file,' said Vivienne. She should know: she had written most of it.

'But that's what it comes down to. It's a shame the work-houses have closed. Mrs King is just the sort who needs the structure and discipline they provided.'

Good heavens, no wonder Mrs Wardle liked the Poodle so much. Vivienne had no intention of treating the last remark as if it deserved a sensible reply.

'You are, of course, welcome to sit in on my visit to Mrs King, but please confine yourself to the role of observer. I have gone to a lot of trouble to gain Mrs King's trust.'

'Gain her trust? She should trust you automatically and be grateful for your assistance.'

'I believe that assistance is most useful when it is given and received in a spirit of cooperation and respect. The days of Lady Bountiful doling out orders along with the gruel are over, and not before time.'

The Poodle threw her a sour look and said nothing more.

Alighting from the tram, they made their way to Limits Lane, where they walked down the cinder path to the Kings' dilapidated little cottage. Looking grey and exhausted, Mrs King let them in. The Poodle turned her up-tilted nose even further up at the sight of the hardened dirt floor, but at least she refrained from commenting. Not that she needed to. Her face said it all.

'How are things, Mrs King?' Vivienne asked. 'Is Katie back at school full time now?'

'Aye.'

'That's good. And how are you coping without her here to help?'

'I know I have to get my act together.'

'Yes, you do,' the Poodle murmured loudly enough to be heard.

Tempting as it was to glare at her, Vivienne kept her gaze on Mrs King. 'Your family suffered a terrible loss, but I know you want to do your best for your remaining children. Now that Katie is attending school as required, all the children will be eligible for free school dinners.'

'We don't want charity.'

'It isn't charity. It's what your husband fought for in the war – a better world for his children. With a hot meal inside them once a day, they'll fare better and that will ease your burden a little.'

Mrs King bit her lip. Vivienne could tell by the gleam in her normally dull eyes that she was on the verge of swallowing her pride and accepting. The poor lived in fear of the stigma attached to public assistance.

Looking vulnerable and upset, Mrs King opened her mouth to speak, but the Poodle got in first.

'If you don't say yes, Mrs Atwood will organise the free school dinners without your consent; and if she doesn't, I will.'

Vivienne couldn't get the Poodle out of there quickly enough. 'How dare you speak to Mrs King in that way?'

'Some people need to be chivvied along and clearly those children need the hot meals.'

'Yes, they do,' Vivienne agreed through gritted teeth, 'and I'll ensure they receive them. But they would also benefit from a mother who feels she is starting to cope. Had Mrs King been permitted to give her consent, it would have made it easier to persuade her at our next meeting to accept other assistance. But after the way you spoke to her, it'll be a long time before she is open to such a thing again.'

Vivienne put on a spurt, stalking past all the gracious houses and big gardens on Edge Lane, taking the fork in the road onto High Lane, past St Clement's Church and shortly after that to Church Road, where St Anthony's stood on the corner. Even though she was angry with the Poodle, she experienced an unusual self-consciousness. Might she one day walk through the orphanage gates as its superintendent?

'We're here to check on the progress of a little girl whom I arranged to move here from a much larger orphanage. She hasn't been an orphan for long and the other orphanage overwhelmed her, poor kid.'

'Bad effects?'

'She withdrew right into herself, though I understand she was a bubbly little thing before that. Also, I'm sorry to say, bed-wetting. Hannah is a fastidious child, and the bed-wetting was particularly hard for her to cope with.'

She led the Poodle upstairs and introduced her to Miss Allan. Ginny escorted them along the passage to Mrs Rostron's door at the far end. She knocked and waited for Mrs Rostron's response before opening the door for them to enter. Vivienne performed the introductions and Mrs Rostron invited them to sit down.

The office contained two chairs for visitors, one that stood at all times in front of Mrs Rostron's desk and one that stood against the wall out of the way. Vivienne politely waved the

Poodle into the first seat before turning to bring forward the other. Before she could sit down, the Poodle started talking.

'I'm delighted to be here, Mrs Rostron. I'm interested in working with children and hope to specialise.'

'A worthy ambition.'

'Thank you. We're here to ask you how Hannah is getting along, the child who was brought here from the larger orphanage. I understand she found it very hard living there. Is she finding her feet now?'

Vivienne listened in astonishment as Boodle the Poodle parroted her own concerns regarding Hannah. Honestly, the woman was behaving as if she was the one who had recommended bringing the child here.

Determined to wrest back control, Vivienne asked, 'And the bed-wetting, Mrs Rostron?'

'Yes, I wanted to ask about that,' the Poodle put in. 'Forgive me if this is inappropriate, but might I speak to one of your senior staff about how bed-wetting is tackled here?'

'It's not at all inappropriate,' said Mrs Rostron. 'Nanny Mitchell is on duty today. I'm sure she'll be pleased to discuss the matter with you.'

Before Vivienne knew quite what was happening, the Poodle had wangled a guided tour.

'There's no need for you to wait for me, Mrs Atwood,' she said with the sweetest smile imaginable. 'I may be some time. I have so many questions.'

Suddenly it all slotted into place. Vivienne wasn't the only person to know that the superintendent's post was coming up in the near future. Mrs Wardle must know as well – and she had her follower lined up as successor to Mrs Rostron. Mrs Wardle was forever sticking her nose into orphanage business. If her poodle became the new superintendent, Mrs Wardle would as good as run the place.

'Miss Hesketh, could I prevail upon you to help me out of a fix?'

'Of course, Mr Greenfield.'

Prudence Hesketh smoothed her features as she looked up at the colleague who had appeared in front of her desk. He was a good-looking young man in his thirties – and just when had she reached the age of thinking that thirties counted as young?

'It's the letters following on from yesterday's meeting.' Mr Greenfield looked at her hopefully.

'I'm aware of the correspondence you mean,' Prudence said in her precise way. She took pride in accuracy. 'I took the minutes.'

'That's why I've come to see you. It's an awful imposition, I know, but it's my son's birthday today and I promised him I'd be there to see him blow out his candles. In my previous job, I travelled all the time and I was somewhere else on his birthday every year. I wouldn't normally dream of asking, but you can see how important it is.'

Prudence nodded. She didn't smile. One didn't smile at work. When she was a thirteen-year-old office junior, Miss Isaacs, a fearsome old lady in black bombazine, had said that girls who smiled in the office made themselves look like tarts and flirts and they deserved what was coming to them, though she never specified what this might be. For Prudence, it had been easy not to smile. She was a serious girl. Moreover, she carried a dark anger inside her against Pa, who had abdicated his responsibility as head of the household, which meant that Prudence had to arrange for the coal to be delivered, the garden gate to be repaired and the chimney to be swept. She hadn't minded the responsibility itself. Nothing if not efficient, she had always been proud of her ability to cope; but she had never been in any doubt that, since Mother's death, these jobs should have been organised by Pa.

'If you bring me the paperwork, Mr Greenfield,' she said now, 'I'll see to it.'

'Thanks most awfully. I thought you were the best person to ask, because of not having children or a husband at home to cook for.'

Oh, the number of times that had been said to her over the years! The number of times she had been called upon to work late on Christmas Eve, the number of times she'd been nudged into taking her annual holiday during term-time, because she couldn't possibly need to take it in the school holidays, could she? And everybody who had said these things to her, who had asked these favours, made these assumptions, had been right, of course. Miss Hesketh, spinster of the parish of St Clement's in Chorlton-cum-Hardy, didn't have to take a family into account in her ordered, respectable life.

Along with all those other people, Mr Greenfield was correct. She didn't have a husband to cook for – but she did have a daughter to go home to. She had to close her eyes for a moment, overwhelmed even now by the knowledge. Years ago, abandoned by the man who had made her pregnant, she had handed over her new baby to her friends Elspeth and Graham Thornton for them to bring up as their own. Parting with her child had broken her heart, but what choice had she had? She had forced herself to concentrate on the gratitude she felt at being certain her baby would grow up with the best possible parents. Not that she would be there to see it happen. Part of the arrangement had been that all ties must be cut.

Then, last year, her long-lost daughter had come back into her life, bringing her more happiness than she would have believed possible. Through her new relationship with Vivienne, she had been able to bring belated happiness into her sister Patience's life too, by reuniting her with her long-ago first love, Niall Henderson, who was the brother of Vivienne's real father. Patience and Niall had become engaged before Christmas, though it was being kept quiet until after Niall had introduced Patience to his daughters, who all lived up in the north of Lancashire. Arrangements had been made for all five of them to travel down to Manchester together to meet their stepmother-elect. At present, only a small handful of people were aware of the engagement, because Patience, dear, sweet Patience, who never took anything for granted, didn't wish it to be announced before she had met Niall's girls.

As everyone else put papers and files away in their desks and got ready to leave for the day, Prudence stayed put, doing the extra work, knowing that by the time she reached home, she would just have time for tea and then she would have to start working all over again, teaching office skills in the business school she and Patience ran in the evenings. There was something a little shaming about being obliged to run a school in their home – but that was the whole point. It wasn't their home, not any longer. The house had belonged outright to Mother, who had left it in her will to Pa; but when he had passed away at the beginning of last year, it had turned out that he'd left the house, not to Prudence and Patience, not to Mother's daughters, oh no, but to Lawrence, the son of his first marriage, who had no blood claim on the property at all. Setting up their business school had been a plot to prevent Lawrence from slinging them out of the house into rented rooms, by announcing to the local press that the school was Mr Lawrence Hesketh's idea. Since this fed into his ambition to become an alderman, he had been forced to play along.

Prudence worked steadily on the letters for Mr Greenfield. If he had stayed to write them, a girl from the typing pool would have been obliged to stay as well, but Prudence could do her own typewriting. She typed the envelopes and placed them in the out-tray. Someone from the post room had to stay until seven every evening to make a final tour of all the out-trays, gathering letters for the late evening post.

Prudence went home. The moment she opened the front door, Patience appeared.

'There you are, Prudence. Did you have to stay late?'

There was concern and kindness in Patience's face – her habitual expression. More than once over the years, someone had looked at the pair of them and asked, 'Are you twins?' immediately followed by, 'No, I can see you aren't.'

Prudence knew exactly what those people meant. Superficially, she and Patience were similar, thin and plain with washed-out colouring and eyes of pale blue, yet somehow they looked different. Somewhat to her shame, Prudence knew the differences were all on the inside. Patience's gentle, loving nature bestowed a softness on her outward appearance while Prudence's critical attitude, which many saw as unsympathetic, lent her a sternness.

But she wasn't as hard-edged as she used to be – not since Vivienne had come into her life.

'I had some work to finish,' she told Patience. 'I can smell bacon.'

'Bubble-and-squeak with bacon and fried bread,' said Patience.

'And something fruity, with vanilla.'

'Mincemeat pudding.'

Prudence removed her coat. 'I hope you didn't wait for me.'

'Of course we did.' Vivienne appeared. 'We're a family and families eat together. Miss Patience is a marvel at keeping food hot without letting it dry out.'

Yes, they were a family. A secret family. Only Niall, who was both Vivienne's uncle and Patience's intended, and Lawrence knew. Prudence felt uncomfortable about Lawrence's knowing, but it had become necessary to tell him and there had been a certain satisfaction in observing his profound shock at the idea of his strait-laced sister having had a baby out of wedlock. There was no fear of his ever telling anybody, not even his wife, Evelyn. He would be too ashamed.

After their meal, there wasn't time for their usual cup of tea in the sitting room.

While Patience cleared away, Vivienne offered, 'Should I teach your lessons for you this evening, if you're tired?'

'That's kind, but I'm fine, though you could help me sort out the dining room.'

While Vivienne put the table felt on one end of the table and positioned the two typewriters on top, Prudence retrieved her box of pretend invoices and delivery notes from the sideboard.

'There's something I'd like to discuss with you,' said Vivienne, 'though not this evening, obviously. I'm thinking of applying for another job and I'd like to talk it over with you.'

'Of course,' said Prudence, but her heart gave a thump. Another job? Where? Surely her beloved – yes, beloved – daughter wasn't going to move away? Yet why shouldn't she? She had lived and worked in London before coming to Manchester to join the new Board of Health. Why shouldn't she consider another post somewhere else?

Oh, but it might well break Prudence's heart to see her go. No, it wouldn't. As always, common sense prevailed. It would be deeply disappointing, but not heartbreaking. Their relationship would change, that was all. Instead of sharing the same roof, there would be letters and visits, all the more precious because of the lost pleasure of living together.

When Vivienne shared the news the following evening, when there was plenty of time to talk it over, Prudence surprised herself by feeling she could have wept with relief.

'I didn't say anything before because I wanted to be completely sure,' Vivienne explained, 'but I've thought hard about it, and I want to apply. It means a lot to think that Mrs Rostron herself wishes me to, but I haven't had a post like it before.'

'No, but your work has always brought you into contact with the general public and particularly with families in need.'

'That's true. At the Board of Health, I've worked closely with families facing all kinds of difficulties – including situations that have resulted in children being sent to orphanages, including St Anthony's.'

'Exactly,' said Prudence. 'You have worked well with Mrs Rostron and the fact that she has encouraged you is a good sign. Moreover, you are known to the Orphanage Committee, not least through your idea to change the name to St Nicholas's.'

'In fact, the only disadvantage I've ever come up against regarding St Anthony's is that it means I get a double dose of Mrs Wardle, because she sticks her nose in at the orphanage every bit as much as she does in the Board of Health office. Mrs Rostron never permits so much as a flicker to cross her face, but it must drive her mad.'

'But tolerating Mrs Wardle as the orphanage's official visitor must be a very different thing to being under her thumb at the Board of Health,' Prudence pointed out. 'Mrs Rostron copes with her and you could too.'

Vivienne smiled. 'I'm glad you approve.'

'I more than approve,' said Prudence. 'I'm delighted and proud.'

Not to mention unutterably relieved. If Vivienne were to be given this post, then she would carry on living in Wilton Close and what could be better than that? Prudence shook her head. What a selfish old bat she was.

Chapter Twelve

ON HER WAY home from work, Vivienne popped into the stationer's and purchased a notebook. After tea, she started preparing her letter of application by making notes about her relevant experience. She put the notebook in her bag to take to work with her the next morning.

Before she went to the office, she returned to Holly Lodge to see Miss Mason. She had liked her at their first meeting and felt they would work well together. She generally had a good instinct for these things.

Miss Mason answered the door to her, dressed in the office woman's attire of white blouse and dark skirt, worn with a simple jacket with no braid, turned-back cuffs, decorative top-stitching or extra buttons purely for trim, in fact with none of the fashionable details that characterised Vivienne's own clothes. She had never worn the 'uniform' of the lady clerk. The simple attire made Miss Mason look the same as a thousand other working women, but, oh, wouldn't she look a treat in something jewel-coloured that would show off the radiance of her skin and deepen the colour of her eyes.

'Good morning,' said Vivienne. 'I hope I'm not too early.'

'Come into the office. Have you found out anything that might help Holly Lodge?'

Vivienne took a seat. 'I hope so. I know Holly Lodge is due to be a home for old soldiers, but how would you feel about having some younger men as well? Ex-soldiers, of course.'

'It wouldn't be up to me. It would be for Mr Peters to decide.'

'I realise that, but I wanted to discuss it with you first. Then you can decide if you wish to talk to Mr Peters about it.'

'I appreciate your not going over my head. Tell me what you've found out.' Miss Mason tilted her head slightly to one side, looking interested.

'Many men emerged from the Great War with shattered nerves. Many will always require nursing care, but others don't, though they would benefit from being kept an eye on, shall we say? These men that I hope might find a home here have no families to take care of them, but they are in need of the feeling of security that comes from living in a settled home and being part of a – well, a family, if that isn't an inappropriate term.'

Jess Mason smiled. 'It's not inappropriate at all. There's a real sense of companionship among the men at Oak Lodge. I like the thought of fostering a family feeling.' Then she frowned. 'I'm sure Mr Peters would wish me to make it clear that Holly Lodge won't provide nursing care.'

'I understand that – and so does the charity I have consulted. They place men who served in the Great War in what they consider to be the best place for each man, so I can assure you that Holly Lodge wouldn't be offered any hospital cases. And when I say that, I don't just refer to physical infirmity, but also to mental problems.'

Miss Mason pressed her lips together so tightly they formed a white line. 'I feel mean saying we can't help men like that.'

'That isn't Holly Lodge's purpose,' Vivienne said gently.

'They say it was the war to end all wars. I hope they're right. What other justification could there possibly be for all those deaths and for the terrible injuries of the men who returned? The limbless, the blind, the maimed; men with useless lungs. Men who turn into quivering wrecks every Bonfire Night because of the loud bangs. And you hear stories, though I don't know how true they are, of men shut away in asylums who'll never be allowed out.'

'Shellshock,' said Vivienne. 'It doesn't sound too bad, put like that. It sounds like something you should recover from, something temporary. They should call it endless-shock, because that's what it seems to be. Not that I'm any kind of expert on the subject, mind you.'

'As far as I'm concerned,' said Miss Mason, 'your idea of placing Great War men here is a good one. Of course, Mr Peters has a clear vision of what he wants Holly Lodge to be.'

'Namely, a second Oak Lodge.'

'Yes, so I imagine that three or four younger soldiers would be the maximum.' Miss Mason's brown eyes narrowed and she seemed to gaze into the distance. 'And perhaps a lower age limit – say, forty – so that the gap between the old soldiers and the younger ones isn't too big. And the younger ones would need to be regular soldiers, not conscripts. That would make them the same as the old ones.' She focused on Vivienne. 'Sorry. I'm thinking out loud.'

'Don't let me stop you.'

'I'm trying to come up with ways of making the idea seem right to Mr Peters.'

'I'm delighted to hear it,' said Vivienne, feeling her day had got off to the best possible start. 'Thank you for being so open-minded.'

Soon after that, she left. She was due to be in the Town Hall for the remainder of the day, writing up her recent visits in the morning and attending a meeting in the afternoon. Miss Byrne and Miss Cadman looked up as Vivienne walked into the office.

'You might wish you'd stayed away,' said Miss Byrne. 'Mrs Wardle isn't pleased with you.'

'Why not?' asked Vivienne. She could have asked 'Why not this time?', but that wouldn't have been professional.

'Something to do with a letter from the owner of Holly Lodge,' said Miss Cadman. 'It seems he's asked if you can be the liaison with the Board of Health.'

It seemed wise to feign innocence. 'Really? I'd be happy to, of course.'

And that was what she told Mr Taylor a short while later when he summoned her into his office.

Returning to the main office, Vivienne found that her colleagues had left to attend appointments. They were to be out for the rest of the day, so the office would be quiet.

At midday she went to the canteen, where she sat alone so as not to be caught up in conversation. She ate quickly, then returned to her desk to spend the rest of her dinner hour working on her application for the position of superintendent. The office was empty apart from herself, so there was no one to ask awkward questions.

Shortly before one o'clock, Mrs Wardle came bustling in. The silk rosebuds swaying to and fro on her hat toned in with her silk jacquard costume. When she set eyes on Vivienne, she stopped dead and seemed to rear up in annoyance.

'So you got round Mr Peters, did you? Well, he'll live to rue the day, that's all I can say. I suppose I'll have to pick up the pieces when the time comes.'

'I'm perfectly sure that time will not come,' Vivienne said quietly.

'What are you doing?' Mrs Wardle demanded. The glass eyes on her fox fur seemed to gaze accusingly at Vivienne. 'Are those your notes about the King woman? Let me see.'

Vivienne closed her notebook. 'This is private.' She slipped it into her top drawer beneath some envelopes.

'You aren't paid to do private things in the office.'

'I believe you'll find I can do whatever I please during my dinner hour.'

Mrs Wardle made a humphing sound. 'Just so long as you don't bring the Board of Health into disrepute.' She made it sound as if Vivienne routinely knocked back a liquid lunch and spent the afternoon dancing the Charleston on the desks.

As one o'clock struck, Vivienne took out her file and looked through it in preparation for her meeting. Miss Boodle came into the office and exchanged greetings with Mrs Wardle. Vivienne glanced up with a polite smile before bending her head over her work once more. Presently it was time for her to leave.

The meeting was chaired by her boss – her real boss – Mr Taylor. It was only when you saw him away from the office and safe from Mrs Wardle's hectoring that you realised how good he was at his job. At the end of the meeting, Vivienne left, armed with a list of families with whom she needed to make contact. She loved being out and about, meeting people and finding ways to help them. It was something she would miss if she was fortunate enough to get the post at St Anthony's, soon to be St Nicholas's.

The moment she entered the office, even without looking, she knew Mrs Wardle and Miss Boodle had gone. Miss Cadman and Miss Byrne had both returned and the atmosphere had none of the tautness that characterised it in Mrs Wardle's presence. The three of them chatted about various cases they were working on and then it was time to go home. When Vivienne tidied her desk and opened the drawer to retrieve her notebook, she couldn't help exclaiming.

'Is something wrong?' Miss Cadman asked her.

'No, nothing.'

But it was. It jolly well was. She had placed her notebook underneath the envelopes and now it was on top of them. It had to have been Mrs Wardle. No one else would have looked in her drawer, let alone removed her notebook. Presumably Mrs Wardle had been curious about the private business Vivienne had declined to discuss with her earlier. Curious? Downright nosy, more like. The cheek of it! But that wasn't the worst part. No, the worst thing was that Mrs Wardle – bossy, disagreeable, superior Mrs Wardle – now knew about Vivienne's ambition to be the superintendent of St Anthony's.

Tom went out for a drink with Aaron. Aaron's local was the Bowling Green, known to its regulars as the Bowler, which was near Soapsuds Lane. Several pubs hereabouts had their own bowling greens and Tom and Dad had played in many a crown green match here over the years.

'What are you working on at the moment?' asked Aaron.

Tom mentioned a couple of jobs that had come the way of Perkins and Watson. 'And we're about to lay out an allotment in Limits Lane, where the old cottage burned down last year.'

Aaron nodded. 'The two Layton lads had to move into the orphanage after the fire, because their family didn't have a home any longer.'

Tom remembered Gabriel Linkworth saying that Belinda Layton's younger brothers might end up living with them in due course, but he didn't mention it. As a builder, you heard all kinds of private business and you had to be trustworthy about not passing it on.

From their table in the corner, Tom saw Zachary Milner walk through the door. He was a slim, pleasant-faced fellow, with a suggestion of energy about him that Tom felt drawn to, because it meant Milner was a grafter and Tom respected that. Milner went to the bar and bought himself half a pint. Aaron caught his eye and waved him over.

'You don't mind, do you?' Aaron asked Tom. 'It's time you and he got to know one another. He's a good chap.'

'Fine by me,' said Tom, taking a sup of his bitter.

He knew Zachary Milner slightly, because his shop was a few doors along from Soapsuds House and he was on friendly terms with Aaron and Molly.

'You know my brother-in-law, Tom Watson, don't you?' Aaron said as Zachary joined them. 'He and his father are the builders who knocked the two cottages together to make Soapsuds House.'

'You've got the fire extinguisher shop,' said Tom. 'How's business going?'

'So-so.' Zachary nodded. 'I'm building it up gradually.'

'Best way,' said Tom. 'Take it steady. I'm lucky to have joined an established family firm.'

'How's the building trade these days?' Zachary asked.

'Holding up.' Tom described a couple of jobs Perkins and Watson were currently engaged in, putting in a new snug in a pub and adding an extension to a hotel. 'If either place hasn't got fire precautions in place, I'll mention your name. Let me have a few business cards, will you?'

'With pleasure. Thanks very much.'

'I admire you, setting up in business on your own,' said Tom. 'There's another job in the pipeline, at a place called Holly Lodge. If Perkins and Watson get that contract, I'll mention you there as well.'

Zachary smiled and the skin crinkled around his hazel eyes. 'Thanks for the offer, but I've already got that job. I did the fire safety for Oak Lodge, Mr Peters' other place in Seymour Grove.'

Tom nodded. 'I've heard of it.'

'An old soldiers' place, isn't it?' asked Aaron.

'That's right,' said Zachary. 'Me and Nancy – that's my fiancée,' he added for Tom's benefit, 'we visit there regularly because we love the old fellows. It's good to know that Mr Peters is setting up an old soldiers' home here in Chorlton too.'

The hairs stood up on the back of Tom's neck. 'Here in Chorlton? You don't mean – Holly Lodge?'

'Yes, of course.'

A cold feeling passed through Tom. Yet why should it come as a shock? He ought to have realised. Now that he'd been told, it seemed obvious. Of course Holly Lodge was going to be a home for old soldiers. What else would it be?

Pull yourself together, man!

But it played on his mind and his dreams intensified. Not that he came any closer to remembering them, but he awoke with their tendrils bound tightly around him before they evaporated. God, he was pathetic.

When a letter came from Mr Peters, offering the Holly Lodge work to Perkins and Watson, Tom deliberately disappeared to make tea for Dad, Uncle Bill and himself. After he placed the mugs on the desk, he spent a few moments turning the pages of the diary, keeping his gaze fixed on the various jobs.

'This Holly Lodge job,' he remarked ever so casually. 'Do you want to take the lead on it, Dad?'

'Me? No, son. It's yours. You did the quote.'

'That doesn't mean I have to be in charge of it.' Ever so casual, ever so casual.

But Dad and Uncle Bill were both busy with their own projects. Besides, they saw no reason for him to take a step back. Well, they wouldn't, would they? Not if he didn't explain, and he could never do that. Even if he wanted to – which he didn't and never would – how could he possibly find the words? So he was lumbered with the project.

But as he thought it through over the weekend, he realised what an ass he was. Holly Lodge wouldn't become an old soldiers' home until after all the work had been done. Before then, it was a building just like any other – a building he would work on and bring back to life and then walk away from. He nodded to himself. He could do that. He'd have to be pretty bloody feeble not to be able to manage that.

Finishing work one day early in the week, he returned to the office, where he found Mr Peters drinking tea with Uncle Bill.

'This is the chap you need to ask,' said Uncle Bill in his genial way.

Tom shook hands with Mr Peters. 'Ask me what?'

'My old soldiers at Oak Lodge are interested in what's going on with Holly Lodge. Once the work gets under way, would it be in order for me to bring them across a few at a time, so they can see what's going on? We'd be careful to stay out of your way, naturally. It'd be interesting for the old boys, something new to talk about. What d'you think?'

What did he think? What did he *think*? He wished himself a hundred miles away. That was what he thought. But he agreed to the proposal – he had to. It wasn't as though the work he and the lads would be doing meant that it wouldn't be safe for the old chaps to enter the building.

Besides, they were old men. Their wars had been different wars. He would cope. He would get by. It wouldn't be so bad. Unsettling, yes, but he'd get through it and come out the other side. It would be a kind of test. He would do what he had to and afterwards... afterwards he would feel better about himself.

He went to Holly Lodge to talk about a possible starting date.

'I've got here a list of the various jobs and the order in which they'll be done.' He handed it to Jess. 'I hope it'll make you feel a bit more in control.'

'I don't follow.'

'Having workmen on the premises is a disruptive business and it's not just the physical bother, having the floorboards up and so on. It's the feeling of upset that can get to people, the feeling that the place is being invaded and isn't their own any longer and everything is upside down. At Perkins and Watson, we do try to make the experience as straightforward as we can, so, for example, we make a point of cleaning up after ourselves at the end of each day. Even so, most folk find it unsettling to some degree, especially the elderly.'

Jess's fine eyebrows arched. 'I hope you aren't suggesting I'm old.' There was humour in her brown eyes.

'No – no, not at all.' Curse him, was he blushing? When had he last done that? 'I just meant—'

'I know what you meant and I appreciate the courtesy. I'm sure most builders wouldn't give it a second thought.'

She smiled at him. She had the sweetest smile. Yes, the sweetest. It wasn't the sort of smile he would have expected from her, with her clever, serious face and those watchful eyes. On the watch for the next snub that came her way from a patronising man? Maybe. But that smile – oh, that smile showed the real Jess, he was sure it did. It suggested gentleness and warmth – two attributes that were of no use whatsoever to a woman working in a man's world. Was that what the real Jess was like underneath?

Tom cleared his throat to scatter the inconvenient thoughts, snatching at the first words that came to him.

'I gather that Mr Peters intends to bring his old soldiers along to see the work as it progresses.'

'That's right,' said Jess. 'It'll be interesting for them to see the place take shape before the new batch of old soldiers move in. And there will be young soldiers as well – at least, I hope there will.'

Something inside Tom went still and cold. 'Young soldiers?'

Jess laughed. 'Only compared to the old boys at Oak Lodge. Middle-aged men, regular soldiers, not conscripts.'

'You mean, soldiers who were... damaged in the Great War and can't return to active duty?'

'Exactly.' Her eyes were shining. To her, it was obviously a splendid idea.

But to Tom...

He left Holly Lodge as soon as he decently could, the thoughts, the impressions, the anxiety pressing hard against his brain. The inside of the top of his skull was red-hot while from the neck down he was icy cold. Well, that was that, wasn't it? If Holly Lodge was due to have Great War soldiers visiting, Perkins and Watson couldn't do the work. He would make up an excuse. He could quickly look at those two requests that had come in earlier today, provide quotes for them and then pretend they had come in before Holly Lodge.

'We've got too much on at the moment.' That was what he would say. 'I'm sorry to let you down, Mr Thorpe.'

Already the words were in his head. He clung to them. He hated lying, but what choice was there? Was it cowardly of him? Of course it was. Pure yellow-bellied cowardice, but so what? He had lived for a long time with the knowledge of what he was.

Chapter Thirteen

WHEN THE OFFICIAL advertisement for the post of superintendent at St Anthony's Orphanage appeared, Vivienne's application was all but finished. She had already written to her old bosses to ask for references. Her first job after being widowed had been at Projects for the Ignorant Poor, after which she had worked for a local corporation housing department. She knew she could rely on receiving good references from these two sources, but the most important job she'd had before coming to Manchester, which would provide her with the most relevant reference, had been with what had at the time remained of the wartime rationing department in one of the London boroughs, which had worked to provide additional milk for expectant mothers and free school meals for the children of the poor. While she had been there, she had quietly extended the scope of her duties, which, so long as she concentrated on families – in other words, on women's work – her boss had been happy for her to do.

She received good wishes and promises of references from her previous employers, along with a patronising though no doubt well-meant remark about the wisdom of her choice to follow a path suitable for a woman instead of trying her hand in a masculine area such as housing or town planning.

'I'm surprised to hear you laugh at that,' said Miss Prudence.

'I have to,' said Vivienne. 'It's either that or blow my top.'

Now the time had come to tell Mr Taylor what she intended to do. Usually she was a self-confident person, but she felt tense and uncertain as she knocked on his door. He wasn't necessarily entitled to know she was applying for the post, but she wished to inform him as a matter of courtesy. Moreover, she wanted permission to use his name as a referee.

'I wish you well in your application, Mrs Atwood,' he said, 'though I should be sorry to lose you. You're an asset to the Board of Health and I've come to rely on you – which is what I'll say if I am called upon to write a reference.' He smiled and his bright-blue eyes crinkled. 'What am I saying? If? I mean, *when* I am called upon.'

'It's good of you to say so,' said Vivienne, 'but I don't want to take anything for granted.'

'It won't be easy for anybody to fill Mrs Rostron's shoes,' said Mr Taylor, 'but if anyone can, I have every faith that that person is you.'

Vivienne also told a few special people whom she could trust not to spread it around. As well as Miss Prudence and Miss Patience, she wanted Molly to know.

'Though you mustn't say a word in front of Danny. He's still got lots of friends at St Anthony's.'

'Don't worry. Your secret is safe with me.' Molly gave her a hug. 'Best of luck. I think you'd make a splendid superintendent.'

After some thought, Vivienne confided in Miss Kirby as well. She was a long-standing and dear friend of Miss Prudence and Miss Patience, a spinster who had taken care of her ailing mother for many a year while working as a teacher. Just when her mother had passed away and her life ought to have become easier, she had been required to leave her post so that it could be given to a returning soldier, which meant that, instead of having a final few years to save for her retirement, she now eked out a precarious living, renting a couple of small rooms. Vivienne wasn't particularly close to Miss Kirby, but the Miss Heskeths thought highly of her and Vivienne thought she would appreciate being allowed into the secret.

Miss Kirby repaid her faith by discussing various families whose children she had taught over the years, giving Vivienne examples of the difficulties faced by families coping with poverty, illness, unemployment and violence.

'Might I suggest you make notes about each of these cases,' said Miss Kirby, 'and the ways in which they might be helped, supposing these circumstances were to come up again. That way, at your interview—'

'If I'm interviewed,' said Vivienne.

'—if anyone says you haven't worked in child welfare, you can show your notebook and explain you have consulted with a retired teacher who spent her long working life teaching in a deprived area; that this has broadened your understanding of children's lives; and, using examples provided by this teacher, you have considered ways in which individual children can be provided with practical help and moral guidance. This will show you are serious about wanting to dedicate your life to working with children.'

'Thank you,' said Vivienne. 'That's a good idea. I appreciate your support.'

'It's my pleasure,' said Miss Kirby. 'I'm honoured that you chose to tell me about your hopes. I know how proud the Miss Heskeths are of you, and I am too. Oh, my dear, I hope I haven't spoken out of turn in saying that. You look upset.'

'I'm fine. I just thought how proud my husband would have been, though of course if he were here to be proud, this wouldn't be happening, because—'

'Because you'd be looking after your own home and probably your own children.' Miss Kirby nodded understandingly. 'None of us expects to live our lives alone, but for some of us, it just happens that way.'

Determined not to let that thought pull her down, Vivienne concentrated on her job. It felt a bit odd to be carrying around thoughts of her application in her head while she attended meetings and went on visits in her professional capacity. Each time she filled in a form or made notes in a case file, she couldn't help wondering if she was approaching the final time of doing these tasks. Was that big-headed of her? She hoped not. She hoped it was a sign of her keen interest in the superintendent's post.

She found herself casting a few secret glances in Miss Boodle's direction. The office diary now showed two appointments for Miss Boodle at St Anthony's.

'One appointment is for a general discussion,' she said in reply to a question from Miss Cadman, 'and the other concerns a child I'm interested in, a little girl called Hannah. This is her second orphanage placement. The first didn't suit her at all.'

Miss Cadman frowned. 'That rings a bell. Wasn't Hannah the name of the girl Mrs Atwood asked St Anthony's to take?'

'I believe so,' said the Poodle. 'It's important to ensure a second mistake hasn't been made with the child – isn't that so, Mrs Atwood?'

Temper fizzed through Vivienne's bloodstream, but she wasn't a hotelier's daughter for nothing. She smiled at Miss Boodle. 'Naturally. Hannah's welfare is the most important thing.'

Even so, the thought of Miss Boodle getting a foot in the door at the orphanage left Vivienne feeling jittery, or was she being silly? She herself was an established figure there; she had been visiting for the best part of a year. All the same...

Vivienne went to Holly Lodge later that day. As she arrived, she cast a glance over her shoulder in the direction of St Anthony's, but she refused to drop in without an appointment. She had too much pride for that, which was just as well, because Mrs Rostron would see through such a ploy immediately. Later this month, the legal side of things would have been attended to and the orphanage would officially change its name to St Nicholas's. Two weeks on Saturday, there was to be a special assembly for all the children, and Vivienne, as the person who had thought of the new name, was to be the honoured guest... but now she couldn't help wondering if Miss Boodle had been invited too. What if she had? Honestly! As if it mattered.

Vivienne pulled herself together before she knocked on Holly Lodge's door. Miss Mason appeared and invited her inside.

'Take a seat in the office and I'll fetch some tea.'

But Vivienne followed her into the kitchen, watching as she put the kettle on and took the milk jug from the marble cold-slab in the pantry.

'How are you settling in?' Vivienne asked. 'It can't be easy spending your days in a nigh-empty building.'

'It's not the most comfortable thing,' Miss Mason agreed, but she smiled as she said it. 'Actually, it's not the lack of furniture I mind so much as the surprise on people's faces when they realise the manager is a woman, but I'm used to people's attitudes. I know all about being polite, no matter what the circumstances. I used to work in a hotel before I came here.'

'Really?' asked Vivienne. 'My father is a hotelier.' She didn't say that her family owned a string of smart establishments. 'So I understand exactly what you mean. A colleague was rather rude to me today and I could practically hear Dad's voice inside my head telling me, "No matter how mad they make you, always remember your manners." He made sure everyone knew that.'

'The first rule of the hotel trade,' said Miss Mason as she prepared the tea-tray.

'Shall I help with that?' Vivienne offered.

'Second rule of the hotel trade. The guest never lifts a finger.'

Following her back to the office, Vivienne thought Miss Jess Mason must have been rather good in her previous job.

'What made you leave the hotel?' she asked as they sat down.

'It was a family concern and the son needed a job. Otherwise I'd still be there now. Not that I want you to think that Holly Lodge is second-best in any way. I love being here and I'm lucky to have this opportunity.'

Vivienne smiled. 'In spite of the patronising remarks.'

'It's part and parcel of being a working woman.' Miss Mason shrugged. 'I'm don't know why I'm shrugging. It's not as though I've ever mastered the art of ignoring the remarks.'

'I don't think one ever does. You just have to be polite, because if you aren't, you provide more ammunition for the men who like putting you down.'

'Like the colleague who was rude to you earlier today.'

'Actually,' said Vivienne, 'that was a woman. To be honest, it might have been a genuine remark, though I don't think it was. I think it was calculated to snub me.'

'The worst sort. Women should stick together. It's all the more important now that so many more women have to go out to work.'

'Surplus girls, you mean.'

'Yes,' said Miss Mason. 'Not that I see myself as one. I'm a career woman. I choose to work – well, I have to, obviously, to support myself – but it's also what I want to do.'

'I'm the same. I was widowed in the war.'

'I'm sorry to hear that.'

'Thank you. It left me with a big gap to fill.'

'Which you fill with work,' said Miss Mason. 'I can understand that. Didn't you want to work in your father's hotel?'

Vivienne made a decision. 'I don't want to mislead you.'

Miss Mason frowned. 'I'm sorry?'

'May I speak frankly? I think you and I could become friends and I don't want to start off by letting you think things that aren't so. My father doesn't have just the one hotel I let you imagine. My family owns several.'

To her surprise, Miss Mason laughed. 'That explains it. I thought you were better dressed than a Board of Health employee might be expected to be.'

Vivienne felt the two of them being nudged from acquaintanceship into friendship.

'I hope you'll call me Vivienne,' she said.

'And I'm Jess.'

They nodded at one another.

'I'm pleased to make a friend who doesn't think that being a career woman makes me unwomanly,' said Jess.

'Is that what you've been told before?'

'Once or twice.' Jess tilted her chin, dismissing it.

'Would you like to meet more women who take the same view as I do?'

Jess laughed and frowned at the same time. 'Why do I feel as if I've just been invited to a suffragette meeting?'

Vivienne laughed too. 'It did sound a bit like that, didn't it? It wasn't meant to. I lodge with a pair of ladies who run a business school in the evenings. They teach office skills – to surplus girls, actually. I know you don't consider yourself to be one, but technically you are. Attending the school could be useful for you.'

'What do they teach?' Jess looked interested.

'Typewriting, filing, writing business letters, using the telephone. Invoices, delivery notes, book-keeping.'

'I can do all that – apart from the book-keeping.'

'Did you go on a business course?'

'No,' said Jess. 'I picked up some of it in my first jobs and I was taught what I needed to know by Mr Hitchcock at the hotel.'

'Why not learn it properly? I don't mean to be pushy, but there's a big difference between picking something up as you go along and learning it in a formal way.'

Jess nodded thoughtfully. 'And if I have to leave here, it would be a good qualification to add to my next applications.'

Vivienne frowned. 'What d'you mean, "have" to leave?'

'I'm here on trial. Mr Peters gave me the job – rather reluctantly, I may say – because I was the best candidate, but he would really have preferred a man.'

Frustration rippled from Vivienne on a sigh. 'If only employers would accept that we're as good as men. I was once told in an interview that my application was excellent, but they didn't want me because I might re-marry and have a family.'

'What a cruel thing to say to a widow.'

'Cruel, yes, and also how unprofessional. But women are told that all the time. By and large, we don't get the chance of interesting, fulfilling positions, because the best jobs are seen as men's work and, besides, why employ a woman who'll only let you down by getting married? Even these days, with such a shortage of potential husbands, people still think it isn't worthwhile to employ a woman.' Vivienne smiled ruefully. 'I shall now climb down from my soap-box.'

'Perhaps we ought to get down to business,' Jess suggested.

Vivienne opened her file of information on Great War soldiers who might be suitable for Holly Lodge and gave Jess their details to look at.

'Have these men been told?' Jess asked.

'No. Don't worry. They won't be told anything until Mr Peters says yes – if he says yes.'

'Good. I'd hate to have their hopes built up.'

Vivienne gathered her things. 'I must be getting along. I've another appointment. I'm very pleased to have had the chance of a proper talk with you.'

'Likewise,' Jess said, then hesitated. 'Do you mind if I ask you about your hair? Who cuts it for you?'

'I go to a hairdresser called Miss Travers. I can let you have her address. Are you thinking of having the chop?'

'I'm building up to it. Some girls wear very short bobs these days, practically at ear-length, but I think that looks severe.'

'You could have a longer one and then have it cut shorter if you like it. You're lucky to have such dark hair. Mine's pure mouse.'

Jess saw her to the door.

'Goodbye... Vivienne.'

'Goodbye, Jess.'

Vivienne smiled as she walked away. Whatever else happened today, this was a good day, because she had made a friend.

Chapter Fourteen

JESS ANSWERED THE door to a young man, who raised his bowler hat to her, showing sandy hair. He had a slim build and wasn't more than average height, but there was nothing puny about him. He possessed a cheerful energy and Jess found herself smiling instinctively. He introduced himself as Zachary Milner from Milner's Fire Safety Services.

'Mr Peters told me to expect you,' said Jess.

'I know it's too soon to install the extinguishers,' he said, 'but I'd like to have a look round so I can plan how many you'll require and where they should go.'

Jess showed Mr Milner round the house while he made notes in a little book and told her that training the staff in the correct use of extinguishers and fire blankets was part of the service he offered.

'It's a family firm, is it?' Jess asked.

'No, I set it up myself.'

He didn't look all that old to be running his own business and Jess was impressed. If Mr Peters had chosen to employ him, he must be reliable.

From one of the downstairs rooms, Mr Milner glanced out of the bay window and Jess saw him smile. Seeing that she had noticed, he said, 'That's my young lady,' and there was such a note of love in his voice that Jess went to the window to have a look. On the pavement over the road, a pair of nursemaids from the orphanage escorted a group of young children in pairs, holding hands.

'The redhead or the dark-haired girl?' Jess asked, seeing what showed of the two girls' hair beneath their hats.

'Nancy would be pleased to hear herself called a redhead. She worries that her hair is more of an orange colour, but her mum says it's the colour of copper saucepans.'

'Copper. Yes, that's a better description than red.'

'We're engaged,' Mr Milner said proudly. 'Of course, it'll be ages yet before we can get married, but that's the way of the world. I'm happy to spend time saving up so that I can look after her properly, and any children that come along.'

Lucky Nancy, having such a steady young man by her side. Not that it made Jess wish for a man of her own. She was happy with things as they were – well, as happy as it was possible to be when you were a woman in what you were constantly being reminded was a man's world.

The end of the day came round and she went home. Could a room in a B and B be called home? It was clean and comfortable, but it wasn't appropriate long term. It would be too costly, for one thing, but Jess hadn't had any luck so far in finding a room to rent. Each time she followed up an advertisement, her heart sank a little as she made her way there. She had heard of 'bedsit-itis', which was something that surplus girls were meant to suffer from. It meant that such a large part of their wages went on their living expenses that there was barely anything left for a social life and so they were doomed to long evenings alone in their rooms.

But Jess had lived like that before in the days before the Sea View Hotel and she would manage it again, because she had no option. It wasn't easy finding a room, though. Some people refused to rent to a woman, because men, brought up to go out to work and earn money, made better lodgers. Others refused to have a woman renting a room in a house where there were already male lodgers.

'Asking for trouble, that is,' one landlady said, eyeing Jess up and down as if she had turned up on the doorstep dressed as a harem girl.

A couple of landladies who were prepared to rent to a woman demanded references from previous landlords, only to declare that Mr Hitchcock didn't count and Jess's previous landladies were from too long ago. Jess trailed back to the B and B, where she found a letter in the M pigeonhole in the hallway. It was from Mrs Nolan and Jess's spirits lifted. Tom Watson's idea about writing to her future stepmother had paid off. Jess didn't know Mrs Nolan's address, so she had written to *Dear Dad and Mrs Nolan* at Dad's house, which meant that Dad had all the pleasure of the correspondence without any of the responsibility. Once, that might have galled Jess, but now she simply felt glad to be on good terms with Mrs Nolan.

The letter contained the date of the wedding – Saturday the twenty-fourth, just two weeks away – and Mrs Nolan wanted Jess to be her attendant. Well! That was a surprise, but a nice one. It showed that her stepmother-to-be wanted them to be on good terms. It was an honour to be asked. Mrs Nolan said she wasn't having 'anything fancy' for herself and asked Jess simply to wear a smart dress. She made it sound as if Jess had a dozen to choose from. Jess smiled. She had her office clothes and her Sunday best, and that was it, really, when it came to smartness. When she worked at the Sea View, she had made herself a couple of frocks to wear on her days off. One was a two-piece with a straight, hip-length top with elbow-length sleeves, and a calf-length skirt. The original pattern had had a pleated skirt, and not just pleats but knife-pleats, which had called for masses of extra fabric, leaving her with a choice between incorporating the knife-pleats but having to choose a cheaper fabric or else forgetting them altogether and having a few extra coppers to afford better material. She had opted for the latter, not least because all those teeny-tiny pleats would have stretched her dressmaking abilities to the limit. The garment was toffee-coloured. Very sensible, but not exactly festive. Jess couldn't suppress a sigh. How lovely it must be to have money to spend on clothes, but she had always had to be sensible in her choices. Mind you, if she were to add some frothy lace to the cuffs, that would liven the costume up a bit without making it too fancy. And perhaps now was the time to be brave and have her hair cut.

Mr Peters came to Holly Lodge for one of his visits. Some were planned, but at other times he simply turned up. Honestly, did he expect to catch her out, knitting or poring over a women's magazine?

'I've had an idea about the garden,' said Jess. 'We've got plenty of space and we can be creative about how we use it. I wondered about putting in some raised beds – you know, long wooden boxes on legs, so that the older gentlemen could potter about and do a spot of gardening at waist-height.'

'Hm. That's not a bad idea,' said Mr Peters. 'They might enjoy that. I'll have a word with the men at Oak Lodge and see if they like the sound of it. If they do, we could have some over there too.'

Jess was glad that her idea had been well received, though that didn't fool her into thinking it would make Mr Peters more receptive to what she said next. 'I'd like to book some time off, if you don't mind.'

Mr Peters lifted his eyebrows. 'Already? I'm not sure I like the sound of that. It smacks of taking advantage.'

'It's for a special occasion, sir. My father is re-marrying in a fortnight's time and naturally he would like me to be there.'

'This would involve your going to...'

'Annerby,' Jess reminded him. 'The wedding is on a Saturday afternoon, so I'd need that morning off and the Friday afternoon as well.'

'Can't you travel up on the Saturday morning?'

'If I have to, though it would mean an early start.'

Mr Peters released a huff of breath. 'I'm sorry to sound ungracious, but it never occurred to me that you would ask for time off during your probationary period. It is, however, a special occasion and I am not an unreasonable man. You must, of course, travel on the Friday.'

'Thank you,' breathed Jess.

'And you can travel back on the Sunday, ready for work on the Monday morning.'

'Yes,' said Jess. 'Thank you,' she said again.

But Mr Peters must have detected something in her face, because he said, 'What is it, Miss Mason? Spit it out.'

'As well as attending the wedding, I shall need to pack up the belongings I still have in my father's house. I can do that on the Sunday – it really wouldn't be appropriate to do it on the Saturday morning before the wedding,' she added.

'I suppose not. At least, I suppose Mrs Peters would say not.'

'And my father will also expect me to attend chapel on Sunday morning. So with that and the packing up, and with the Sunday train timetable being different and the journey taking longer... well, I'd hoped you wouldn't mind if I travelled back on the Monday.'

'Indeed?' Mr Peters thought for a moment. 'As I say, I'm not an unreasonable man. And I'm quite sure my wife would come down firmly on your side in this, since there is a wedding involved. Very well, Miss Mason. You may take the time off, but please be aware that there is no question of your receiving any pay for that time.'

'I didn't expect it,' Jess murmured.

'And you should not ask for any further time off during the rest of your probation.'

'I understand, Mr Peters.'

Then he surprised her by offering, 'Shall you require somewhere to store the things you'll be bringing back from Annerby? I'm sure we can find you a suitable corner somewhere in Oak Lodge. I don't suppose you have much space in your room at the bed and breakfast.'

'Thank you,' Jess said sincerely. 'It will be a small trunk, nothing more.'

It sounded very straightforward, put like that, but there was something unsettling about it. She hadn't lived at home since 1919, but it still seemed odd to think of moving the last of her belongings out – as if Dad's house wouldn't be her home any more. Well, it wouldn't, would it? Once Mrs Nolan became Mrs Mason, the house would be hers and Jess would only go there as a visitor. A welcome visitor, she hoped, but a visitor all the same.

That thought made it all the more important for her to find herself a home. She couldn't follow up any possibilities this evening, though, as she had to attend her interview at the business school, which was to take place quite early in the evening.

'So that it is finished before lessons start,' Vivienne had explained.

It wasn't far from Holly Lodge to Wilton Close, which was a daft reason to be positive about the interview, but Jess couldn't help it. Wilton Close was an attractive little cul-de-sac containing two pairs of semi-detached houses on each side and another pair of semis at the top. Each had a front garden, with snowdrops and winter aconites peeping out among the evergreens.

Jess opened the gate and walked up the path. A thin, older lady opened the door to her. Jess's first thought was that she didn't look like anything special, but then she smiled and Jess quickly reviewed her impression. This lady might not be a bobby dazzler, but she had the loveliest smile and it made her pale-blue eyes look kind.

'You must be Miss Jess Mason. Dear Vivienne has told us about you. I am Miss Patience Hesketh and my sister and I run the business school. She is my older sister, so you should call her Miss Hesketh and address me as Miss Patience. Do come in.'

Miss Patience ushered Jess from the hall into a pleasant sitting room. After working in a hotel, Jess was accustomed to eyeing up places for smartness and cleanliness. The Miss Heskeths' sitting room was smart, but in a faded sort of way that suggested there was less money now than there had been in former times.

'This is my sister, Miss Hesketh,' said Miss Patience.

Miss Hesketh was, on the face of it, similar in appearance to her younger sister, but there was a no-nonsense air about her that ensured the two of them could never be mistaken for each other.

'How do you do, Miss Mason?' she said. 'Please sit down. Forgive me if we do not indulge in polite chit-chat, but I'm sure you are aware that lessons will begin in an hour's time.'

Jess nodded, thinking that Miss Hesketh wouldn't be the sort for polite chit-chat even if they had the whole evening stretching before them.

'Perhaps you could start by telling us a little about your

previous work experience,' suggested Miss Patience. 'Vivienne says you worked in a hotel.'

'That's right.' Jess described the types of tasks she had undertaken at the Sea View. 'And before that I worked for two different local corporations.'

'Whereabouts?' asked Miss Hesketh.

'In the north of Lancashire. I come from a place called Annerby.'

That provoked a response that surprised her. Both ladies sat up straighter and looked at one another.

'Annerby?' said Miss Patience.

'We have a friend, a family friend, who lives there,' added her sister.

Something clicked into place in Jess's mind. She remembered what Vicky Rodwell had said about her father's special friend in Chorlton-cum-Hardy. 'It wouldn't be Mr Niall Henderson, by any chance, would it?'

'Why, yes,' Miss Patience exclaimed. 'Do you know him?'

'Only by sight, but it was his daughters who found me the advertisement for the job I now have, working for Mr Peters at Holly Lodge.'

'His daughters?' Miss Patience. 'Well, what a small world. How extraordinary.'

'How are they known to you?' enquired Miss Hesketh.

'Through doing war work in the local hospital,' said Jess.

'To return to the subject,' Miss Hesketh said with a glance at her sister. 'Miss Mason is here to be interviewed, not to discuss mutual friends. Please could you describe your existing office skills and what benefit you think you will derive from attending our school, Miss Mason.'

Jess had prepared an answer to this and to other questions that were asked. She also posed some questions herself.

Finally, she saw a look pass between the Miss Heskeths and then Miss Patience smiled at her.

'Thank you for coming to meet us, Miss Mason. We shall be happy to offer you a place in our school.'

'Thank you.'

'The fees cover two evenings a week and you will have two lessons on each evening,' said Miss Hesketh. 'I teach the specific office skills and my sister provides coaching in using the telephone and giving spoken information in a concise and professional manner.'

'Having worked in the hotel, I am quite used to using the telephone,' said Jess.

'Yes, I rather thought so from what you said earlier,' said Miss Hesketh. 'We will have to adapt things to suit you. Perhaps instead of twice a week for two lessons, you could come twice a week for one lesson; or possibly one evening for two lessons with me. We shall have to decide what is best. I suggest you come tomorrow evening for a trial session and we'll see how we get on. Would that suit you?'

'Thank you,' said Jess. 'May I ask something before I leave? I don't want to be nosy, but are you the friends Mrs Rodwell told me about, the ones whom she and her sisters are coming to visit?'

'Mrs Rodwell?' queried Miss Hesketh.

'I told you, Prudence,' Miss Patience said. 'Vicky – the oldest Henderson daughter.' To Jess, she said, 'Yes, they are coming the weekend after next.' She laughed, a sound in which nerves were evident. 'All five of them are coming.'

'I'll be away at a wedding that weekend.' Jess smiled to herself. The Henderson sisters would be coming here while she was heading home to Annerby.

'And now, if you'll excuse us, Miss Mason,' said Miss Hesketh, 'we need to prepare for this evening's lessons.'

'Of course.' Jess stood up. 'Thank you for seeing me and for offering the trial session.'

She left Wilton Close feeling pleased. Joining the business school might give her the chance to meet some young women and perhaps make more friends. It wasn't easy moving to a new place and starting again. Going to the business school would add a little more structure to her life. And, of course, there was her new friendship with Vivienne. Things were looking up.

But they stopped looking up the next morning when Mr Peters turned up at Holly Lodge, marching in looking vexed, leaving her to scuttle after him into the office. Before she could offer him a seat, he swung round to face her.

'Well, this is a fine thing,' he declared. 'Perkins and Watson have turned down the Holly Lodge work – and from what I gather, it's because they don't want their work to be overseen by a woman.'

Jess went back to Wilton Close for her trial lessons at the business school.

'You have clearly picked up a reasonable working know-ledge of office work,' was Miss Hesketh's verdict. 'Certainly enough to get by comfortably.'

'I want to do more than get by,' said Jess. 'I'd like some formal tuition. One of the reasons is so that, when I next apply for a post, I can say I attended your school.'

'Fair enough,' agreed Miss Hesketh. 'One of the services we offer our pupils is to find them some unpaid hours of office work in order to extend their experience, which most girls find useful when they're applying for jobs, but in your case, I don't think it's appropriate. The sorts of places where we now send our girls wouldn't really extend your experi-ence significantly – unless you feel that additional experience would be of use to you? No? I thought not.'

As Jess was about to leave, Miss Patience appeared and drew her into the sitting room. 'I have a few minutes before my next lesson. Do come in and have a chat. How did you get on with my sister?'

They talked for a minute or two, then there was a light tap on the door and Vivienne walked in, accompanied by a good-looking young woman with strawberry-blonde hair and eyes of an unusual greeny-hazel. She smiled at Jess, who found herself smiling back.

'Don't worry,' Vivienne said to Miss Patience. 'We shan't interrupt your lesson. I just wanted to see how Jess got on. Are you going to join the business school?'

'Yes, I am, though only with Miss Hesketh, not with Miss Patience.'

The strawberry-blonde lady laughed. 'You'd find it much easier to have Miss Patience's lessons and steer clear of Miss Hesketh. She can be scary.'

'This is my friend, Molly Abrams,' said Vivienne. 'She used to have lessons here too. Molly, this is Jess Mason, who works at Holly Lodge.'

'Pleased to meet you,' they both said.

'How are things going there?' asked Miss Patience.

Jess's frustration came bubbling up. 'It was all going beautifully – until today. I was told this morning that Perkins and Watson, the building company that was supposed to be doing the work on the house, have pulled out.' She noticed a glance pass between Molly and Vivienne.

'That's a shame,' said Molly.

'Apparently it's because they don't want to work alongside a woman.'

There was a charged silence.

Jess looked round. 'That's what I've been told, anyway.'

'I ought to tell you that Molly is Tom Watson's sister,' said Vivienne.

'Oh.' Jess could have kicked herself. 'I'm sorry. I didn't mean any offence.'

'I'm sure you're mistaken about the reason,' said Molly.

'Well, I must admit it didn't tie in with my impression of your brother,' said Jess.

'Perhaps you misunderstood, dear,' suggested Miss Patience.

Misunderstood? She most definitely hadn't misunderstood when Mr Peters had wiped the floor with her. To him, it was yet another reason why it wasn't advisable to employ a woman in a responsible role. It had all felt so grossly unfair, but she'd had to stand there and take it. It had been a nasty few minutes.

And the worst bit was that she'd let it get to her to the extent that she had poured out her grievance in front of other people, including Tom Watson's sister. It had made her commit the cardinal sin of behaving in an unprofessional manner.

Chapter Fifteen

I T HADN'T BEEN easy dodging the remarks from Dad and Uncle Bill about not taking on the Holly Lodge work. Fortunately for Tom, an existing job had hit an unexpected snag, which meant extra work. It had started out as a simple job, but the resident, impressed with the quality of the work done so far by Perkins and Watson, had asked, 'Do you look at roofs? We've got damp patches on two of the bedroom walls and I wonder if some of the roof tiles are cracked or missing.'

Tom climbed the ladder and it had turned out that there was nothing wrong with the tiles, but one of the chimney pots was loose, allowing rainwater to get into the house down the side of the pot. This had soaked the chimney breast inside the loft, which in turn had led to the formation of the damp patches in the bedrooms below. Now the chimney needed to be repointed and the chimney pot had to be replaced. Repairs were needed on the chimney breast too. It was work that Tom would oversee personally. One of the reasons Perkins and Watson enjoyed such a good reputation was that they didn't just set up a job and then leave their lads to get on with it.

'Mr Perkins and the two Mr Watsons, whichever one of them it is that's in charge of your work, he'll be there, running the show. Not all building firms operate that way. You can rely on them.'

It helped Tom explain why he had pulled out of the Holly Lodge job, something that had puzzled and displeased both Uncle Bill and his dad.

'We don't let folk down,' said Uncle Bill. 'We're famous locally for our reliability.'

'Sometimes,' said Tom, feeling a complete heel, but knowing he had to fight his corner, 'being reliable means being honest and saying no. Look, I know it isn't the best outcome for us—'

'—or for Holly Lodge,' Dad cut in.

'—but it turns out that I can't give Holly Lodge the attention it deserves, not at present. There were a couple of other requests for jobs that came in just before Holly Lodge and the quotes I gave were accepted. Neither of you can take on Holly Lodge either, so we have to let it go. I'm sorry, but that's how it is.'

In common with most firms, Perkins and Watson worked on Saturday mornings, but on this particular Saturday morning, Tom was free so he nipped round to St Anthony's to help Aaron unblock some gutters.

On Saturdays, the older orphans were allowed, with permission, to leave the premises to visit the library or the recreation ground or to see school-friends. What must it be like for them to spend time in their friends' homes? And how did they feel when they returned to the orphanage? The children who hadn't gone out came outside for an extended playtime and the boys congregated around the ladders at the top of which Tom and Aaron were working.

The two men looked at each other and grinned.

'Nothing else for it,' said Aaron and they both descended their ladders and instigated a rowdy game of chase.

When playtime finished, the bell rang and the boys headed for the girls' playground, which was where everyone went to line up. A girl with copper-coloured hair walked past Tom and Aaron, wrapped up in a winter shawl. She smiled at Aaron.

'This is Nurse Nancy, Zachary Milner's young lady,' said Aaron.

'How do,' said Tom.

'Are you off out?' asked Aaron.

'Yes, I'm taking some of the children to the meadows for a nature walk,' she said. 'We might find some chickweed and shepherd's purse they can draw.'

'It won't be long before you can take the girls to collect flowers for pressing,' said Aaron.

Nurse Nancy went on her way. Tom and Aaron finished their job and put the ladders away. Aaron fetched a couple of mugs of tea from Mrs Wilkes, the cook, and Tom followed him to his workshop, which was located in front of the high walls at the rear of the orphanage. The rich aromas of wood, oils and beeswax greeted Tom as he entered and he sniffed keenly.

'If ever you feel like a change, Perkins and Watson would be proud to employ an excellent chippy like you. You'd earn more too.'

'I'm happy where I am for now, thanks. Watching the kids growing up is a privilege. You can't put a price on that.'

'I suppose not,' said Tom.

After they had supped their tea, Aaron walked him to the gates. Tom didn't mean to look in that direction, but his gaze swung towards Holly Lodge.

'How come Perkins and Watson pulled out of that job?' asked Aaron. 'I thought it was a settled thing.'

'Too much work on,' said Tom. 'I don't want to let anyone down.'

Aaron nodded. 'You should tell Miss Mason that. She thinks it's because she's a woman.'

Tom almost spluttered in surprise. 'That's ridiculous. What makes you say that?'

'She's friendly with Vivienne and, through her, she met Molly.' Aaron grinned. 'Small world.'

For a moment, Tom was pleased at the thought of Jess Mason taking a step into his world – but only for a moment. Tempting as it might be to edge closer to her, it wouldn't do at all. Even so…

'I can't have her thinking that about me,' he said. 'Do you happen to know if she'll be at Holly Lodge at the moment?'

'I've no idea, but there's one way to find out.'

Exchanging goodbyes, they shook hands and Tom walked to the corner and crossed over. Looking at Holly Lodge, he couldn't suppress a pang of regret for the lost job. It would have been a pleasure to work here, bringing modern touches to the place in a sympathetic way that was in keeping with the character of the handsome old house. It was precisely the sort of work he loved most.

He rang the doorbell. He knew exactly what he was going to say. 'I apologise for the interruption, but my sister says you think Perkins and Watson withdrew from this job because—'

The door swung open and Tom's thoughts dropped straight out of his head. She had changed her hair. Gone was the bun with the two flat-to-the-head plaits that met at the back. Now her hair hung loose in that newish style that he didn't know the name of and which up until this very moment, he would have said he wasn't keen on. Most women wore this style to chin-length or even shorter these days. Jess's hair was a little longer, not quite touching her shoulders. The style showed how thick and glossy her hair was, the same sort of deep, rich brown as the speckled wood butterfly. She wore a fringe, but while the current fashion was for short fringes cut straight across, Jess's was a little longer at each side, the tapering creating a softening effect.

'Can I help you?' she asked when Tom failed to speak.

He wanted to say, 'You look stunning.'

He wanted to say, 'Your hair is gorgeous.'

He said – he had to clear his throat before he could say, 'It's about Perkins and Watson not doing the work here.'

'What about it?' Her voice was crisp. She wasn't going to give an inch – and why should she?

'I've heard that you think it's because you're a woman. That's not the case.'

'It's not the case that I'm a woman?'

She didn't say it sarcastically or as a challenge, but there was no humour in her voice either. Her tone was bland, if anything. But her eyes – ah, they told their own story. There was a look in them that Tom hadn't seen before, not when she looked at him, anyway. He had seen it when she looked at Mr Thorpe. A guarded look, with a flicker of annoyance – and perhaps a touch of weariness, or was he imagining that? The weariness of a capable woman who was yet again being put in her place by a man. His heart yearned towards her.

'It's not the case that Perkins and Watson – that I – pulled out for that reason. That isn't a reason to do such a thing. It's perfectly absurd.'

'Then why did you pull out?'

It was on the tip of his tongue to tell her about the extra work in the current job. How easy it would be to make it sound more than it was. Except that it wouldn't be easy at all. He didn't want to lie to her. Simple as that.

'The decision wasn't in any way because of you.'

Was that the best he could do? She wasn't impressed. Neither was he.

'Thank you for telling me,' she said. 'Good morning.'
She shut the door.

Jess felt out of sorts after Tom Watson's fleeting visit. How bizarre, turning up like that just to say that pulling out of the job was nothing to do with her being female, and then declining to give the real reason. It was such an odd thing to do. She ought to be glad to see the back of him, but she wasn't, not really, even though she was displeased and frankly confused by the decision for Perkins and Watson to pull out. If it wasn't for the reason Mr Peters had given her, and she was perfectly sure it wasn't, then why? Tom Watson ought to have provided a solid, professional reason. The lack of one didn't fit in with what she knew of him – but then, what did she know? At the start, he had been polite and good-natured and he hadn't talked down to her, the latter being something that had meant a lot to her. Had that clouded her judgement? Was his good nature really nothing more than a casual approach to life in general? She didn't want to believe it, because she had thought so much better of him than that. And why did her opinion of him matter so much to her anyway?

She determined to put Tom Watson from her mind. There were plenty of other things to think about – such as enjoying pancakes with the old soldiers at Oak Lodge on Shrove Tuesday and taking her first lessons at the business school. That felt more important now, after what Tom Watson on behalf of Perkins and Watson had done, regardless of what the real reason was. It had left her feeling vulnerable. If Mr Peters thought that having a female manager was a disadvantage, he wouldn't keep her on.

*

Jess enjoyed her lessons in Wilton Close. She felt she had something to prove, having made such a point of telling the Miss Heskeths how experienced she already was.

'It's all in the detail,' said Miss Hesketh. 'If you check every detail, you won't let mistakes get through.'

Jess was sure Miss Hesketh could spot an error a mile off and said as much to Miss Patience when that lady drew her into the sitting room for a chat while she was herself between lessons.

'My sister is a stickler, as I'm sure she would be the first to admit,' said Miss Patience.

'Well, I know all about the importance of paying attention,' said Jess. 'There are various kinds of things you learn when you work in a hotel. For instance, when a guest pays in cash, you mustn't let them distract you while you're counting their money. If they do distract you, you should go back to the beginning and start counting again. That's because there are some folk who use that distraction as a way of making you lose your place so that they end up paying less.'

'Goodness,' said Miss Patience. 'Would someone really do that?'

'I'm sure you always see the very best in everyone,' said Jess.

'I like to think so,' was the simple reply.

What a lovely lady she was. Jess wondered about Mr Niall Henderson and the Hesketh sisters. What was their connection? But it was none of her business.

Before she went back to the B and B, Vivienne had a word with her.

'Come for tea on Thursday. It has to be on the early side because of the ladies doing their lessons, but you shan't mind that, shall you? Then we can go to an amateur production of *The Importance of Being Earnest* in the church hall.'

'Thank you,' said Jess, pleased. 'I'd love to. It'll make a

pleasant change from looking for somewhere to live, which is rapidly turning into my least favourite occupation.'

Looking forward to Thursday evening carried her through the next day or two. On her way to tea in Wilton Close, she purchased a bunch of fragrant narcissi and presented them to Miss Patience.

'What have I done to deserve these?' asked Miss Patience.

'Something tells me you're the one who makes the tea,' said Jess.

Vivienne laughed. 'You see,' she said to the Hesketh ladies. 'I told you she'd fit in.'

Tea was a simple but tasty meal of curry omelettes followed by apple fritters sprinkled with sugar and lemon juice. The four of them chatted easily together and Jess saw why it suited Vivienne to live with these two middle-aged spinsters.

'That was delicious,' Jess said when they had finished. 'Thank you.'

'You're most welcome,' said Miss Patience.

'Vivienne tells us that you are looking for somewhere to live,' said Miss Hesketh.

'Yes. I'm in a B and B at present. Good bedsits are hard to find.'

'And soulless, I imagine,' said Miss Patience.

'We may be able to help you – as a short-term measure,' said Miss Hesketh. 'I don't know if you are aware of it, but we sometimes take in a pupil as a lodger for the duration of the business course. We would be happy to offer you a room while you are studying with us.'

Jess drew in a breath of surprise and delight. 'That's very kind of you.'

'Take a look at what we're offering before you go all dewy-eyed over our generosity,' said Miss Hesketh. 'Will you do the honours, Vivienne?'

'With pleasure.'

Vivienne stood up and Jess followed her upstairs, where Vivienne opened the door to a small bedroom. It contained a dressing table with a looking-glass. Although there wasn't sufficient space for a hanging cupboard, there were hooks and hangers behind a pretty curtain.

'Tom put up the hooks and the curtain-rail – Molly's brother,' said Vivienne. 'He put up the shelves as well. What do you think?'

'It's lovely. It will be so nice to feel I'm actually settled somewhere instead of living out of a suitcase, even if it is only for as long as the course lasts.'

Vivienne laughed. 'You'll have to sign up for book-keeping so you can stay longer.'

They went back downstairs.

'What do you think?' asked Miss Patience.

Jess's arms itched to give her a hug, but it wouldn't be appropriate. 'I love it. Thank you for the offer. When might I move in?'

'Would Saturday suit you?' asked Miss Hesketh. 'That's ample time to get the room aired, isn't it?' She glanced at her sister for confirmation.

'It will be nice for you to leave the bed and breakfast and live in a family environment,' said Miss Patience.

Jess felt a pang in which sorrow mingled with gratitude. 'I haven't really had that since Mum died.'

'Stop it, Patience,' said Miss Hesketh. To Jess, she said, 'My sister is busy planning all kinds of ways to spoil you. But I look at the time. We need to get ready for lessons and you two should be on your way.'

Jess thought she wouldn't be able to concentrate on the play, because of being too distracted by the idea of moving to Wilton Close on Saturday – the day after tomorrow! A real home, albeit a temporary one. Nevertheless, once the play started, it soon had her captivated.

Her high spirits stayed with her as she travelled to Oak Lodge the next morning to see Mr Peters. She intended to raise the subject of having a few younger soldiers at Holly Lodge, but Mr Peters seemed to be in a talking mood rather than a listening one. He gave her a lot of instructions to do with the builders, which she put down to his vexation at Perkins and Watson for pulling out, though it wasn't really fair of him to take out his annoyance on her.

To her dismay, Mr Thorpe was present.

'Fear not, Mr Peters,' he said in his lofty manner. 'I'll supervise the builders. It's a good thing that Mr Jones was available. I know him of old, a solid chap and a good worker. We can't expect Miss Mason to shoulder that responsibility, can we?'

'I am perfectly capable,' said Jess.

Mr Thorpe smiled at her, but the smile was a trap. 'Really? You have supervised building work on a previous occasion, have you?'

'Well, not as such,' she was forced to admit.

'By which I assume you mean you haven't,' said Mr Thorpe. 'I stand ready, Mr Peters.'

Mr Peters looked thoughtful. 'That might not be a bad idea, especially with Perkins and Watson having pulled out because of not wanting to work with a woman.'

'Who told you that?' asked Jess. He hadn't given her the chance to ask before.

'That's irrelevant,' said Mr Peters, but not before Jess had caught the glance he sent Mr Thorpe's way.

'It was you, wasn't it?' she challenged the landlord's agent.

Mr Thorpe laughed and shrugged. 'Just like a woman, eh?' he said to Mr Peters. 'Taking it to heart.'

'Mr Watson told me that wasn't the reason,' said Jess.

'He was merely sparing your feelings,' replied Mr Thorpe.

'I don't believe so,' she replied stoutly – and meant it. That conversation with Tom Watson on the Holly Lodge doorstep had been odd, to say the least, not to mention deeply unsatisfactory, but she believed Tom Watson's denial even though he had failed to provide her with the real reason.

To her annoyance, Mr Thorpe chuckled. 'What's this? Feminine intuition?'

Jess wanted to retaliate, but she could see Mr Peters was becoming irritated and she had too much to lose.

'Is there anything else you wish to discuss this morning?' Mr Peters asked Jess.

She definitely wasn't going to bring up the idea of the younger soldiers in front of Mr Thorpe, so she said, 'No, thank you.'

'Very well. Thank you for coming – and you too, Mr Thorpe.'

Mr Thorpe opened the door and Jess left the room.

In the hall, having shut the door behind them, Mr Thorpe remarked, 'You really don't do yourself any favours, Miss Mason.'

'Excuse me,' she said with dignity. 'I'm going to spend some time with Captain Wingate and Captain Styles and their friends before I go back to Holly Lodge.'

'You do that.' Mr Thorpe's voice was kind. Kind? 'I'm sure they'll be interested to find out if you're still employed.'

Jess managed not to utter a word, but her face gave her away.

'The sweepstake, of course,' said Mr Thorpe. 'Don't tell me you're unaware of it. All the old boys have picked a date as to when they think you'll either give up and leave or else be helped on your way by Mr Peters. Whoever is closest to the actual date of your departure wins the pot. Miss Mason? Going so soon?'

Jess marched straight across the hall and out of the front door. It nearly choked her to do it, but she managed to hang onto her tears and not let them fall until she was round the corner.

Chapter Sixteen

SHUTTING THE DOOR on her new bedroom, Jess went downstairs and into the sitting room. Miss Patience looked up from her sewing. She was doing a rather lovely piece of crewel-work.

'Have you unpacked everything?' she asked. 'That's good.'

'I haven't got all that much,' said Jess, 'though I'll be bringing the rest of my things back from Annerby after the wedding.'

She expected Miss Patience to bend over her needlework once more, but instead she frowned, looking at Jess. 'I don't mean to sound big-headed about our home, but I had expected you to be... well, excited, I suppose, about moving in. More pleased.'

'Of course I'm pleased,' Jess exclaimed. She hadn't intended to say anything, but somehow Miss Patience's kindness brought it all pouring out about the sweepstake. She couldn't hide how hurt she felt. 'I thought they liked me. We seemed to get on so well. The kindness of the old soldiers at Oak Lodge made me glad to be working at Holly Lodge.'

'I'm sure they do like you, Jess dear. May I call you Jess? So much more cosy since we're to live together. They obviously never intended you to know about the sweepstake.'

'I had pancakes with them on Tuesday. We were making jokes about having pancake races. They made me feel welcome, but they were probably wondering whether I'll still be there at Easter.'

'If you felt welcome, you can be sure they like you. I know it doesn't lessen the upset about the sweepstake, which I agree is rather horrid, but please try to concentrate on the good things. After all, you're going to have to go back and face them again, aren't you?'

Jess groaned. 'Worse luck. But you're right. I have to brazen it out. No matter how beastly it is, I mustn't be upset or I'll look like a silly, over-sensitive female.'

'There's nothing wrong with being sensitive. I would say it's one of the qualities that makes you good at your job.'

Unexpectedly, Jess felt a release of tension. She even laughed a little. 'Miss Patience, I think you're going to be very good for my morale.'

That was the moment when she knew she had done the right thing by coming here, not simply for the sake of having a pleasant home, but because she was going to be taken care of and it was thanks to the warmth of Miss Patience's personality and the gentle fuss she made of those around her, wanting them to be comfortable and happy. Jess hadn't felt truly looked after for a long time.

Miss Patience was obviously a born home-maker, which was a huge shame in a way, with her being a middle-aged spinster and having to make do with her sister and a couple of lodgers.

But a little later in the weekend, Miss Patience had a surprise for Jess.

'I've discussed it with my sister and we've agreed that since we've taken to you sufficiently to invite you to live with us, and also because dear Vivienne thinks highly of you as a friend, it is right and proper that we should confide my situation.'

'Only if you're comfortable doing so,' said Jess. What could this be about?

'The fact is,' Miss Patience told her, blushing as she spoke, 'I'm... well, I'm engaged to be married.'

Did she look as surprised as she felt? Jess hurriedly re-arranged her features.

'You are one of a small number to have been told,' Miss Patience went on. 'I don't wish it to be generally known until I've met my intended's family – and that is another reason for you to be told, Jess dear.'

When Jess heard that Miss Patience was engaged to Niall Henderson, the father of the Henderson sisters, it didn't matter how much she tried to hide her surprise. She gawped – there was no other word for it. But then, seeing Miss Patience's discomfort, she pulled herself together.

'All I can say is, he's a lucky man. I hope it isn't presumptuous of me to say so on such a short acquaintance, but I think you're a lovely lady, kind and sweet-natured. I hope you'll both be very happy. And thank you for confiding in me.'

'Oh, my dear.' Miss Patience pressed a thin hand to her chest.

Later, Vivienne took Jess into her bedroom for a quiet word. Being at the front of the house, the room had the same gracious bay window as the sitting room beneath and was handsomely furnished, with a matching set of bedstead, wardrobe, chest of drawers and dressing table. There was a wicker chair on one corner, with a fringed shawl thrown over the back of it, and a row of books stood along the back of the chest of drawers. Art nouveau pictures hung from the picture-rail and a teddy and a doll sat on the pillows.

'I wanted to explain about Miss Patience and Mr Henderson,' said Vivienne. 'They knew one another when they were young. They fell in love, but circumstances came between them and they hadn't seen one another in years until a few weeks ago. Mr Henderson has been on his own for some years, as you must know, and Miss Patience never met anyone else, so...' She lifted her shoulders in a graceful shrug, the warmth in her hazel eyes clearly showing her pleasure at recent events.

Jess didn't say so, but she couldn't help comparing the engagement of Miss Patience and Niall Henderson with that of Dad and Mrs Nolan, the former obviously a love-match... and the latter? She had assumed that Dad's forthcoming marriage was one of convenience on both sides, but had she made that assumption because she didn't want Dad to love anyone but Mum? That was an uncomfortable thought. Or had she assumed it was a marriage of convenience because of Dad's and Mrs Nolan's ages? Could she be one of those small-minded people who thought that love was only for the young?

For the young? Not in her case. Love certainly hadn't done her any favours.

Chapter Seventeen

IT WAS A short distance from Wilton Close to Holly Lodge, which meant that on Monday, Jess could linger a little over breakfast and still walk to work in plenty of time before the new builder, Mr Jones, was to arrive at eight o'clock; but even though she got there at a quarter to, she found to her chagrin that she was the last to appear. Mr Thorpe and a short, stocky man wearing an old bowler were standing back from the building, looking up at it and pointing, nodding their heads in agreement while a couple of labourers in corduroy trousers and flat caps stood to one side, having a cigarette before they were called upon to begin.

Glancing round, Mr Thorpe noticed Jess, but carried on talking, thereby keeping Mr Jones's attention fixed on the house. Annoyance flared inside Jess as she marched up the path, heels tapping on the flagstones.

Affecting to see her for the first time, Mr Thorpe said casually, 'Oh, there you are,' though he did at least have the good manners to touch the brim of his hat to her. 'Jones, this is Miss Mason. She works here. She'll look after you, make sure you have tea and so forth.'

'How do, miss.' Mr Jones lifted his bowler.

'How do you do?' Jess adopted her most formal voice. 'You must be Mr Jones. I'm pleased to meet you. I'm Jess Mason and I'm the manager of Holly Lodge.'

The builder glanced at Mr Thorpe, confusion evident in his expression.

'Mr Peters' little experiment,' Mr Thorpe murmured before addressing Jess. 'Jones and his lads are here to do some preliminary bits and pieces before the building work proper starts.' He winked at her, the cheeky devil. 'Get the kettle on.'

He shook hands with Mr Jones and departed. Seething, Jess unlocked the front door. She went straight to the office and fetched the list Tom Watson had given her.

'Mr Jones, before you get started, may I ask you one or two things?'

'Like how many sugars we all take?' quipped one of the labourers, grinning at his mate.

'You lads take the tools upstairs,' said Mr Jones. 'I'll be up in a minute. Now then, miss, what can I do for you?'

He spoke politely enough, but Jess could see she didn't have his full attention. She didn't let it rile her.

'I have here a list of the various jobs to be done and the order in which they might best be tackled. I wonder how my list compares with yours.'

She affected not to notice the surprise in Mr Jones's eyes turning to respect. She poured a thousand blessings on Tom Watson's head. She would have liked to thank him, but presumably she wouldn't see him again now.

After they had talked through the list, Mr Jones went upstairs to give his men instructions, but didn't remain on the premises. He was on his way out when Jess stopped him.

'Aren't you staying?' she asked.

'Not for this part, but don't worry. I'll be here for all the important bits.'

Jess rather thought she would prefer a builder who regarded every aspect of the work as important, but it wasn't her place to say so.

The two labourers spent the day dismantling some built-in cupboards and taking down sets of shelves as well as stripping off ancient wallpaper. Jess made tea at intervals, happy to do so now that she had established her credentials as a person of authority.

As the end of the day approached, the men called goodbye to her as they headed across the hall to the front door and let themselves out. Jess ran upstairs, interested to see what had been achieved, and found that they had left a right old mess behind them. Most of the wood was stacked up against various walls instead of all in one place, and what wasn't stacked had been left lying around; and as for the wallpaper—

She raced downstairs and threw open the door, ready to yell after the men and drag them back by their ears if necessary, only to find herself face to face with Mr Jones on the doorstep.

'Afternoon, miss. Ready to go home, are you?'

'What? No, not yet.' She looked over his shoulder. 'I wanted to get your men back. They've left the place in chaos.'

'Oh, aye? Let's have a look, shall we?'

Mr Jones headed upstairs, but far from being vexed, he simply looked around as if he couldn't see what the fuss was about. 'Bless you. You really are a little woman, aren't you? Don't fret yourself, love. We'll have a big clear up when we finish. All this will go on a bonfire.'

'I don't just mean all the pieces of wood and the wallpaper,' said Jess. 'Look how filthy the place is.'

'And if it was cleaned up, it'd only get dirty again tomorrow.'

And that was that as far as Mr Jones was concerned. When he had gone, Jess wished she'd given him the sharp side of her tongue, but it was probably a good thing that she hadn't or she would be for ever marked as the little woman who cared more about clean floors than getting the job done.

The thought of all the dirt that looked set to accumulate filled her with dismay and annoyance. It went against the grain to let the house get into a state, but she would lose status if she cleaned up. What Holly Lodge needed was a cleaner, but not all the time, and anyway Mr Peters wasn't going to employ any more staff until he was preparing the house for opening.

Then she remembered what Miss Hesketh had said about pupils at the business school being found part-time office work as part of their studies and it sparked an idea. Putting on her hat and gloves but not bothering with her coat, she ran over the road to the orphanage, hoping Mrs Rostron would be available.

'I'll only take five minutes of her time,' she told the for-midable secretary.

'Mrs Rostron is a busy woman. Perhaps you'd like to make an appointment.'

'Of course, if I have to, but I was hoping to see her today. It – it might be of benefit to one of the girls here.'

The secretary sniffed. 'I'll find out if she can see you.'

A minute later, Jess was seated in Mrs Rostron's office.

'What's this about?' asked the superintendent. 'Miss Allan says it might be useful for one of the girls.'

'I hope so,' said Jess. She explained about the mess the labourers had left behind them.

'So you've come here looking for a girl to do your charring for you.' There was disapproval not merely in Mrs Rostron's voice, but in every line of her body.

'Not at all,' Jess cried. 'I'm sorry. I started my explanation in the wrong place.'

'Then kindly begin in the right place.'

'I wonder if you have a capable girl who might benefit from some basic office experience. You're aware of the building work over the road. There'll be invoices and delivery lists, dates in the diary – a variety of things to do with office work. I'll share all of that with a suitable girl.'

'And you'd also expect her to roll her sleeves up and clean up after the workmen every day.'

Jess lifted her chin. 'Yes, I would. I wouldn't be asking her to do anything I haven't myself done on previous occasions. I used to work in a seaside hotel and if a chambermaid was sick, I did what was needed. I've also given Holly Lodge what my late mother would have called a good bottoming.'

'I see.' Was that a smile on Mrs Rostron's lips? 'If something needs doing, you do it; and you'd like to give a chance to a girl with the same sort of attitude.'

'It would help both of us,' said Jess.

'I'm sure we can find someone suitable, but, of course, it would have to be a girl who isn't already a half-timer.'

Jess hadn't thought of that. When they reached twelve, children were allowed to get afternoon jobs if they could, so their time was divided between school and work. Presumably the best and most capable children would have afternoon jobs.

'I think I have just the girl for you, Miss Mason,' said Mrs Rostron. 'Abigail Hunter. She's one of our fourteens. That is how we refer to our oldest children, the ones who are in their final year at school. Abigail had a half-time job for a year after her employer's daughter left the shop to get married; but the daughter's husband unfortunately suffered a bad accident, so the daughter had to return to work in the family shop.'

'And that meant Abigail had to leave.' Jess nodded. 'And you think she'll be suitable?'

'It so happens the orphanage has a relationship with a local business school.'

'The Miss Heskeths' school?' Jess asked. 'I attend that. In fact, I'm a pupil-lodger as of a couple of days ago.'

'A former pupil, Mrs Abrams, takes classes here each week. It's a relatively new scheme. When our children leave here, we have to find jobs for them that also provide accommodation. We send a lot of boys into the army and many of our girls go into service or else into shop-work in the department stores that have staff dormitories. It remains to be seen whether we are able to find suitable places for the girls who have received training in office work.'

'I don't want to make it sound more than it is,' said Jess, 'but gaining some experience at Holly Lodge might help to stand Abigail in good stead in the future. It might help her become an office junior.'

'As long as the place of work includes accommodation,' said Mrs Rostron.

'I could offer Abigail work five afternoons a week, plus Saturday mornings,' said Jess. 'What is she like?'

'She's a bright girl. Mrs Abrams says she is quick at filing and at spotting mistakes on pretend invoices.'

'That sounds promising.'

'I should also inform you that we had a problem with her when she started having lessons with Mrs Abrams. Abigail has a competitive streak and she always wanted to finish her work before the other girls did, which led to her making mistakes. We solved this problem by telling the class that Miss Hesketh herself might visit at any time and would want to check their progress.' Mrs Rostron smiled wryly. 'Fear of Miss Hesketh was all it took to pull Abigail into line. I'm telling you this because it's only right that you should know that Abigail is capable of letting herself down. But if you're willing to give her a chance, Miss Mason, I believe this could be the making of her. There's one matter we need to discuss:

payment. I realise that the business school pupils are required to provide their services for free in order to gain the necessary experience, but I cannot agree to that for one of the children under my care, no matter how useful the experience might be. It would set an unfortunate precedent. If Abigail Hunter is to work at Holly Lodge, she must receive some remuneration.'

'I understand that, though I'm afraid the payment won't be much.' Jess would have to pay the girl out of her own pocket.

'As long as she doesn't earn significantly less than the other half-timers of the same age,' said Mrs Rostron. 'And you should pay the wage to me, not to Abigail. The children's earnings are saved for them, so they have a small nest-egg when they leave. One more thing: please address her as Abigail, not by any diminutive of the name. We do not encourage pet names or nicknames.'

'Very well.' The poor children!

'I think that covers everything,' said Mrs Rostron. 'I suggest that I send Abigail over to you in, say, half an hour and if you find her to your liking, I can send a letter to her headmaster tomorrow, saying she will be going half-time again, starting immediately.'

Jess stood up and shook hands. When she let herself back into Holly Lodge, she heard footsteps overhead and found Mr Peters prowling around, having a good look.

'They've left something of a mess,' he remarked.

Did Mr Peters think that was her fault? 'Mr Jones says he doesn't clear up until the end of a job.' Something made her add, 'Tom Watson said that Perkins and Watson tidy up at the end of every day.'

Mr Peters looked at her. 'Ah, but they don't wish to be seen working under a woman's eye.'

'Mr Watson assured me that wasn't the reason they withdrew.'

Mr Peters made a swiping motion with his hand, as if dashing the matter aside. 'Where have you been?'

Jess explained about Abigail.

'Do I understand correctly?' asked Mr Peters, using the tone of displeasure with which Jess was all too familiar. 'You have taken it upon yourself to employ somebody? Did it not occur to you to discuss it with me?'

'As the manager of Holly Lodge,' Jess said in her politest voice, 'I made a decision regarding its day-to-day running. That's what you expect of me, isn't it? You can't want me to run to you over every small matter.'

Mr Peters huffed out a breath. 'What you mean is, I wouldn't require a man to come to me over every small matter. In fact, I would expect a man to show initiative. But employing someone does not constitute a small matter.'

'I haven't employed her in quite the way you mean, sir. What I mean is, you aren't expected to pay her. I got the idea from the business school I now attend. They place their pupils in unpaid work for a few hours a week as part of the course. That doesn't apply to me,' she added hurriedly in case Mr Peters got the wrong impression. 'I'm experienced enough not to need it.'

'I see.' Mr Peters looked thoughtful. 'So this orphan girl will be here to gain experience by helping you; and you have said nothing that will expect the superintendent to believe I intend to pay her.'

'If I had hoped you would pay,' Jess said, 'naturally I would have spoken to you first.'

'Very well,' said Mr Peters. 'Carry on, Miss Mason.' It was almost a military command. Perhaps he had picked it up off his old soldiers.

Jess was relieved to get rid of him before Abigail arrived. She was a slender girl with light-brown eyes in a narrow face and hair of a shade Mum used to call dirty blonde, which she wore in a plait down her back. She wore a grey dress beneath a white pinafore. Poor kid. If that was how the orphans dressed, it must instantly mark them out as such.

Jess took Abigail upstairs and showed her the mess left by the builders.

'If you come here, one of your jobs will be to clean up each day. I know that doesn't sound appealing, but I promise I'll also show you all the invoices and so forth and you can type letters for me – on the understanding, of course, that you respect confidentiality. I can't pay you much, I'm afraid.'

'So I'm cheap labour, am I?' Abigail asked bluntly.

Jess hid her surprise. The dull uniform might give an impression of quiet obedience, but Abigail clearly had a mind of her own. Good for her. Nevertheless, Jess knew she had to put her foot down. She couldn't have the hired help answering back.

'Firstly, don't be cheeky, and secondly, I think you'll find I'm cheap labour as well. Women are, I'm afraid. It doesn't matter how good you are at your job; you'll never be as highly regarded as a man, or earn as much as he does, even for doing exactly the same work. That's the way of the world.'

Abigail looked abashed.

In a kinder voice, Jess asked, 'Would you like the job? I hope you'll say yes.'

Her reward was a warm smile. 'Yes, please, and I promise to do my best. I'll bring a work apron with me. You get into trouble if you get your pinafore dirty, especially if Nanny Duffy's on duty. I can't wait to be fourteen.'

'So you can leave school?'

'So I can wear a skirt and blouse and put my hair up. At St Anthony's, you can always tell the girls' ages by their hair.'

Jess would have liked to know more, but she didn't want to encourage chatter. It would set a poor example. If Abigail settled in and proved her worth, that would be the time to unbend a little, but not until. Give her her due, Abigail was a hard worker. On the next couple of afternoons, Jess gave her some typing to test her ability and also talked to her about the clerical work involved in hotel work. Truth be told, she felt guilty, because at present the work she mostly needed from Abigail was cleaning.

And Abigail was nothing if not good at cleaning.

'We all are,' she said, 'all us girls at the orphanage. So many of us have to go into service, you see, so we have to be good with a mop and bucket and know the difference between a library brush and a banister brush. That's why I like the lessons with Mrs Abrams. It makes me think I've got something more interesting to look forward to.'

'And most of what you do here is cleaning,' said Jess with a sigh. 'There will be more clerical work, I promise, once the building work, as opposed to the stripping out, gets going. By the way, I shan't want you here on Friday, because I won't be here.'

She was looking forward to going to Annerby for the wedding, but before that Mr Peters wanted to see her so she could bring him up to date with affairs at Holly Lodge and it so happened that she did have something new to discuss with him, because she wanted to introduce the idea of having Great War veterans at Holly Lodge.

Jess wished Mr Peters was coming to Holly Lodge for her appointment with him, but instead she had to go over to Oak Lodge, which she wasn't at all keen to do. The thought of the sweepstake brought embarrassment sweeping up the back of her neck and across her face.

Maybe it was cowardly of her, but she went slinking into the building via the back door under the guise of having a chat with Rose and the cook; and she headed for the office at exactly ten o'clock so she didn't have to hang about in the hall.

'What are those papers?' Mr Peters asked.

Jess explained about having some younger soldiers at Holly Lodge. 'But it would still be primarily for old soldiers, of course,' she added hastily as Mr Peters' brow darkened. 'These,' she held out the sheets of paper Vivienne had given her a while ago, 'are the details of some possible candidates.'

Mr Peters did not take the papers from her and she was obliged to place them on his desk.

'You've done it again, haven't you, Miss Mason?'

'I beg your pardon?' It came out almost as a whisper.

'And the simple fact that you have to ask shows that this wasn't an honest mistake. It is a part of your character – and not a part that I care for. You went behind my back at the start of the week by employing that orphan girl—'

'I explained that—'

'Yes, indeed, I'm learning that you have an explanation for everything. I expect you have an explanation for keeping this information from me too. Kindly enlighten me.'

'I wanted to present you with all the information to help you make your decision, sir.'

'For me to make the decision you want me to make, you mean. Had you truly relied on my judgement and my ability to make the best decisions for my business, you would have done me the courtesy of sharing the idea when it was precisely that – a fresh idea, not yet properly formed. Then it would have been for me decide whether to pursue the matter further. You have overstepped the mark, Miss Mason.'

'I'm sorry, sir.'

'I suggest you return to Holly Lodge and make sure everything is in order before you set off on your jaunt. Good day to you.'

Mr Peters made a point of pulling a ledger towards him and leaning over it, ignoring her as she rose from her seat. Should she remove the papers she'd brought? But when she reached out to take them, Mr Peters glanced up.

'Leave those,' he snapped. 'Since you have involved the Board of Health in this, as well as a charity, I am now obliged to consider the matter. I'll tell you this, Miss Mason. I do not care to be manipulated.'

'That was never my intention, Mr Peters.'

'Shut the door on your way out.'

Jess hesitated, but Mr Peters returned his attention to the columns of figures in the ledger, so she crept from the room, not entirely sure whether she still had a job. Presumably she did – but she might not when Mr Peters had had a chance to think things over. For a moment, she wondered if she should stay here and work instead of going to Annerby, but no, she couldn't possibly miss Dad's wedding.

She left the building. It was another chilly day, with frost lingering and the tall ornamental grasses adding an almost eerie note. The starry yellow flowers on the winter jasmine that had provided a welcome dash of bright colour on Jess's previous visits had now mostly faded. Taking a moment to wrap her knitted scarf more snugly around her neck and chin, she heard the front door open behind her.

'Miss Mason.'

Oh no. If only she hadn't already stopped, she might have been able to hurry away, pretending not to have heard. Forcing a smile, she turned round to face Captain Styles and Captain Wingate.

'Were you leaving without seeing us?' Captain Styles asked.

'I'm sorry. I'm in rather a hurry.'

'But you always pop in and say how do,' said Captain Wingate, 'even if it's only for a minute.'

'Is something the matter?' asked his friend.

Something slumped inside Jess. She didn't want to say anything about the sweepstake, but they could see something was wrong and she didn't want to lie to them.

'I know about the sweepstake. I know you're all just waiting for me to be sacked.' She felt a chill that had nothing to do with the temperature outdoors. She had come pretty close to being sacked only minutes ago, she was sure.

The two old men exchanged shamefaced glances.

'It's true that we set up a sweepstake,' said Captain Wingate, 'but it was when you first got the job.'

'Before we got to know you,' added Captain Styles. 'Please forgive us – all of us. We're old codgers, always on the look-out for something to make the time pass.'

'It's worse than that,' said Captain Wingate. 'We're old-fashioned old codgers. None of us thought a young lady could be a manager, but we were wrong.'

Tears welled up behind Jess's eyes. 'Thank you. That's made me feel better. But you still might get to use your sweepstake, I'm afraid. Mr Peters isn't at all pleased with me at the moment.'

Both men stood up straight.

'Come with us.' Captain Styles turned to the door and held it open.

'No, really, I must be on my way.'

But they wouldn't listen to her protests and, at their insistence, Jess reluctantly went back into the hall. Mr Peters was just coming out of the office.

'Mr Peters, a word, if you please,' said Captain Wingate. 'Would you come into the residents' sitting room, please? You too, Miss Mason.'

Several elderly men were in there, reading the newspapers or playing cards.

Captain Wingate stood in the middle of the room. 'Your attention, men, if you please. It's to do with that blessed sweepstake. It was wrong of us to set it up – callous, if I may say so – and the only excuse is that we did it before we knew Miss Mason. But we know her now and we all enjoy seeing her and I'm sure I speak for all of us when I offer her our hearty apologies.'

There were a few sheepish glances among the murmurs of agreement.

'Thank you,' said Jess. 'I'm fond of all of you too.'

'Sweepstake?' said Mr Peters.

'That doesn't matter now,' said Captain Styles. 'What matters is that Miss Mason is in fear of losing her job and we want you to know, Mr Peters – all of us here in this room and all the fellows who aren't here – we want you to know that we think jolly highly of Miss Mason and we want her to stay. What d'you say, sir?'

Chapter Eighteen

THE FRONT DOOR opened and Mrs Nolan walked in, her arms full of bed linen, followed by a down-at-heel-looking chap carrying a box of pots and pans. 'Put it down there and fetch in the next one,' she told him.

Jess's mouth dropped open. 'You can't come in. Dad's here. It's bad luck for him to see you before the wedding.'

Mrs Nolan snorted. She dumped the linen on an armchair and turned to face Jess. 'Don't be daft. Marriages aren't made of luck. They're made of common sense and doing the right thing by the other person and having the same attitude to money. Besides, your dad has seen me in my wedding dress umpteen times, because it's my Sunday best.'

Her helper walked in with a box of crockery, which he set on top of the first box.

'Fetch in the rocking chair,' Mrs Nolan ordered. 'Ah, there you are, love,' she added as Dad appeared. 'Give Len a hand, will you? I've fetched my bits and bobs over this morning, because if I'm still in the house at midday, I'll owe another week's rent.'

'Come on, Jess,' said Dad. 'Lend a hand.'

Mrs Nolan's bits and bobs turned out to be a substantial amount. As well as her linen, crockery and kitchen things, she had brought her sewing-box, a selection of knick-knacks, an aspidistra and her stack of sheet music. The rocker was followed into the house by a footstool, a hearthrug, two or three small tables, a surprising number of cushions all trimmed with tassels and braid, two pairs of curtains and a dressing table.

The sight of Mum's parlour filling up with another woman's possessions made Jess's heart beat faster, but she told herself not to be silly. Mum was long gone and Dad would be much better off being looked after than living on his own. It would mean she could live away from home without feeling guilty and that was something to be grateful for, but in those moments her heart ached for her darling mum.

'What about your other things?' Dad asked. 'The kitchen table and the cupboard in your parlour?'

'I've sold most of my furniture. My neighbour's lass is getting wed, so she and her intended came round to buy my belongings, so that'll give me summat to put in my rainy-day pot.'

Looking pleased with herself, Mrs Nolan put her sewing-box on the floor beside what had once been Mum's armchair and arranged her fancy cushions on the furniture. Jess couldn't help smiling to see a tasselled cushion on Dad's armchair. How long would Dad keep his opinion of cushions as 'dratted pointless nuisance things' to himself?

'Where's the rocker going?' Dad asked.

'Put it in the window for now,' said Mrs Nolan. 'Jess, can you carry these things upstairs and put them in your old room? We'll use it for storage for the time being.'

Her old room. Not hers any more, but her old room. It would be daft to have feelings on the subject. It hadn't really been her room since she moved out to go to her first job – except that it had still been hers, hadn't it? It was where she slept during her visits home. It was where she slept when she was between jobs. A chilly feeling slithered down her spine. The old boys at Oak Lodge may well have saved her bacon yesterday, but what if Mr Peters didn't choose to keep her on at the end of her trial period? Would there still be a place for her here?

A small, battered trunk stood at the foot of the bed, filled now with the possessions she had left at home. Not that she owned that many things, but there wasn't much room to have your own things about you when you lived in rented accommodation. Even at the Sea View, all she'd had was a bedroom. Now the trunk contained her books, her album of pressed flowers, the linen she had saved up for and lovingly embroidered when she was a romantic young girl with dreams of marriage – oh, and a shawl of Mum's that Dad had given her yesterday. Jess had instinctively crushed it to her face, longing to breathe in Mum's scent one more time. Mum had always smelled of rose-water and soda crystals and fresh moorland air; she'd smelled of laughter and home and kiss-it-better; but the shawl hadn't smelled of anything. Well, of course not, after all this time in the bottom of Dad's hanging cupboard, but it was disappointing all the same.

When she went back downstairs, Mrs Nolan was fussing in front of the mantelpiece, positioning a couple of ornaments. Jess hurried over the road to Mrs Douglas's, where she was staying so as to be very much out of the way on the wedding night. A minute later, she returned to Dad's house, carrying a parcel.

'Here.' She offered it to Mrs Nolan. For some reason that escaped her, Jess suddenly felt shy and awkward. 'Since you're sorting out your knick-knacks, you'd better have this now. It's my wedding present to both of you.'

'Well, now, isn't that nice?' Mrs Nolan unwrapped it, giving Jess a sharp glance. 'It's a rose-bowl. Look.' She held it out for Dad to see. 'Jess has given us a lovely rose-bowl.' She looked at Jess. 'Does this mean you want to swap it for your mother's?'

Heat rose in Jess's cheeks. 'Yes, if you don't mind, but that's not the only reason I chose it. It comes with my sincere good wishes and I hope you'll love it as much as my mum loved hers.'

Mrs Nolan nodded. 'I call that proper gradely of you.' She turned to Dad. 'Isn't that so?'

'Aye, it is,' Dad confirmed. 'Our Jess is a good lass when the fancy takes her.'

When the fancy takes her? Jess could have crowned him. But others would say he had a point after the way she had 'abandoned' him to pursue a career. Thank goodness for Vivienne. It had given Jess a real boost to have a friend who understood the wish to work and get on in life.

'Righto.' Mrs Nolan brushed her palms together. 'We'll leave the rest for now. It's time me and Jess got changed.' She pecked Dad's cheek. 'We'll see you in chapel, love. Don't be late.'

'And don't you leave me standing at the altar,' Dad quipped, immediately followed by, 'Eh, lass, I'm that sorry...' He turned to Jess, looking stricken.

Jess forced a smile. It didn't hurt any more. 'No harm done – and take that look off your face.' Reaching up, she pretended to lift the corners of Dad's mouth. 'Smile. It's your wedding day.'

She and Mrs Nolan went over the road. Mrs Douglas was thrilled to death to have the bride and her attendant getting changed under her roof and after the practical business of sorting out Mrs Nolan's belongings followed by Dad's gaffe, her pleasure was infectious and just what Jess needed.

Even so, in a corner of her mind, Jess couldn't help but be aware of the time when she had been supposed to be the next person getting married from Mum and Dad's house. But that was a long time ago, and today was going to be a happy day.

Prudence sat on Patience's bed, biting her tongue as Patience gazed into her wardrobe. They both had large, sturdy wardrobes with fancy carving that were completely at odds with the small number of garments within. The wardrobes, along with all the good furniture, had been inherited part and parcel with the house by their mother years ago. It was partly thanks to the beautiful and enduring quality of the Victorian furniture that they were able to keep up the appearance of being well-heeled.

Patience was in a flutter over what to wear to meet Niall's daughters. As if she had masses of choice! Prudence faced no such dilemma. Her wardrobe was straightforward. Her blouses were crisp and white and everything else was dark. She dressed smartly and sombrely for work and kept her best blouse and navy wool skirt for Sundays. So much less taxing than the anguish that Patience regularly put herself through with her longing for pretty things.

'What about my cream and green check? But that's not really a winter garment and I don't want to appear frivolous. What do you think? I don't want Niall's daughters' hearts to sink into their shoes when they set eyes on me.'

Standing up, Prudence plucked a garment from the wardrobe. 'Your forest-green skirt. Vivienne has a cream blouse with a matching long-line cardigan that would go well with it.'

'I can't wear Vivienne's clothes.'

'Why not? I'm sure she wouldn't mind being asked.'

'What if she intends to wear the cream for the assembly at the orphanage this afternoon?'

'She's going to wear her olive-green dress. And you may borrow Mother's cameo brooch.'

'Are you sure?' breathed Patience. 'I should love that.'

It had honestly never occurred to Prudence before. Patience would have cherished Mother's cameo, which would have undoubtedly seen the light of day a lot more had she been its owner. As it was, Pa had automatically given the brooch to Prudence as the elder daughter, neither of them questioning the rightness of this.

Patience looked anxious. 'I can't meet Niall's daughters wearing Vivienne's clothes and your brooch. What will they think?'

'Unless they're psychic, they'll have no idea you're in borrowed plumes.' Prudence took a moment to soften her tone. 'They'll just think you're in attractive plumes.'

'I'm being silly, aren't I?'

'Let's be grateful you're meeting them for lunch and not a glamorous night out at the opera. Decking you out for that really would have been a challenge.'

'What shall you wear?' Patience asked.

'Never mind me. Let's get you sorted out.'

Prudence felt honoured to have been included in the invitation. When the letter had arrived from Niall, explaining the arrangement to Patience, he had also penned a short letter to Prudence.

I hope you will come too, not simply for Patience's sake, so she feels less outnumbered, but also for your own. You and Patience have lived together all your lives and I should like my daughters to meet and appreciate their stepmother-elect's sister. My hope is that you shall wish to be an aunt to them.

'Remind me of the names,' said Prudence.

'The oldest is Vicky, who is married to Alexander. They

have three children, the oldest of whom is ten. Then there's Leonora and her husband, Marcus. They also have three and their oldest is eight.'

Prudence ticked them off inside her head as being the first wife's daughters from husband number one.

'Vicky and Leonora both married men some years older than themselves and their husbands are the sons-in-law who bought Niall's share of the law firm when he decided to retire. Madeline comes next. Her husband is William and they have a three-year-old boy and a new baby daughter. Then Anastasia and Edward; they have an eighteen-month-old and a new baby. And the youngest is Bonnie, so called because she won the bonny baby competition at the village fête. She was christened Margaret, but please don't call her that. Everyone calls her Bonnie.'

Prudence started to say 'Of course I will' in a semi-indignant tone, but stopped herself. There was no *of course* about it. Only a matter of weeks back, she would have rejected the silly pet name and made a point of using Margaret, but not any longer. Since being reunited with Vivienne, she had – she didn't *want* to say softened, but she couldn't think of a more appropriate word off-hand and what did it matter, anyway?

She said mildly, 'Then Bonnie it will be,' and went to knock on Vivienne's door to seek the loan of the cream blouse, which Vivienne was, as Prudence had known she would be, happy to lend.

Vivienne looked perfect in her olive-green dress, its sash buckled at her hip. She took Prudence's hands in hers and kissed her cheek. 'I hope all goes well at the lunch.'

'They'll love her,' said Prudence. 'How can they not?'

She squeezed Vivienne's hands, marvelling that this beautiful, clever, confident young woman was her daughter. Her *daughter*, whom she had trained herself to know she would never see or hear of again. She was every bit as amazed and grateful as she had been last summer. And her pride just kept on growing. Handing over her baby daughter had been the hardest thing she had ever had to do. Although she had been in no doubt that Elspeth and Graham would be excellent parents, somehow that had never quite provided her with the level of comfort and satisfaction that it had been supposed to.

'I hope the assembly is a success,' she said.

'Bound to be. Anything organised by Mrs Rostron always is. And it's not just the assembly; that isn't until this afternoon. The children are putting on a concert and then there's to be a special dinner.' Vivienne's hazel eyes were grave. 'It will be a lot to live up to, if I get the post.'

'Yes, it will,' Prudence agreed, 'but that is for another day. For now, make the most of this afternoon. It's all because of you, don't forget. You were the one who thought of the new name. It's an extraordinary thing to be able to say that you named an institution. I'm immensely proud of you.'

'Thank you, dearest Miss Prudence. That means a lot. And now I must go.'

Their hands fell away from one another's and Vivienne reached for her handbag and gloves.

'I'll say goodbye to Miss Patience and be on my way.' At the door, she turned back with a saucy grin. 'Take note of all the tiny details. I'll expect you to spill every single bean about my cousins when you come home.'

Prudence shook her head indulgently – indulgently? She, Prudence Hesketh, indulgent? Since when? Silly question. She knew precisely since when.

She got ready and went downstairs, Patience following soon after. Prudence stood at the window and presently a taxi drew up outside and Niall got out.

'Ready?' Prudence asked Patience. 'You look just right.'

'I wish we had better coats to wear on top.'

'We'll thrust them at the cloakroom attendant and no one will be any the wiser.'

In the hall, while Patience fussed over her coat and hat, Prudence opened the door, greeting Niall with a smile, but he had eyes only for Patience.

'Your chariot awaits.' Niall's face glowed with loving pride at the sight of his intended. 'You look lovely.'

Niall escorted them outside and helped them into the waiting vehicle.

As they drove off, he said, 'I've hired a private dining room in the Claremont and I've sent the girls out shopping. They won't be back until about half an hour after we get there.'

Prudence approved. What a thoughtful man he was. This way, Patience and Niall could establish themselves in the room before the daughters appeared, instead of Patience having to walk into a room filled with strangers.

They walked up the Claremont's front steps and the uniformed doorman opened the door to admit them into the lofty, pillared foyer with its gleaming woodwork, handsome armchairs and vast flower arrangements.

The private room was ready for them, one half of it given over to a large circular table, all starched linen, shining cutlery and beautiful glassware, and the other half with chintzy armchairs and low tables.

By the time Patience had worked off her nerves by admiring every detail, there wasn't long to wait for the daughters to arrive. The door opened, but instead of a multitude pouring in, only two appeared. By the looks of them, they must be the oldest, both of them beautifully dressed. They were both blonde, but one was a sandy blonde with light-green eyes, the other a darker blonde with blue eyes.

Niall rose to his feet to perform the introductions.

'Patience and Prudence, may I present my daughters, Vicky and Leonora. Girls, this is the lady I told you about, who is so dear to me, Miss Patience Hesketh. Just in case you are too fierce, she has brought her sister with her.'

That broke the ice and the daughters laughed.

'We promise not to be fierce,' said Vicky. She was the sandy blonde.

'As a sign of good faith, we're arriving in batches rather than storming in like the barbarian hordes,' added Leonora. 'The others will be along in ten minutes.'

By the time Madeline, Anastasia and Bonnie (ridiculous name, but never mind) appeared, Patience was happily finding out all about Vicky and Leonora's children. Prudence made a mental note for future reference: if a conversational gambit was required, mothers could talk about their offspring until the cows came home. Was it silly to feel left out? She would never be free to talk about her own daughter. She shrugged that off. This was no time to be maudlin. She concentrated on memorising which name went with which face. Madeline and Bonnie were both dark-haired and dark-eyed like their father while Anastasia was the one with blue eyes and honey-blonde hair.

Presently it was time to take their places around the table for a delicious lunch. Afterwards, they returned to the armchairs. As staff cleared the table, another maid carried in a tray of tea, which she unloaded efficiently onto the long low table in the middle. Niall's daughters glanced at one another.

Niall looked at them, one dark eyebrow climbing up his broad forehead. 'Who's going to be mother?'

This time, the girls laughed as they exchanged more glances. It was Anastasia who spoke up.

'We've been talking behind your back, Daddy, ever since you told us and we think that, if marrying this lady will make you happy, then we'll be happy, too.'

'Mother passed away before Leonora, Anastasia and I got married,' said Madeline. 'It would be nice if Bonnie could have a mother of the bride.'

'Steady on,' said Bonnie. 'I haven't even got a young man yet.'

'What Madeline means,' said Leonora, addressing Patience, 'is that Daddy has sung your praises and we'd like to welcome you into our family.'

'Besides,' added Vicky, 'it'll save all of us having to look after the old curmudgeon. That'll be your job.'

Niall laughed. 'That's enough of that, miss. Curmudgeon, indeed.' He looked affectionately at Patience. 'Do you think you could cope with this lot? Not to mention all the husbands and children.'

Patience's eyes were bright with tears. 'I think so.'

'Right,' said Niall. 'Let's do this properly. Let me shove this table out of the way.' He went down on one knee in front of Patience, causing a ripple of delight among his daughters. 'Patience Hesketh, will you do me the honour of becoming my wife and will you do my girls the inestimable favour of taking care of their old curmudgeon of a dad?'

Everyone looked at Patience – everyone except Prudence. She looked at Niall's daughters, observing their smiles, which were full of hope and pleasure. Patience would do well in this family.

'Yes,' said Patience and anything else she might have said was lost in the delighted cries of her stepdaughters-to-be, who all jumped up and crowded round to pull her to her feet and pass her from one to the next for hugs and kisses, leaving Niall to rise to his feet, laughing.

'Is my fiancée in there somewhere?' he asked. 'Move aside. It's my turn.'

Patience flushed bright pink as he kissed her cheek, leaving his face close to hers for a lingering moment.

'I hope the wedding is going to be soon,' said Bonnie.

'It will be in the spring,' her father answered. 'Possibly at Easter.'

'Oh, good,' said Bonnie. 'We won't have long to wait.'

Before Prudence could start to feel like a spare part, dark-eyed Madeline dropped down beside her on the sofa and linked her arm.

'We're all looking forward to having an aunt. Our children all have heaps of aunties, but we sisters don't have a single one, so we're hoping you'll be happy to step in.'

Surprise fluttered through Prudence – pleasure, too. 'Thank you. I'd be honoured.'

It looked like Patience wasn't the only one who was about to gain an instant family.

Vivienne smiled to herself. She had been quite right about Mrs Rostron's having put a lot of effort into today. As the Orphanage Committee's guest of honour, she had sat on the front row of chairs behind most of the children, who were sitting cross-legged on the floor, while various groups of children took turns to stand up at the front and sing, accompanied by Nurse Eva on the piano. In between the songs, Mrs Rostron and Mr Lowe, the Chairman of the Orphanage Committee, had read out entries from the orphanage's log book, stretching back over the years.

After the concert, the guests had been served coffee in the staff dining room and Vivienne chatted to Molly. Meanwhile, the children's dining room was turned back from a spacious hall into a place for eating, something Aaron and Danny both lent a hand with. After that, the guests had returned to the children's dining room, where the youngsters stood in silence behind their places, and Mr Lowe had led everyone in grace. Then, leaving the children still politely standing, the adults had filed back into the staff dining room. Behind them, as the door was being closed, came the sound of the children taking their seats and starting to talk.

'Please join us on the top table,' Mr Lowe invited her.

Vivienne thanked him, though it felt rather uncomfortable going onto the raised dais at one end of the staff dining room and taking her seat. Mrs Wardle, a couple of places along from her, clearly entertained no such reservations. The rosebuds on her hat swayed complacently as she surveyed the rest of the room, where those nursemaids who weren't required to be with the children were standing waiting for the dignitaries to be seated.

Mrs Wilkes had prepared a special meal for the Orphanage Committee and its guests. Chicken in sage with apple rings and potatoes roasted in rosemary was followed by a lemon syllabub that was light as air. Vivienne couldn't help noticing that the nursemaids, and presumably the children also, were given shepherd's pie and baked custard.

Afterwards she sought permission to enter the kitchen to thank Mrs Wilkes.

'It was a delicious meal, Mrs Wilkes,' Vivienne said, 'and cooked to perfection. I hope the nursemaids and the children enjoyed their meals just as much.'

Mrs Wilkes was normally a stern individual, but just now there was a twinkle in her eye. 'Don't you worry about that, Mrs Atwood. They all had a dollop of my special chutney alongside their shepherd's pie and the baked custard had honey in it. I know how to turn summat ordinary into summat special when it's called for.'

Vivienne smiled. 'I apologise. I should never have doubted it.'

While the children's dining room was cleaned and all the tables and benches were carried over to the sides of the long room, Vivienne joined the Orphanage Committee in looking at the children's latest art and crafts work.

'Congratulations,' Vivienne said to Nurse Nancy, who was standing to one side. 'I know much of this is thanks to you.'

'Not really,' Nancy said modestly. 'The children love it. All I do is come up with ideas and scrounge materials from where I can.'

'These pieces of felt with the beads sewn on are delightful.'

'We call those our treasure squares,' said Nancy. 'Sewing beads on is easy and the children like choosing them. It makes sewing fun.'

Behind them came a snorting sound and Vivienne made sure her smile didn't falter as she turned to Mrs Wardle.

'Fun!' said Mrs Wardle, her rosebuds quivering with disapproval. 'What nonsense. They should learn by sewing samplers. That's the traditional way. It's worked for years – centuries, even.'

As Mrs Wardle sailed on her impressive way, Vivienne whispered to Nancy, 'Don't take it to heart. The treasure squares are delightful.'

'And they're useful too,' Nancy answered, looking upset. 'Plenty of the boys are happy to make them because of the "treasure" and that means one day they'll be able to sew on their own buttons instead of the girls being obliged to do it for them.'

'Ah, but being able to doesn't mean they'll be prepared to do it,' said Vivienne, 'though I applaud you for trying.'

Soon it was time for the assembly. Vivienne took her place once more on the front row of chairs behind all the crossed-legged children. Mrs Rostron stood behind a lectern with everyone facing her. There was an air of excitement and a few of the smaller children wriggled, but a raised eyebrow from the superintendent was all it took to subdue them.

'Good afternoon, everybody,' she said clearly.

'Good after-noon, Mrs Rost-ron,' chorused the children. 'Good after-noon, every-one.'

Vivienne smiled. It sounded just like school. Then she stopped smiling. This wasn't school. This was home for these children. What must it be like growing up in an institution?

'Today is a very important day,' said Mrs Rostron. 'As you know, a decision was made at Christmas to change the orphanage's name.' There was a ripple of anticipation around the room and she waited for it to settle. 'The Orphanage Committee had to go through a certain legal process to be permitted to do this, but now everything is in place and the change has been approved. We can now call this St Nicholas's Orphanage.'

The children clapped and cheered until Mrs Rostron held up her hand for quiet.

'We have a special guest with us today – Mrs Atwood from the Board of Health.'

All the children turned round to look at her.

'I'm sure you all remember our nativity play on Christmas Eve and the announcement afterwards about the change of name from St Anthony's to St Nicholas's.' As Mrs Rostron continued speaking, the children turned back to face the front. 'Who can tell me what that has to do with Mrs Atwood and why we are so pleased to have her here with us today?'

Hands shot up and Mrs Rostron chose a child of about eight or nine.

'Stand up, Taylor.'

It took Taylor a moment to untangle his feet and rise. 'Please, Mrs Rostron, the new name was Mrs Atwood's idea.'

'Exactly so. Thank you, Taylor. You may sit down.' Mrs Rostron looked over the children's heads at Vivienne. 'Mrs

Atwood, we are all grateful to you for your idea, especially the children, though I can't imagine why...'

She shook her head in mock-confusion and the children tittered. Practically every hand in the room went up, some children waving their hands madly in an effort to be picked.

'Layton Two,' said Mrs Rostron.

Jacob Layton stood up, grinning broadly. He was taller than he had been when he'd first arrived here nearly a year ago, thanks to Mrs Wilkes's cooking. 'Please, Mrs Rostron, it's because we're the Christmas Orphanage now.'

The children all turned to one another with big smiles all over their faces. There was some laughter and whispering, which died down when Mrs Rostron spoke again.

'Mrs Atwood, I would like you to come to the front, please.'

Surprised, Vivienne stood and made her way to stand beside the superintendent. Wondering what was going to happen, she smiled at the sea of faces in front of her.

'The children want to mark this occasion by presenting you with a memento,' said Mrs Rostron. 'The nursemaids talked to them about what might be suitable. The Orphanage Committee asked the nursemaids to suggest something silver-plated that could be engraved, but the children had other ideas.'

'I'm sure it will be lovely, whatever it is,' said Vivienne, touched.

'O'Malley, who is the oldest orphan, and Daisy, who is the youngest, not counting the babies, will now present it to you,' said Mrs Rostron.

Nurse Carmel went on her knees at one end of the front row, whispering to a small girl, who promptly burst into tears.

'Well, perhaps not,' said Mrs Rostron. 'Daisy's place will be taken by Hannah, because it is thanks to Mrs Atwood that she came to live here.'

Nurse Carmel sat on the floor next to Daisy and the child quietened. A tall dark-haired boy came forward from the back, waiting for Hannah to sidle out from the middle of her row. Together they approached the two adults standing at the front. O'Malley carried a large parcel wrapped in tissue paper. He paused for Hannah to take hold of it too and then they presented it to Vivienne.

'Thank you very much,' she said. 'Shall I open it now?'

'Please do,' murmured Mrs Rostron.

Through the paper, Vivienne felt something that moved. She unfastened the paper and found a long string of different-coloured beads. She lifted it free of the wrapping and held it up.

'It's for your Christmas tree,' said Mrs Rostron. 'Every child here has threaded a bead onto the string and so has every member of staff.'

Vivienne gave a soft gasp of delight. 'Thank you – thank you all. It's beautiful and knowing that you made it especially for me makes it even lovelier. I promise I'll put it on my tree every single Christmas and I'll remember all of you when I do.'

'I think we should give Mrs Atwood three cheers,' said Mrs Rostron.

'No,' Vivienne said quickly. 'If you don't mind, I think we should give three cheers for the Christmas Orphanage. Hip – hip—'

'Hooray!' roared the children.

Chapter Nineteen

T OM HAD SPENT the morning working in Limits Lane, where Gabriel Linkworth wanted to establish the allotment for the benefit of the lane's residents. It was a generous thing to do and Tom approved. The folk of Limits Lane were poor, their dwellings old. Mr Tyrell, Linkworth's late uncle, had owned the cottage at the far end before the lane sloped down onto the meadows. It had been a bigger property than the others and the plot of land was a decent size for this project.

Last year, after the fire that had reduced the cottage to a ruin, the land had been cleared so as not to leave an eyesore, but it had needed more attention this year before work could start; a different sort of clearing, not the removal of rubble but the satisfying clearing of land that was going to be worked on. Tom had done his research. Early spring was the best time to get a new allotment up and running and this one was going to be better than most, because it possessed its own water supply in the form of both an old well and a new water-pump.

Tom had consulted various allotment-holders about the best way to lay out the ground and Linkworth had approved of his plans. There would be different sections for vegetables and fruit bushes, marked by narrow paved paths, and Tom had ordered the materials to construct a sturdy shed and some raised beds. The whole allotment would be protected by a wooden fence. If everything went according to plan, the folk of Limits Lane would be working on their allotment before the Lady Day fair pitched camp down on the meadows.

As a rule, the Perkins and Watson men finished at dinner-time on Saturdays, but this was a relatively small job for the firm, and Crosby and Reeves, who were working with Tom today, had agreed to do a bit of overtime so as to make good headway. Mum had made some sandwiches and pasties for Tom to take with him for the three of them and they worked through until the middle of the afternoon.

Now Tom was heading for home, but instead of going all the way by the roads, he walked across the meadows to the end of Hawthorn Road. He always enjoyed walking on the meadows. He headed up Hawthorn Road past the long lines of terraced houses with a shop on every corner and came out opposite the Bowler. He strode up to Chorlton Green, where his face broke into a broad grin at the sight of Molly, Aaron and Danny. He stopped to meet them on the corner of Soapsuds Lane.

'Well, don't you all look smart,' he said by way of greeting. They weren't in their Sunday best, but they had clearly made an effort.

'We've been to St Nicholas's,' said Danny. 'We can call it that now because its name has been changed officially. It's the Christmas Orphanage.'

'Is it indeed?' Tom chuckled. 'You'll be wanting to go back and live there if it's the *Christmas* Orphanage.'

'Never!' Danny exclaimed. 'I wouldn't leave Mum and Dad for anything.'

'Come and have a cup of tea with us,' said Molly.

Tom held out his arms sideways. 'I'm a bit grubby.

Molly laughed. 'You're talking to a builder's daughter.'

They went to Soapsuds House. Aaron and Danny disappeared upstairs to change into comfortable, everyday clothes and Tom joined Molly in the kitchen.

'The change-of-name ceremony went well, then?' he prompted.

'It was lovely, and Vivienne was the guest of honour. I'm so proud of her. She stayed behind to talk to the children, then she's coming here to fetch me and we're going to Wilton Close to see the ladies.' Molly paused to warm the pot. 'I gather that Perkins and Watson was due to do some work at Holly Lodge, but then couldn't.'

'That's right.' Tom hated lying to his sister, but he had to give her the same story he'd told Dad and Uncle Bill.

'Shame,' Molly replied. 'It looks like a handsome place from the outside. I know you. You'd have loved working on it.'

'And I know you, Molly Abrams. Are you fishing for information? I know you've met Miss Mason. Aaron told me.'

'He told me he mentioned to you about Miss Mason hearing you didn't want your work to be overseen by a woman. He also said you couldn't get over the road fast enough to set her straight.'

'I couldn't have her thinking that about me,' Tom said defensively.

Molly's eyes twinkled. 'Course you couldn't. Pretty, isn't she?'

'I hadn't noticed.'

'Oh aye? Then you must be blind. She's very good-looking. But would you like to know what I liked best about her?'

He shouldn't ask. He shouldn't encourage this conversation. 'What?'

'As soon as I said she must be mistaken about you, she agreed.'

'She did?' His heart thumped.

'She said – what was it? Something like it didn't tie in with the impression she'd formed of you.'

'Really?' Jess Mason had said that about him? Tom wanted to beam his head off, but he didn't dare show his delight to his sister.

'Yes, really,' said Molly, adding mischievously, 'And you didn't even have the good manners to notice how pretty she is. Shame.'

The afternoon had been an undoubted success and when Niall dropped them off at home before returning to the Claremont by taxi, Patience was positively glowing with happiness. It did Prudence's heart good to see it and she had no compunction about saying so once they were settled, she in her usual armchair, Patience on the sofa.

'I am happy,' Patience confirmed softly. 'Now that I've met Niall's daughters and we all like one another, I can finally let myself truly believe that all this is real. It mattered so much that they would accept me. I've been on tenterhooks all this time.'

'Of course they accepted you,' Prudence said stoutly, feeling fiercely protective of her gentle sister. 'How could they not? Firstly, their mother has been gone for some years; secondly, they seem a sensible lot; and thirdly, you're you.'

'Oh, Prudence, bless you.'

'Well, it's true. I know I've never been one for singing anyone's praises, but – but maybe I should have been. If I'd told you more often what a dear you are, perhaps you wouldn't have worried so much about Niall's daughters and what they were going to think of you.'

'Anyway, we all got along and that's what counts,' said Patience. 'Did you like them?'

'Yes, I did. They made me feel welcome.'

'Did you – did you wish Vivienne could be there? After all, she is part of the Henderson family as well as the Heskeths'.'

On the verge of laughing it off, Prudence changed her mind. Patience had been honest about her own feelings, so she would be too. 'Now it's my turn to say "Bless you." Thank you for thinking of it. Keeping my relationship with Vivienne a secret is something I've had to accept, though you're right. There are times when it is harder than at other times. You'd think it would come naturally, wouldn't you, after all these years?'

'It's different now,' said Patience. 'She is by your side, so of course you would like to acknowledge her.'

Prudence shook her head, not denying the assessment, but wondering at herself and her own obtuseness. She had always thought herself so clever. Oh yes, the capable, critical Miss Hesketh, no problem too tricky to be solved. She had spent years more or less dismissing Patience because of her gentle nature, seeing it as a form of weakness, but that gentleness was filled with insight and compassion. Tolerance, too – Patience must have employed an awful lot of tolerance over the years when dealing with her tetchy sister.

The front door opened.

'That'll be Vivienne,' said Prudence.

'And Molly, I hope,' Patience added. 'I asked Vivienne to bring her if she's free.'

In came the two young women, cheeks pink and eyes sparkling from a brisk walk on this chilly afternoon, though at least part of Molly's radiance might be due to her interesting condition. She wore a tweed skirt with a light-green knitted jumper that made her strawberry-blonde hair look more golden than usual. Prudence found herself paying more attention to other women's clothes these days, now that it gave her such pleasure to see her beautiful daughter so well dressed. Her own appearance didn't matter to her any more than it ever had, but she couldn't get enough of seeing Vivienne.

Molly went straight to the sofa and sat beside Patience, taking her hand. 'How was it?'

'It all went very well,' said Patience.

'What Patience means,' said Prudence, 'is they all liked her.'

'Of course they did,' said Vivienne.

'They fell in love with you at first sight.' Molly kissed Patience's cheek. 'How could they not?'

'Molly, dear,' Patience murmured.

'If I kiss you as well,' said Vivienne, going to her, 'will I get a "Vivienne, dear"?' Sitting on her aunt's other side, she kissed her.

'You get a "silly girl",' said Patience.

'Then I'll redeem myself by putting the kettle on.' Vivienne got up. 'No, you stay put, Molly. I won't be a minute – but, Miss Patience, you're not to talk about it until I get back.'

'And don't forget we want to hear about the assembly as well,' said Prudence.

'Just wait until you see Vivienne's present,' said Molly.

Soon they were all drinking tea and discussing the afternoon at the Claremont, Vivienne insisting on hearing all about that before she would utter a word about the assembly. Prudence left most of the talking to Patience. It was her story to tell, her excitement to share.

'Does this mean the engagement is official now?' asked Molly. 'Shall you start telling people?'

'Well – yes, I suppose so.' Patience laughed, sounding nervous and happy at the same time. 'Goodness, what will people think? An old biddy like me.'

'That's quite enough of that sort of talk,' said Vivienne. 'Age has nothing to do with it.'

'Folk who care about you will be pleased,' Molly predicted staunchly. 'And any that aren't pleased aren't worth bothering about.'

'Hear, hear,' said Vivienne.

'You're right,' said Patience. 'I shan't be silly about it. I'm extremely lucky and others should be glad for me.'

'If anyone says that to you, Miss Patience,' said Molly, 'you can tell them from me that Mr Henderson is the lucky one.'

Prudence listened in satisfaction. How their lives had expanded since they had opened their business school early last year. Yes, they had set up the school in the most difficult and distressing circumstances imaginable, thanks to that shocking will left by Pa when he had left the house to Lawrence instead of to them, but the strange thing was that so much good had come about because of it. Life was a lot more interesting now. It was fulfilling too.

'I have to go home in a minute and make tea for my boys,' said Molly, her voice showing her love for her family. 'Shall you be seeing Mr Henderson again this evening, Miss Patience?'

'No, Molly dear. It's Saturday, so Miss Kirby is coming round. I wouldn't dream of letting her down.'

Molly squeezed her hand affectionately. 'Only you could set aside the excitement of making your engagement official in order to see your old friend. That's why you're so special.'

'Get on with you.' Patience flapped a hand, pretending to shoo Molly away, but it was obvious she was pleased.

Prudence was glad the two young women had made such a point of being here to share the moment. They had definitely added to the day's pleasure.

'Now,' said Prudence when Vivienne came back into the sitting room after seeing Molly out, 'tell us about the assembly – and what's this special present that Molly mentioned?'

'I'll fetch it,' said Vivienne. 'I left it in the hall.' She popped out for a moment and returned with a long string of coloured beads. 'As far as the children are concerned, they now belong to the Christmas Orphanage, so they wanted me to have a Christmas decoration to remember them by.'

'How charming,' said Patience, holding out her hands for Vivienne to put the garland into. 'Tell us all about it.'

Vivienne described the occasion, but it was clear she didn't want to steal her aunt's thunder and it wasn't long before she asked, 'Are you going to tell Miss Kirby your news?'

'Yes, I am,' said Patience. 'Strictly speaking, I ought to tell Lawrence and Evelyn first, but it would feel ungracious not to tell Miss Kirby since she is a friend of so many years' standing and is coming to us this evening. I thought perhaps I'd make some fruit scones and what do you say to a few sandwiches? Just to make a little occasion of it.'

Usually when Miss Kirby came to their house, they had tea and a slice of cake. It could be difficult having a friend who was hard up. One wanted to be generous and, to be blunt, to feed her up a bit, but it would be wrong to offer her more, because it would put her under an obligation to offer similar hospitality to them when they visited her in her rooms. On her meagre means, Miss Kirby couldn't run to anything fancy. For those who lived their lives amid the ranks of the genteel poor, appearances were everything and it would be the height of bad manners to place a fellow genteel poor person in an uncomfortable position.

That evening, Patience and Vivienne laid out the supper before their visitor arrived.

'This looks festive,' Miss Kirby commented as she walked in.

'Do sit down,' said Patience. 'We wanted something special this evening because we – that is, I – have news for you.'

'Good news, I hope,' Miss Kirby said politely, 'though I think it must be, judging by this.' She indicated the food.

'I hope you'll think it's good.' Patience started to sound flustered. Her cheeks were bright pink. 'I'm – well, I'm engaged.'

Miss Kirby blinked. 'I'm so sorry. I think my ears must be at fault. It's the oddest thing. It sounded as if you said you were engaged.'

The ground was damp, but it didn't stop Jess kneeling beside Mum's grave on Sunday morning. The wedding had gone off well yesterday, as had the little reception afterwards. Mum and Dad's house was no longer Mum and Dad's house, but she would get used to that. The main thing was that Dad would be looked after. Life would be better for Mrs Nolan too – Mrs Mason, rather. Everyone knew that widows in their station in life had it hard.

Mrs Nolan had carried a small bouquet of snowdrops and greenery and she had given Jess a posy of the same flowers. Now Jess laid her posy on Mum's grave. She hadn't told anybody her intention. She didn't want anyone thinking she had taken against her new stepmother. Giving Mum the flowers just seemed like the right thing to do. It made her feel part of the occasion and that was important to Jess.

Some folk talked to the dead person when they visited a grave. Jess had glimpsed it many a time, heard it sometimes too, a soft murmur that made her look straight ahead so she didn't appear to be earwigging. Jess had never talked to Mum, though. She considered herself to be a practical person and speaking to the dead wasn't for the likes of her. Even so, she was aware of a part of herself, deep down, that wanted to talk to her mum, but there was too much to say and she wouldn't know where to start.

She touched the headstone with her gloved fingers, then sat back on her heels for a few moments before coming to her feet, her gaze still on the stone Mum shared with Dad's parents.

'Look who's here,' said a voice behind her.

Jess turned to find the newlyweds, arm in arm; Dad in his Sunday suit and bowler, the new Mrs Mason in a dark-brown coat, her hat sporting a small feather.

'Great minds, eh?' said Mrs Mason, lifting her own bouquet a little so as to draw Jess's gaze.

Jess realised. 'You're putting your flowers on Mum's grave.'

'Aye. Me and your dad thought it'd be a nice gesture,' said Mrs Mason, but Jess wasn't fooled: she knew it would have been wholly her stepmother's idea. 'She were a good wife to your dad and a loving mother to you, by all accounts. It's a shame she were took so young.'

'Yes.' Jess forced the word around a sudden painful constriction in her throat. 'It was.'

Mrs Mason bent and laid her flowers beside Jess's. 'There.' She looked at Dad. 'You go on ahead and we'll catch up in a minute. Me and your Jess need to have a word.' She tucked her hand in the crook of Jess's elbow. 'Come on, lass. Let's sit on that bench.'

'Thank you for giving Mum your flowers,' said Jess once they were seated.

'It seems to me that being respectful of the first marriage is a good way to start the second one.'

Jess nodded, thinking also of what Mrs Mason had said about doing right by your spouse and having the same attitude to money. She had no idea whether this was a love-match, but she had no doubt Dad would be in a safe pair of hands.

'What did you want us to talk about?' she asked.

'We need to settle what you're going to call me. I've been Mrs Nolan so far, but I can't be Mrs Mason, can I? I know you called your mother Mum, so how about Mother for me?'

The child inside Jess rebelled. 'What about Mother Agnes?'

'Mother Agnes? Are you barmy or summat? That sounds like I run a convent. Now listen, you've got to call me something and I won't be Agnes, not to a slip of a girl like you, so it's got to be summat along the lines of Mother. I can't be Mum, so that leaves Mother or Ma. Your choice, so have a think. Now then, let's see if we can catch up with your dad, shall we?'

As they left the graveyard, arm in arm, Jess felt a surge of liking for her father's new wife.

'If you want to keep my dad happy,' she said, 'always put a drop of Lea & Perrins in the gravy.'

'Oh aye?'

'I think my mum wouldn't mind you knowing.'

Chapter Twenty

PRUDENCE SPENT A quiet afternoon at home. Vivienne had gone out and so had Patience. Niall had collected her in a taxi to meet with his daughters again. The daughters were due to travel home to Annerby in the morning.

'You're welcome to come too,' Patience had said when she was waiting for Niall to arrive.

'Thank you, but I'll stay here. You need to get to know them all.'

'So do you. They're going to be your nieces.' Patience shook her head. 'I can't get used to the idea of having all those stepdaughters. It's bewildering. Wonderful but bewildering.'

'And you've yet to meet the husbands and children. You're going to be a grandmother.'

'I know,' Patience said softly. 'It's everything I hoped for when I was young. The dream vanished years and years ago, but now it's come true. I don't know what I did to deserve to be so lucky.'

'My dear Patience, firstly, luck isn't something that comes to one through being deserving; and secondly, if anybody could be said to deserve it, that person would be you.'

'Bless you. That sounds like the taxi. Are you sure you won't come?'

'Positive. Go and enjoy your new family's company.'

Alone in the house, Prudence felt the strangeness of her situation. She was on her own here so infrequently, especially since they had started taking pupil-lodgers, but this afternoon felt different, a foretaste of her life without Patience. Aside from that brief time in Scotland which had ended for Prudence with the birth of her daughter, they had lived together beneath this roof their entire lives and she would miss her sister keenly. Oh, she was eminently sensible and practical and she wouldn't make a fuss out of it, but Patience's absence would make a huge difference to her.

Patience was a good companion, an attentive listener. Her propensity to see the best in everyone had long acted as a reminder to Prudence that her own critical nature wasn't as agreeable as it might be. Yes, there had been many occasions when she had felt vexed because it seemed that all the difficult decisions were left to her to make, but the truth was that she had set herself up as the head of the household after Mother died and Pa abdicated responsibility, and that was how she had always liked it.

But she would be lonely without Patience. That was the truth. No matter how dear Vivienne was to her, she would miss Patience deeply and lastingly. She gave herself a shake. Times were when she had regarded having the house to herself as a luxury. Now she was feeling it in a different way, a way that was acutely painful but which she would have to get used to.

Going into the dining room, she removed her box of lesson plans and resources from the sideboard cupboard. She had taken to spending a couple of hours on Sunday afternoons sorting out the following week's lessons. She had been brought up to believe that it was wrong to work on a Sunday; but whoever had made that rule back in the mists of time had apparently not put in the hours of work each week that she did. It was no picnic working all day in the office and then working at home in the evenings as well, and she had to fit in her planning somewhere.

That was another thing. When Patience left, what would happen about the telephone lessons? Prudence considered her own lessons to be infinitely superior and more useful than telephone lessons, but the use of the telephone was a skill that wasn't taught on other secretarial courses. It set their school apart and raised the tone.

Her sharp ears caught the snap of the letter-box and she got up to look into the hall, where an envelope now lay on the mat. She went to pick it up. It was addressed simply to *Miss Patience Hesketh*, with *By hand* written in the top left. Prudence knew the handwriting immediately.

She opened the door just as Miss Kirby reached the gate. Prudence called to her to come back.

'I hope I didn't disturb you,' said Miss Kirby.

'Not at all. Won't you come in? I'm on my own at present. Keep me company for a while.'

Prudence hung up her friend's coat and put extra coal on the fire. Coal was one of the things Miss Kirby scrimped on. Prudence prepared a tray of tea with Patience's home-made apple and cinnamon cake and took it into the sitting room.

She experienced a glimmer of something akin to sisterhood as she took in her friend's familiar appearance. Miss Kirby's long-line linen jacket and ankle-length panelled skirt, together with the felt hat with its turned-down brim, had been her Sunday best since the middle of the war. They were two of a kind, she and Miss Kirby, ladylike spinsters with little money, clinging to their smartness, though Miss Kirby's situation was considerably more precarious. Being genteel poor wasn't a problem Patience would have to face any longer. Niall would keep her in comfort for the rest of her days.

Miss Kirby glanced at the letter, which Prudence had propped up on the mantelpiece.

'It's a letter of congratulation,' she said. 'I hope you can both forgive me for expressing my surprise yesterday evening.'

'Frankly, I think Patience will have to get used to other people's surprise pretty swiftly,' said Prudence. 'The engagement of a maiden lady of her age is going to cause astonishment all round – and I told her so after you'd gone.'

'Well, my good wishes are sincere.'

Prudence picked up the cake knife. 'Do have a slice. I'm going to.' She was full from the Sunday roast, but if she didn't have some cake, Miss Kirby wouldn't.

'Tea and cake, a good fire and a good friend,' said Miss Kirby. 'What a treat for a Sunday afternoon.'

Prudence was about to say, 'It's better than planning lessons, which is what I'm supposed to do,' but stopped herself. Suddenly it was important not to mention the business school, because she'd had an idea that, tempting as it was to broach it with Miss Kirby, needed to be discussed first with Patience.

What would Patience think? Vivienne, too. Prudence valued her opinion. Was it a viable idea – or was she clutching at straws?

When Niall brought Patience home early that evening, Prudence and Vivienne were in the sitting room. The happy couple sat together on the sofa, Patience smiling and Niall looking at ease and pleased with life.

'Did you have a good afternoon?' Prudence asked.

'Very much so,' sighed Patience. 'The girls are delightful and they've made it clear that I'll be welcome among them and their families.'

Prudence smothered a pang. She and Patience had relied on one another for such a long time, but now Patience was moving on. And, after all, Prudence had Vivienne.

'I've had an idea about the business school,' said Prudence, 'about when you're gone, I mean. I wonder about asking Miss Kirby to be a tutor. She doesn't have any office experience, but, as a teacher, she had years of keeping records and writing reports. I'm sure she'd have something to offer our pupils.'

'I agree,' said Patience. 'You could pay her out of the fees. I know it wouldn't be much, but it would make a difference to her.'

'That sounds perfect, if I may say so,' Vivienne commented.

Patience and Niall looked at one another and laughed.

'Here you are, Prudence, making plans for the business school,' said Niall, 'while, on the way home in the taxi, Patience was talking about what will happen on the domestic front.'

'The domestic front?' Prudence repeated.

'Typical Prudence,' Patience said affectionately. 'Who's going to run the house after I move out?'

'I hadn't thought of it in those terms,' Prudence admitted. 'I've only thought of it as regards how I'll miss Patience's company and, just this afternoon, how to adapt the school.'

'You're going to miss me?' asked Patience, going predictably misty-eyed. 'I'll miss you too.'

'No you won't,' Prudence said stoutly. 'You'll be too busy with that vast new family you're marrying into.'

'Tell Prudence your ideas about the house,' said Niall.

'It's just an idea,' said Patience. 'I wonder whether, instead of coming in just to do the rough, Mrs Whitney might do more hours and look after the light housework as well.'

Prudence pictured the tuition fees trickling through her fingers. They had been meant to form a nest-egg.

'And then there's the cooking,' added Patience.

'We'll manage,' said Vivienne.

Prudence and Patience exchanged a look – more than that, a thought, years of understanding. They had spent their lives managing ever since Mother died and Pa stopped going out to work, just about getting by, doing their best to adhere to the rules and expectations of the middle class. It was all about standards.

'What you really need,' said Patience, 'is for Mrs Whitney to carry on doing the rough and you to have a cook-general to do the light work and run the kitchen.'

And there went the rest of the tuition fees, sacrificed on the altar of the great god, standards.

The doorbell rang.

'I'll go.' Vivienne stood up and left the room.

There were voices in the hall. It was Lawrence and Evelyn.

'My goodness,' said Patience and Niall squeezed her hand.

Evelyn came in first, decked out in a heavily beaded evening dress of dark blue. She was followed by their younger girl, Felicity, wearing a cream velvet dress that could only be described as tubular. The height of fashion, no doubt, and probably hideously expensive, but honestly, girls nowadays. Then Lawrence followed Vivienne in. He was also in evening dress.

'Good evening,' he said, sounding very full of himself. 'We're on our way out, as you can see, but we've come to— Oh, I beg your pardon. I didn't realise you had company.'

Patience and Niall rose. Prudence realised that Lawrence and Evelyn were looking to herself to perform the introductions. It was a small detail, but it made her see that she was the one who had always taken control of every situation under this roof.

'Patience has someone she would like you to meet,' she said mildly.

Patience drew herself up taller, looking utterly serene.

'Evelyn, Lawrence, Felicity, I'd like to introduce Mr Niall Henderson, a very old friend who yesterday became my fiancé. Niall, may I present—'

'*What?*' Lawrence exclaimed. 'Fiancé, did you say? But that's imposs—'

'That's enough, Lawrence,' Prudence broke in. 'Save your surprise until you get home. Just now, allow Patience to finish the introductions and then you may congratulate her.'

'Yes,' said Patience, quiet but determined. 'Please don't be rude in front of my fiancé.'

Lawrence's mouth dropped open, but Niall saved the situation. He shook hands and was pleasant and charming.

'Patience and I,' he said, giving her a loving look, 'met years ago on the banks of Loch Lomond and I've never forgotten her. We met again recently and I knew I couldn't let her go.'

'That's ever so romantic,' said Felicity. 'I never knew things like that happened to...' Her voice trailed away.

'To people of our advanced years?' Niall suggested and his kindly laughter made the situation feel easy and natural.

'Have you set a date?' Felicity asked.

'We're thinking of Easter,' said Patience.

'Easter!' Lawrence exclaimed, as if that somehow made it even more preposterous.

Evelyn asked after Niall's family and Patience proudly announced she was to be not just a stepmother but a step-grandmother.

'My daughters are delighted,' said Niall.

Prudence willed Evelyn to say the right thing.

'And so they should be,' said Evelyn. 'Patience will love her new position and she'll flourish in it. She's always been a devoted little home-body, haven't you, Patience?'

'Speaking of new positions,' said Lawrence, puffing up

his chest. 'We're here to tell you my good news. Alderman Edwards is stepping down because of ill-health and...' He jutted out his chin. 'I shall take his place.'

'Alderman Hesketh,' said Evelyn.

'Congratulations, Lawrence,' said Prudence. 'You've wanted this for a long time.'

'It's a great honour,' said Lawrence. 'To know that my services to the community have been recognised is deeply gratifying.' He looked round as if expecting applause. Then his gaze homed in on Prudence. 'If Patience is getting married and leaving home at last, this is the end of the business school; and you, Prudence, shan't want to be rattling around in here all alone, shall you? This is the perfect time for me to take possession of my house and move in with my wife and daughter.'

Prudence's heartbeat raced. 'It needn't be the end of the school. I'm hoping to engage a new tutor.'

'Ah, an outsider, you mean, and why should I make provision for that?'

'Because the world believes you are the brains behind the school; because the world believes you set it up out of concern for surplus girls.'

'Exactly so – thanks to you,' said Lawrence. 'Frankly, I don't care what you do about the school, but you won't be doing it under my roof. You've used the school as the means to prevent me from moving in for the past year and I've had enough. You can find rented rooms, Prudence.' He gazed into the air, as if having a vision. 'I can see the article in the newspaper: "Alderman Hesketh said, 'This is an appropriate time to move into the family property which my father left to me. Not only is it suitable because of my new status, but my sisters' circumstances have recently altered. One of them has married and the other will continue the good work of the business school for surplus girls from her new accommodation.'" Or possibly, "One is getting married and, as a result, it is with deep regret that I must announce the closure of the business school." Either way suits me.'

He looked round at everyone. Patience clutched Niall's hand and gazed in anguish at Prudence.

Lawrence looked at Prudence as well. 'Which is it to be?'

Chapter Twenty-One

JESS CAUGHT AN early train back from Annerby on Monday, though you'd never have guessed it from the time it eventually arrived at Manchester Victoria, a delay having made it over an hour late. So much for her careful plans. She had intended to take a taxi home to Wilton Close and freshen herself up before hurrying to Holly Lodge for the afternoon. As it was, she had to dump her trunk in Left Luggage and go straight to work. Even so, she was late. She just hoped Mr Peters wouldn't have taken it into his head to perform one of his unexpected visits. It would be just like him to turn up today to make sure she had arrived on time.

Mr Peters wasn't there – but Mr Thorpe was. He walked down the steps, heading for the gate just as she came through it. Oh glory. Jess's heart sank. She would rather have faced Mr Peters' annoyance at her tardiness.

'You've deigned to put in an appearance at last, then,' said Mr Thorpe. 'What was it? Another shopping expedition?'

'Certainly not,' she snapped.

He glanced at her carpetbag. 'Looks like it to me.'

'Then you're mistaken, aren't you?' Jess aimed for a breezy tone. She had no intention of explaining herself to this odious man. He wasn't entitled to it and he didn't deserve it. She glanced around. Abigail should be here, waiting for her. She had half expected to find her sitting on the front steps.

'Looking for the girl?' Mr Thorpe enquired. 'Since there was no sign of you, I sent her away.'

'You had no right to do that. She's my assistant.'

'Your assistant? A kid from the orphanage?' said Mr Thorpe. 'Now I've heard it all. I thought you'd hired a cleaner. Allow me,' he added before she could speak.

Jess thought he was offering to carry her bag for her, but no, he retraced his steps and unlocked the front door.

'You've got a key,' she exclaimed. Marching inside, she immediately turned to face him, effectively barring his way.

'Of course I have,' he said. 'I'm the landlord's agent.'

'Don't tell me you carry all the landlord's front door keys around with you.'

'Normally, I don't need to, Miss Mason. Normally, a woman wouldn't be put in charge of somewhere like Holly Lodge. It so happens I called here earlier – or attempted to, I should say.' Mr Thorpe stared at her, waiting.

Jess all but ground her teeth, but forced herself to abide by the first rule of the hotel trade. 'I'm sorry if you were inconvenienced, but,' she couldn't resist adding, 'it's not as though you had made an appointment.'

'That may be so, but it's just as well I happened to be here, because the builders' merchant attempted to make a delivery – and he *did* have an appointment.'

Jess's mouth dropped open. She snapped it shut. 'No, he didn't.'

'Indeed? I suggest you take that up with your boss. I think you'll find that Mr Peters informed him the delivery could be made any time after midday.' Mr Thorpe bared his teeth in a supercilious smile. 'When I was here shortly before one o'clock, I regret to say I didn't have the key to Holly Lodge in my possession or I would have signed for the delivery myself, as a favour to Mr Peters, you understand.'

Jess didn't respond. What could she say?

'So I put a telephone call through to Oak Lodge, informed Mr Peters of your absence and offered to fetch my key and be here between half past one and half past two so that the builders' merchant could return. Mr Peters was most grateful, as you can appreciate. It saved him from having to rush over here to stand in for the flibbertigibbet he was unwise enough to employ.' Another of those lofty smiles. 'Oh, I do beg your pardon. Did I make it sound as if you're a flibbertigibbet? Slip of the tongue.'

It was wrong of her – it was unprofessional and ill-mannered – but Jess shut the door in his face, then almost stamped across the hall to dump her carpetbag and take off her coat and hat. When the bell rang, she marched back and threw the door open.

'What do you— Oh! I'm sorry. I thought you were someone else.'

'Oh aye?' A thin-faced man in a flat cap and workman's jacket stood on the step. He had large, wonky teeth. 'Screech like a harpy at your usual callers, do you? Oh, Mr Thorpe. Good to see you, sir,' he added as Mr Thorpe strolled from behind him and into the hall as if he owned the place. 'Thanks for coming back to open up.'

'Pleasure,' Mr Thorpe murmured. 'It's a shame you were let down earlier, Baxter.'

'Where do you want everything, sir?'

Jess stepped forward. 'I'm the manager. You should be dealing with me.'

'You're the—' The man, Baxter, stared at her. Then he glanced enquiringly at Mr Thorpe, widening his eyes as if to ask if she were mad.

Mr Thorpe merely shrugged his shoulders and smirked, moving off to the side.

'Well, I've seen it all now,' Baxter exclaimed.

'What have you brought?' Jess asked, determined to assert herself. She gave Baxter a hard look, daring him not to answer.

'The baths and basins. Lengths of pipe, cast-iron drainpipes. Nails, screws and what-have-you. Where do you want it?'

The two largest rooms stood one to each side of the hall. Jess opened the door to the one she visualised becoming the men's sitting room.

'In here, if you please. Is there sufficient space?'

Baxter looked in, pulling his mouth this way and that, as if he'd been asked to do the impossible. Then, without a word to her, he returned to the front door, calling, 'Right we are, Chalky,' as he ran down the steps, leaving the door wide open.

Moments later, there was another ring at the doorbell. Good heavens, Baxter and Chalky weren't going to ring politely every time they brought something inside, were they? Jess returned to the door to find another man, older this time, wearing the same sort of jacket and cap.

'Holly Lodge? Delivery from the timber merchant. Let the boss know, will you, love?'

Jess adopted her calmest expression. 'I am the boss.'

The fellow's eyes narrowed, then his mouth crinkled humorously. 'You almost had me believing you for a moment there, love. Now go and fetch the manager, will you?'

'I am not "love". I am Miss Mason and I'm the manager.'

'No! Honestly?' The man looked over Jess's shoulder into the hall. 'Oh, Mr Thorpe. I didn't see you there, sir. Wood delivery.'

'Hayes, old chap. Always good to see you. You'd better ask Miss Mason what she wants done with your delivery.'

'You mean to say she really is...?'

'Difficult to believe, isn't it?'

Hayes pulled off his cap. 'Beg pardon, miss. No offence intended.'

Well, that was something. Jess opened the door to the other front room, which she thought of as the dining room. 'Is there enough space in here?'

'Aye. Me 'n' Mr Rigby will fetch it all in.'

'Shove over, mate,' said a voice behind him and Baxter backed through the doorway, carrying one end of a bath, with another man at the other end. Hayes hurried outside, calling to his own colleague. The two pairs of delivery men went in and out, dodging round one another, laying things on the floors of their respective rooms.

'That's your lot,' said Hayes. 'Here's the delivery note, if you want to check it.'

He fixed his gaze halfway between Jess and Mr Thorpe. Jess wasn't having that. She took the sheet of paper and walked into the dining room, her gaze shifting between the list and the lengths of wood.

'Over there is the timber for the new window frames,' said Hayes, 'and these pieces are various lengths.'

'Give it to me.' Mr Thorpe twitched the delivery note out of Jess's fingers. 'If Miss Mason checks off the delivery, we'll have to wait while she finds a tape-measure.'

Hayes grinned. 'You wouldn't expect a lady to know one length from another just by looking.'

After a minute, Mr Thorpe said, 'Yes – yes – that's everything,' but instead of handing the list back to Jess, he signed it with a flourish. The gall of the man!

Jess thanked Hayes and Rigby and headed for the other room. Mr Thorpe wasn't going to get his hands on this list, not if she had anything to do with it. She stood in the room, waiting for the last items to be brought in and put down.

But no sooner had she been presented with the delivery note and started to look for each item than the postman, taking advantage of the open front door, walked in and handed her the afternoon post. As Jess glanced at it, she realised he had given her next door's as well in error, so she had to run after him, somewhat to Baxter's annoyance. Then, just when she had made a fresh start on the delivery list, one of the butchers she had spoken to about supplying Holly Lodge turned up, full of apologies for not having got back in touch sooner with the necessary information.

'Oh my giddy aunt.' Baxter rolled his eyes. 'Tell you what, miss. You talk to the butcher and let Mr Thorpe go through the delivery note. At least he'll know what's what.'

'I'm perfectly capable of recognising a bath,' Jess replied, though, truth be told, she was feeling flustered. Everything seemed to be happening at once. 'Mr Goodwin,' she said to the butcher, 'if you'll kindly leave your prices with me, I'll be in touch. Thank you for coming.'

'Get a move on, can't you, miss?' said Baxter. 'You've already messed up our delivery schedule by not being here earlier when you were supposed to be. Tell her, Mr Thorpe.'

'Alas…' murmured Mr Thorpe.

Jess skimmed down the list. 'The nails and screws?'

'Them paper bags over yon. Bath taps in the boxes in the corner.'

Jess signed and the unpleasant Baxter went on his way, accompanied by Chalky. Good riddance. All of a sudden, Holly Lodge felt very quiet.

'There,' Jess said in a bright voice calculated to rub Mr Thorpe's snooty nose in the dirt. 'That's all in order.'

'You reckon?'

'I do indeed. If you've quite finished sniping, perhaps you'd like to leave now.'

'Leave? And miss the anguish when you realise your mistake?'

'The only mistake I made was permitting you to set foot inside,' Jess retorted. He was just taunting her – wasn't he?

'If you say so.'

'What mistake?' she demanded. She didn't want to ask, but she had to. Suppose she really had made an error? She was sure she hadn't, but what if she had?

'The delivery from the general builders' merchant,' said Mr Thorpe.

'What of it?'

'Did you sign to confirm that all items had been delivered?'

'You know I did.'

'Signed for the bath plugs and basin plugs, did you?'

Jess scanned her copy of the list. 'Yes.'

Mr Thorpe didn't speak. Jess looked at him. He looked at her until she gave in and went back into the sitting room and started looking round.

'You won't find them.' Mr Thorpe stood in the doorway.

'You could have told me,' she flared.

'What? Treat you as a silly little flibbertigibbet, you mean?' Mr Thorpe laughed, a satisfied sound. 'Don't worry about the plugs. I'll sort out the oversight. I'll drop in at the builders' merchant's at the end of the day and tell them. They'll take my word for it. I'm sure they'll understand that it's the sort of thing that's bound to happen when a woman thinks she can do a man's job. Good afternoon, Miss Mason.'

Jess remained where she was, seething. She felt like kicking Mr Thorpe down the front steps, but more than that, she felt like kicking herself. What a stupid mistake – and it was all her fault. She seemed to hear her own voice in her head, telling Angela Hitchcock, 'Always take your time when going through invoices and delivery notices.' Miss

Hesketh had said the same thing almost word for word when talking to her pupils and Jess had had to glance down at her hands to hide her complacency, but look at her now. Checking every item on the delivery list was such a basic thing to do and she had let herself get pushed into not doing it properly. As if that wasn't bad enough, Mr Thorpe was going to have the pleasure of doing her down. It wouldn't be just the builders' merchant he would tell. He was bound to inform Mr Peters as well.

And she had only herself to blame.

Chapter Twenty-Two

JESS STOOD ALONE in Holly Lodge, with the silence seeming to ring all around her. Should she go across the road to the orphanage in search of Abigail? Mr Thorpe had had no business sending the girl on her way like that. But Abigail might not have returned to the orphanage. What if she had taken herself off to indulge in a spot of window-shopping? Jess would land her right in the soup if she went and asked for her. She sighed. It was probably best to leave well alone.

Later, the doorbell sounded. Jess answered the door and there was the disagreeable Baxter on the step. He pulled off his cap.

'I'm sorry to bother you, Miss Mason, but, um, there's been a mistake.'

'I know,' said Jess.

'You know?' Baxter's face lost its colour.

'The plugs.' Jess's spirits lifted. 'Have you brought them?'

'I don't know about anything about any plugs, miss… madam.' Baxter smiled at her, showing off his uneven teeth. 'I'm here about summat else. My mistake, not yours. It can happen to the best of us, wouldn't you say? I fetched you the wrong pipes.'

'The wrong drainpipes?'

'No, the ordinary pipes for the indoor plumbing. My own fault entirely. I can't apologise enough for the inconvenience, miss, but if I could just come in and get them…'

She ought to be glad he was being polite at last, but it was as if he was being *too* polite. Something about him made Jess's skin crawl and she didn't trust him. Instinct told her there was something going on here.

'I'm afraid it isn't convenient at present.' She held the door, ready to close it. 'You'll have to come back later.'

Baxter bit his lip. 'Are you sure I can't just…? I'll only be a minute.'

'Quite sure. Now please excuse me.'

Jess shut the door. Her heart was beating quickly. What was this about? Nothing, in all probability. It was very likely just her getting the creeps because Baxter had been rude earlier and now was trying to be smarmy.

She entered the sitting room. There were four sets of indoor pipes, each set bundled together with thin rope. Jess looked at them, then she hunkered down for a closer inspection. She felt like laughing at herself. What a twit – as if she had the first idea what she was doing! Then she noticed something. Was that…? She ran a fingertip along it – yes, a long hairline crack. Making up her mind, she undid the knots in the rope and set the pipes clattering free on the floor. In the bundle of twelve, there were three with cracks. She freed another set and found another four with cracks. Four! That made seven out of twenty-four. She tried the other sets and found that nearly a quarter of all the pipes were faulty.

But Baxter hadn't said that a dud lot had been delivered. In fact, more than three-quarters of them looked perfectly good to her admittedly untrained eye. Was it normal for a certain number of pipes to be cracked? No, that was a ridiculous idea. There was something going on here, but Jess didn't know what it was.

Tom Watson would know.

The thought popped into her head before she could blot it out. She didn't like to approach him after the way he hadn't provided a proper explanation for pulling out of the Holly Lodge job. That had made her uncomfortable because she had trusted him. But there was no one else she could ask.

She had Perkins and Watson's address from their paperwork. Their office was on Wilbraham Road. Jess quickly finished up for the day, tidied her desk and put on her outdoor things. After a moment's thought, she picked up her carpetbag and took it with her. She would drop it off at home before heading to Perkins and Watson's. After everything that had happened this afternoon, she could hardly believe she had started the day in Annerby.

When she was walking along Wilbraham Road in the direction of Chorlton Station, she asked a stranger for directions to Perkins and Watson's and was told simply to carry on.

'You'll find them just the other side of the railway bridge.'

Soon she was at the entrance to a yard with varying lengths of timber propped up against the walls and pallets of bricks over to one side, half-covered by a tarpaulin. Across the yard stood a small, brick-built building. She went to knock on the door, but, before she could do so, a man of around Dad's age came over to her.

'Afternoon.' He touched his cap to her. 'Can I help you?'

Jess smiled. He was an older version of Tom Watson, with the same blue eyes and physical presence, muscular without being heavy-set, though his hair was salt and pepper, not white.

'Mr Watson senior?' she asked.

He grinned. That smile was the same too. 'I don't think I've been called that before.'

'My name is Jess Mason. I work at Holly Lodge. I was hoping for a word with your son.'

'You were headed the right way before I interrupted you.' Mr Watson opened the door and leaned in. 'Tom! Visitor for you. A pretty one an' all. No offence, miss.'

'None taken.' She liked Mr Watson. She sensed he would be a lot easier to get on with than her own dad.

She stepped inside – and there was Tom. Yes, Tom. Not Tom Watson, as she had meticulously thought of him because she knew him through work and he was therefore someone to be regarded as a colleague and nothing more; someone moreover by whom she wished to be taken seriously as a working person.

Here he was now, jacket off, sleeves rolled up, waistcoat unbuttoned, looking workmanlike and casual both at the same time. He was bare-headed too and that white hair above the relatively young face made him appear both distinguished and vulnerable, a combination that touched her heart. Jess felt as though she had unexpectedly stumbled across the real Tom. And of all the things to think, what entered her head was, *No wonder I felt so let down when Perkins and Watson didn't want the Holly Lodge work*. Her disappointment hadn't been because she liked him as a colleague and someone she would be glad to work with. It had been because she found him attractive. She *liked* him.

If there had been any question in Tom's mind as to the warmth of the feeling he had for Jess Mason, then the colossal bump his heart delivered at the unexpected sight of her in the office would have brought it home to him. For a moment he was too dazzled to speak. She was neat and trim in her sensible coat, the unfashionable length of which showed its age, and her new hairstyle framed her face beneath her felt cloche hat. She looked as if she had hurried here, because her cheeks glowed and her eyes were bright. Had she hurried on his account? Even as his heart lifted at the idea, his head told him not to be so ruddy daft. Of course she hadn't.

He pulled himself together. 'Miss Mason, what brings you here?'

'I hope you don't mind. I've come to ask for your help.'

Mind? He was surprised, but his surprise was nothing compared to his delight.

'Of course. Have a seat.' He held the chair for her. Should he remain on this side of the desk, leaning against it so as to be close to her? No, that wouldn't be gentlemanly. He took his place behind the desk. 'What's this about?'

He listened closely as she explained about Baxter and the cracked pipes, then he nodded.

'I've a pretty good idea what's happened and it sounds to me as if this Baxter fellow has a nice little sideline going.' He glanced at the clock. 'I'd like to take a look at the pipes, if I may, just to make sure.'

'Thank you,' said Jess. 'I wouldn't want to have made a mistake, especially if a man's reputation depends on it.'

'We'll nip round in the van, then we'll go to the builders' merchant.'

'To see Mr Baxter?'

'No. He's just the delivery driver.' Delivery driver and part-time scoundrel, by the sound of it, though Tom didn't say so out loud.

They went to Holly Lodge and Tom examined the pipes – well, not so much examined them as gave them a glance that told him all he needed to know.

'Right,' he said decisively. 'Let's go to the builders' merchant.'

'Should we take the damaged pipes with us?'

'No, leave them here.'

Jess climbed into the van once more. Tom turned the starter-handle on the front and got in behind the wheel. He was aware of Jess looking at his profile.

'You look serious,' she said. 'Now you've seen the pipes for yourself, will you tell me what you think has happened?'

'You're correct about the pipes having cracks and I'm sorry if you thought I doubted your word.'

'Not at all. It's not as though I've had occasion to look at pipes before. You said something about Baxter having a sideline.'

'It seems that way to me. Here's how it works. This builders' merchant, Durrell's, is a reputable company. The odd faulty item might slip through now and again, but the number of cracked pipes you've received – that's deliberate. I've heard of this kind of thing happening. What Baxter does is this. He takes one or two good pipes out of a bundle and replaces them with substandard cracked pipes. The pipes are delivered in quantity to building sites and when the time comes to use them, no one will particularly notice if a few are faulty. They'll just set them aside and use the good ones. Meanwhile, Baxter builds up a collection of good pipes he can sell on.'

'So that's why he was desperate to get them back,' said Jess. 'In a relatively small job like Holly Lodge's, the cracked pipes would stand out a mile.'

'And Durrell's would have been on the receiving end of a serious complaint,' said Tom, checking the traffic before he turned a corner. 'It's a good thing you didn't let this Baxter softsoap you.'

Her shoulders moved as she shuddered. 'Nasty individual. The funny thing is, if he'd been off-hand with me, like he was first time round, I wouldn't have thought twice about letting him in.'

Tom pulled up outside the spacious yard belonging to the builders' merchant and escorted Jess between the pallets and piles of goods. He held open the door for her to enter the office at the front of the warehouse.

Walking in behind her, he heard Mr Thorpe's voice, loud and clear.

'Well, it's only to be expected, isn't it, when you put a woman in charge of something like this? Yes, if you let me have the plugs, I'll pop them round there myself. There's no reason for you to put yourselves out just because women can't do things properly.'

Jess's face went pink, then white. Tom wanted to bundle her up and protect her, but she wouldn't thank him for it – and quite right too. It wouldn't help her in the long run to be seen to need a man to fight her battles.

'Afternoon, Thorpe,' said Tom.

Thorpe turned to return the greeting, but changed it to, 'Well, well, well, who have we here? Are your ears burning, Miss Mason? I've just been explaining that you don't think baths require plugs.'

Thorpe laughed, his manner inviting the men behind the long wooden counter to join in, though a hard look from Tom soon put paid to any inclination they might have had to do so.

'Are you here to confess your error, Miss Mason?' enquired Mr Thorpe. 'I see you didn't feel able to come without moral support.'

'Me, you mean?' Tom kept his tone airy. 'All I did was provide Miss Mason with a lift in my van. I believe she has important information that your boss will be interested in,' he informed the warehousemen, 'so I suggest you fetch him right away.' He picked up the plugs and chains from the counter. 'I'll take these for you, shall I, Miss Mason?'

'Important information?' said Thorpe. 'From Miss Mason? I find that difficult to believe.'

Tom took a couple of steps backwards, removing himself from the immediate situation. It was up to Jess now. He would have given anything to throw her an encouraging look, but he mustn't. He would have given a lot to punch Mr Thorpe on the nose, but he mustn't do that either.

Mr Durrell appeared. A thin fellow with a deeply lined face, he had taken over this business from his father before the turn of the century. He nodded at Tom and Mr Thorpe, both of whom were known to him, and at Jess.

'I believe you need to speak to me,' he said to Tom.

'Miss Mason wishes to speak to you,' said Tom.

Jess lifted her chin. 'Good afternoon. I'm Jess Mason and I manage Holly Lodge in Chorlton for Mr Peters. Something happened this afternoon that I think you should know about.'

'She accepted delivery of baths and basins minus their plugs,' Thorpe said with a chortle.

Jess ignored him. Directing her words at Mr Durrell, she explained about the consignment of indoor pipes and the way in which Baxter had subsequently attempted to remove them. She wisely made no accusations, simply stating, 'So either your company has supplied substandard goods, sir, or else something untoward is going on.'

'Is this why you're here, Thorpe?' asked Mr Durrell. Tom ground his teeth together. Was this what Jess had to cope with all the time?

'No,' she said before Thorpe could utter a word. 'Mr Thorpe is here merely to crow over the mistake I made in not noticing that you hadn't supplied plugs. I'm here to report a serious incident involving cracked pipes and I'd be obliged if you would kindly address your remarks to me. In fact,' she added, casting a sweet smile in Thorpe's direction, 'if Mr Thorpe had been less keen to find fault with me and more interested in the delivery in general, he might have noticed the cracks himself. After all, I'm a complete novice in these matters and a mere woman to boot, and yet the cracks were easy for me to spot.'

Tom felt like cheering. Game, set and match to Jess.

Chapter Twenty-Three

AFTER SOME THOUGHT, Jess wrote up the plugs incident in the log book. She had already recorded the matter of the cracked pipes, though she had taken care how she phrased it. *It appears that...* and *It seems possible that...* meant she could relate what had happened, including the likely ramifications, without actually accusing Baxter outright. She had hummed and hawed over whether to mention the missing plugs, but honesty compelled her to record her error and give Mr Thorpe the credit for spotting it. When Abigail arrived at Holly Lodge on Tuesday afternoon, Jess put her to work in the sitting room, where the cracked pipes had now been replaced by faultless pipes.

'All these things were delivered yesterday. Here's the delivery note. I want you to check the items against the list.'

Abigail's eyes widened. 'You'd trust me to do that?'

Jess smiled. 'It was all checked yesterday when it arrived, but there was a mistake. I want you to find it. It isn't a race,' she added, recalling what Mrs Rostron had said about Abigail. 'You need to work steadily and be sure of what you've done. If you need any help, ask.'

Leaving Abigail to it, Jess went into her office to go over the price lists provided by the local butchers and grocers. She made a note to remind herself to ask Mrs Rostron who delivered the orphanage's milk.

Eventually Abigail appeared in the open doorway, leaning in to knock.

'Success?' Jess asked, though she could see the answer in the girl's face.

'The list shows plugs for the baths and basins, but I couldn't find them anywhere.'

'That's because they're here.' Jess opened a drawer and retrieved them. 'They really were missing,' she added, seeing Abigail's fleeting frown. 'They had to be fetched from the builders' merchant.'

'Shouldn't the builders' merchant have delivered them, since it was their mistake?'

Clever girl, thought Jess. 'It wasn't just their mistake. It was mine as well. When the delivery arrived, several things happened all at once and I allowed myself to get distracted. I ended up signing to say the delivery was complete when it wasn't. What I want you to learn from this, Abigail, is that it's all very well knowing the right procedure to follow, but you have to make sure you actually follow it.'

Next she showed Abigail the log book.

'I can't let you read it, because it's confidential, but it's interesting for you to know it exists and what it's for.'

'Does Mrs Rostron have to keep a log book?' Abigail asked.

'I expect so,' said Jess. 'All sorts of places have to. I know schools do.'

'Maybe I could be a school clerk, then I could keep the log book.'

Jess smiled. 'I think you'll find that's the head's responsibility.'

'So I'd have to train to be a teacher first,' said Abigail. 'There's no hope of that.'

'You'd have to turn into a man as well,' Jess said, trying to make light of it. 'There are far more headmasters than headmistresses.'

Abigail laughed, then turned serious. 'But nearly all teachers are female. It really isn't fair on us, is it?'

'I'm afraid not,' said Jess, 'but we have to make the best of it. That's all we can do.' She hesitated before asking, 'Would you like to take off your pinafore while you're working here? You might feel more professional.' She didn't add that she would certainly look more professional.

Abigail's face lit up, but only for a moment. 'If Mrs Rostron got wind of it, she'd give me a frightful wigging. She'd probably tell you off too.' She sighed. 'I'll just have to wait until I'm fourteen. I'm really unlucky. Lots of the other girls have turned fourteen now and they wear blouses and skirts and they've put their hair up, but I'm one of the younger ones in the school year, so I'm stuck with this pinafore.'

Her dismay seemed so comical that Jess wanted to laugh, but she was sure Abigail wouldn't see the amusing side.

'The builders will be here tomorrow to make a start,' said Jess. 'Mr Jones popped in this morning to make sure all the goods had been delivered.'

'So tomorrow will be when the cleaning part of my job really gets going,' said Abigail. She didn't sound pleased.

'Yes, but there will be other things happening too. Mr Peters will bring his old soldiers over from Oak Lodge to view the progress of the improvements. You'll like the old soldiers.'

'Nurse Nancy from the orphanage goes to Oak Lodge sometimes to see the old soldiers. She goes with her fiancé. She's set up a choir at the orphanage and they're going to go to Oak Lodge to sing.'

'That's worth knowing,' said Jess. 'Perhaps they could come here and put on a little concert one day.'

She would like that. It was important to make Holly Lodge a part of the local community. It was something Mr Peters was keen on, but Jess would have wanted to do it even if it hadn't been one of his priorities.

Mr Peters chose that afternoon for one of his drop-in visits. Jess introduced Abigail.

'Miss Hunter is working hard,' she said.

'I'm pleased to hear it.' Mr Peters smiled benevolently at Abigail. 'It's a good opportunity for a girl from St Anthony's, so make the most of it.'

'Please, sir, it's St Nicholas's now,' said Abigail.

'So it is. You're quite right. Miss Pike mentioned it when she and Mr Milner came to Oak Lodge on Sunday.'

Abigail told Jess, 'Miss Pike is Nurse Nancy.'

Jess turned to Mr Peters. 'Miss Hunter was telling me that Nurse Nancy – Miss Pike – is going to take the orphanage choir to Oak Lodge.'

'That's correct,' Mr Peters replied.

'I'm keen for Holly Lodge to enjoy social functions too,' said Jess. 'I organised plenty of events when I worked at the Sea View.'

'I don't doubt it,' said Mr Peters, 'but it's one thing to do that in a hotel, where, with different guests, you can afford to repeat what you offer. It's very different in a residential setting.'

'I understand that,' said Jess. 'There's an extra dimension to running a home for permanent residents. I'd like to create a stimulating environment with activities, outings and visitors coming in. The old soldiers who are going to live here, and the younger soldiers too, if they come, have all served their country and they deserve the best care and attention.'

'True, true,' said Mr Peters. 'That has always been my own belief.' He glanced at Abigail and then away. 'Is there something Miss Hunter can be getting on with?'

'Of course,' said Jess. 'Would you take some letters to the pillar-box for me, please, Miss Hunter?' It suited her to have Mr Peters on his own, so she could tell him about the cracked pipes – but it turned out that Mr Peters already knew about them.

'I had a visit earlier from Mr Durrell, the builders' merchant,' Mr Peters told her. 'He wished to congratulate me on the calibre of my staff.'

'Really? You mean – me?' She couldn't quite believe it.

'He explained how you had found some damaged goods and how you dealt with the matter.'

'That was good of him,' said Jess.

'Fair's fair,' said Mr Peters. 'Mr Durrell paid a compliment and it's only right to pass it along. I'm pleased, I must say. Appointing you isn't regarded by the local business community as the soundest decision I ever made, so it is most pleasing to receive positive comments about you.'

'Thank you.'

'You haven't done too badly, all told, Miss Mason,' said Mr Peters. 'In fact, I'd go so far as to say you're looking quite promising.'

With Mr Peters' words still echoing in her ears, Jess went home that evening feeling light-hearted, even hopeful. Coming from Mr Peters, 'quite promising' was practically a ringing endorsement. Yesterday, at Wilton Close, she had answered questions about Dad's wedding without really enjoying the conversation, because she was still kicking herself for having made such a foolish mistake over the delivery note. Today, though, she felt ready to join in properly with the others. In fact, she was looking forward to it. It was such a treat to live in an agreeable atmosphere with like-minded people.

Except that there seemed to be something new in the atmosphere this evening, a faint sense of strain. Was it her imagination or might something have happened over the weekend? Had this air of restraint been here yesterday when she had been too preoccupied to notice?

She didn't like to say anything, but Vivienne took her aside to explain when the Miss Heskeths were preparing for the arrival of their pupils. Jess and Vivienne had to make themselves scarce when lessons were in progress. Miss Hesketh taught at the dining table and Miss Patience used the sitting room, so this gave Jess and Vivienne the choice of disappearing upstairs or going out.

'Let's go into my room,' said Vivienne. 'We can play cards, but first I've got something to tell you.'

Jess sat in the wicker chair and Vivienne lounged on the bed.

'Miss Hesketh and Miss Patience have asked me to tell you this,' Vivienne began. 'They would have told you themselves, but there is so little time in the evenings when pupils are here.'

'That sounds serious,' said Jess. 'I hope nothing is wrong.'

'It is serious and you need to know about it because it could affect your own situation. It's to do with this house.'

Had the roof above her little bedroom lost some tiles? Was water going to come seeping in if it rained?

'The house actually belongs to Mr Lawrence Hesketh,' said Vivienne. 'He is the ladies' brother – well, their half-brother, to be precise.'

'I assumed it belonged to the ladies.'

'It used to be the property of their mother, who was the stepmother of Lawrence Hesketh. When Mrs Hesketh passed away, her daughters and stepson were children. She left the house to her husband, who was, you have to remember, the father of all three children. He died early last year – and he left the house to his son.'

'Wait a minute,' Jess began.

'I know what you're going to say. Why didn't he leave it to the Miss Heskeths, since it had originally belonged to their mother? Well, he didn't. He left it to Lawrence Hesketh – and now Lawrence wants to take possession. He says that with Miss Patience getting married, it's time for Miss Hesketh to make other arrangements.'

'That's unfair,' Jess exclaimed.

'Immaterial, I'm afraid,' said Vivienne. 'There are plenty of people who'd say he's done his sisters a big favour by letting them stay on in the house for a whole year. The point is that he wants to move in with his wife and daughter after Miss Patience gets married, and if – when – that happens, the rest of us will be obliged to make other arrangements.'

'What will happen to Miss Hesketh?' Jess asked at once.

Vivienne smiled and her blue-grey eyes were soft with warmth. 'It's good of you to think of her before your own situation.'

'Never mind me,' Jess said dismissively. 'I'm used to moving around. But poor Miss Hesketh, facing the loss of her home.'

Vivienne arched her eyebrows. 'Poor Miss Hesketh? I suggest you don't say that outside this room.'

Jess couldn't help smiling. 'You're right. She wouldn't thank me for it.'

Should she say something to the Miss Heskeths about this distressing turn of events? She didn't want to be impertinent or speak out of turn, but it wouldn't feel right not to acknowledge it. She wouldn't attempt to make conversation out of it. A polite reference was all that was needed.

Later, when she and Vivienne prepared the nightly Ovaltine and took it into the sitting room, Jess said to her landladies, 'I was sorry to hear about your situation with the house.'

'It's such a shame for you, Jess dear,' said Miss Patience. 'I almost feel as if we lured you here under false pretences.'

'I didn't mean on my own account,' Jess exclaimed at once. 'I meant it must be difficult for you.'

'To put it mildly,' said Miss Hesketh in a dry voice, 'but it is how it is and we must put up with it.'

'Perhaps I could have a longer engagement,' said Miss Patience.

'Perhaps you could talk sense,' said her sister, immediately followed by, 'I apologise, my dear Patience. That was deeply rude of me. I think it must be the worry talking – not that that's any excuse for being ill-mannered. As to your idea, it's preposterous and you mustn't even think of it.'

Miss Hesketh sounded as forthright as ever, but Jess couldn't help feeling sorry for her, even though she knew full well that Miss Hesketh would have her guts for garters if she sensed it. But it must be desperately hard to face the prospect of being more or less forcibly removed from the home you had lived in your entire life. Jess had found it a wrench to move out properly from Dad's house, so how much worse must it be for Miss Hesketh at her age?

Chapter Twenty-Four

As the week went by, the work on Holly Lodge took shape quite quickly. Pleased, Jess commented on it when she took mugs of tea to the workmen.

'It's what Mr Watson said would happen.' Something made her add, 'The younger Mr Watson.'

The men chuckled at the idea of 'young' Mr Watson. Then one of them said, 'That's a good building firm, that is. They know their stuff and they never cut corners. They treat their men right an' all. My brother works for them. He's a brickie.'

'And Tom Watson's a decent bloke,' added another chap. 'He's grown up in that firm and the two older fellas trained him well. I remember my old dad saying it was a shame there was only a young Watson and not a young Perkins as well, but I reckon Tom Watson has got more than what it takes. That firm will be in sound hands when Thomas Watson and Bill Perkins retire.'

Jess had to bottle up her smiles so they didn't burst out. After the strange business of Perkins and Watson accepting and then refusing the Holly Lodge contract, it made her feel all tingly with pride to hear Tom being praised for his work. Pride? What business had she to feel such a thing where Tom Watson was concerned? She was being ridiculous. She just hoped she hadn't betrayed herself in front of Mr Jones's workmen. The last thing she needed was to be laughed at behind her back for having a secret pash on Tom.

At the end of each day, she and Abigail went upstairs to look round and it was a pleasure to see what had been achieved – that is, it was a pleasure for Jess and she hoped it was for Abigail too. She liked the girl and wondered what the chances were of being permitted to keep her on in a formal capacity after she left school. Hark at her! She didn't even know if she herself would be staying on. She mustn't let Mr Peters' words of praise go to her head, especially since she knew it wouldn't take much to make him revise his opinion.

On Friday morning, Mr Peters brought some of the old soldiers to view the work in progress. Jess had borrowed chairs from the orphanage for them to take the weight off their feet. Mr and Mrs Peters pulled up outside Holly Lodge in a pair of taxis and Jess threw open the front door in welcome. Shortly afterwards, Vivienne arrived, bringing a pair of middle-aged men, two of the 'young' soldiers who might be moving in. There were introductions all round.

Jess had used some of the petty cash to purchase flour and other ingredients and Miss Patience had lent her a mixing bowl and cake tins, so that she and Abigail could make a Victoria sponge and a gingerbread loaf, the scent of which when it was in the oven had brought Mr Jones's workmen downstairs, but Jess hadn't been able to give them anything more than the promise of a slice if there was any left over.

While they were all upstairs, the doorbell rang and Jess went to answer it.

'I'll put the kettle on while I'm down there,' she promised her visitors.

'And don't forget the ones doing all the hard graft,' Mr Jones's carpenter called after her.

Jess laughed as she ran downstairs. It was wonderful to have Oak Lodge's old soldiers here, admiring everything and taking an interest. It made her realise how much Holly Lodge had come to mean to her. She was still smiling as she opened the front door. Her heart bumped inside her chest at the sight of Tom Watson. She immediately straightened her face. She couldn't have him thinking the smile was for him.

Tom touched the peak of his cap to her. 'How do.'

'Good morning.' How formal she sounded, but that was only right and proper. Then her delight at having the old soldiers in the house broke through and she said impulsively, 'Do you remember my saying that Mr Peters wanted to bring the residents from Oak Lodge over here to see the work as it goes on? They're here now, some of them. They're lovely gentlemen. Do come in and meet them.'

'Well…' A smile started to tug at Tom's lips.

'Oh, please do,' Jess urged him. 'We have a pair of our young soldiers here too; you remember, the Great War veterans.'

Tom shifted uncomfortably. 'No, thank you, I'd better not. I – I don't want to intrude.'

'It wouldn't be an intrusion. They'd love it. They're very sociable, I promise.'

'No, honestly, I…'

Did he feel awkward about meeting Mr Peters after having let him down? Yet it had looked like he wanted to say yes to start with.

Tom started to step away. 'I'd better not keep you if you've got a houseful.'

Jess took a step after him. Pure instinct made her follow him. 'You haven't said why you came.' She pulled the door to behind her.

'Oh, yes, that. I thought you'd want to know that we were right about Baxter and his money-making scheme. He filched good pipes from each batch and given that Durrell's supply a heck of a lot of pipes, it never took him long to build up a decent quantity to sell on.'

'It's generous of you to say that "we" were right,' said Jess, 'when it was you who deduced what was going on.'

'Maybe, but that's only because I know about the building trade, including its less honourable side. It was you who spotted the faulty pipes.' Tom smiled and his blue eyes crinkled at the edges. The faint lines suggested he did a lot of smiling. 'Now that we've admired one another's perspicacity, shall I tell you the rest?'

'Please do,' said Jess. 'How did he get away with it?'

'He had a pair of accomplices. They worked as labourers, getting themselves taken on on various building sites, so Baxter always had a helper around when the dodgy deliveries were made.'

'Very sneaky,' said Jess.

'But it's come to light and it's in the hands of the police now,' said Tom. After a moment he added, 'Thanks to you.'

There was that smile again and Jess felt fluttery inside. She tore her gaze away from Tom's and took a step backwards.

'Thank you for coming here to tell me, Mr Watson. I appreciate it.'

'My pleasure, Miss Mason.'

There must have been something of dismissal in her tone, because he touched his cap to her and walked down the path. Jess wanted to watch him until he disappeared, but she would feel a complete twit if he glanced back and saw her, so she went back inside and shut the door, glad that everybody else was upstairs and there was no one to witness her appearing to be oddly breathless.

She was halfway up the stairs before she remembered her promise to put the kettle on and went down again. She hadn't been in the kitchen more than a minute before Vivienne walked in.

'Let me give you a hand,' said Vivienne. 'It's going well, isn't it? You must be pleased.'

'I am. Thank you for bringing Mr Haddon and Mr Armitage.'

'It seemed like a good way for them to meet Mr Peters. Informal, with plenty to talk about.'

Jess felt a little rush of excitement. Would Mr Haddon and Mr Armitage be her first two residents? She and Vivienne made tea and cut some slices into the sponge and the ginger-bread. As they assembled the trays, Mr Haddon and one of the workmen appeared in the doorway, ready to do the carrying.

All in all, it was a successful occasion. When the old soldiers were putting on their coats and hats, getting ready to leave, the two younger servicemen offered to carry the borrowed chairs back to the orphanage. A line of grey-shirted boys had brought the chairs across the road yesterday after school and Mrs Rostron had said that they would collect the chairs at the same time today. Jess rather thought that Mrs Rostron wasn't somebody whose arrangements she would care to disrupt, so she thanked Messrs Armitage and Haddon, smiling as she declined their kind offer.

All the soldiers shook her hand and thanked her for her hospitality. Vivienne awarded her an approving smile.

'I think that went well, don't you?' Mr Peters murmured, putting on his leather gloves.

'Definitely,' said Mrs Peters even though his remark had been aimed at Jess. 'When they hear about it, our other residents will be anxious for their turn.'

'Not until the end of next week,' said Mr Peters. 'We don't want the work to be held up.'

Mrs Peters laid a hand on Jess's arm. 'Good show, my dear.'

'Thank you.' Jess was more touched by the intimate gesture than by the words.

After the Oak Lodge contingent had gone, Vivienne departed with the two Great War men, leaving Jess feeling pleasantly tired with the satisfaction of a job well done. It would be something good to record in the log book at the end of the day.

Jess had always enjoyed working on Saturday mornings. Many a former Corporation colleague had hated it because it ate into the weekend, but Jess loved it. Knowing it was a half-day added a feeling of lightness to whatever work had to be tackled. Moreover, at the Sea View, she had never had an entire weekend off unless she was away visiting Dad, and early starts and late finishes had been the norm; so a return to office hours now she was at Holly Lodge felt like a great treat. It would be different, of course, once the home opened, but for the time being she appreciated the favourable hours.

She went upstairs to the first floor, where a new fellow, the plumber, had joined the workmen. Lengths of pipe lay on the landing, but Jess wouldn't let herself think of Tom. Ascending the next flight to the second floor, she opened the door to the attic stairs and made her way up. A dusty skylight was positioned above a small landing with a door, through which was a narrow passage with a couple of doors on either side. These had been the servants' bedrooms in days gone by.

She went from room to room. The two at the front had dormer windows looking out over High Lane, those at the rear old sash windows in need of attention. The rooms were stale and dusty now, but with plenty of elbow grease and a lick of whitewash, they could soon be made presentable. Might it be possible that one day in the not-too-distant future, Abigail would occupy one of them? And maybe another girl from the orphanage as well, who could be a maid who doubled up as the help in the kitchen. Those poor fourteens, needing jobs that included accommodation.

But she mustn't stop up here daydreaming. With a smile on her lips, Jess retraced her steps and returned to her office, where Abigail was doing some typing for her. She was a good little typist. It was tempting to take her to the top floor, but it would be wrong to get her hopes up.

Jess and Abigail tidied and cleaned up as usual after the men had finished, then Jess locked up and went home. It was a mild spring day and pastel-coloured primulas made a pretty show in the gardens she passed while the bright yellow of lesser celandine created a dramatic little splash against its dark foliage, and here and there, large rubbery leaves of elephants' ears were starting to send up the tall stems that would bear flowers of richest pink.

Miss Hesketh and Vivienne also worked on Saturday mornings and all three of them arrived home to a dinner of braised cabbage and bacon followed by what Miss Patience called treacle tart, though she made it with golden syrup.

Afterwards, Jess and Vivienne washed up and put the kettle on. While the four of them were drinking tea in the sitting room, the doorbell rang. Vivienne got up to answer it and, a moment later, she showed Molly in. Jess hadn't seen Molly since that toe-curling moment when she had announced that Perkins and Watson had withdrawn from the Holly Lodge job, supposedly because of not wishing to work alongside a woman, only for her to discover she was in the presence of Tom's sister. But that hardly signified to Jess now. What struck her now, what she couldn't help being aware of, was that Molly's easy-going presence made her wish Tom could be here too.

Molly was accompanied by a chirpy-looking young lad with blue eyes in a narrow, oval face with a dent in his chin. His short back and sides was sandy. In his hands he held his cap, which was a man's, not a boy's.

'Jess, dear, you haven't met Danny before, have you?' asked Miss Patience. 'This is Danny Cropper Abrams, Molly's son. Danny, this lady is Miss Mason. She is our new pupil-lodger.'

Shaking the boy's hand, Jess gave him a smile. 'I've got the bedroom your mum used to have.'

'Miss Mason runs Holly Lodge, the big house over the road from St Nicholas's,' Vivienne told Danny. 'It's going to be a home for retired soldiers.'

Danny nodded. 'Like Mrs Rostron running the orphanage. Dad says it's all right for women to be in charge. My real dad didn't think women could do things like that.'

'But then your real dad had never met Mrs Rostron, had he?' said Molly.

Danny grinned. 'If he had, he might have changed his mind. Mrs Rostron's all right. She must be, or Dad wouldn't work for her.' He looked at Jess. 'I hope you're as good at it as Mrs Rostron.'

'Clumsily put, but I think he means it as a compliment,' Molly told Jess.

'I certainly hope I'm as good at my job as Mrs Rostron is at hers,' Jess said to Danny.

As Molly sat down, Jess pretended not to notice how she shifted in her seat to get comfortable. She must be about six months along.

'Can you squeeze more out of the pot?' Vivienne asked Miss Patience. 'Or shall I put the kettle on again?'

Soon the visitors were provided with tea.

'We're here on a mission,' said Molly. 'Danny can tell you about it.' She looked at Jess. 'He isn't normally forward in company, but the Miss Heskeths are as good as family.' She nodded to her son to say his piece.

'It's to do with St Nicholas's. There's a funfair on the meadows every year to coincide with Lady Day. That's the twenty-fifth of March. The farmer at Turn Moss Farm lets the fair people have one of his fields. It's the first fair of the season.'

'We'll have to hope for good weather,' said Miss Patience. 'Not too chilly.'

'The kids won't care as long as it's dry,' said Danny.

'You said you were here on a mission,' said Vivienne.

'The orphans are taken to the fair every year,' said Danny. 'Not the babies, obviously, but the ones who are big enough. We need lots of grown-ups to come with us.'

That puzzled Jess. 'You make it sound as if...' She didn't like to finish the sentence.

'I used to live in the orphanage until Mum and Dad adopted me,' Danny told her, 'and I've still got friends there. Some of them go to the same school as me.'

'So Mrs Rostron needs lots of grown-ups,' said Vivienne.

'Very brave and patient grown-ups,' said Molly in mock-resignation, 'who can face an interminable afternoon in the company of children as high as kites.'

'I think I might be able to manage that,' said Vivienne. 'Just about.'

Danny grinned at her.

'How about you?' Vivienne asked Jess. 'If you haven't got plans, that is.'

Jess glanced at Molly. Was it a good idea to be associated closely with Tom's sister? Oh, what the heck. It was for the orphans. 'Happy to.'

When Molly and Danny had gone, Vivienne caught Jess on her own to say, 'You looked a trifle self-conscious while Molly was here. Please don't worry about what was said that other time. Molly's the last person to hold it against you. She's much too sensible – and so are you.'

'I shan't give it another thought,' said Jess.

So Vivienne had sensed her unease, had she? It was true that Jess had felt self-conscious, though not for the reason Vivienne had attributed it to. It was because Molly was Tom's sister and Danny was his nephew. As well as liking them for their own sakes, their relationship to Tom also made Jess feel drawn to them, but that was something she had to beware of. It was no good her liking Tom Watson. For a start, she was nothing to him, but more to the point, she had her career to think of. She wasn't one of those young women who worked because they had to, all the while hoping for the right man to happen along. No, to Jess, her work was more than a job, much more. It was her career, her future, something to which she had dedicated herself. She had worked hard to get where she was now and if Mr Peters kept her on, she would have secured the job of her dreams.

And to be a working woman in this kind of post, with this kind of responsibility, you had to be single. Simple as that. There was no place in her life for the way Tom Watson made her feel.

Chapter Twenty-Five

MOLLY WAS VIVIENNE'S dearest friend and she was becoming increasingly fond of Jess too. Vivienne couldn't think of anything better than for her two good friends to become friends with one another. Molly worked a few hours each week at St Nicholas's, teaching basic office skills to some hand-picked girl-fourteens and on one Sunday afternoon a month, she came over to Wilton Lane to see Miss Hesketh and report to her on the girls' progress. This Sunday was one of those days and Vivienne hoped that the slight discomfort she had sensed in Jess yesterday would be swept away for good if she got to know Molly better.

Vivienne explained to Jess about Molly's monthly visit, adding, 'Would you mind making yourself available?'

'Why?' Jess asked before answering her own question. 'Abigail Hunter.'

'Afterwards we all usually have a cup of tea and a good old gossip together.'

Jess laughed. 'I can't imagine Miss Hesketh having a good old gossip.'

In the afternoon, Miss Prudence and Molly spent some time together in the dining room, discussing Molly's various pupils. Then Jess was invited in to join them to describe how Abigail Hunter was coming along at Holly Lodge. Meanwhile Vivienne helped Miss Patience get the tea and biscuits ready.

She took ginger biscuits from one tin, where they were kept in isolation so that their robust aroma couldn't tarnish anything else, and, from another tin, some sly cakes, so called because although they looked plain on the outside, they were filled with delicious fruit.

Presently the dining room door opened, signalling the end of the meeting, and soon the five women were settled comfortably in the sitting room.

'Is everything going well with your lessons, Molly dear?' asked Miss Patience.

'Yes, thank you,' said Molly with a smile. 'At yesterday's lesson, Abigail told us about the old soldiers from Oak Lodge visiting Holly Lodge and how she helped Jess make cakes for them.'

'Making use of her office skills, I see,' murmured Miss Prudence.

'Making use of the ability to adapt to whatever the situation requires,' replied Jess.

'Which is itself an important skill,' said Miss Prudence.

Molly addressed Jess. 'My husband is the caretaker at St Nicholas's and he wondered if you might let him bring a few boys over to see the work in progress. I don't mean to put you on the spot. It's just an idea.'

'If it was up to me, I'd say yes,' Jess answered at once, 'but I have to check with Mr Peters. He wouldn't want anything to hold up the work.'

'Aaron is a carpenter and joiner,' said Vivienne, 'and he's a skilled furniture-maker too.'

'We have a spiral staircase in our house that he built,' Molly added proudly. 'You'll have to come and see it.'

'Thank you,' said Jess. 'I'd like that.'

Vivienne glowed inwardly at the prospect of her two friends growing closer.

Molly looked at Miss Patience. 'The most important topic of all: do you have any wedding plans to share with us?'

Vivienne turned her attention to her secret aunt. She was enormously fond of her. She admired her too for the way she had, after the great disappointment of her young life, devoted herself uncomplainingly to the care of her father and sister. She had certainly made the best of things, but had she suffered and yearned throughout all those long years? She more than deserved her happy ending.

'Next week, I'm going to look for something to wear,' said Miss Patience.

'What sort of thing?' asked Jess.

'Just something ordinary,' said Miss Patience. 'Smart, of course, as befits the occasion, but ordinary. Suitable for my age.'

'That doesn't sound as if it will do at all,' cried Molly. 'Something ordinary – for your wedding dress?'

With a glance at Miss Prudence, Miss Patience said, 'I don't want to be mutton dressed as lamb.'

'I wish I'd never said that,' said Miss Prudence.

'Prudence, you've said it to me more times than I can count – and you're quite right. One doesn't wish to look ridiculous.'

'That settles it,' said Molly. 'You and I are going shopping together, Miss Patience, and we shall find something utterly lovely and appropriate and not in the slightest bit lamby. Believe me, with hair this colour, I know all about finding the right clothes.'

'But you always look so nice, Molly dear,' said Miss Patience.

'If I can do it for me, with my frightful hair,' said Molly, 'I can do it for you at your advanced age.' Her warm smile made the words affectionate and not at all hurtful.

'It really should be one of you young ones getting married,' said Miss Patience, 'not an old thing like me.'

'Well, I'm already spoken for,' said Molly.

'Oh, Vivienne dear,' Miss Patience exclaimed. 'I'm sorry. I didn't think.'

'It's quite all right.' They were words Vivienne had uttered so many times in recent years, but it wasn't all right, not really. She rather thought it never would be. 'I'm a career woman now and content with my lot – like Jess.'

'I'm happy to work and support myself,' said Jess. 'That's why I value my role at Holly Lodge. Once the house opens, the job will be interesting and varied, with plenty of responsibility and scope for me to employ my imagination.'

'Was it always your intention to carve a career for yourself?' enquired Miss Prudence. 'That's an uncommon ambition for a woman.'

Jess hesitated before admitting, 'No, it wasn't always my intention. I learned the hard way that it's the right thing for me.'

There was a short silence.

'We don't mean to pry,' said Miss Patience.

Jess looked round at them all and something in her expression said she had made up her mind. 'I was engaged during the war. He was a local chap. Drew – short for Andrew. Drew Bryce. We'd been walking out together for a time and when war broke out and he volunteered, he wanted us to get married right away, but my dad said no. I was under twenty-one, so there was nothing I could do about it. Other couples were rushing to get married, but Dad wouldn't listen. I think Mum would have let me, but it wasn't up to her.'

'I'm sure your father was only trying to do what he believed was best for you,' Miss Patience murmured.

'When the war ended,' Jess went on, 'I imagined Drew coming home immediately, but that was daft, because of course you can't just send an army home all in one go. It takes time. I didn't see him again until... until after Mum had died of the influenza.' She stopped speaking for a moment, then carried on. 'I pictured our future together while I waited for him. I'd have to take care of Dad, so I thought Drew and I could live in Dad's house; or maybe Drew would want somewhere of our own and Dad could move in with us. Anyway, it was all pie in the sky. He didn't want to marry me any more. He'd met a nurse in a field hospital and he wanted to marry her instead.'

'Oh, Jess, I'm so sorry,' exclaimed Molly.

'You poor love,' said Miss Patience. 'What a blow.'

'Then it turned out that he'd already married her. According to him, when he told me he wanted to marry her, that was his way of trying to let me down gently.'

Indignation boiled up inside Vivienne. 'The beast. Trying to get himself off the hook, more like.'

'Trying to make out he was less of a cad,' said Molly.

But as sympathy swelled in the room and she and the others all leaned forward slightly as if to commiserate, Jess sat up straight and forestalled them.

'You're not to feel sorry for me. I got over the disappointment and – and – yes, I will say it, the humiliation – a long time ago. I'd already had a job during the war and had discovered that work suited me, so I looked around for an interesting, worthwhile position... and that has led me in the end to Holly Lodge. I enjoy working. I love it. It can be jolly frustrating not being paid as much as a man and not being allowed the same opportunities, but I've now found the ideal post, where I can be happy and fulfilled – as long as all goes well and Mr Peters keeps me on, of course.' She smiled round at them. 'It's not the life I expected when I was young, but it suits me very well. I'm a dedicated career woman now, and proud of it.'

*

'Congratulations, Miss Boodle. That is excellent news.' Mrs Wardle looked up from the letter that the Poodle had shown her and beamed at her protégée, the little sprays of lilac on her hat swaying in a satisfied way.

Vivienne looked up from the paperwork on her desk, aware of Miss Cadman and Miss Byrne doing the same. Mrs Wardle looked from each of them to the next in an unhurried manner. She couldn't have looked more complacent if she'd tried.

'Shall we share your news?' Mrs Wardle glanced archly at the Poodle. 'Or should we leave them guessing?'

It was the Poodle's turn to look at her colleagues. There was a brightness in her dark eyes. Vivienne had never seen that sensual mouth expand into a wide smile, but there was a definite twitch at its corners just now. The deliberately suppressed smile made her look even more pleased with herself than a dazzling beam would have done.

'I'm happy to tell them,' said Miss Boodle. 'I applied for the position of superintendent at St Nicholas's Orphanage in Chorlton and I've been offered an interview.'

'Congratulations,' said Miss Byrne and Miss Cadman.

'Congratulations,' said Vivienne a split second later. She felt dazed. She forced a smile and it really was an effort. An interview – for the Poodle? When she herself had heard nothing...

'Apparently,' said Miss Boodle, 'as well as being interviewed, I'll have to—'

'Now then!' Mrs Wardle waved a pudgy finger in mockscolding. 'We don't want to make anybody jealous, do we?'

Heat rushed up the back of Vivienne's neck and poured around to flood her cheeks. Her smile felt as if it had stuck to her face. All she could do was bend over her report once more and try to look as if it was of consuming interest when really the words were swimming in front of her tear-filled eyes. She longed to brush aside the wetness, but that would be a dead giveaway.

It hurt unbearably not to have been offered an interview. Was it her own fault? Had she read too much into Mrs Rostron's encouragement? Had that given her a sense of entitlement that had now rebounded on her in the most appalling way? Her heart struggled to beat through the weight of her humiliation.

She remembered Jess's words about being a dedicated career woman and the way she had talked about the manager's post at Holly Lodge being the perfect role for her. That was how Vivienne had felt about the superintendent's post at St Nicholas's. It was – or it had been – a post she would gladly have immersed herself in indefinitely. It would have brought a special meaning into her life – and now it turned out she had been considered unsuitable. She had never imagined that. She had imagined, and dreaded, somebody else out-performing her at the interview stage, but not once had she seriously thought she might not be shortlisted. How damnably big-headed.

Not only had she failed to get an interview, but one had been offered to Miss Boodle. That was a kick in the teeth. Vivienne had rather looked down on the Poodle because of her close association with Mrs Wardle, but was there more to Miss Boodle than she had thought? There must be, because she had been selected for interview and Vivienne... hadn't.

As if failing to be selected by the Orphanage Committee for an interview wasn't bad enough, Vivienne had an appointment at St Nicholas's that very afternoon. Talk about adding insult to injury. The prospect of facing Mrs Rostron made her want to curl up in a corner. She even considered, just for one moment, ducking out of the appointment, but that would be unprofessional and would go against everything she had been brought up to believe in.

No, she would attend; she would be her usual self, polite and efficient, a good listener. She prided herself on being a person others liked to deal with, because they knew they could rely on her to get things done. She had always enjoyed being Mrs Atwood from the Board of Health – and now she would continue to enjoy it and make the most of it.

When she arrived at the orphanage, Mrs Rostron greeted her in her customary unfussy way, not even bestowing an extra glance that might have meant something. Was this how it was to be? Were they going to behave as if Mrs Rostron's post wasn't up for grabs? As if Mrs Rostron had never drawn it to Vivienne's attention?

'I've just been speaking to Mr Taylor on the telephone,' said Mrs Rostron. 'Two candidates for the post of superintendent have a professional connection with St Nicholas's and the others do not. Therefore, those that do will not be permitted from now on to come here before the day of the interviews. We have to be completely impartial.'

'Of course,' Vivienne murmured.

Golly, this was going to be tougher than she had thought. Not only were they going to ignore her own situation, but apparently she was expected to show a polite curiosity in that of the successful candidates.

Mrs Rostron raised her eyebrows, betraying a flicker of impatience. 'I have to say, Mrs Atwood, that I did expect a greater show of interest from you.'

Vivienne couldn't think what to say, but she had to come up with something. 'It makes sense for the candidates with experience of St Nicholas's to stay away. You have to be seen to be fair.'

'Quite so.'

Mrs Rostron continued to regard Vivienne with a penetrating look. Vivienne attempted a smile, trying to conceal her confusion. Honestly, what else was she supposed to say?

'You do understand what I've told you, Mrs Atwood? I cannot have candidates coming here in advance of the interviews.'

'Yes.'

'Then, not to put too fine a point on it, why are you not getting to your feet and excusing yourself from our meeting?'

'I'm sorry?'

'Mrs Atwood, did you read your post this morning?'

'I had an early appointment,' said Vivienne. 'I had to leave home before the first post arrived.'

'Indeed?' A small smile played across the superintendent's lips. 'Then might I suggest you go back and read your letters. You should find something to your advantage.'

Chapter Twenty-Six

FOR SOME REASON, folk sometimes found it odd that Tom
knew so much about plants – as if builders were only
supposed to know about foundations and mortar and gable-
ends. But Tom had grown up helping Dad on his allotment.
Not that he'd been all that fussed about it as a lad, but then...
then the war had come and he had eked out his life surrounded by death and destruction, by injury upon injury, by
blood-soaked bandages and crushed bones and moaning and
young lads – aye, and grown men too sometimes – calling out
for their mothers... When that was what his life became, he
had longed for the beauty and grace of plants; he had yearned
to see new growth.

Now, home once more, he enjoyed a spot of gardening.
There was something forgiving about the earth. You could
curse yourself for pruning a shrub with too heavy a hand, but
given time, the shrub would grow back again, as beautiful
and flourishing as ever. There was solace of a kind in that. He
didn't think about it too deeply; he couldn't bear to; but there
was a sort of comfort for... what he had witnessed.

It was early evening and the springtime air was crisp with
the scent of the privet hedges that fronted the line of cottages.
He had already trimmed the hedge and now was weeding the
flowerbed, tidying it up and getting it ready for the growing

season. He didn't wear gloves. He wouldn't be much use as a builder if dirt bothered him.

Finishing the bed where he was working, Tom stood up to stretch his back and roll his shoulders before tackling the next bit. As he rose, he glanced up and down the road, nodding a greeting to a couple of passers-by out for an evening stroll, and then he saw Jess walking along the opposite pavement.

She was dressed in a hip-length sweater in a soft pinky shade he didn't know the name of, with a tie-belt and a sailor-style collar. The effect was casual, but not too casual. Appealing, in fact. There was something boyish about it that made her look extraordinarily feminine. Instead of the smart, efficient office worker he was used to, she was natural and graceful, very easy on the eye. Her waist was slender, her wrists dainty. And her face – he'd seen her serious; he'd seen her trying not to look vexed when Mr Thorpe goaded her; he'd seen the curiosity and intelligence in her eyes over the matter of the cracked pipes. But he hadn't seen her this way before, relaxed, unguarded. Exquisite.

He couldn't help himself. It was sheer lunacy, of course, to have anything to do with her. Nothing could possibly come of it, because... well, because. He shouldn't do it, shouldn't attract her attention. If he knew what was good for him, he would duck down behind Mrs Carter's privet and get on with pulling up weeds.

He waved. 'Lovely evening,' he called.

His breath caught. Would she smile a greeting and carry on walking? She saw him – hesitated – and then crossed the road. She carried a couple of books under her arm. Tom touched his cap to her as he started to breathe again. Warmth poured through him. It was wrong; it was hopeless; but since he knew it was hopeless, didn't that make it all right? Safe? It wasn't as though he was fooling himself, was it?

'Out for a walk?' he asked. Talk about stating the obvious. What a stupid thing to say.

'I'm going to the library.' Jess nodded at the cottage behind him. 'Is this where you live?'

'No, it's my gran's friend's cottage. I help out in her garden now and again. She'd be the first to tell you she's a bit creaky these days.'

'It's good of you.'

Tom frowned. He hadn't been fishing for compliments. 'I like gardening.'

'So do I.' Jess's brown eyes shone. 'My dad has an allotment and I used to help him.'

'That was how I started too, though I wasn't as enthusiastic back then as you sound.'

'Oh, I loved it.' Jess sounded almost bubbly. 'Since I left home, I've lived in digs and haven't had a garden I could work in, but that's one of my dreams. I moved recently and the house has a pretty garden. I'm hoping to be allowed to get my hands on it.'

'My sister said you've moved in with the Miss Heskeths.'

'That's right. In fact, I've got her old room, which means I ought to thank you for the shelves.'

Tom grinned. 'You're welcome. How are things going at Holly Lodge?'

'I love it,' she said frankly. 'I know this is going to sound barmy, but I feel in a way as if it belongs to me.'

'That's not barmy at all,' said Tom, enchanted.

'I didn't feel like this when I was at the Sea View. That's the hotel where I worked before. I loved the job and took pride in it and always worked hard, but I never had this proprietorial feeling for the Sea View that I'm developing for Holly Lodge.' Jess frowned, considering the matter. 'Maybe that's because Mr Peters is at a distance and the Hitchcocks were always on the premises. Mrs Hitchcock always liked to make sure I kept in my place.'

'But with Mr Peters over at Oak Lodge, that's left you free to make your own mark on Holly Lodge,' said Tom.

'That's right. I have made my mark.' Jess uttered the words as if this hadn't truly occurred to her before. 'Abigail – the young soldiers – my plans to be involved in the local community.' She looked at him. 'Is it silly to love an empty old house?'

'Not at all. I know how it feels. I love to see how a building changes and grows when Perkins and Watson work on it. I'm not just talking about brand-new places that we build from scratch. I mean anywhere that we work on.'

'Yes, I remember the way you talked about the Holly Lodge work before you had to pull out.' It was an honest comment. Nothing in her tone suggested she was making a sly dig at him.

'The thing about an empty building having improvements is that it stops being empty because you start to fill it with your own hopes and dreams.'

'That's true,' Jess said warmly. 'I've made all kinds of decisions about Holly Lodge. I know which room I want to be the sitting room and which I think is best for the dining room. I've even chosen where to put the Christmas tree. I just hope I'm still there when the time comes.'

'So do I,' said Tom.

She looked at him. She didn't speak, just looked. Could she tell what he was thinking? Oh crikey.

'What I mean is,' Tom said quickly, 'I hope Mr Peters keeps you on.'

'I see. Yes, of course.' Jess looked faintly embarrassed. 'Well, I'd better be getting on.' She lifted her library books a fraction. 'Good evening, Mr Watson.'

Oh, the temptation to offer her his first name. 'Good evening, Miss Mason,' he said politely, touching his cap to her.

He watched as she set off along the road, then realised what he was doing and returned his attention to the flowerbed. It wouldn't do at all for Mrs Carter to tell Gran that he was mooning after a young lady. Gran would be thrilled to pieces and it would be all over Chorlton before he knew it.

But Mrs Carter evidently had seen, and she did tell Gran, as Tom discovered the following day when he had to drop in at home in the course of the afternoon. As he entered the house, he heard women's voices and stuck his head round the parlour door. A sea of faces turned in his direction. Mum, Gran and Auntie Faith, all three of his sisters, plus their cousin Dora, who had got married last year a month after Molly.

'What's this? A mothers' meeting?'

'What we want to know—' Gran began.

'Don't, Gran,' said Christabel.

'Mrs Carter said you spent more time yesterday making eyes at a girl than you did turning over her flowerbeds.'

'She said nothing of the sort,' Mum corrected her, flinging him a hopeless look.

'So who was she?' Gran demanded.

'Miss Mason, the new manager at Holly Lodge,' said Tom.

'I notice there's no pretence that you don't know who I'm talking about.' Gran sounded triumphant. 'You didn't even ask what she looked like.'

'Since she was the only lady I spoke to,' said Tom, 'I don't need any clues; and for the information of the family gathering, I know her through work and that's all.'

'Does that mean there's nothing going on?' asked Auntie Faith, disappointed.

'Nothing at all.' He hoped his face didn't show the *Worse luck* that he was thinking.

'That's just as well, actually,' Molly chimed in. 'I know Jess – Miss Mason – a little and I do like her. But she was saying only last Sunday that she's devoted to her work, and that's the way she sees her future unfolding.'

Tom lowered his head. His heart felt as if it was shrinking, but what right did he have to feel such bitter disappointment?

'It's just as well I'm not looking for a wife, then, isn't it?' He managed to sound light-hearted.

But when he left the room and closed the door quietly behind him, he was forced to lean against the wall and close his eyes for a minute before his strength returned and he could carry on.

After she had told the story of Drew and herself to the Miss Heskeths, Molly and Vivienne last Sunday afternoon, Jess had suffered from second thoughts and wished she hadn't done it. She couldn't bear the idea of anyone feeling sorry for her or thinking that her career, because it had begun through her having been jilted, must be second-best. But it was pointless wishing she hadn't confided.

Then Vivienne had enthused about her forthcoming interview at the orphanage and as well as being pleased for her friend, Jess had felt better about herself. Vivienne hadn't started out as a career woman either. It was something she had turned to after the heartbreak of being widowed. No one thought the worse of her because of it; nobody looked down on her. Her new life, her change of direction, was accepted and even respected. Vivienne had well-wishers and Jess, newly accepted into Vivienne's circle, realised that these same people wished her well too, as did the Henderson sisters, who had given her their moral support all along.

She shook off the vague regret that had descended on her and concentrated instead on feeling grateful for the new friendships that had made her feel able to confide what had happened to her when she was younger. It felt now as if it had happened to someone else. She had grown up a lot in the intervening time and felt herself to be a better, more interesting person because of the life she had lived since then. Jess wanted to be a good friend as well and provide Vivienne with the support she deserved.

At her forthcoming interview, she would not only be seen by the members of the Orphanage Committee, but she would also have to conduct an assembly for the children.

'St Nicholas's has assemblies just the same as schools do,' Vivienne explained. 'The children and staff come together every day for prayers and announcements. The superintendent has to be more than a skilled organiser and administrator with the children's welfare at heart. He or she is also the figurehead whom everyone looks up to. Being able to hold assemblies is part of that.'

Jess shivered. 'I wouldn't mind the interview, but I'd fall flat on my face if I had to conduct an assembly.'

'It's going to be a challenge,' Vivienne admitted, 'and not just because of the assembly. The interviews are to be held on a Saturday so that the school-aged children will be available to attend.'

Jess winced on her friend's behalf. 'So after having lessons and assemblies all week at school, they'll have to put up with more assemblies on the Saturday. Poor kids.'

'Not just that, but an assembly from each candidate,' said Vivienne. 'On top of that, it's the Saturday when the orphans are being taken in batches to the funfair, so they'll be even less pleased at being lumbered with extra assemblies. Some will be fidgeting because they're dying to go to the fair and others will be fed up because they've been brought back early from the fun.'

Vivienne looked so glum that Jess hugged her.

'I'm not sure how much use I can be,' said Jess, 'but I'm happy to help if I can. When you've written your assembly, you can try it out on me if you like.'

'You'll play the part of the children, you mean?' Vivienne shook her head, pretending to look stern. 'I'm not sure about that. I expect you were one of the naughty children at school.'

'Who, me?' Jess laughed. 'I was good as gold.'

'I believe you. Thousands wouldn't.'

Jess didn't say so, because she didn't want to jinx Vivienne's chances or make Vivienne think she was taking anything for granted, but she couldn't help picturing Vivienne as superintendent of St Nicholas's and herself as the manager of Holly Lodge, and all the good things they could bring about for the children and the old soldiers alike through cooperation and neighbourliness. How wonderful it would be if Vivienne got Mrs Rostron's job. Mind you, Jess's plans and dreams also presupposed that Mr Peters decided to keep her on beyond her trial period, so maybe she shouldn't get too deeply involved in her imaginings.

But it was impossible not to dream.

The building work was going well in Holly Lodge and the materials in the two downstairs rooms were gradually vanishing upstairs. Jess loved seeing the progress at the end of each day and she remembered what Tom had said about watching a place grow. She understood exactly what he had meant. Seeing the improvements take shape made her love Holly Lodge all the more. It would be a terrible wrench if she had to leave. She clung to the memory of those words of praise from Mr Peters, then worried in case she was deluding herself.

On Friday morning, same as last week, Mr and Mrs Peters brought over some of the old soldiers from Oak Lodge to view the ongoing improvements. Jess and Abigail once more provided refreshments and Jess had to take Mr Peters on one side and request more petty cash.

'I've kept a tally of everything I've spent and on what.' She showed him her accounts book.

'Rather a large proportion of the expenditure seems to have gone on tea, sugar and flour.'

'If you think I shouldn't offer refreshments to visitors...' Jess murmured.

'Don't be silly,' said Mr Peters. 'Of course I don't mean that.'

'Besides,' said Jess, 'those items will form part of the day-to-day expenditure when Holly Lodge opens for business. Then the petty cash will be for when I – when the manager – runs out of ink.'

When she had started speaking, she had intended it to be a light-hearted remark, but she felt anything but light-hearted by the end. It was hard having a job she loved but that she didn't know for certain was hers.

The visit was another success. As it drew to a close, Jess asked Mr Peters about some of the orphan boys being allowed to see the work in progress.

'Mr Abrams, the caretaker at St Nicholas's, would bring the boys and be in charge of them.'

Mr Peters frowned. 'I'm not sure. I don't want people trooping in and out willy-nilly. It's not a sideshow.'

'With Mr Abrams's background in carpentry, he'd be able to explain things to them without needing to interrupt the workmen too much,' said Jess. 'And it would be good for our relationship with the orphanage.'

'Yes, that is important,' Mr Peters agreed. 'Very well, then – but don't take advantage of my good nature, Miss Mason.'

'I wouldn't dream of it, sir.'

As soon as the Oak Lodge party had gone, Jess went across the road to St Nicholas's. First of all, she made sure Mrs Rostron was happy for some of her older lads to have this opportunity.

'It might foster an interest in the various building trades,' said Mrs Rostron, 'but it would be hard to find apprenticeships that included accommodation. If a plumber or a bricklayer or whoever were to offer to take on one of our boys, he and his family would need to be looked into closely. Nevertheless, that is no reason to refuse the boys this chance.'

'If nothing else, it's something interesting for them to see.'

'I'll leave it to you, Miss Mason, to liaise with Mr Abrams. I believe he is in his workshop at present. Miss Virginia will show you the way.'

A long, low building, the workshop was situated in front of the high walls at the rear of the orphanage premises. The door stood open and the rich scents of wood and oils hung in the air. Virginia leaned in to knock and Mr Abrams appeared. Jess knew his first name was Aaron. He moved with the confidence of a man accustomed to physical toil. His eyes were nut-brown. Because he was in his own domain, he was bare-headed and his dark hair showed a suggestion of a curl.

'My name is Jess Mason,' Jess said before Virginia could do the honours. 'I'm the manager at Holly Lodge.'

Aaron shook her hand. 'And you're my Molly's new friend. No need to explain why you're here. I take it Mr Peters and Mrs Rostron have agreed?'

'Yes, so now the nitty-gritty is down to us.'

Aaron smiled, looking friendly and good-humoured. Jess wasn't attracted to him herself, but she could see why Molly had fallen for him. She could see too why young Danny adored his dad.

They soon made arrangements. Aaron was to bring a group across tomorrow morning.

'Would you mind making it a relatively short visit?' Jess asked. 'Say, fifteen or twenty minutes.'

'Fine by me.'

'I know it's not very long, especially if the boys are interested, but I don't want Mr Peters to think I'm taking advantage.'

'You're doing us a favour by letting us in,' said Aaron. 'I'll tell the lads they must pay attention from the start.'

The visit the next morning was a success. The boys were on their best behaviour and Aaron knew enough of what was happening to answer most of their questions, though the workmen were happy to explain what he couldn't.

'I hope these horrors haven't bothered you too much,' Aaron said to the workmen as the visit ended. 'I tried to get my brother-in-law to come along. He's a builder and he could have talked to the boys about what's happening, but he said Mr Jones probably wouldn't appreciate having Perkins and Watson breathing down his men's necks.'

'He's a good bloke, is Tom Watson,' said one of the men.

Jess had to look away. So Tom had chosen not to come today, had he? But it sounded as if the workmen wouldn't have minded. She knew from what they had said before about him that they respected him. So did that mean he could have come if he'd wanted? And the fact that he wasn't here meant he hadn't wanted to. Even though she knew there was no place in her life for a man, it still hurt to know he wasn't looking for reasons to see her again.

Aaron and his little troop left soon afterwards. Jess had some things to do and she stayed on after the workmen had finished. Dear Miss Patience, always the looker-after, had provided her with a sandwich and a slice of juicy apple pie to tide her over since she wouldn't be home for her meal.

When it was time to leave, she decided to enjoy the mild spring afternoon by taking a detour through the recreation ground near to Wilton Close. A courting couple strolled past, hanging onto each other's every word; and two old ladies in shawls sat together on a bench, indulging in a good old chinwag. A group of children was playing an elaborate game that involved running about with twigs and putting them down in special places, while over near the bandstand, more children played French cricket with a man – with Tom Watson.

Jess stood and watched – not just watched, stared. She couldn't help it. There was Danny, and all those girls must be his cousins. They were laughing, Tom most of all. Jess wrenched her gaze away and walked quickly back the way she had come before Tom or Danny could spot her.

Her heart thumped. Tom Watson was a family man through and through. It reminded her of the life she had lost – the marriage she had expected to have. She might have moved on and left Drew well and truly behind, and she might have different ambitions now, but she had grown up not simply expecting to get married because it was what girls did in order to provide for themselves, but actively wanting to get married because she had always visualised herself as a mum.

It brought it home to her that any sort of friendship with Tom would be dangerous. She had known all along he wasn't meant for her. He was a family man and she was a career woman… wasn't she?

Chapter Twenty-Seven

IT ALWAYS IRRITATED Prudence when someone displayed an 'it's not fair' attitude to their problems and their life in general, but she couldn't help feeling the deep unfairness of her own situation. The house in which she had spent her entire life apart from her brief spell in Scotland ought to belong to her and Patience now, not to Lawrence. The fact that the law found it acceptable that Pa had left it to Lawrence made Prudence seethe. She would never feel that the house belonged to her brother. Never. The law could say what it liked, but morally this house should have been left to Mother's daughters. She felt like grabbing her hair in clumps or scrubbing her face with her hands, but all she did was pinch her lips together.

'You could,' Patience had suggested tentatively, 'come to Annerby with me. I'd love you to live with us. You'd be most welcome.'

Good grief – though Prudence managed not to utter the words aloud. 'It's kind of you to invite me, but I've supported myself all my adult life and I have no wish to depend on someone else now.' She reached for her sister's hand. 'But thank you for asking.'

Part of it was pride. She knew that. She, the older sister, the capable one, the organiser, the decision-maker, couldn't possibly be reduced to living as a guest under her sister's roof. No matter how dear Patience was to her, Prudence couldn't have swallowed that. As the middle-aged bride of a well-to-do gentleman, Patience was going to cause a stir in Annerby, and not all of the stir would be flattering. Some of it would be catty or scornful; some might call her – what was that new expression? – a gold-digger. And just imagine what the cats would say about Prudence if she arrived in Annerby clinging to her sister's skirts. Under no circumstances was that to be borne.

No, Prudence was a strong person and she'd always had an independent streak – more than a streak. It was deeply ingrained in her. She would make her own arrangements. Of course she would. The cold fingers of dread touched her and she had to shut her eyes. She would have to find rooms to rent. What could she afford? The only reason she, Patience and Pa had been able to reside in Wilton Close all these years was because Pa had owned the property. Had there been rent to pay on top of the household bills, they could never have afforded it. Even without rent to pay, money had been tight.

It felt strange having this dark future hanging over her at the same time as things were so joyful for Patience. Of one thing Prudence was certain: she didn't want to take the edge off Patience's happiness.

'The wedding invitations will go out soon,' Patience remarked to Prudence and Vivienne. 'I'd like to invite Lucy and Dickie, only I'm not sure what Lawrence would make of it. His plan was that they would remain abroad for a whole year.'

'Lawrence can go and boil his head,' Prudence said forthrightly. 'Of course you want Lucy to come. Let her and Dickie decide if it's the right thing to do.'

'And then there's dear Molly as well, you see,' Patience added. 'I don't want to make things difficult for her.'

Prudence was silent. How would Molly feel meeting the girl whose illegitimate baby she had been supposed to adopt? Everyone had been stunned when Lucy had changed her mind practically at the last moment. She was now a happily married mother.

It was Vivienne who spoke. 'I'll have a quiet word with Molly. She won't make a fuss about it. She'll just appreciate the fact that you were concerned for her.'

'Thank you, Vivienne dear,' said Patience. 'That makes me feel much better.'

'Does it really?' Prudence enquired. 'Didn't my suggestion about Lawrence boiling his head make you feel better?'

The others smiled, which was what Prudence had intended, but it didn't raise her own spirits. The week dragged by. Without telling anyone what she was doing, Prudence made herself scan the 'for rent' columns in the evening paper each day, though it was a struggle to read them because despair blurred her vision. That it should come to this. She, Prudence Hesketh, who had always taken such pride in residing in the family property, was now doomed to end her days in rented accommodation. There was nothing wrong with rented as such. Renting was normal; most people rented. But it was a question of what one could afford and Prudence, who had lived her life in a comfortable house in which the boxroom – the boxroom, if you please! – was big enough to get by as a small bedroom, could not stump up the rent on anything even vaguely similar. The come-down was going to tear her in two.

Of course, if Vivienne was happy for them to share, then the outlook would improve enormously. Her breath seemed to get bottled up inside her chest as her heart filled with hope. Could she suggest to Vivienne that they find somewhere together? Or would Vivienne, an attractive young woman, baulk at the idea of sharing with an older person? But sharing would make sense in so many ways – though what would Graham make of it? It was one thing for Vivienne to move into Wilton Close in order to get to know her real mother, quite another for the two of them to set up home together. Would it hurt Graham if his beloved daughter did that? Besides, if Vivienne got the job of superintendent, she would want to live near the orphanage, whereas the idea of living anywhere in the vicinity of Wilton Close made Prudence's skin crawl with humiliation. Quitting her beautiful house for rented rooms would be painful enough without the additional injury of having to see familiar faces every day. Her pride wouldn't permit it. And what did that say about her as a mother? Shouldn't she be prepared to swallow any amount of indignity for the sake of her daughter's company?

Whenever she reached this far in her thinking, she was forced to stop. It was unlike Prudence not to face her problems head on, but just the thought of this one made her feel ill and defeated. She went to bed with her heart thudding dully in her chest and woke up feeling hot behind her eyelids. What sort of future was she likely to have as a middle-aged spinster of limited means? Should she swallow her pride and join Patience in Annerby? What – and live under Niall's roof as some sort of hanger-on? Never! She wasn't a coward and she wasn't going to run away. Neither was she the sort to take the easiest way out. She had her self-respect.

At that moment, it seemed her self-respect was all she had left.

One of the great joys of Prudence's life was the way in which Vivienne, when she wanted a private word, would come into her bedroom and throw herself on the bed for a chat. Such intimacy, so cosy and casual, was something

Prudence had never experienced before. Certainly there had never been anything of the kind between her and Patience, though she knew Patience wouldn't have minded it. Wouldn't have minded? Patience would have welcomed it with open arms. It was Prudence, responsible, decisive, straight-backed Prudence, who had never permitted such things. Maybe she hadn't been straight-backed so much as stiff-necked.

Now, the evening after returning from their respective offices, Vivienne came into Prudence's room, having given a brief knock.

'Can I come in?' she asked, walking right in.

Prudence had already undone her severe bun, combed her hair and put it back up again, just as she always did when she arrived home from the office. Vivienne had changed into a cherry-red jumper with a large roll-collar, and a straight skirt that showed off her trim figure. She dropped onto the bed, sitting sideways with one foot on the floor.

Was this how it was meant to be between sisters? Was Prudence now, at this late stage in her life, finally learning what a sisterly relationship could be like? And she was learning it from her illegitimate daughter. What a lot she had missed out on, and in so many ways.

'I need your help,' Vivienne announced. 'Uncle Niall has sent me some money.' Only in front of Prudence or Patience, and only when nobody else was present, could she refer to him as Uncle Niall and acknowledge their secret relationship. 'A big, fat cheque, as a matter of fact.'

'That was generous of him,' Prudence remarked.

'It's not for me. It's wedding dress money,' said Vivienne. 'He didn't want to embarrass Aunt Patience by trying to get her to accept it.'

Prudence nodded. 'Typical Niall. He was always a generous man.'

'He doesn't want her to feel at a disadvantage when it comes to choosing her wedding finery.'

'Having seen his daughters, I'm not surprised,' said Prudence. 'They were all very well turned out.'

'So we must ask Molly and Aunt Patience to save their shopping spree for Saturday afternoon, so you and I can go too.'

'I'm not sure,' Prudence began.

'Well, I am,' said Vivienne, 'and we're going, both of us. It's the only way to make sure Aunt Patience spends the money.'

'I suppose so.'

'It'll be fun.' There was a twinkle in Vivienne's eyes.

'I've never been a great one for fun.'

'No, I don't imagine you have,' said Vivienne. 'You had so much responsibility thrust upon you at a young age, but it's never too late to start.'

Prudence thought about it. What would be considered appropriate wedding garb for a woman knocking on the door of fifty? But that wasn't a generous question, was it? If she approached this with her usual 'mutton dressed as lamb' attitude, she would spoil the proceedings. How many times down the years had she poured cold water on Patience's small pleasures? Well, she wouldn't do it again.

She smiled at her beloved daughter. 'Then let's have a little foray into the world of fun, shall we?'

And it was fun – well, it was light-hearted and enjoyable, which presumably, to a less serious person, counted as fun. At the end of their morning's work, Prudence and Vivienne had lunch together in a pleasant café before meeting up with Molly and Patience. Vivienne had taken Patience aside a day or two ago to tell her about the wedding dress money. Prudence didn't know what had been said, but she knew Vivienne would have charmed Patience out of any reservations she might have.

They visited a couple of exclusive shops, telling the assistants no more than that a dress was required for a special occasion, so as to spare Patience's blushes. She had already made it clear that, at her age, she didn't want to look like a bride – but was she thinking of the bride she had hoped to be thirty years ago? A feeling of guilt made Prudence's chest feel tight. Even though she had learned last autumn that it had been Pa who had sent Niall on his way all that time ago, it didn't alter the fact that she had believed for thirty years that Niall had left at her instigation and she still felt remorse. It might have been Pa who had done the deed, but she had certainly intended to do it.

'We need to choose a colour,' said Molly. 'I know you don't want white, but what about cream?'

'Too close to white,' said Patience. 'Besides, with my washed-out colouring—'

'You're not washed-out,' Molly said firmly. 'You're pale.'

'Pale and interesting,' said Vivienne. 'Isn't that what people say?'

'And don't forget you're going to be radiantly happy,' Molly added.

'I know how appealing you find pretty things, Patience,' said Prudence. 'Let's find a suitable garment in a colour you like and then...' She floundered for a moment. 'And then Vivienne and Molly can work out how to make it look...'

'Look not like mutton dressed as lamb,' Patience finished.

'I didn't say that,' Prudence replied crossly.

'No, but you're right,' said Patience. 'I don't want to look silly. I want to look...' Now it was her turn to let her words fade away.

Vivienne slipped an arm through Patience's. 'We'll dress you as Lady Bracknell,' she said with a twinkle in her eye. 'You are, after all, going to be the matriarch of a substantial family.'

'I don't see myself as a grand matriarch,' said Patience. 'Can you imagine anybody less imposing?'

'That's true,' Vivienne agreed, 'but neither can I imagine anybody more affectionate or considerate. Your stepdaughters will soon find they have someone new to confide in and before you know it, your new grandchildren will come running to you when they want to be spoilt. That's much better than being a matriarch.'

'Thank you, Vivienne dear,' Patience whispered, looking misty-eyed. 'My new grandchildren. I can still hardly believe it.'

Molly smiled. 'That's why we need to choose a dress – so you can start believing.'

After an hour or so, the right dress was found. It was in a colour Vivienne called dusty rose, with a simple round neckline and a skirt that fell to mid-calf length. Molly took Patience into the fitting room to help her get changed.

When they emerged, Patience was protesting about the sash at her hips.

'These dropped waistlines do nothing for me. I'm so thin – and the sash makes me look thinner.'

Vivienne took charge. 'We need a different sash,' she told the black-clad assistant. 'A wide one that can be worn at its fullest on one side, covering the dress from waist to hip, then caught up on the other hip through a buckle – a sparkly buckle – so that it falls like a gathered scarf.'

'That sounds complicated,' Patience said doubtfully.

'It will make you look utterly spiffing. It'll show off the dropped waistline that none of us has a choice about these days, but in such a way as to flatter your narrow figure. Every woman in the church will swoon with envy.'

After that came gloves with a froth of lace at the wrists, a hat trimmed with rosebuds and leather shoes fastened with buttons at the side.

'You'll have to wear the shoes around the house to break them in,' said Molly.

'This is all lovely,' said Patience. 'Thank you so much for your help.' She smiled around at them. 'I'd never have managed on my own. I wouldn't have known where to start and I wouldn't have enjoyed it half so much.'

'We haven't finished yet,' said Vivienne with a touch of mischief.

'What else can I possibly need?' asked Patience.

'I'm talking about Miss Prudence,' said Vivienne.

'Me?' Prudence asked, startled.

Vivienne spoke softly into her ear. 'You don't imagine he sent money just for Miss Patience, do you?'

Prudence looked at the smart dark-blue dress hanging from the top of her wardrobe door. As plain as it was, it was without question the best dress she had ever possessed. The style was simple but the tailoring was exquisite, the drape of the fabric perfection itself.

'You needn't imagine you're going to get away with wearing your old mac on top of this,' Vivienne had declared in the shop.

Before Prudence had fully grasped what was happening, she possessed a single-breasted jacket with narrow sleeves, new shoes and a felt hat with an upturned brim. Somewhat to her surprise, she had felt rather good wearing such costly garments.

A brief tap on her bedroom door heralded Vivienne's arrival. She slipped inside.

'Have you forgiven me?'

'You silly girl. There's nothing to forgive. Mind you, I'm still in a state of shock. Once I've recovered, I might want to tell you off.'

'Don't scold me. Scold Uncle Niall. Did it really not occur to you that he would send enough money for you as well?'

'No,' said Prudence, 'though it shouldn't surprise me.'

She remembered how, all those years ago, Niall had offered her an income to support his brother's illegitimate child. He had gone against his family's wishes to do so, but it hadn't stopped him. He wasn't just a generous man. He was principled too.

'May I?' Vivienne sat on the bed. She didn't cast herself onto it as she normally would, but sat demurely on the edge.

'What is it?' Prudence asked. She pulled out the stool from beneath her dressing table and perched on it.

'This time next week, I'll know whether I've got the super-intendent's post at St Nicholas's.'

'I know. It's on my mind as well.'

'Regardless of whether I get the job, I'm going to need a new home. Molly and Aaron have invited me to stay with them if I need to, while I make arrangements.'

'That's kind of them,' said Prudence.

'They're good friends. I appreciate the offer, but I'm not the sort to accept short-term solutions. I prefer to think ahead and plan accordingly.'

Was that the widow talking? The young wife whose whole future had been snatched from her?

'The thing is,' Vivienne continued, 'if I get the St Nicholas's job – if – then I'll view it as a long-term prospect. I can't imagine ever wanting to move on from it and leave it behind.'

'You're fortunate to have something you'd be willing to devote yourself to so wholeheartedly,' said Prudence, but at the same time, something cut into her heart. What if Vivienne didn't get this job that meant so much to her? Prudence knew how deeply she personally would feel hurt on Vivienne's behalf. Above everything, she wanted good things for her daughter.

'Yes, I am,' Vivienne agreed, 'if I get it.'

'You mustn't doubt yourself. That's not the right attitude to take into an interview.'

'I know, but at the same time I'm scared to hope for too much. Anyway, I didn't come here to talk about that. I have a suggestion I'd like you to consider.'

'Of course,' said Prudence.

'If I don't get Mrs Rostron's job, I can't honestly say how long I'll stay at the Board of Health. It might be for years; it might be for ever; or it might be that another opportunity comes along. But if I do get Mrs Rostron's job, I know I'll stay here in Chorlton indefinitely, very likely for ever. What I'm building up to asking is if you think it might be a good idea for the two of us to find somewhere to live together after your brother takes over this house.'

'Oh, Vivienne,' breathed Prudence.

'That's why I hesitated to mention it before the interview – because if I fail to get the post, then our living together wouldn't necessarily be a permanent arrangement.'

'I realise that.'

'So would you like to think it over?'

'Very well,' said Prudence. 'All right, I've thought. Let's do it.'

Chapter Twenty-Eight

Enjoying the sight of the bright-yellow trumpets of daffodils and the hazy-blue swathes of grape hyacinths as she walked past the gardens on High Lane on her way home at the end of her day's work, Jess could almost wish it was further from Holly Lodge to Wilton Close so she could keep on admiring the spring flowers that said that the darker days of winter had been left well and truly behind. Then she recalled that her days in Wilton Close were numbered. Apparently Mr Lawrence Hesketh wanted to move in as soon after Miss Patience's wedding as was feasible. Would the work on Holly Lodge be finished by then? Would the basement flat be ready to move into? If not, Jess would find herself back in the B and B, because no landlady would take on a lodger for such a short amount of time. Anyway, there was no saying that she would get the chance to move in to Holly Lodge, was there? If Mr Peters decided to declare her unsuitable…

She was about to sigh, but then she didn't. It was no use moping. That's what Mum would have said and she'd have been right. All the same, it was unsettling knowing that both her job and her home were in doubt.

But that evening it seemed that maybe the problem of the digs had been settled. Vivienne and Miss Hesketh were going to look for a place to share and Vivienne suggested that Jess join them.

'We hope for your sake you won't need to.' Vivienne held up crossed fingers. 'We hope you'll be confirmed in the Holly Lodge post and be able to move into the flat there.' She laughed. 'Maybe we'll end up coming to stay with you until we find somewhere permanent.'

'It's kind of you to offer to have me,' Jess said, mulling it over, 'but if I'm not kept on at Holly Lodge, who knows where my next job will be?'

Vivienne nodded sympathetically. 'Either you get a job and a home – or you lose both. It's a difficult situation to find yourself in.'

'I would say it's all or nothing, but I don't want to sound dramatic.'

Jess had never said anything previously, but she couldn't help feeling intrigued by the friendship between Miss Hesketh and Vivienne. Now she said, 'Tell me to mind my own business if you like, but I've noticed how well you and Miss Hesketh get along – but even so, to choose to live together?'

'Strikes you as odd, does it?' asked Vivienne.

Aiming for a light-hearted note, Jess said, 'I've never been on terms like that with any of my landladies. I can't deny, though, that the two of you, in spite of the differences in age and personality, seem well suited.'

'Maybe I am just one of those people who gravitate towards folk older than herself.'

'Anyway, you're lucky,' said Jess. 'You seem to get on better with your landlady than I do with my parents.'

'Your father and stepmother, you mean?' said Vivienne.

'Yes. I don't mean my mum. She was wonderful. We were very close.'

'I was close to my late mother too. What sort of relationship do you have with your stepmother?'

'Not bad at all,' said Jess. 'I have Molly's brother to thank for that, as a matter of fact.'

'Tom? How so?'

Jess explained how Tom had encouraged her to get on friendly terms by writing chatty letters.

Vivienne nodded approvingly. 'That sounds like Tom. I've got a lot of time for him. He's a lovely man.' She smiled and frowned at the same time. 'I know "lovely" isn't a word one normally applies to a man, and most men would be miffed by it, but Tom really is lovely. He's kind and thoughtful and he's so good with his sisters' children. He's got a good head on his shoulders too; he thinks things through.'

'He always seems very likeable,' said Jess. How pale that sounded compared to Vivienne's warm praise, but she couldn't afford to look eager. Although she would dearly have loved to hear more about Tom, she turned the subject back to the original question. 'I now get along with my stepmother better than I do with my dad in some ways. I love Dad and he loves me, but we seem to have become more aware of one another's shortcomings in recent years and there's been a lot of friction between us, even some downright ill-feeling at times. The fact that I chose to leave home in order to work didn't help. Do you mind if I ask whether your father minds you living and working away from him?'

'It's different for me,' said Vivienne. 'I left home when I got married. Before I was widowed, I was already engaged in war work, so I just carried on working and I've never stopped.'

'I never married,' said Jess, 'and that makes a difference to how people see you. When we lost Mum, suddenly everyone else had my future mapped out for me as the spinster daughter living at home and taking care of Dad.'

'Did it make you feel guilty?' Vivienne asked.

'Goodness, yes, all the time – but I felt annoyed too. Nobody seemed to see it from my point of view. It's not as though Dad was old and feeble. He was a working man with friends and enough money to pay for the lady over the road to clean the house and do his washing and some baking for him.'

'Has the guilt gone now that he's remarried?'

'Yes, it has,' said Jess. 'I like knowing that he's being looked after. I know most people thought me selfish to pursue a career, but I really did worry about him, though I could never say so because the obvious reply would have been "Come home, then." Either that or "Liar. You can't be worried or you wouldn't stay away." I felt I couldn't win, whatever I did.'

'Not a nice feeling,' said Vivienne.

'No,' Jess agreed, 'but things are much better now I've got my stepmother. They're better for Dad and they're better for me, because I don't need to worry about him.'

'It's good that you don't feel guilty now,' said Vivienne. 'It's just a rotten shame that you have the worry of your future hanging over you.'

'Thanks again for offering to put me up if I need it. It's reassuring to know I have that option.'

'If you do need it,' said Vivienne, 'you'll be most welcome and I would hope that you'd be able to find a new job nearby. I don't like to think of you moving away.'

'Neither do I,' said Jess. 'I haven't been in Chorlton long, but I feel more settled than I've felt for a long time. I'd hate to leave.'

She thought about that. It was thanks to her post in Holly Lodge and her home in Wilton Close that she felt that way – and now she was definitely going to lose the latter and possibly the former as well. But she had the offer of digs with

Vivienne and Miss Hesketh and that made her feel warm inside. She knew she had made good friends.

When Tom was next at Soapsuds House, he found that Danny and Aaron intended to go and see the Lady Day fair being set up. They invited Tom to come along with them, or, to be accurate, the invitation came from Danny.

'Did Uncle Tom say yes?' Molly asked her son.

'Uncle Tom always says yes,' Danny replied.

Molly cast an amused glance at Tom. 'You aren't exactly famous for saying no to your nephew and nieces, are you?'

'I wouldn't want to be,' said Tom. 'Good old Uncle Tom, that's me.' He couldn't say so, but knowing he would never have children of his own meant that his sisters' children were his world.

'Uncle Tom is better than Uncle Angus,' said Danny.

'Now then,' Molly remonstrated, though Tom was aware that she didn't entertain the highest opinion of Uncle Angus. 'It's not fair to compare them. Uncle Angus lives a long way away. He does what he can.'

What he had to, more like – what Molly and Aaron made him do. He was Danny's late father's brother and by rights Danny should have gone to live with him after Mr Cropper passed away, but instead of rushing to his orphaned nephew's side, Angus Cropper had taken a few days to present himself at the orphanage and when he finally did, Aaron, who had paid young Danny a lot of attention in recent weeks and developed a strong bond with him, had, according to Molly, given Angus Cropper a right old roasting.

One of us, sir, has behaved as a father should – and it isn't you.

Molly had repeated Aaron's words to Tom, pride shining in her eyes as she quoted him.

Tom now turned to Danny. 'Are any of your mates coming with us?'

'Jacob, Henry and Charlie. They're all in my class.'

'Four of you, eh?' Tom shook his head, sucking in a breath between his teeth and producing a hissing sound. 'Will two grown men be enough to keep you in check?'

'I'm sure you'll do your best,' Molly said wryly. 'Just make sure none of them runs off to join the fair.'

'I shan't,' Danny said at once. 'My running away days are over.'

'I'm pleased to hear it.' Molly spoke lightly, but Tom could see the look in her eyes. When Danny's real father had been sent away to spend his final weeks in a sanatorium, the motherless Danny had been dumped at St Anthony's. He had attempted several times to run away to be with his dad. In the end, it had been Molly who had broken every rule imaginable in order to make sure he was near to his father as Mr Cropper breathed his last.

With one thing and another, it was no wonder that Molly, Aaron and Danny were such a strong and devoted family. Molly and Aaron had earned the right to be Danny's new parents and that had given the lad a powerful sense of security. Tom's admiration for his sister and her husband was boundless.

And if his heart swelled with envy now and then, he was careful not to let it show.

It was a fine evening for a walk. Tom, Aaron and the four lads headed down Edge Lane past all the big houses with their spacious lawns and flowerbeds behind brick walls over which grew tall stems of golden forsythia, rich-pink blooms of flowering currant and fragrant catkins of winter hazel.

High-spirited at the thought of seeing the fair take shape, the boys were laughing and jostling one another, but their mucking about wasn't excessive and Aaron didn't rein them in. Jacob and Henry were both in orphan grey. Some parents didn't encourage friendships with children from the orphanage, but Molly and Aaron didn't care for that attitude.

They turned the corner into Limits Lane, which had a line of cottages down one side of its cinder path. The cottages were in Stretford, but if they had been built on the opposite side, they would have been in Chorlton – hence the name of the lane.

They walked past the cottages, coming to the fenced allotment area at the end.

'Uncle Tom built this,' Danny proudly told his friends.

'The cottage that used to be here burned down,' Jacob announced. 'Me and my family were in it and we could have burned to death.'

'Cor,' said Henry. 'Did you set fire to it?'

'Nah, course not,' Jacob said scornfully.

'By accident, I mean,' said Henry.

'Someone set fire to it from the outside,' said Jacob, 'but they never found out who. It happened in the dead of night.' Holding up his arms and wiggling his fingers, he made ghostly noises.

Standing beside the wooden fence, Tom pointed out the areas of soil with narrow paving in between and the sturdy shed in the corner.

'The onions, shallots and artichokes should be in now,' he said. 'Early potatoes too. This piece of land will make a big difference to the folk of Limits Lane.'

But they were too near now to the fair for the boys to be interested in Gabriel Linkworth's allotment – or Mr Tyrell's Garden, as Gabriel and Belinda wanted it to be known. At the bottom of the lane was the rugged slope down onto the meadows, an extensive length of land that ran along the banks of the River Mersey on both sides. Further along, the land was called Chorlton Ees, ees being the ancient name for water-meadows, but hereabouts the meadows were known as Turn Moss, the same as the local farm.

Excited, the four lads broke into a run, each eager to be first to reach the fair. They had already been given instructions to go no nearer than the outlying wagons and caravans that surrounded the attractions, but there was still plenty to be seen from that distance. Tom and Aaron strolled behind, letting the boys run ahead. They weren't the only ones here. A number of families had come to have a look and there seemed to be plenty of unaccompanied youngsters as well.

'Evening, Tom – Aaron.'

Tom looked round to find Vivienne – and with her was Jess. His heart bumped. Coming across her unexpectedly sent warmth radiating throughout his body. Jess looked lovely in a simple straight skirt and top in a warm brown shade that reminded Tom of toffee, over which she wore a jacket. Her shorter hairstyle, which he had found out from Christabel was called a bob, had grown a little and now brushed her shoulders. Together with the straw hat she wore with a green scarf tied around the crown, the effect was pretty and relaxed.

'Have you brought Danny to see the fair getting ready?' Vivienne asked. 'I saw Jacob Layton too.'

'He's with us,' said Aaron, 'plus another couple of lads. It seems we aren't the only ones.' He glanced about, acknowledging the various parents and their offspring.

'We've brought some children as well,' said Vivienne, 'so that Jess can get to know them before she's put in charge of them on Saturday.'

Jess pretended to look at the empty space beside her. 'As you can see, I'm getting to know them really well.'

Tom smiled. One of the things he liked about her was her sense of humour. It was never far away, not even when she was riled. That made him ask, 'How are you getting along with Mr Thorpe these days?'

'Not too badly,' she told him. 'He's been considerably more civil ever since that time at Durrell's. Best of all, he has stopped dropping in at Holly Lodge every five minutes. As far as I'm concerned, that means we're getting on extremely well.'

'Good.' Tom liked to think of her being happier in her work.

'Since we've all lost our kids,' said Aaron, 'shall we walk around together?'

Tom could have slapped his brother-in-law on the back and hugged him for making the suggestion. He kept his mouth clamped shut, determined not to blurt out the agreement that swelled inside him.

'Yes, let's,' said Vivienne and Tom could have hugged her too. What was wrong with him? It was hopeless. He'd known that all along. Nothing could possibly come of being friendly with Jess Mason. He ought to leave these three and run off after the boys, but he couldn't miss out on the chance to be in Jess's company, he just couldn't. He found her entrancing.

Keeping an eye on the children from a distance, they walked around the fairground's perimeter, peering past the wagons to where canopied stalls were being erected for the coconut shy, the hook-a-duck and the hoop-la. Small tents promised fortune-telling and ale. They stopped to watch a pair of tall wooden A-frames being hoisted into position with a strong bar across the top from which the swing-boats were subsequently hung.

'Dad! Uncle Tom! They're building the helter-skelter.' Danny came running back to them. 'Come and see. Can I go on it on Saturday?'

'Manners, son,' said Aaron.

'Oh – sorry.' Danny pulled off his cap. 'Good evening, Mrs Atwood. Good evening, Miss Mason.'

'Good evening, Danny,' said Vivienne. 'What's this about a helter-skelter?'

It was interesting to see the tall, stripey cone being erected in sections with the winding staircase on the inside and the curving slide attached to the outside. A craggy-faced old man sat on a wooden chair, smoking a cigar, watching as the structure gradually took shape.

'Are you one of the fair people?' Aaron asked.

'Aye, I am now.' The man's voice was deep and fruity. 'I used to be a travelling showman, but no one wants them these days.'

'What did you do?' asked Vivienne.

'I exhibited living curiosities.' He drew out the last two words, rolling them richly on his tongue.

'Such as?' asked Jess.

'A real mermaid, for one, and an eight-foot tall queen of the Amazon, for another.'

Would it be impolite to laugh at how gullible their fore-bears had been? Tom knew none of them wanted to offend this old man.

Looking at them, he said grandly, 'I once exhibited... a pincushion.'

'A pincushion!' Vivienne exclaimed.

'You see, it's not what you exhibit so much as the story you tell about it.'

'I can imagine you spinning a wonderful yarn,' Jess said admiringly. 'You have such a rich voice.'

'My voice had more resonance in my younger days, but a compliment from a pretty lady is always welcome.'

'You must have seen a lot of changes,' said Aaron.

Before the old boy could reply, some girls came running towards them, pig-tails flying. They were in orphan grey with white pinafores and they ran straight to Jess, each clamouring to be closest to her.

'Miss! Miss! There are horses. Come and see the horses.'

Taking her by the hands, they started to draw her away. She looked over her shoulder. 'Duty calls.'

Tom watched her go. The way those children had treated Jess was the same as the way his nephew and nieces treated him.

'I thought you said she hadn't met them before,' he remarked to Vivienne.

'She hasn't,' Vivienne answered with a smile, 'but children know when they've found a friend.'

Looking at Jess with the little girls, Tom thought what a good mother she'd make.

Except that she wouldn't, would she? She was married to her job. And, anyway, he wasn't husband material.

Chapter Twenty-Nine

Tom was in the bath. He had slid under the water; his face was submerged. No it wasn't. He was waking up and his face was wet because it was soaked with tears. He'd been crying again. Again. Crying in his sleep like a baby. Shame thickened in his throat. That moment of dreaming of being in the bath hadn't been his real dream, he knew that. It had been nothing more than a distracting flicker in the moment of waking. No, the real dream remained out of reach in the depths of his memory, and thank God it did – or was that another instance of his cowardice? He had heard of men who thrashed about in the night. So bad were their dreams of war and death, of blood and guts and mud and agony, that they couldn't be still as their bodies fought to escape the terrible images in their minds. Tom's body did no such thing. The weight of what he saw in the night was such that it pressed him deep into the mattress, rendering him unable to move. He wasn't even enough of a man to yell and writhe.

Those other men, the ones who shouted and twisted, their consciences were clear. That was why they could try to escape from their dreams, albeit without success. Tom's conscience wasn't clear. That was what held him immobile. It was yet further proof of his cowardice.

All those men who had fought, all the poor buggers who had lost limbs, lost their sight, come home with rotten lungs... all those men who hadn't come home, who had taken one in the chest or the head, those whose bodies had been flung high into the air when a shell landed, those whose brains or guts had come pouring out in a mud-filled crater...

Those men had done their duty. They had suffered, poor blighters, but they had fought for king and country. Their families could hold up their heads and be proud. Their families could wear their red paper poppies every November, with enormous sorrow, yes, but with pride and a sense of honour, because their menfolk, their sons and husbands and brothers and neighbours, had done their duty.

And what had Thomas Benjamin Watson done? Travelled up and down in a bloody train, that's what.

Aye, a bloody train in more ways than one.

Most folk who spared a thought – and let's face it, the majority of the population had no idea about such details of the war – but those who were aware probably knew that it was by and large the task of the Friends' Ambulance Unit to gather up the wounded and ferry them back behind the lines to the field hospitals. And most people would have said that the Friends – bloody pacifists, bloody conchies – had it easy, doing a job like that. That was what the soldiers thought, the men in the trenches, and who could blame them? What was looking after the injured on a train journey compared to the horrors of their own experiences? The Friends weren't going to get killed. They weren't going to leave widows and orphans. Ruddy pacifists.

It was Friends on the ambulance-trains, Friends and doctors and orderlies... and Tom. Each train was assigned a 'real' soldier to oversee matters and Tom was hauled out of the trenches and put on train duty. Why him? How come he'd been chosen? Luck, probably – or lack of it. You couldn't have a train staffed just by medics and stretcher-bearers, not when to all intents and purposes it belonged to the Army. There had to be a soldier or two as well, and Tom had been picked. Wrong place, wrong time.

'Lucky bugger,' said his mates – said *some* of his mates. Others didn't utter a word. They looked at him accusingly because he was going to have a cushy duty. Anything that didn't involve waiting for the whistle and going over the top was cushy – and shameful.

The oddest thing was that it wasn't cushy at all. It was appalling. But he could never say so, not to anyone. To the men in the trenches, a day with nothing worse than trench-foot, rats and mud was a good day. Who would see train duty as difficult? But it was. Oh, it was.

It was groans and ramblings and yells. It was the metallic smell of blood that swamped the carriages as wounds were dressed over and over again because the bleeding wouldn't stop. It was the stench of guts and entrails; it was heads cracked open like nuts.

It was men weak with relief and gratitude at having been pulled out of craters in no-man's land. It was men who wished they'd been killed outright.

It was men who had *fought*.

A young lad with a mangled lump of arm dangling from his thin shoulder, his eyes over-bright with fear and pain.

Tom leaned over him, gently dabbing a wet cloth to colourless lips. 'How old are you, lad?'

The boy blinked. His eyes wandered before they focused. 'Regimentally speaking, eighteen, sir.'

Tom flinched, disgusted at the recruiting sergeants who

permitted such things. Then pity overwhelmed him. Pity and
rage and pity again. Regimentally eighteen. He was fifteen at
most. Not a day older.

Tom never told anybody how he spent the war. Never, not once, did he mention it in his letters home. Letting his family worry about him going over the top was preferable to admitting his terrible shame.

The trains were for all ranks. One mutilated wretch was the same as the next. One bloody stump, one pulverised bone the same as all the rest. One smashed jaw, one set of empty eye-sockets, one abdomen just barely stitched together. Every single one the same, and every single one new and individual and excruciatingly painful to see.

That had been Tom's war. Line upon line of stretchers and bunks all along either side of every carriage; a narrow aisle down the centre between bunks three high. Men who had given an arm, a leg for their king and country. Men who had given their sight, their lungs... their health, their ability to earn a living and support their families. Men for whom a loud noise would forever afterwards return them in an instant to the terror of the battlefield.

Men who had *fought*.

And the many who died on the train, their injuries too severe. The young officer who had lost both his feet. The men gasping for breath, their lungs packed with fluid. The men who said they didn't feel too bad, but that was because they hadn't yet realised that they had lost a limb. The chap who had taken one in the spine and who had, in the most literal sense, died by inches as one by one his muscles became paralysed.

Men who had *fought*.

The nurses must be exhausted, but they never stopped. One young nurse looked stricken.

'You've just brought in a couple of men from her village,' the sister told Tom.

'Will they live?' he asked.

'One is already dead. Gas gangrene. The other will have his leg off tonight or else he'll die of the same, and he still might anyway.'

She moved on. Tom felt cold to his core.

As he left, the young nurse stopped him outside the ward.

'Are you a doctor?' she demanded belligerently. Of course she knew he wasn't. 'Are you a conchie?'

He shook his head.

'But you're on the ambulance train. An able-bodied soldier on the ambulance train. You should be ashamed. You should be dead.'

She started to walk away. Then she came back and spat in his face.

Chapter Thirty

ON SATURDAY MORNING, Jess opened her curtains onto a bright, fine day. Her first thought was that the children were going to enjoy the Lady Day fair. She was grateful to Vivienne for giving her the chance to meet the youngsters she was going to be in charge of, especially since she wouldn't be at the fair herself – which drew Jess onto her second thought: Vivienne's interview. She dressed quickly and went to knock on Vivienne's door to see if she would like some help getting ready.

'I'm going to wear a jumper and skirt this morning,' said Vivienne. 'What do you think of this for this afternoon?'

She indicated a blue dress that was hanging from the top of the wardrobe door. It looked plain beside her normal attire.

'To be honest,' said Jess, 'I prefer your olive green.'

'So do I,' Vivienne agreed, 'but I want to look smart and professional and, frankly, not too stylish. I can't have Mrs Wardle suggesting I'm more interested in fashion than in the children.'

'I know what you mean,' said Jess. 'What you wear at work affects the way others think of you.' She smiled. 'Not that that's much of a problem for me. I've never had the wherewithal to have the choice between professional and stylish. In any case, why can't a woman be both?'

They went downstairs to breakfast.

'Would you like to do a final practice of your assembly?' Miss Patience asked Vivienne. 'I'm happy to be the audience.'

'That's kind of you,' said Vivienne, 'but I don't want to do it so many times that I go stale.'

'You made a good choice of subject,' observed Miss Hesketh.

'I hope the other candidates have all chosen Lady Day,' said Jess, 'so that the children are heartily sick of hearing about it by the time it's your turn.'

Vivienne fingered the collar of her jumper. It wasn't like her to exhibit nerves. 'Going last will be an experience in itself. I've got used to being at the top of the alphabet in recent years.'

'Aren't the candidates going in alphabetical order?' asked Miss Patience.

'It's in the interests of impartiality,' Vivienne explained. 'Both Miss Boodle and I have experience of working with St Nicholas's, and we're both at the start of the alphabet, so names were drawn out of a hat and mine was last.'

Before Jess set off for her Saturday morning at work, she hugged Vivienne and wished her luck.

'I'll be thinking of you.'

'You shouldn't,' Vivienne said lightly. 'When I'm being interviewed, you'll be at the fair with the children, so concentrate on looking after them. Make sure you have a good time too.'

'I hope it all goes well for you,' said Jess, 'especially the assembly.'

Vivienne cast her gaze up to the heavens. 'That's the part I'm most concerned about. Not the assembly itself, but knowing that all the children will want is to go on the hoop-la and the donkey rides.'

Jess felt a little quivery inside as she walked to Holly Lodge. She was nervous on Vivienne's behalf and was also unsettled on her own. By the end of today, Vivienne would know whether she had secured the job she wanted so dearly. Jess would have to wait a further week to find out whether her future lay in Holly Lodge.

What a shame. Not that Tom said so to the householder. This wasn't a rented property. It was owned outright and if the gentleman of the house wanted to have the beautiful old original fire surround and hearth removed and replaced with small, plain new tiles in the most hideous up-to-the-minute design, then he was perfectly entitled to do so. Perkins and Watson had done a number of jobs on this house, and, as far as Tom was concerned, this was an easy task to end on. The old surround was heavy and had to be removed with care, not to mention a great deal of muscle power; then the wall and the hearth had to be made good, ready for the tiler to set to work.

Tom then went to check on another job that was being undertaken for a Mr Golland. Two of the Perkins and Watson men were erecting a fence in between his garden and that of his neighbour, in place of a hedge. What should have been a straightforward job had turned into something of a nightmare during the week because Mr Benson, on the other side, who wasn't responsible for this boundary, had sworn up and down that the fence was going to encroach on his property. The matter had only been resolved when a solicitor, armed with the deeds, had brought a tape-measure to sort things out.

'Don't get embroiled in any arguments,' Tom had instructed his chaps. 'These two aren't on good terms, but that's their problem. It's not up to us to act as referees.'

With Tom's help, the final fenceposts were erected and the last panels were fixed into position. Mr Golland came outside to admire the end result and Tom couldn't help wondering if Mr Benson was glowering at them from behind his curtain.

After that it was nearly time to knock off. Tom went to the office for half an hour to finish up and then it was time to head home for Saturday fish and chips with Mum and Dad. He would far rather have been on his own, though he would never have said so. He didn't want to hurt their feelings and neither could he bear to face their questions. As he sat chatting, passing the salt and shaking on some extra vinegar, he wasn't really engaged in the conversation. This was his life. A grown man in his thirties, living at home with no hope of moving out to marry and have a family of his own.

He was a coward. He had spent the war chugging up and down on a train. He hadn't fought. He hadn't lived through the horror of the trenches, but he had seen, day after day and night after night, the terrible injuries inflicted on the brave men who had.

This was why he couldn't marry. He wasn't a real man. He hadn't fought. Thousands upon thousands had died in unimaginable pain and he – he hadn't even fought. He had been ashamed then and he was ashamed now. He would be ashamed for the rest of his life. He had never told his family and he could never tell a wife. The burden would be too great for her and the shame of that would eat him alive.

Some words came back to him from long ago, a line of Shakespeare learned at school. *Cowards die many times before their deaths*. He had died countless times during the war.

And that was why he must put an end to seeing Jess Mason. He must stop speaking to her. He must turn away from her. He had known all along that nothing could come of it and because he had known, it had been all too easy to fall into the trap of enjoying her company – because he'd told himself he knew what he was doing and he wasn't fooling himself in any way. It had been safe to be with her.

But it hadn't been safe, had it? Because the end result had been that he had fallen in love. Just thinking of her made his pulse race.

If he was any kind of a man, he would never walk past Holly Lodge again, never drop Jess's name into a conversation with Molly. He would cut her out of his life. But he couldn't do it as abruptly as that. He had to permit himself a secret farewell. He would go to the Lady Day fair this afternoon and drink in the sight of her slender figure and shining brown eyes. He might even speak to her. But that would be the end of it.

It would be a kind of death for him, but for a man who had suffered countless deaths throughout the long years of the war, what was one more?

Chapter Thirty-One

ALONG WITH THE other candidates, including the Poodle, Vivienne had been shown round St Nicholas's. The others had asked lots of questions. Vivienne hadn't, because she already knew the answers, but had that been a mistake? Had it made her appear over-confident? Or socially inept?

After that, she had to sit and wait while the others were interviewed and held their assemblies. The children would be fed up to the back teeth by the time it was her turn. At last, she was summoned to her interview. Mrs Rostron's office not being large enough, the interviews were being held in, of all places, the over-furnished sitting room that was used for teaching the girls how to clean.

The interviewers were all members of the Orphanage Committee. There were five of them. Mr Lowe, the chairman of the committee, was a gentleman of rather slight build with earnest blue eyes and pure white hair. He was quietly spoken and unfailingly courteous. He rose to greet Vivienne and wave her into a seat. It was a chintz armchair and she sat on the edge, not wanting to give the impression of getting too comfortable.

Mr Lowe sat down. He had bagged a handsome leather armchair.

'You are acquainted with Mrs Wardle, of course.'

'Mrs Atwood works under me at the Board of Health,' said Mrs Wardle in a dismissive voice that left no room for doubt as to her opinion of this particular candidate. The violets on her hat quivered in agreement.

'I am responsible to Mr Taylor,' Vivienne said to the other interviewers, 'who, as I'm sure you are aware, is in charge of the local Board of Health. We are all appreciative of Mrs Wardle's voluntary contribution.'

Mrs Wardle swelled up, causing further trembling of the violets, but before she could speak, Mr Lowe intervened.

'And this is the Honourable Mrs Granger.'

Wouldn't Mrs Wardle love to be an Honourable! Mrs Granger was a stylish, middle-aged lady with good breeding in every line. The gentlemen were Colonel Lavender and Mr Bennett, both of whom were old codgers, retired gentlemen with their fingers in plenty of charitable pies.

The interview opened with questions about her previous experience.

'So, really and truly, you've had barely any experience of working with children,' Mrs Wardle commented. 'You went from Projects for the Ignorant Poor to the housing department of a local corporation, neither of which is relevant.'

Vivienne directed her best professional smile at Mrs Wardle. 'But after that, I did start working with families. I joined what used to be the rationing department during the war and was involved in the provision of food to poor families, such as free school meals or extra milk, and advice as well. Ultimately, that was what brought me to the Board of Health. I particularly wished to work with families.'

'Indeed?' Mrs Wardle smirked. 'Then may I suggest you have applied for the wrong job? A family is the one thing an orphan doesn't have.'

'That's not strictly true,' said Vivienne. 'Many orphans do have relatives, even if those relatives aren't in a position to care for them; and not all orphans lose their parents in baby-hood. Children come to orphanages at all ages and from all sorts of backgrounds. I might not have worked directly with children, but I am aware of the many issues that surround them.' She reached down to pick up her handbag, removing the notebook she had worked on with Miss Kirby. 'I have spent some time discussing real children with a retired teacher who used to work in a school in a deprived area. If you would care to look, you'll see that I have given a lot of thought to the best ways to help these children, should they come to live in an orphanage.'

'Anyone can be an expert when the problems are hypo-thetical,' Mrs Wardle said with a dismissive sniff.

'I don't claim to be an expert,' Vivienne replied. 'I know I have a great deal to learn, but I hope the notebook shows how serious I am about preparing myself as best I can for this role.'

Questions of a personal nature followed.

'You are a widow,' said Colonel Lavender. 'Is that correct?'

Vivienne stiffened, but it wasn't the first time she had been asked this when seeking a job. 'Yes, sir.'

'Good. We couldn't employ a married woman, of course.'

'Any children in the picture?' asked Mr Bennett.

'No.'

'Good.'

She could have kicked him for that. Good? Her husband was dead and she was childless. What was good about that?

'Obviously, we couldn't have family responsibilities getting in the way,' said Mr Bennett. 'We need a superintendent who will be devoted to the work.'

'It'd be a lot simpler to have a man,' remarked Colonel

Lavender. 'Then we wouldn't have to fuss with women's matters.'

'I believe that what you refer to as "women's matters" shouldn't set you against employing a female superintendent,' said Vivienne. 'It's a question of who is the right person for the post.'

'Indeed it is.' Mrs Wardle looked round at her fellow committee members. 'Miss Boodle gave a very good interview and her assembly was outstanding, as I'm sure you'll all agree.'

Mr Lowe cleared his throat. 'Mrs Atwood, we've asked each candidate to tell us three things he or she would do to improve St Nicholas's.'

Vivienne had anticipated this type of question. 'Funds permitting, I'd employ a qualified nurse.'

'The nannies are perfectly capable of dealing with minor ailments,' said Mrs Wardle.

'Nanny Mitchell and Nanny Duffy have years of experience and the children are in excellent hands,' said Vivienne, 'but with a hundred and twenty children under the same roof, I believe it would make sense to have a nurse on the premises to oversee general health and hygiene as well as to take care of any child who falls ill.'

Mr Lowe scribbled something down, but Vivienne couldn't read his expression. 'What else?' he asked.

'I'd amend the Roll of Honour.'

That made them all sit up straight, eyes popping.

Colonel Lavender made a gobbling sound like a turkey before he managed to bluster, 'Disgraceful! The Roll of Honour is a – a – an honourable thing. It can't be tampered with.'

'I don't propose to tamper with it,' said Vivienne. 'I attended the Remembrance Day service here last November and was deeply moved when Mrs Rostron read out the names of some of the fallen soldiers who had once been boys here. I would like to see the Roll of Honour extended to include the women and girls from St Nicholas's who lost their lives in the war – nurses, ambulance drivers. Many women gave their lives. I think it appropriate to remember them.'

'It was the men who fought,' said Mr Bennett. 'If women were killed, that was unfortunate, but you can't give them the same status as the men.'

'I think it would set a good example,' Vivienne replied, 'unless, of course, you believe that boy orphans are of greater value than girl orphans.' Had she gone too far? But it needed saying and these old duffers ought to hear it.

There was a charged silence.

'And your third suggestion?' asked Mrs Granger.

'I would like to review the rules concerning what the children are called. Currently the girls are known by their full first names, and not by any diminutive forms, and the boys are known only by their surnames, while families of boys have surname and number.'

'What's wrong with that?' demanded the colonel.

'It's a system that was instituted in the last century and is very much of its time, but is it really appropriate for the twentieth century? Is it appropriate for a place we want the children to think of as their home?'

'She'll be waxing lyrical about one big, happy family in a minute,' Mrs Wardle murmured.

'And why not?' Vivienne challenged her. 'It's normal for a teacher to have a class of sixty, so we have the equivalent of two classes here, which really isn't that many children. It's a small enough community that everyone knows everyone else. Why not aim for a friendlier atmosphere?'

'Because there have to be rules, that's why not,' snapped Mr Bennett.

'Of course there have to be rules,' said Vivienne, 'but I believe that relaxing this one rule could make St Nicholas's more cheerful.'

'Thank you, Mrs Atwood.' Mr Lowe spoke in a tone of finality. 'I think we've heard all we need to. It's time now for you to take your assembly.'

None of them looked her in the eye. Had she alienated them or did she still have a chance?

The dining room tables and chairs had been shifted over to the sides of the long room and stacked up, leaving the floor for the children, who sat in lines, cross-legged, smallest at the front, oldest at the back. The nannies and nursemaids sat on chairs down the sides while, at the back, where they could watch everyone, sat the members of the interviewing panel. After that first glance, Vivienne didn't look at the interviewers. She concentrated on the children, some of whom were already blank-faced in anticipation of boredom at having yet another assembly inflicted on them during their precious Saturday. Some children fidgeted.

Vivienne smiled round at them.

'I bet you're feeling pretty fed up by this time, aren't you? How many assemblies have you had to sit through today? And now you've got another one. You'll be pleased to hear that this is the last.'

There was a distinct lightening of the atmosphere and the children perked up. This wasn't the way they expected an adult to speak to them.

'I'm glad to be here this afternoon, because this is a special place. It's a place that looks after children who don't have families of their own or who maybe do have some family but nobody who can take them in. In stories, orphanages can be grim places, but here in St Nicholas's, you are lucky to have a real sense of community.' She paused and let her gaze sweep over the youngest children. 'Community: that's a big word, isn't it?' She looked towards the older ones. 'Is there anyone who can explain to the little ones what I mean by a sense of community?'

Several hands went up.

'A community means where you live,' was the first answer.

'That's right. It is. This is a community of children and the grown-ups who take care of them. But community means more than that, doesn't it?'

More hands went up.

'Does it mean looking after one another?'

'Yes, it does,' said Vivienne. 'And what else might it mean?' She picked a child. 'Yes?'

'Being kind.'

'That's very important. To have a real sense of community, you need people to be kind to one another. What else do you need? For instance, what about rules?'

There were a few groans. Vivienne fixed a couple of lads with a look and the sound subsided.

'What if there were no rules?' she asked. 'That sounds like it might be fun, doesn't it? But think about it. What if St Nicholas's had no rules at all?' She crossed her fingers. This was the moment when it could all go horribly wrong.

Up went hands. Vivienne took the safe option and nodded at Drayshaw One, the head boy.

'If there were no rules, no one would go to bed until late and then they wouldn't want to get up in the morning and they'd be late for school and would get the strap.'

'That's right,' said Vivienne. 'So rules can be a good thing, can't they? They help the community to run smoothly.'

A hand went up somewhere in the middle. It was Hannah, the girl who had come here from that other orphanage.

'Yes, Hannah?' said Vivienne, glad to be able to use a name. 'What would you like to add?'

'I think St Nicholas's has a good feeling of community, because the other orphanage I was at before was much bigger and I felt lost, but now I'm somewhere smaller and I'm not scared all the time.'

'I'm delighted to hear you say so and I'm sure Nanny Duffy, Nanny Mitchell and the nursemaids are too, because taking care of all you children is the most important thing of all. That's another thing you need for a sense of community, isn't it? As Hannah says, you need to feel safe.' Vivienne moved on quickly. This was going well. She mustn't let it drag out. She held up three fingers. 'That's three important things that make St Nicholas's a special community: kindness, following the rules and feeling safe. I'd like you all to do something for me, please. Put your thinking caps on and think of someone here who did something that made you feel you're part of a community, someone you'd like to say thank you to.'

Hands flew up.

'Nanny Mitchell, please will you choose someone,' asked Vivienne.

'Mary-Anne,' said Nanny Mitchell.

'I want to say thank you to Clara because she read a story to me when I had tummy-ache.'

Vivienne nodded at Nanny Mitchell, who chose another child.

'I want to say thank you to Elizabeth because she helped me with my sewing when I got stuck.'

'That was a generous thing to do, wasn't it?' said Vivienne.

Jacob Layton's hand went up, but he pulled it down at once; then he put it up again, only to pull it down again.

'Layton Two,' said Vivienne, 'would you like to thank somebody?'

Jacob went bright red. 'My brother Mikey, miss – Layton One, I mean – for setting a good example for me to follow.'

Vivienne looked at the forest of hands in front of her. 'There are lots of you who want to say thank you, so perhaps you can find your special person afterwards and thank them. We've nearly finished our assembly now and you've had excellent ideas about what makes a good community, so it's my turn to say a big thank you to all of you for joining in so well.'

She smiled at her young audience, then looked at Nanny Duffy as a signal for Nanny to assume responsibility for the children, but before Nanny Duffy could rise from her chair, there was a movement among the children and the older ones started clapping, the younger ones following their lead a moment later. The applause was accompanied by beaming smiles.

Vivienne's eyes filled with tears and her heart expanded with gratitude. Oh, how she would love to work here and be responsible for the welfare of all these children.

Had she done well enough to be offered the post?

Chapter Thirty-Two

J ESS DIDN'T KNOW whether to be amused by the orphan
girls' hair or to feel sorry for them. Abigail had told her
that you could tell all the girls' ages by the way they wore
their hair and Maud, Deborah and Beryl each had two plaits
worn behind their ears, which meant they weren't yet twelve,
while Florence, Beatrix and Rebecca, with single plaits down
their backs, were either twelve or thirteen.

When Jess had arrived at St Nicholas's to collect her
group, a dark-haired girl of about eighteen, wearing the staff
uniform of long-sleeved dress of dark blue beneath a white
bibbed apron, had introduced herself as Nurse Carmel and
suggested that the two of them take their groups together.

'We'll be company for one another,' she said.

Jess had been happy to agree. If she was honest, she'd been
a little nervous of taking her group on her own. It wasn't as
though she had any experience of looking after children.

She had been given four girls to watch over while Nurse
Carmel had two girls and four boys. The boys all wore grey
shirts, short trousers and grey socks.

'At least they don't have to wear ties today,' said Nurse
Carmel, catching Jess looking at them.

Jess knew the boys had to be called by their surnames, but
she asked them their first names because she wanted to show
an interest.

'My name's Gregory, miss,' said Turnbull, 'but no one calls me that. I'm Turnbull.'

Jess thought her heart would break clean in two at that moment, because it seemed so unkind. The children had already bowed and curtsied to her when she met up with them, which Vivienne had warned her to expect. She had found it rather charming, but now she thought of the wider context of the orphans' lives in general and the rules that governed them. Mind you, there were plenty of schools where the children were required to bow or curtsy to the staff the first time they saw them each day, so maybe the orphans didn't feel singled out.

Jess, Nurse Carmel and their young charges walked to Limits Lane together. As they passed the cottages, heading for the slope down to the meadows, they could already hear the jolly sound of the fairground's huge organ that was audible above all the rest of the sounds. Jess and Nurse Carmel paid the modest entrance fees and they all went in. By now the children were bouncy with excitement.

'Listen,' said Nurse Carmel. 'You need to run around as fast as you can and see every single thing, then come back here and tell Miss Mason and me what looks the best. We'll wait for you over by the toffee apple stall.'

The children raced away and Nurse Carmel smiled at Jess.

'I've done this before,' she said, 'and the best way is to let them use up a dollop of energy before we start deciding what to go on.'

Jess and Nurse Carmel chatted while they waited for the children to return. A man on stilts walked past and tipped his hat to them.

'Thanks for letting me join up with you,' said Jess. 'I haven't been in charge of children before.'

'As long as you go home with the same number you arrived with, that's the main thing.' Nurse Carmel grinned. 'You were meant to come here with Mrs Atwood, weren't you? Is it right that you're in digs together?'

'Yes, we are. We live near the rec.' Then, in case Nurse Carmel meant to dig for information as to what sort of superintendent Vivienne might be, Jess veered off in a slightly different direction. 'Apparently, my bedroom used to be Mr Abrams's wife's room when she lived there.'

'She's a good sort,' said Nurse Carmel. 'Did you know she used to have a job at the orphanage? Things have turned out well for her, finding a husband at her age.'

The children came running back, the little girls eager to throw their arms around Jess. She was delighted, though she noticed they didn't attempt to do the same to Nurse Carmel.

'You need to be careful about that,' Nurse Carmel warned her as they all set off, the children dancing ahead. 'Hugging isn't allowed. You needn't look at me like that. I didn't make the rules. All the children have to be treated the same and that means everyone keeping their hands to themselves.'

Jess accepted the reprimand with good grace, but it made her realise that being the superintendent of St Nicholas's would be a very different prospect to being the manager of Holly Lodge. Bringing up children in an institutional environment required specific skills and personal qualities.

She stopped thinking about the orphans' lives and set about enjoying the afternoon and making it as much fun as she could for the children. She applauded their attempts at winning a coconut and waved to them every time they passed by on the beautifully painted golden horses on the carousel.

'It looks like they're having a good time,' said a familiar voice and Jess turned with surprise and pleasure to face Tom Watson, hoping he would think the colour in her cheeks came from sharing the children's excitement. She covered her self-consciousness by introducing him to Nurse Carmel as Mrs Abrams's brother.

'I've seen you around the orphanage sometimes,' said Nurse Carmel, 'when you've lent Mr Abrams a hand.'

The carousel slowed to a halt, its music ending at the same time, and the riders climbed down. Jess and Nurse Carmel's children came flocking towards them.

'Can we go on the rifle range?' Turnbull asked.

'I'll take the boys to that,' Jess said to Nurse Carmel, 'and you take the girls to the skittles.'

'I don't see why we can't fire rifles, said Florence.

'Because you're girls, that's why,' Nurse Carmel said firmly and led the girls away.

'Do you mind if I tag along?' Tom asked, falling in step beside Jess.

The rifle range man and the lad working with him showed the boys how to hold the guns and aim them.

'Are you having a go, mate?' the stallholder asked Tom, who shook his head. 'Had enough of it in the war, did you?'

Tom turned away. Jess felt a little jolt of disappointment. Was he about to walk off? But he didn't. A moment later, the rifle man was busy drumming up more custom and Tom turned back to watch the lads trying their luck. When they had finished, they all walked off together between the swing-chairs and the lucky dip on their way to meet up with Nurse Carmel and the girls.

Jess and Tom chatted as they went.

'Are you here with Danny?' Jess asked.

'He came this morning with his mum and dad. I'm just here to soak up the atmosphere.'

'Everyone enjoys the fair,' said Jess.

'How about the children's company?' Tom asked. 'Are you enjoying that as well?'

'Loving it,' Jess admitted. 'I want to give them all a big hug, but it isn't allowed.'

'You're good with them,' said Tom. 'I noticed it the other evening when you were here with Vivienne.'

'Thank you.'

'I'm sorry to raise it, but if Mr Peters decides against keeping you on, maybe you could think of working with children. It would be another possibility for you.'

Jess frowned. 'I'm sure I could love children if I worked with them, but I love the old soldiers too and that's the work I want to do. The old chaps at Oak Lodge are so interesting and likeable and I dearly want to have my own old soldiers at Holly Lodge, to build friendships with them and make their lives happy and comfortable in their declining years. These children are gorgeous, but I still want to be with my old soldiers.'

'Lucky old soldiers,' Tom said lightly. 'And lucky you, knowing what you want from life. I sincerely hope you get to stay on at Holly Lodge.'

'Thanks. I appreciate that.'

'You deserve it,' he said. 'You're a special person, Jess Mason. You deserve to get what you hope for.'

Jess looked at him in surprise. The warmth in his blue eyes assured her that he meant every word and she felt touched to her core.

Before she could think how to respond, Tom touched the brim of his cap to her, murmured something that might have been, 'I'll leave you to get on,' and then peeled off in a different direction.

'Has your sweetheart gone, miss?' asked young Jones.

'What? He's not— Don't be silly, Jones. Mr Watson is a friend, that's all. Look, there are the girls and Nurse Carmel. Let's hurry.'

It was a good thing, really, that Tom had gone. She couldn't have anyone leaping to conclusions. That wouldn't do at all. It was more than time to set thoughts of him aside and concentrate on her duties as a looker-after. It surprised her how much she was enjoying the afternoon. She had volunteered to help purely to be a good friend to Vivienne and Molly, but now she found that being with her small group was a real pleasure. Their excitement was infectious and she found herself laughing and pointing out attractions, pausing to watch the strongest man competition, hurrying to see the performing poodles, helping the children decide on the best way to spend the coppers that had been entrusted to her on their behalf, and, above all, listening to their happy chatter.

It was a revelation to her how much she liked their company. She was an only child and had never minded being the only one, because her two best friends at school, being the oldest in families of seven and nine respectively, had spent half their time wiping noses, changing nappies and taking their younger brothers and sisters with them wherever they went, while the other half of their time was spent sweeping and mopping, ironing and running errands. They had envied her for being a singleton.

Then, instead of marrying and having a family, Jess had found how interesting work was, soon realising that this new path suited her extremely well. But here, now, with these young orphans, Jess found herself thinking about children in a way she hadn't before. When Drew had chucked her overboard, she had known she faced a life without a family of her own, but it wasn't as though she was one of those girls who had grown up absolutely desperate to be a mum. In due course, her determination to build a career for herself against the odds had shunted the thought of family to the back of her mind. If anything, she had felt, had been made to feel, a certain sense of resistance to the idea of family after being on the receiving end of comments such as 'You poor creature, having to earn your daily bread. That's not natural for a woman' and 'Are you going to let us down by getting married and leaving?' and 'Wouldn't you rather have a husband and children to look after?'

And she had always had to be so careful in how she responded. If she came down too heavily on the side of the working woman, she was regarded as unwomanly and potentially unemployable. Moreover, there was the ever-present danger of sounding like an embittered spinster. Or frigid. A male colleague had called her that once. As a woman who worked from choice as well as necessity, she couldn't win.

She had learned to swallow all that because it was part and parcel of being a female in the workplace; and in so doing, she had focused on making the best of her life the way it was, not on regretting the life that might have been.

But now, with eager children tugging at her hand, she felt an unexpectedly sharp pang of loss... of need. She had honestly never known that children were so likeable, that they could be such fun, that she had it in her to respond to them in this way. Of course, it would be silly to get carried away just because this one experience was going well. But even so...

She would never want to give up her work. She loved it and was proud of it. It was an essential part of who she was. But... but wouldn't it be marvellous to be able to have a family of her own as well? Why couldn't women have both?

Vivienne and the other candidates sat more or less in silence in the nannies' sitting room, the silence all the more obvious because the room wasn't large enough and they'd had to squeeze in. The door opened and everyone looked up. It was Mr Lowe, with Mr Bennett bringing up the rear.

'Miss Boodle,' said Mr Lowe, smiling at her.

Vivienne's heart didn't just sink, it crashed to the floor. Was the Poodle to be spirited away and offered the job?

'And Mrs Atwood,' went on Mr Lowe. 'If you two ladies would come with me, please.'

As they left the room, Mr Bennett remained behind and closed the door. Mr Lowe escorted Vivienne and Miss Boodle back to the sitting room where the interviews had been held. Mrs Wardle, Mrs Granger and the colonel were all there; the colonel lumbered gallantly to his feet. A movement over to one side caught Vivienne's attention – and there, of all people, was Mr Taylor, rising politely to acknowledge the ladies. What was he doing here?

'Please sit down, ladies.'

Mr Lowe waved them towards a pair of chairs beside one another. Mr Lowe took his place, with Mrs Wardle and Mrs Granger to one side of him and Colonel Lavender and an empty chair to the other.

'We'll wait for Mr Bennett,' said Mr Lowe. 'He is thanking the other candidates and informing them that they haven't been successful.'

Vivienne couldn't help glancing at the Poodle, finding that Miss Boodle was glancing her way too. Looking towards the panel, Vivienne received a sneering look from Mrs Wardle, who then smiled warmly at Miss Boodle.

In came Mr Bennett. He resumed his seat next to the colonel.

'Good. We're all here,' said Mr Lowe. 'This is unorthodox, but we have invited both of you back because one of you is to be offered the position of superintendent. The question is, which? Allow me to explain. You have each received two votes from my colleagues on the panel. Under normal circumstances, this would leave me with the casting vote, but, as Mrs Wardle pointed out at some length, this would be inappropriate as I have met Mrs Atwood in her professional capacity on various occasions, whereas I have never had the pleasure of meeting Miss Boodle. Therefore we have decided to offer the casting vote to Mr Taylor, who knows both of you from the Board of Health.'

Mrs Wardle thrust out her bosom and tilted her head, sending her violets bobbing. She looked unbearably smug – and no wonder. She had always been able to bend Mr Taylor to her will. Vivienne lowered her head for a moment, pressing her lips tightly together. She would have loved this job. Today's interview and the assembly she had taken had only made her set her heart on it all the more.

Mr Lowe spoke to Mr Taylor. 'We're most grateful to you, sir. Would you like to put any questions to the candidates?'

'If that would be in order,' said Mr Taylor.

'Absolutely not!' exclaimed Mrs Wardle. Then she feigned a laugh. 'Surely there's no call for that. The panel has done all the interviewing that is necessary.' She fixed Mr Taylor with a beady look and her fox fur seemed to do so as well.

'Mr Taylor has come all this way, at no notice, to favour us with the benefit of his opinion,' said Mr Lowe. 'I believe he is entitled to speak to the candidates, so he can be certain he is making the correct choice.' He smiled at Vivienne and the Poodle. 'I must ask one of you ladies to leave the room. Mrs Atwood, would you please remain?'

'Miss Boodle should have the opportunity to be heard first,' cut in Mrs Wardle. 'I would remind you that when the candidates' names were drawn from the hat, hers came out before Mrs Atwood's.'

'I'm happy to go second.' Vivienne started to rise.

'Please remain seated,' said Mr Lowe. 'Pulling names from the hat was a way of showing fairness to those candidates with no prior experience of St Nicholas's. That consideration no longer applies and we can resort to the traditional method. The alphabet dictates that Mrs Atwood should go first. Miss Boodle, if you wouldn't mind? Colonel, if you'd be so good?'

Colonel Lavender got up and opened the door for the Poodle to leave.

'Please proceed, Mr Taylor,' said Mr Lowe.

A flush appeared in Mr Taylor's cheeks as Mrs Wardle pursed her lips and shook her head. Vivienne felt like dredging up a sigh from the depths. Was there any point in going through with this? It was obvious what the outcome was going to be. Nevertheless, she lifted her chin and fixed a small, professional smile on her lips.

'How do you think the Board of Health could better support orphanages in general?' asked Mr Taylor.

Vivienne experienced a moment of panic. This was a question she hadn't prepared. 'Well...' And that was all the thinking time she had. 'Firstly, through advice and information. Things are becoming more regulated than they used to be and the Board of Health could provide an information service to ensure all orphanage superintendents are kept up to date.'

She was losing their interest; she could see it in their eyes. She sounded like she was spouting a load of flannel. She needed a real example to sound as if she knew what she was talking about – but what? – Oh, Molly, thank you! She cast her mind back to what Molly had told her when she and Aaron had been on the verge of adopting Lucy's baby.

'Take adoption, for example. The system, if you can call it that, has always been entirely informal. To adopt a child, you simply take him or her into your family and that's that.

There are moves afoot to make a proper legal process out of it, which will be formalised by certificates of adoption.'

'I'm sure all the superintendents are fully aware of this,' said Mrs Wardle in a long-suffering voice.

'I agree,' Vivienne said at once. 'What I'm suggesting is that if the Board of Health could provide information as and when it becomes available, then the superintendents would have the reassurance of knowing they were always going to be up to date. There are other matters too on which the Board of Health could provide information.' Inspiration struck. 'Perhaps a member of staff could be responsible for producing a regular newsletter.'

'Indeed,' smirked Mrs Wardle. 'Perhaps that is a project you would care to take on. I'm sure you'd do an excellent job.'

Vivienne caught her breath. Mrs Wardle was as good as telling her she would be remaining at the Board of Health.

'Has Mrs Atwood answered the question to your satisfaction, Mr Taylor?' enquired Mr Lowe and when Mr Taylor nodded, the chairman addressed Vivienne. 'Thank you, Mrs Atwood.'

Vivienne got up. The colonel opened the door and let her out and the Poodle in – she had better stop thinking of her as the Poodle. It wouldn't do to be disrespectful towards the superintendent of St Nicholas's, not even in her thoughts. Crikey, but Mrs Wardle was on the brink of getting her chubby fingers in a big pie.

After about ten minutes, the door opened and Vivienne was invited back in. She stood up, smoothing the skirt of her blue dress, and entered the room, smiling round in a general way and not looking directly at either Mrs Wardle or the Poodle – Miss Boodle.

'It's been a long day for you, ladies,' said Mr Lowe, 'and I'd like to congratulate you both on a splendid performance. St

Nicholas's would be fortunate indeed to have either of you as superintendent.' He turned to Mr Taylor. 'Have you reached your decision, sir?'

'We hardly need trouble Mr Taylor to state his choice,' put in Mrs Wardle. 'It is only too obvious who deserves to be the next superintendent of St Nicholas's.' She looked round, eyebrows raised confidently.

Mr Taylor cleared his throat, avoiding Mrs Wardle's eyes as he said, 'I have indeed decided, Mr Chairman. Based on my knowledge of these two ladies, I believe you should offer the post to – um – Mrs Atwood.'

Mrs Wardle sat bolt upright. 'Mrs Atwood! That's an outrage!'

'Mrs Wardle, please,' protested Mr Lowe. 'My good lady.'

'Don't my good lady me,' snapped Mrs Wardle. 'This is a ridiculous decision. Ridiculous, I say. Why, I have spent more time with Miss Boodle and Mrs Atwood than Mr Taylor has. He hides away in his office most of the time. I am telling you categorically that this is the wrong decision – a foolish decision – a calamitous decision, I may say, calamitous. In fact, Mr Chairman, I'll go so far as to say that if you offer the post of superintendent to this – this person – I'll be obliged to resign from my position on the Orphanage Committee. There! What do you think of that?'

Mrs Wardle and her violets trembled with indignation, but at the same time she rolled her plump shoulders and smoothed the front of her dress, which made her look complacent. She was in no doubt as to the outcome of this situation – and she wasn't the only one.

Then Mr Lowe jumped up from his chair and practically leaped across the room, somehow managing not to knock over any of the ornaments. He grasped Mrs Wardle's right hand in both his own and pumped it up and down vigorously.

'My dear Mrs Wardle, may I say on behalf of the committee how deeply grateful we are for your many years of service and how sorry we are to accept your resignation.'

'What? What?' Mrs Wardle blustered.

'I completely understand, madam… such a busy lady… so many commitments, so many demands on your valuable time… The committee recognises the great contribution you have made over the years to so many worthy causes through your charitable interests and endeavours. You are indeed a shining example to us all and we salute you. The whole Orphanage Committee salutes you and we send our very best wishes to whichever good causes are next to benefit from your insight and experience.'

Crikey, he would be leading a rousing chorus of 'For She's a Jolly Good Fellow' in a minute. Somehow or other, Mr Lowe had drawn Mrs Wardle to her feet and got her almost to the door.

'… an inspiration to us all… so devoted to good works…' At last Mr Lowe ran out of steam.

'Well!' exclaimed Mrs Wardle. Then she rallied. 'When I said—'

Colonel Lavender stood up. 'Dear lady, save your speech. We shall, of course, hold a farewell party in your honour and that is where you shall make your speech. And now, will you permit an old soldier to walk you out?'

Mr Lowe threw the door open and the colonel escorted a gasping Mrs Wardle from the room. Mr Lowe shut the door and leaned against it for a moment before pushing himself upright and blowing out a breath.

'Now then, where were we?'

Chapter Thirty-Three

As HE WALKED away, Tom knew that Jess had had no idea he had just said goodbye to her. Of course she hadn't. She didn't know how he felt, and that was how it should be. He didn't look back. He didn't let himself. It would be unbearably difficult if she was watching him go – and just as hard if she wasn't. Maybe harder.

He walked past the various stalls and rides, trying to make himself take an interest. A grinding sound as he passed the helter-skelter made him glance up.

'Nothing to worry about,' said the fairground man collecting the money at the helter-skelter's base. 'Just the bolts settling, that's all.'

A few ragged-looking boys with one pair of shoes between them looked longingly at the delights surrounding them. Tom dug his hand in his pocket and pulled out his loose change.

'There's enough here for you all to have a go on something. Can I trust you to share it out fairly?'

'My mam says not to take anything off strangers,' said one boy, sticking out his chin defiantly, though Tom could see the fear flickering in his eyes.

'Quite right too,' said Tom.

Not wanting to appear threatening, he took a step backwards. A couple of the boys instantly took a step forwards, desperate to get their hands on the windfall. Tom's heart ached for these lads, who had so little.

'Tell you what,' he suggested. 'There's a bobby over there. I'll give the money to him and he can give it to you. You trust a policeman, don't you?'

Or maybe they didn't. Maybe their dads sailed close to the wind and their families lived in dread of a knock on the door. It wasn't just the rent man some poor folk hid from. At any rate, it was the best Tom could come up with. It was either that or chuck the coins on the grass at their feet. He didn't suppose the boys would care, but he would. It would feel demeaning to treat them in that way.

The bobby cheerfully accepted the money and Tom left him doling it out. Those poor kids. They probably only got one meal a day. Well now, if he had intended to cheer himself up after leaving Jess for the final time, he hadn't succeeded. A brisk walk home was what he needed and he wouldn't go via Limits Lane, but would take a tramp across the meadows as far as Jackson's Boat before peeling off and wending his way home. Get rid of some energy: that was the best thing. It was what had helped him through since coming home after the war. Fresh air. Exercise. They cleared your head and lifted your heart, even if only temporarily.

Walk on, Tom. Don't look back.

But in spite of his long-legged pace, it felt less like walking than trudging through the deepest, darkest mud because he was leaving Jess behind for ever. In his head, he knew it was the right thing to do, but his heart had other ideas.

Suddenly, alongside the jaunty music of the fairground organ came a loud yell, as of a number of voices raised in the same moment. Tom jerked around. They weren't cries of excitement. He knew fear when he heard it. There were more voices now, a ragged succession of shouts, less distinct than that first collective yell – and then came a prolonged groaning sound that made the hairs stand up on the back of Tom's neck. The helter-skelter: that grinding sound he had heard earlier. He ran in its direction, pushing his way through the crowd. He saw what had happened before he reached it. A section of the slide on the outside of the helter-skelter had parted company with the tall structure. Two children were on the piece that had come adrift and were clinging to its raised sides, their faces white with terror. Above them on the upper part of the slide that still clung to the helter-skelter, other children also hung on for dear life.

As Tom stopped at the foot of the colourful structure, the helter-skelter man appeared from the little doorway at the top of the cone-shaped building. Sitting down and bracing himself against the sides of the slide so that he couldn't slip downwards, he made his way to the first of the children, prised her fingers off the edge and helped her to climb up past him towards the doorway, where another fairground man pulled her to safety and sent her down the spiral staircase. Presently, the girl emerged at the bottom, where a fairground woman with a brightly coloured headscarf helped her down the final steps to the ground.

A woman darted forwards. 'Josie! Oh, Josie!' She pulled the girl into her arms and held her close.

'Move out of the way, love,' said a fairground man whom Tom recognised as the man from the rifle range. 'Not to worry, folks,' he called to those nearest. 'We've got people on the steps inside to help the kids down.'

Tom realised someone was beside him and Jess clutched his arm.

'The girl trapped on the bit that's broken loose is Maud from the orphanage. I don't know the boy.'

But Tom did. It was the lad whose mum had wisely warned him against accepting anything from a stranger.

There was a crowd at the foot of the helter-skelter, where grateful parents were fussing around the children who had been below the broken section when it came adrift and had come safely down the slide. Fairground folk were trying to get them to move away.

Catching hold of Jess's hand and pulling her behind him, Tom forced his way through and spoke to the rifle range man.

'What about the two who are stuck?'

'They'll be rescued. The kids up above them on the slide have to be helped back up to the top, then Jay-Boy up there will get the last two to safety. Don't fret. Are you the parents? Jay-Boy has been shinning up and down helter-skelters and Ferris wheels since he was a lad, putting them up and taking 'em down again.'

'Oh aye?' Tom said sharply. 'He didn't make a very good job of erecting this helter-skelter, did he?'

Jess tugged his arm. 'Now isn't the time.'

She was right. Tom backed off a few steps, looking up. Maud and the boy must be terrified. There was another grinding sound and the section where they were jerked, causing cries of fear and dismay from below. Then the section settled again, but now it was further from the main structure.

Above the broken part, Jay-Boy hung on, steadying himself.

'He won't get to the kids from up there,' Tom said grimly, 'not now it's shifted again.' Cupping his hands around his mouth, he yelled up to Jay-Boy, 'Go back! You can't do anything. I'll come up and get them.'

Before anybody could prevent him, he had leaned forwards, grasped hold of the sides and placed his foot on the surface, briefly testing it for slipperiness and finding that the gradient of the slope was going to prove more of a problem. There was no time consider it. If he did that, he would be hauled away by fairground men. He started up the slide, bending forwards and holding on tight to the raised edges.

As the slide curved around, he realised someone was behind him. He glanced over his arm to see behind and below, expecting to find a fairground man intent on dragging him back to earth, but instead he saw Jess.

'Go back,' he called. 'This will be dangerous.'

'You'd better keep your eyes on what you're doing, then,' she retorted.

There was another groaning sound from above and the slide vibrated, the tiny movement travelling up through Tom's hands and feet and through his limbs. When it subsided, he pressed on, following the curve and trying to keep his gaze on the stripes painted on the tower instead of on the drop on his other side, which was giving him a swimmy sensation in his belly.

Tom was strong and fit; the physical nature of his job had seen to that. Even so, his muscles burned in protest and being bent practically double didn't help. If this was hard for him, how much tougher must it be for Jess? But he knew she wouldn't give up.

At last, coming to where the section had started to break away, he halted, leaning his back against the central structure. Beyond him, the slide ended in thin air. On the section that had come loose, the bolts had partly worked free from the nuts that were meant to hold them. How much longer could they bear the weight?

'Keep still,' he called across to the children. He made himself smile at them. 'I know it's scary, but think what a tale you'll have to tell your friends. I know you're Maud, but what's your name, lad?'

'Timothy,' said the boy.

'Timothy, eh? I'm Tom. Tim and Tom. That's a good sign, isn't it?'

Tom looked back. Jess had arrived behind him. Instead of standing like he did, she crouched on the slide. Was she scared of heights?

Tom turned back to examine the dislocated part of the slide, weighing his options. In terms of distance, a fit child would be able to make the leap to safety – but only in terms of distance. It wasn't just a matter of jumping. It was standing up and preparing, neither of which was possible on that sloping surface that, in any case, wasn't stable.

He turned to Jess.

'The children can't get from there to here without help, so this is what we'll do. I'll lie down on my front and edge forwards over the gap—'

'No,' breathed Jess, her eyes widening.

'Yes,' said Tom. 'I need you to sit on my legs to keep me stable. I'll grab hold of the other section and the kids can use me as a bridge one at a time.'

He thought she was going to protest, but then a steely look entered her eyes and she nodded. He explained to the children.

'Do you think you can manage that?' he asked.

'Yes,' said Timothy. 'Please hurry. It's – it's hard hanging on.'

'Here we go, then,' said Tom.

Jess moved down the slide a short way to give him the room he needed. Knowing that what he was about to attempt was completely mad and not quite believing he was actually doing it, Tom lay down on the slope and pulled himself up towards the break in the slide. His hands closed around the edge and he sucked in a deep breath, knowing that in the next moment he would be looking straight down at a drop of thirty feet. Just like being on a roof, he told himself, and he'd been on plenty of those – but it wasn't like that at all. This was frightening because so much was at stake, but at the same time Tom felt oddly calm. He knew exactly what he had to do.

Instead of looking down at the sea of anxious faces below, he lifted his head and focused on the other part of the slide. Bringing his arms forward to reach out made his pulse race. Thank heavens for Jess's weight on his legs. She was crazy to have followed him up here, but he was glad she had. He couldn't do this without her.

In those first moments, every instinct urged him to set his arms whirling like the sails on a windmill. Instead he reached out, making him feel he was on the verge of toppling over and hurtling to the ground, but Jess, who had lifted her weight a fraction to allow him to move forwards, now sat down firmly again and he felt steadier. His muscles roared as he forced his torso not to drop forwards. He stretched his arms – inched further out over thin air – and with a final grunt of effort, grasped the other section of the slide. It wobbled but he held on, knowing he'd be in serious danger of getting socked in the head if he didn't. The children screamed, but they hung on.

Timothy was nearest. Gasping with the strain his body was under, Tom couldn't speak, but Jess called across to the boy in a commendably steady voice.

'Timothy, edge your way down to the bottom and then use Mr Watson as a bridge. Lie on your tummy and slither along his back like a snake and I'll pull you onto here the moment you're in reach.'

Timothy did as he was told. When he was making his way along Tom's back, Tom felt as if his spine would crack and break clean in two. He pushed the breath out of his body in long puffs, aiming to keep a clear head.

Then the weight vanished as Jess helped the boy off.

'Slide down.' There was a pause, then she called, 'Your turn, Maud.'

Silence, apart from the roaring in Tom's ears.

Then – 'I can't,' Maud whimpered.

'You must,' Jess called. 'Sweetheart, I know how frightened you are, but this is the only way. The top end of the bit where you are is sticking out too far for you to go upwards, so you have to come this way. Can you be brave for me?'

Nothing happened.

Tom felt as if every joint in his body was going to be wrenched out of its socket. Twisting his head, he called to Jess. 'You'll have to climb across me and get her. *Do it!*'

He clamped his teeth, bracing himself. Jess lay down and pulled herself along his length. How much longer could he hold on? As long as it took, that was how long, as long as it took.

The strain eased as Jess heaved herself off at the other end, Tom ducking his head to keep it safe from an inadvertent kick. He clamped his eyes shut, not so as to avoid looking at the sheer drop beneath him, but so as to concentrate on holding on. What the devil were Jess and the child doing? He needed them to get back across the gap.

He heard Jess say, 'You have to, Maud. There's no other way, darling,' and he shouted, 'Pick her up – carry her – walk back.' The breath hitched in his throat. 'Just – walk across.'

There was a pause, then Jess called, 'Right. Here we come.'

'Quick,' ordered Tom. 'Quick as you can.'

He managed not to groan as Jess's foot sought purchase on the back of his shoulders. Then she stumbled along his length. As her weight vanished, he felt as if his body was rising to meet the empty air above him. His arms and shoulders seemed locked in position, his hands apparently frozen to the edges of the sticking out piece of the slide. Fear ran through Tom at the prospect of peeling his fingers free and letting go. What if his centre of gravity was in the wrong place, was too far into the gap, and his own weight dragged him downwards—?

There was a scrabbling sensation on his back and then hands grasped hold of the waistband of his trousers and heaved, trying to haul him backwards. Tom removed his fingers from the other section – felt his upper half drop – then he wriggled backwards with all his strength, helped by Jess. One of his braces pinged free – his ribs seemed to catch on the sharp edge – Jess gasped, 'Come on!' – and his head swam, though not because he was about to fall. It was relief, because enough of him was on the slide for him to know he was safe.

He drew himself onto his knees. Somehow the effort had brought him in between Jess's position and Maud's and Jess was now nearest to the drop. From slightly further down the slope, Maud stared at him.

'I couldn't move,' she said. 'Miss Mason gave me a piggy-back across you.'

'You're safe now,' Tom told her.

'Here.' Jess took off her jacket and Tom passed it to the child. 'Sit on this and use it as a mat. That way, you'll get down without hurting yourself.'

'Are you coming too?' asked Maud.

'Good grief, yes,' said Tom. 'I think we've all had enough of heights for one day.'

'Off you go, chick,' said Jess and the child arranged the jacket and slid away.

Tom and Jess looked at one another. Jess had lost her hat and the breeze had blown her hair in every direction, but to Tom she had never looked more beautiful. Her brown eyes, which had been cloudy with a mixture of fear and determination when the two of them had reached this place after their arduous climb, were now big and bright with relief and satisfaction at having sent young Maud to safety.

'I can't believe I did that,' she said. 'I can't believe I crawled across you to fetch Maud – and I can't stand heights.' Her voice sobered. 'I can't believe you did what you did either. You turned yourself into a human bridge. That took some courage.'

Tom shrugged. 'It was the only way.'

'It's the bravest thing I've ever seen.'

Tom felt himself withdraw. He didn't move; he was pretty sure his expression didn't change, but he shrank inside himself. Brave? Him? That was the last thing he was.

'It wasn't brave.' He spoke in a flat voice. 'I just did what had to be done.'

'Yes – in a horribly dangerous situation,' said Jess. 'That's bravery in my book.'

'Let's get down,' said Tom. In his head, he added, *before you see me for what I really am*. 'If I squeeze over to the side, can you get past me? Then you can go first.'

Jess grinned. 'Always the gentleman.'

The helter-skelter vibrated and the bolts holding the top of the section where they were groaned and came away, the top piece parting company with the central structure. Caught unawares, Jess flailed her arms, trying to grab onto something and then—

As she toppled over the edge, Tom hurled himself after her, seizing her arm, his shoulder joints snapping as he took her weight. He looked down. Beyond her dangling body was that thirty-foot drop to the ground. He focused on her eyes, huge with fear.

'Hold on,' he gasped, heaving her up and trying to manoeuvre himself backwards at the same time. The strain set every muscle and sinew on fire with effort and pain, but what was that compared to the possibility of losing this wonderful girl? Clever, funny, kind, determined Jess. The love of his life.

Tom inched down the slope, pulling with all his might to bring Jess to safety. She threw out her free arm, scrabbling to catch hold of the edge. Tom heaved himself backwards and gradually drew her up and over the lip, onto the slide and into his arms. He enfolded her, wanting only to keep her safe and secure for as long as they both should live.

Never mind his vow to walk out of her life. Never mind his unworthiness. Both were hopelessly outweighed by the strength of his feelings for her. He couldn't let her go. He could never let her go.

Chapter Thirty-Four

WITH HER HEART pounding and adrenaline swooshing through her veins, Jess clung to Tom. He had caught her – she had nearly fallen but he had caught her and now she was in his arms and there was nowhere else in the world she would rather be. It was the madness of the moment, of course, just an emotional reaction to the terrible fate from which he had saved her.

But it wasn't, and she knew it. It was more, oh, so much more than that. It was the realisation of the depth of her feelings for him. It was the knowledge that this was where she longed to be, now and always. She drew back her head and looked at him, the expression in his blue eyes a mixture of tenderness, wonder and passion that left her in no doubt that he felt the same. Jess had held her feelings for him at bay, or tried to, for some time now. Could it be that he had been doing the same with his own feelings for her?

'Thank you,' she whispered. 'You saved me.'

'I couldn't have borne it if you'd fallen.'

'Really? Or is it just the emotion of the moment speaking?'

'Really,' said Tom. 'A thousand times really. I love you, Jess Mason. I love the spring in your step and the light in your eyes. I love you so much that I'm going to tell you the truth about myself and – and if you never want to see me again, I love and respect you enough to accept your decision.'

'Never see you again?' Jess repeated, startled. 'What d'you mean?'

'Not now,' Tom said gently. 'We'll talk about it later, I promise. Let me have this precious time with you to dream my dreams... whatever happens later.'

He pulled her closer and she tucked her head under his chin. They stayed like that for a minute, then Tom's broad chest rose and fell on a deep, slow sigh.

'We'd better get ourselves down from here,' he said, 'or someone will come up to fetch us.'

He released her and Jess reluctantly moved away. Tom removed his jacket and Jess took it. Tom held her steady as she moved to sit on it. She stuck her foot against the slide's wall to act as a brake.

'Keep your arms tucked in,' said Tom. 'Off you go. I'll be right behind you.'

Jess released her foot and allowed herself to travel down the curving pathway to the bottom, where willing hands were waiting to help her to stand up. She took a few steps to get clear and leave space for Tom, who appeared moments later. Jess had a mad urge to run into his arms, but there was a squeal from behind and Maud and the other children came dashing towards her, flinging themselves at her. She caught them in her arms, trying to hug them all at the same time.

'Maud, let me look at you,' said Jess.

Maud's face was tear-stained, but she seemed none the worse for her ordeal.

'You were very brave,' Jess told her. 'I'm proud of you.'

Glancing around, she saw Tom talking to young Timothy while a few lads, presumably Timothy's friends, hovered nearby. Then a constable approached Tom and, after a moment, they both came over to her.

'This is Miss Mason, who helped me rescue the children,' said Tom. 'You'll want to speak to her as well as to me.'

The constable didn't look so sure about that. Were only men supposed to act decisively in a crisis? But Jess didn't care what the bobby thought. She had done the right thing – and the end result had been that she'd found herself head over heels in love. It was difficult to think about anything else.

'We'll go to the police station and give our statements,' said Tom. 'Just now, I suggest you make a list of the men who erected this helter-skelter, Constable, and in particular take the names of those who fastened the bolts.'

Nurse Carmel appeared at Jess's side. 'Here's your jacket. We'd best take the children back to St Nicholas's. Mrs Rostron won't want anybody else coming to the fair until after it's all been checked for safety.'

Jess, Tom and Nurse Carmel walked the children home to the orphanage, where Jess and Tom left them at the front gates.

'Police station next?' Jess asked Tom.

'We can do that later. You and I need to talk.'

'You mean, about whatever it is that might make me turn away from you? Nothing could ever do that.'

'Don't say that. Don't sound so sure.'

'But—' Jess began.

Tom smiled, but there was sadness in his eyes. 'Don't paint yourself into a corner. Leave yourself a way out.'

Jess couldn't imagine wanting a way out, but this wasn't the moment to say so. As they left the orphanage, she let Tom choose the route and made no comment as he took her to Chorlton Green, then along past the Bowling Green pub and the farm, finally walking down a bushy path onto the meadows.

'Let's go to Jackson's Boat,' he said. 'Do you know it?'

'I've heard of it, but I've not been there yet.'

'You know it's a bridge, not a boat? It's always been one of my favourite places.'

They headed towards the riverbank and walked along the pathway, beside which the deep riverbank ran steeply down to the Mersey. The bridge wasn't far ahead.

'Do you mind sitting on the grass?' Tom asked.

'Not at all.'

The ground was dry, but Jess wouldn't have cared if it had been sopping wet. She wanted to hear what Tom had to say. He removed his jacket and laid it down for her to sit on. He sat beside her, but whereas she was facing him, he positioned himself sideways to her, knees up with his elbows on them and his hands lightly dangling in between as he looked towards the bridge. Why couldn't he look at her? But at last he did.

'I'm going to look at you to say this and... you can make of me what you will. You couldn't have a lower opinion of me than I have of myself.'

'Tom,' she began, but he carried on speaking.

'I've never talked about this before, not to anybody. I thought I never would, but you're entitled to hear it so you decide what to do. It's – it's about the war and what I did. More to the point, it's about what I didn't do. I didn't do anything. I didn't fight. I wasn't in the trenches – well, I was for a short time, but then I was given different duty. I was sent off to be a guard on an ambulance train.'

'I don't understand.' Jess frowned. 'You say that as if...' Her voice trailed off. She didn't know how to finish the sentence. She didn't know what to make of the haunted look in his eyes.

Gradually Tom described being on the trains, the rows of bunks and stretchers, the smell of blood and injury, the cries of agony, the men who had left limbs behind, those whose lungs had been all but destroyed by mustard gas.

'There were young lads who'd lied about their ages because they wanted to go to war and have an adventure. And they ended up lying on stretchers with smelly stumps where their limbs should have been. They cried for their mums.'

'Poor boys,' Jess whispered.

'Aye, boys. That's all they were. But each one of them was more of a man than I was, because they had fought. They'd done their bit. Me – all I did was travel up and down between the front and the field hospitals. But them – they weren't much more than children; they weren't all that much older than Danny is now; but they had *fought*.'

'You did what you were told to do, what you were ordered to do.'

'You can't imagine it,' said Tom, distress twisting his face for a moment. 'The blokes on the trains, those that weren't doctors, were conchies, pacifists, the lowest of the low. They were the ones I spent the war with. I went out there to fight and all I did was see thousands upon thousands of men with horrific injuries they had got in the course of doing their duty. I just travelled up and down on a train and every injury made me… made me hate and despise myself even more. I shouldn't be asking you to take me on. You deserve someone better. You deserve a man who can hold his head up when the war is mentioned.'

Jess's heart overflowed with tenderness and concern for Tom's suffering. Could she find the right words?

'Shall I tell you what I think? I truly believe that what you did was difficult and important – let me finish – and I think it put you under an enormous strain. Did you ever try to evade your train duty? Well, did you?'

'Of course not.'

'Did you tend the men's wounds?'

'I got the orderlies to show me what to do.'

'And when the boys cried for their mums, what did you do?'

'Look, there's no point in talking about it,' said Tom.

'What did you do?'

'I told them their mums were on their way. The boys were rambling and I said their mums would be here soon. I told them to hang on and be brave... and I told them that if they didn't feel brave, their mums wouldn't mind because they loved them so much.'

'You gave them comfort,' Jess said softly.

'They were just kids. And what are a few words here and there compared to facing the enemy and having your leg blown off?'

'You were part of what happened. You went there thinking you were going to fight and when you were called upon to do something else, you didn't attach any value to it.'

'It didn't have any value,' said Tom.

'The mums of those boys would disagree with you. The doctors and the orderlies would disagree with you.'

Tom shrugged. 'You're being kind and I appreciate it, but—'

'I'm not saying it to be kind,' Jess insisted. 'I'm being honest. I'm remembering my own experiences during the war. I worked in a hospital, so I saw some of the injuries – the amputations, the blindness, the men who could barely breathe. There were times when I felt so overcome by worry and desperation and pure heartbreak that it was all I could do to put one foot in front of the other to walk to the sluice-room. But the hospital where I worked was in Annerby, right up in the north, so the men who were brought there were well enough to survive that long journey. What I mean is, as terrible as some of their injuries were, they weren't anything like as bad as those of the men in hospitals on the south coast.

And then there were the men who couldn't be repatriated, because they'd never have survived the Channel crossing. And that's before you start thinking about the men who died in the field hospitals or on the ambulance trains. I found it hard enough to see the patients in the Annerby hospital, but you had to see all of them, all the men, all the injuries. That was your job for months on end, for several years. I know you feel bad because they were injured and you weren't; I know it made you feel less of a soldier, but it doesn't make you any less of a man. What you did took extraordinary strength, all the more so because you thought badly of yourself for doing it. I can't even start to imagine how hard it must have been for you. All I can do is remind you that you were given a job to do and you did it. You did your duty and that's the most any soldier can do.'

There was a silence. Jess waited. Then, without looking at her, Tom told her about a nurse who had spat in his face.

Something inside Jess collapsed in despair. How could she get through to him? Leaning forwards, she took his face in her hands and kissed his forehead, kissed the small vertical lines between his eyebrows. She kissed first one cheek and then the other before she leaned her forehead against his.

'You're a good man, Tom Watson. You're a loving family man. That's what I've heard about you.'

'From people who don't know the real me.'

'We all have secrets.' Jess moved so they were looking at one another. 'I'd been friends with Vivienne for some time before I told her I used to be engaged to a man who married someone else before he got round to breaking it off with me. Did Vivienne fall out with me over it? Did she think that because I hadn't opened my heart right at the beginning, that meant I couldn't be a true friend? Of course not. Keeping one part of your life private doesn't make the rest of your life a lie.'

'That's the way it feels to me,' said Tom.

'Really? So you aren't a loving family man?'

'Of course I am, but—'

'But nothing,' said Jess. 'Listen to me. This is the Tom that I know. He's polite and kind and he's always treated me with respect, which is more than I can say for many of the men I've come across in the course of my work. He's highly professional and he takes pride in his job. The men who work for Mr Jones have nothing but praise for you. Did you know that? And you truly are the best sort of family man. You helped me build a friendship with my stepmother and I've seen you with Danny and your nieces. That's the Tom Watson I know. Are you telling me I'm wrong?'

'You've picked out the best bits,' Tom said wryly.

'And now I know there's another Tom deep inside, who has never come to terms with what he did, what he was *ordered* to do, during the war. I know that this clever, affectionate, principled man whom I love battles with a deep-seated fear that he is a coward, a fear so strong that it has become an actual belief.'

Tom hung his head. Jess gently lifted his chin and looked into his eyes.

'I want to help you, Tom, but I know that telling you that you aren't a coward won't change the way you think and the way you feel. But let me make a suggestion that I hope with all my heart might help you, or at least begin to help you. I think you should tell your family— No, don't pull away. Listen. Without the advice you gave me, I would now be distanced from my father and stepmother. That advice came from your being part of a strong, loving family. So turn to them now. Let them see how you suffer – and let them love you.'

*

Vivienne almost danced home, such was her delight at having been appointed to the post of superintendent of St Nicholas's. After Mrs Wardle's unexpected departure, Mr Lowe had led the congratulations and Miss Boodle had been gracious in defeat. A certain gleam in the Poodle's dark eyes hadn't escaped Vivienne's notice. Was Miss Boodle reconsidering her position as Mrs Wardle's acolyte? Vivienne found she didn't care one way or the other. Not only had she been awarded the job she had longed for, but Mrs Wardle, who would have been the one fly in the orphanage ointment, had inadvertently resigned from her position on the Orphanage Committee. Talk about the cherry on the cake!

Miss Prudence and Miss Patience both appeared in the hall as Vivienne opened the front door.

'I've got it!' Vivienne exclaimed.

'Oh, my dear,' said Miss Patience. 'Congratulations.'

Vivienne knew that if she wanted to be hugged – and she did – then it was up to her to instigate it. She put her arms around Miss Patience, who she knew wouldn't rebuff her. That gave Miss Prudence a moment to think about it before Vivienne held out an arm in invitation and Miss Prudence entered the embrace, accepting a couple of seconds of warmth before stepping away.

'That's very good news,' said Miss Patience.

'Better than very good. Excellent,' said Miss Prudence. 'Come into the sitting room and tell us all about it.'

Vivienne told them all about the original interview, then described how her assembly had been received, ending with the additional interview. It warmed her heart to see the pleasure and satisfaction in the ladies' expressions.

'I'll write to my father this evening and tell him,' said Vivienne.

'I'm sure he'll be delighted for you,' said Miss Patience, 'and very proud.'

'Yes, he will,' said Vivienne.

She glanced round at the sound of the front door opening. A moment later, Jess popped her head into the room to say hello.

'Come in and hear dear Vivienne's news,' said Miss Patience.

'You look dishevelled,' observed Miss Prudence.

'Did you go on the fairground rides with the children?' asked Vivienne. 'I hadn't realised it was so breezy.'

'Never mind me,' said Jess. 'How did you get on? Should I take it from the happy smiles that...?'

'That you're looking at the new superintendent of St Nicholas's,' said Vivienne.

As Jess came towards her, she stood up to receive her friend's hug.

'Well done,' said Jess. 'Congratulations. I know how much it means to you.'

'Thank you,' said Vivienne. 'But what about you? You must have thrown yourself into all the activities to have come home looking so wind-blown.'

'Actually, there was a bit of an incident,' said Jess, 'but no one was hurt, so it's nothing to worry about. The children are fine. I don't want to spoil your special moment.'

But they insisted on her telling them and listened first in shock and then in admiration as Jess described what had happened on the helter-skelter.

'I'll have to go along to the police station shortly to make a statement,' she said.

'Shall you and Tom go together?' Vivienne asked.

'I don't think so,' said Jess, and was that a faint flush in her cheeks? 'I think he has something important to do.' She perked up, smiling warmly at Vivienne. 'But the most important thing at the moment is your new job, you clever thing. I want to hear all about your assembly.'

'The ladies have already heard the whole story,' said Vivienne. 'Tell you what. I'll come to the police station with you and tell you on the way – assuming you're well enough to go, that is. You may be in shock. Your eyes are huge.'

'Honestly, I'd rather go now and get it over with,' said Jess.

'You'd better go and repair your appearance before you go, Jess dear,' said Miss Patience.

As Jess disappeared from the room, they all looked at one another. 'Are you sure we shouldn't keep her at home?' asked Miss Patience.

'No, let her get it over with since that's what she wants,' said Miss Prudence. 'Then Vivienne can bring her home and you can cosset her to your heart's content, which is probably just what she needs.'

'What an adventure,' said Vivienne. 'I'm so relieved nobody was hurt.'

'We shall have two things to celebrate this evening,' said Miss Prudence. 'Jess's courage and your new position.'

'My new job.' Vivienne shook her head. It was still sinking in. 'After this, all we need is for Jess to be confirmed in her post at Holly Lodge.'

Chapter Thirty-Five

T OM WALKED HOME. He had taken Jess back to Wilton Close, saying goodbye to her at the garden gate, and now he was walking to Cavendish Road, off which was the quiet close where the Watsons lived. His mouth was dry and an odd, cold feeling had taken up residence in his chest. Was he really contemplating telling Mum and Dad the truth about his war? His deep reluctance was still there, but at the same time he knew Jess was right. Mum and Dad loved him and would do anything for him. If he told them, if he permitted them to glimpse his suffering, might it ease his mind a little?

Opening the front door, Tom hung up his cap on the hall-stand. For once, he took a moment to look at his reflection in the age-spotted mirror. He looked... ordinary. Most men did, but you didn't know what was happening inside their heads and their hearts, did you? You couldn't tell what they lived through in their dreams.

'I'm back,' he called.

'In here,' Mum called.

Tom opened the door to the parlour and walked in, ready to face his parents – and stopped dead at the sight of Molly sitting in one of the armchairs. She wore a loose green blouse, with a long string of beads under her collar and hanging down the front. Her complexion was radiant. Tom had always considered her to be good-looking, but her condition had bestowed an extra glow of loveliness on her. Although he tried to hide his shock at seeing her, she was too quick for him.

'You look surprised to see me,' she said and laughed. 'I am a frequent visitor here, you know.'

'Have you brought Danny with you?' Tom asked.

'No, it's just me. Danny is helping Aaron with some woodwork.'

'He'll make a decent apprentice one day,' said Dad.

'You can't wait to get him into the family business, can you?' said Mum.

'Don't get me wrong,' said Dad. 'I love all our girls, but I feel like a dog with two tails every time I think of having a grandson.'

Mum looked fondly at Molly. 'Maybe there'll be two grandsons soon.'

'I don't mind what you have, Molly,' said Dad, 'but if your sisters are anything to go by, it'll be a girl.'

Molly was looking at Tom. 'You look like you've been dragged through a hedge backwards.'

Tom glanced down at himself. Jess had straightened his tie, but now he became aware of his grubby waistcoat and shirt and his scuffed shoes.

'Oh – this,' he said. 'Yes. Something happened at the fair.' He described the incident, trying to play it down, but there was no fooling Dad. It wasn't the sort of thing a builder could possibly fail to understand.

'You mean the bolts hadn't been fastened correctly?' Dad demanded. 'That's disgraceful. It's downright dangerous – as everyone found out.'

'No one was hurt,' said Tom.

'Thanks to you and Jess, by the sound of it,' said Molly.

'I'm glad I wasn't there to see it,' said Mum. 'I don't think I could have watched you do that. You were very brave, Tom.'

'I'll go and tidy myself up,' said Tom.

Upstairs, he sat on his bed. Had he missed his chance? He had been prepared to speak out when he got home, but Molly's presence had thrown him and now the incident at the fair would be at the forefront of everyone's minds. Did he even want to talk about the war?

There was a light tap on the door and Molly walked in and sat beside him.

'Are you all right?' she asked. 'You must be feeling shaken up.'

'I'm fine, thanks.'

'It was a courageous thing to do. I'm proud of you. Danny will think you're a hero – and he'll be right.'

'I didn't think about it. I just did it.'

Molly nodded, looking thoughtful. 'Are you going to tell me what this is really about?'

A chilly feeling ran through Tom. 'I don't know what you mean.'

'Yes you do,' said Molly. 'I saw your face when you walked in. You looked… determined in a way I've never seen before. Then you saw me and you looked shocked.' Gently she touched his temple. 'There's something going on in there. Do you want me to leave so you can talk to Mum and Dad?'

Her perspicacity took him by surprise, but only for a moment. Of all his sisters, Molly had always been the one most able to see through to the heart of the matter.

'Yes, go – please. No – stay.'

'Are you sure?'

'The honest answer,' said Tom, 'is that I don't know. But stay anyway.'

Molly leaned against him. 'Love you, Thomas Benjamin Watson,' she whispered.

He kissed her hair. 'Love you too, Margaret Louise Abrams.'

Standing up, he offered her his hand. She took it and they went downstairs together. In the parlour, Tom waited for Molly to be seated. For his own part, he didn't know whether to sit down or stay standing. Ought he to stand so as to show the importance of what he was about to say? No, you stood when you were proud and he definitely wasn't that. Mum was sitting on one end of the sofa; Tom took the other end.

'You look serious, son,' said Dad.

Tom inhaled slowly and pushed out a silent breath. His heart drummed in his chest.

'I've got something to tell you.' He had to stop. The words wouldn't come.

'Do you want to talk to your father man to man?' asked Mum.

'No, it's something I want all three of you to know. It's to do with the war.' Again he stopped. His jaw was clamped so tightly that it felt as though it would take a chisel to force his mouth open again.

There was a silence in which he was aware of the others looking at one another.

'Tom, I don't know if this is the right thing to say,' Molly began, 'but I had a conversation with Mum some time back. It was last year – when I was still engaged to Norris. Do you remember, Mum? You said that everyone who came back from the war came home with something or without something. Is that what this is about, Tom?'

With something or without something.

This was his now or never moment. Stumbling at first, Tom talked. Spoke the truth. Owned up to the lies and omissions in his letters from the front. He didn't look at their faces. He didn't want to see the shock, the disappointment. He couldn't bear to see in their expressions how he had let them down.

He talked of the regulation eighteen-year-olds with missing limbs, bandaged eyes, crushed bones; the stench of blood and entrails and gangrene; those that died in agony, the lives that slipped away; the nurse who had spat in his face.

'No,' Mum whispered. 'Oh, no,' and she moved along the sofa, arms out, wanting to hold him in her embrace, but somehow that was too much; it was all too much; and Tom practically toppled over into her lap, his head pounding with the voices of the men and boys who in their darkest moments had cried out for their mothers. Now here he was, needing his own mother as much as any of those soldiers had needed theirs. She gathered him in her arms and leaned over to kiss the side of his head, murmuring, 'Oh, Tom, my Tom, my boy.'

And here was Molly, kneeling on the floor in front of him, her arms around him; and Dad, beside Molly, his strong arms around her and Mum, holding them all together with Tom in the middle.

Tom's body heaved as he sobbed, for himself, for his sorrows and regrets, for every man he had seen on the ambulance train. It wasn't dignified. It wasn't manly.

But perhaps it was the beginning of healing.

Tom didn't sleep that night. His mind was alert and crisp. It shocked him to think he had shared his experiences with his family. He had never imagined for one moment he would do that and now he had told Jess, his parents and his favourite sister. Having Molly there had helped, because she had come home from her war work in London burdened by her own secret, which she had hugged to herself in secret longing and shame until last year, when events – or, more accurately, her former fiancé – had pushed her into opening up to Mum, Dad and Tom. Until this weekend, Tom had seen Molly's wartime secret as something that filled him with love and concern for her; but during the long hours of that night, he began to see it in a different way. Maybe it was time to seek strength and solace from knowing he wasn't the only Watson to have suffered.

Strength and solace. That was what he needed. That was what he had to concentrate on – probably for the rest of his life. He longed for a normal life with a wife and family of his own, so it was up to him to focus on strength and solace. He had to make this right, not just for himself but for Jess if he intended to marry her, which he most certainly did, and for the children he hoped they would have together. To be the best husband and father it was within his power to be, he had to find strength and solace.

It wouldn't be easy. It would never be easy. The memories were too horrific for that. He knew they would never loosen their grip, so it was up to him to change the way he thought of himself. Above all else, he had to try to listen and accept when the people he treasured most in the world told him he had done his duty with steadfastness and honour. Did he believe them? In his head, he could see their point of view, but his heart and his sense of self had other ideas. Would he ever see himself as Mum and Dad saw him, as Molly saw him, most of all as his darling Jess saw him? Maybe, maybe not. At the moment, it felt like a definite 'not', but the simple fact that he wanted to stop seeing himself as a coward was a revelation.

Strength and solace. And Jess. A life with her was worth fighting for.

Chapter Thirty-Six

ON SUNDAY MORNING, Vivienne was concerned to see Jess looking hollow-eyed.

'Didn't you sleep?' she asked.

'Not much,' Jess admitted. 'I couldn't get comfortable. I think the bumps and bruises are starting to come out.'

'You should stay at home this morning,' said Miss Patience, 'and not attend church.'

'There's nothing wrong with me,' said Jess. 'I'm a bit stiff, that's all. Besides, I don't want to miss hearing your banns being read for the third time.'

'You need to rest,' Miss Patience said firmly. 'No arguments.'

'I'll stay at home with you,' said Vivienne, 'and go to evening service.'

Between them, she and Miss Patience settled Jess on the sofa with her feet up and several cushions supporting her back, her lower body covered by a woollen blanket.

'There's really no need,' Jess tried to tell them.

'Let yourself be looked after,' said Vivienne.

After the Miss Heskeths had departed for church, Vivienne made tea and settled down for a chat.

'I'm not surprised you didn't get much sleep,' she said.

'I suppose it was a mixture of physical discomfort and the realisation of what you did.'

Jess wriggled more upright. 'Yes to both, but there was something else as well. Can I tell you something?'

'Of course. We're friends.'

'It's Tom Watson.'

'It makes me shiver to imagine what he did yesterday. He showed such courage.'

'That's true. He did,' said Jess. 'But that isn't what I want to say – or maybe it is, in a way, because it's a place to start. When we were up there on the helter-skelter, after the children had been rescued and sent down the slope to safety, something happened that I didn't mention yesterday. The part of the slide where we were shook and – and I fell off the edge, but Tom grabbed me.'

'My goodness,' Vivienne breathed. 'That man deserves a medal. You must have been terrified.'

'I was, but don't let's dwell on that, because it isn't the important part.'

'I can't begin to imagine what's more important than that.'

'I've liked Tom for some time, but I was sure nothing could ever come of it – but that last incident on the helter-skelter changed all that.'

Vivienne felt a shiver of surprise and pleasure. 'You – and Tom? Does he feel the same?'

'Yes, he does.' Jess's face glowed with happiness.

Vivienne left her chair and went to perch beside Jess on the edge on the sofa, leaning forward to give her a hug. 'That's wonderful news. You are two of my favourite people and I'm delighted for you. Am I the first to know?'

'Yes. Please don't say a word. I don't want to steal Miss Patience's thunder just before her wedding.'

'My lips are sealed,' Vivienne promised, 'except to say that I'm honoured to be allowed to know.'

'You've been a good friend to me,' said Jess. 'I wanted to tell you. Besides, I was dying to talk about it.'

'Oho, so if I hadn't been here, you'd have told next door's cat.'

'I've always found Ginger to be a very good listener.' Jess's eyes twinkled, but then she pressed her lips together. 'The trouble is, what about my job? I've worked so hard to get where I am. At last I've found the perfect job – just like you being the superintendent at the orphanage.'

'And it coincides with meeting Tom,' said Vivienne, understanding at once.

'Exactly. I love Holly Lodge and it's even better now that Mr Thorpe isn't hounding me. I can't wait for the residents to move in. But then there's Tom. He means so much to me, but – I know how bad this sounds – but getting together with him couldn't have happened at a worse time.'

'Are you worried you've made the wrong decision?' Vivienne asked. She spoke gently, trying to take the sting out of the question.

'No. Absolutely not. I've never felt more sure of anything than I have of the rightness of being with Tom Watson, but... I can't bear to think of losing my job because of it.'

'Mr Peters will dismiss you the moment he hears,' Vivienne said soberly.

'It shouldn't be like this,' Jess exclaimed, her voice rising. 'I'm perfectly capable of doing my job and having a relationship at the same time.'

'You know that and I know that,' said Vivienne wryly, 'but Mr Peters is a man and men don't see it the same way.'

'It's not just men,' said Jess. 'The world in general thinks that married women have no business going out to work unless they're so poor that they have no choice.'

'Married?' Vivienne lifted her eyebrows.

'Well, frankly – yes.'

'You really have made up your mind, haven't you? And Tom?'

'I know he feels the same. Neither of us is the sort for dalliances.'

Vivienne sighed, sharing her friend's distress and frustration. 'What a dilemma.'

'With bells on,' said Jess.

As Vivienne turned the corner into Soapsuds Lane on Sunday afternoon, the door to Soapsuds House opened and Aaron and Danny emerged, clad in jackets and caps. Then Molly appeared, standing on the doorstep, arms wrapped across the front of her blue dress and cardie as she saw her menfolk off. Danny spotted Vivienne and waved, which made his parents look round. Vivienne picked up her pace.

'Where are you off to?' she asked Danny.

His blue eyes were bright in his narrow, oval face. 'We're collecting some of the lads from St Nicholas's to go onto the meadows for races and French cricket.'

Aaron kissed Molly's cheek. 'See you later, love.' He stepped aside to let Vivienne into the house. 'C'mon, son.'

Aaron and Danny set off. Molly shut the door and smiled at Vivienne.

'It does my heart good to see them together,' said Molly. 'They adore one another. Give me your coat and go through.'

It wasn't long before they were settled with cups of tea beside them.

'Tell me all about yesterday,' said Molly.

'I will, with the greatest pleasure,' said Vivienne, 'though you have to keep quiet about it for now, until the children know.'

Molly drew in a soft breath and her greeny-hazel eyes shone. 'You haven't...'

'I have.'

'Been appointed the new superintendent? That's marvellous. Congratulations. Tell me everything. I imagine La Wardle gave you a hard time.'

'Definitely.'

Molly grimaced. 'That's one thing I don't envy you – having to deal with her swanning onto the premises whenever she feels like it.'

Vivienne laughed. 'Ah, that's the best bit.'

'Better than your being appointed?' teased Molly.

'Nothing's better than that. Just wait until you hear what happened to the mighty Mrs Wardle.'

'Start at the beginning. I want to hear all about your interview and the assembly. Much as I want to hear about Mrs Wardle, I'm far more interested in you.'

Vivienne described the interview and her assembly.

'It sounds like it went very well,' commented Molly. 'Clever old you.'

After that came the final contest between Vivienne and Miss Boodle followed by the routing of Mrs Wardle, which Molly listened to with ever-widening eyes until she and Vivienne ended up howling with laughter. When Vivienne stopped because her sides were aching, Molly's continued laughter set her off once more.

When they had exhausted themselves, there was a short, happy silence.

'Mr Lowe and Mrs Rostron are telling the staff about my appointment. It will take a while because of shifts. The children won't be told until Tuesday after tea, so please don't say anything to Danny before then.'

'I won't, but I will tell Aaron, if you don't mind. He won't pass it on.'

'I know. I wouldn't dream of asking you to keep a secret from your husband.'

Molly gave her a beaming smile. 'This is the most wonderful news and I'm proud of you. My friend, the superintendent of St Nicholas's. Danny will be chuffed to bits when he hears.' She sighed happily. 'That's made this weekend perfect – and now we have next weekend and the wedding to look forward to.'

Chapter Thirty-Seven

P RUDENCE LAY AWAKE, thinking of Jonty. She didn't often think of him. She had taught herself years ago not to. Back then, she had believed he had let her down in the worst possible way. In the turn her life had taken, there had been no room for thoughts of him. They would have been a waste of time. She had needed to concentrate on her own situation and that of her unborn child. Allowing herself to dwell on Jonty would have made her weak and that was the one thing she couldn't afford to be.

But now, in the days leading up to Patience's wedding, the old memories were inevitably resurfacing and Prudence found they were no longer as painful as they had once been. For one thing, she now had a strong and lasting relationship with Vivienne, the daughter she had been forced to give up and whom she had never expected to see again. Moreover, thanks to Niall, she now knew that Jonty hadn't been the out and out cad she had for so long believed him to be. Did that make his initial abandonment of her less serious? Did it soften her heart towards him? No to both. She had assigned him to a frozen part of her heart thirty years ago, and there he remained, as if she had put him in a box and closed the lid on him.

Now, though, she opened the box and took out the memories to have a look at them; to have a look at Jonty, yes, and at herself too, that younger self who had been so deeply, so recklessly in love that she had thrown all social caution, all morals, to the four winds. She had believed Jonty had loved her every bit as much as she had loved him. What a fool she had been. What an easy target.

And what a swine he had been, using her like that, taking advantage of an innocent girl's first love. He might have felt wretched about it later and changed his mind, losing his life in the process, but that didn't stop his having been an utter swine in the first place, when she'd needed him most.

Jonathan Henderson. Handsome, charming, with a twinkle in his eyes, and a featherlight touch that had made her tingle all over. He had turned her into a new person. Then his departure, and her having to part with her new baby, had turned her into another person again. Or not exactly a new person, but back into the Prudence she had always been – serious, determined, critical – only more so. More serious, more judgemental, less tolerant. She had spent the greater part of her life being that person, that version of herself.

Now, Vivienne had been restored to her and she knew that the hardness inside her was gradually softening. That was what Vivienne had done for her. She had created the beginning of a softening.

No, not softening. Healing.

Jess hadn't seen Tom for a few days. Much as she longed to be with him, she knew she had to give him time to speak with his family and think about his life and his past... and his future. Oh, how she wanted to be a part of that future. The first step was for Tom to accept his past.

On Wednesday, Abigail arrived at Holly Lodge after her school dinner, full of excitement at the news that Mrs Rostron was leaving St Nicholas's and the new superintendent was going to be Mrs Atwood.

Jess didn't like to say she already knew. She smiled at Abigail's delight. 'Are you pleased?'

'I'm not pleased that Mrs Rostron is leaving, but I'm glad about Mrs Atwood. Everyone is. We all like her. She's helped some of the children, so we know her. She thought of changing the name to St Nicholas's too.'

'I hope all the children are as delighted as you are,' said Jess.

Abigail's face fell. 'It won't make much difference to me. I won't be there to see it. Mrs Rostron is leaving at the end of May, so I'll have just a few weeks of Mrs Atwood before I have to leave at the end of August.'

Was that a flicker of fear in her eyes? Jess wanted to throw her arms around the girl and hug her. If only she could promise her a job here at Holly Lodge, along with a bedroom on the top floor, but she didn't dare so much as hint. Such an offer was not in her gift.

Later on, when Mr Jones's workmen left, Jess and Abigail walked around the various rooms, seeing what had been done. Glancing from a window, Jess saw Tom coming along the road.

She turned to Abigail. 'You may leave now.'

'It isn't time yet,' said Abigail.

'I won't dock your pay. Off you go.'

When the girl left the house, Tom held the gate open for her, though his gaze was on Jess at the door. Jess was almost breathless with delight to see him. When he walked up the steps and into the house, she shut the door and then found herself in his arms.

'I've missed you,' Tom murmured.

'I haven't exactly been hiding away,' she said lightly.

'I know,' said Tom, his eyes serious. 'I wanted to stay away until my head cleared. Then I realised it might never clear, not the way I'd like it to, so here I am.'

'Muddled head and all.'

'Muddled head and all,' Tom agreed.

'Did you tell your family?'

Tom nodded. 'Don't ask if it helped because I still feel too overwhelmed by it to think about it closely.'

'You did it,' Jess said softly. 'That's what matters. You're so brave.' She held him tight. 'You've suffered so much.'

'No, I haven't. Not like all the injured men you see out and about.'

'There are different kinds of suffering. One thing we do know now about war and fighting is that it can leave terrible scars on the mind.'

'You can't call what happened to me shellshock.'

'Maybe not,' said Jess, 'but it was war-shock. It was heart-shock.'

Letting her go, Tom glanced away, but not before Jess had glimpsed the sheen of tears in his eyes.

'There's something I want you to know – something I need you to know,' said Tom. 'When Perkins and Watson pulled out of the work here – when *I* pulled out, it wasn't because of other work. It was because I couldn't bear the possibility of meeting war veterans. When I thought it would just be old soldiers, I felt I could cope with that, with old men who'd fought in long-ago wars. But coming face to face with men who served in the war in which I...'

Jess's heart swelled with love and sorrow. Not pity, but honest sorrow. 'I understand.'

'And I know my decision ended up making life harder for you. Thorpe wouldn't have been able to lord it over you in the same way if I'd been here. I'm sorry that happened.'

'Not your fault,' Jess said softly.

'No?'

'No. Just Mr Thorpe's fault for being an arrogant twerp.' She reached for Tom's hand. 'Let me show you the work Mr Jones's men have been doing.'

Tom was happy to be shown round. 'The men who live here will be lucky to have such a spacious and well-appointed home. Jones is making a good job of it.'

'Each bedroom is a decent size and there's a bathroom on each floor,' said Jess. 'It's just that when the house opens, I wonder whether I'll still be here to see everyone settling in. There's always been a question mark over whether I'm going to be kept on. Now, though, there's a socking great "but". Not only am I female, but I'm about to start walking out with a man – and that will be the biggest "but" of all in Mr Peters' eyes.'

Chapter Thirty-Eight

PRUDENCE WOKE EARLY on Easter Saturday. She peeped through the curtains onto a bright day of light-blue skies that Patience would probably have called forget-me-not. Well, Patience could be as fanciful and romantic as she liked today and Prudence would support her at every turn, doing everything she could to ensure her sister enjoyed the perfect wedding day. Prudence had felt unsettled on and off all week, knowing that these were the final days of living together in the old way, but she hadn't said anything. Above all else, she hadn't wanted to spoil anything for Patience, who had acquired a radiant glow of quiet happiness. Dear Patience. She had waited such a long time for this.

The house was quiet. Prudence dressed in a plain skirt and blouse and hung her new dress from the top of the wardrobe door. Then she went downstairs to unbolt the front door. That had been one of her daily tasks ever since Pa had abdicated all responsibility for domestic matters. Going into the kitchen, she found Vivienne, wrapped in a dressing gown with a tie-belt and embroidered lapels, preparing tea.

Vivienne looked round. 'Oh, you've come down, I was going to bring everyone tea in bed.'

The old Prudence would have scorned such luxury, but the new Prudence took control and smiled. 'You still can. I'll sit in Patience's room.'

Vivienne laughed. 'I don't mean tea in separate beds. I mean all piling into my double together. Actually, it's a good thing you're up and dressed. Now there'll be enough space for Miss Patience, Jess and me, and you can sit in the wicker chair. Much more dignified.'

A few minutes later, the four of them were in Vivienne's room, with Patience, still in her hairnet, in between the two girls in Pa's old bed.

'Make the most of this, Miss Patience,' said Jess. 'It'll be the one quiet moment of the day. Things will soon get busy.'

'I hope everything goes smoothly,' said Patience. 'I hope everyone has a good day.'

'Today of all days,' decreed Vivienne, 'you should be thinking about yourself, not everyone else.'

'The day Patience doesn't think about everyone else,' said Prudence, 'we'll know we've got an imposter on our hands.'

'Jess and I will see to the breakfast and the washing up,' said Vivienne. 'Miss Patience, you must take your time getting ready. We'll help you get dressed and do your hair.'

'It's really happening, isn't it?' said Patience. She laughed, the sound containing a mixture of nerves and joy.

'Yes, it is,' said Prudence.

Patience looked at her and Prudence returned the look with affection.

When Jess and Vivienne rolled out of bed and disappeared downstairs with the tea-tray, Prudence went to sit on the bed.

'This should have happened thirty years ago,' she said.

'It's happening now.' Patience took her hand. 'That's what matters.'

'Wait there.'

Prudence freed her hand and left the room. In her bedroom, she opened her dressing table drawer and took out the small box that had lived there ever since Mother's death. She took it back to Vivienne's room and handed it to Patience.

'Here. I want you to have this.'

Patience didn't need to open the box. 'To wear for the wedding? Thank you, Prudence. That's very thoughtful. You know how I love it.'

'Yes, I do – and I don't mean you to wear it just for today. I mean you to have it for keeps. Pa only gave it to me because I'm older than you. If he'd had a shred of common sense, he'd have given it to you, because you always loved pretty things and jewellery even when you were a child.'

'Oh, Prudence, are you sure?' Patience took the lid from the box to reveal Mother's cameo brooch.

'Positive,' said Prudence. 'I should have handed it over years ago, but I didn't because I'm the older sister and I thought that made it mine, but how often do I wear it? I'm not a jewellery sort of person. Mother's brooch isn't to do with who was born first. It's to do with which of us will derive the most use and pleasure from it – and we both know that was never me. So take it, please, with my love and warmest wishes.'

To her surprise, Patience handed it back to her.

'Wear it today,' she said. 'To please me, and then give it to me afterwards. I think that's the right thing to do.'

The house was busy. The old Prudence hated it and, truth be told, the new Prudence wasn't enamoured of it either. She didn't care for fuss and noise; she hated to feel she wasn't in control of every little thing. But whereas the old Prudence would have been thin-lipped and scornful and probably rather ratty, the new Prudence tried hard to take it in her stride.

The bridesmaids had arrived. Vicky, Niall's eldest

daughter, had brought the four oldest granddaughters, of whom the youngest two were apparently only six years old. To Prudence's eyes, they looked too small to be relied upon, but she forbore to say so. Vicky and Leonora had been in charge of decking them out appropriately and they wore light-pink dresses with headbands of silk rosebuds. Bonnie, Niall's youngest and only unmarried daughter, was also a bridesmaid and she wore a pale-green dress with a hip-sash, the skirt fashioned into scalloped layers.

One of the smallest bridesmaids gazed up at Prudence. 'Are you our new granny?'

Vicky and Bonnie both swooped on the child.

'No, Maisie, this is your Great-aunt Prudence. She is your new granny's sister, just like Evie and Clara are your sisters. Now, come and sit down and keep your dress perfect.'

Prudence retreated to her bedroom to get ready, deciding it might not be a bad idea to take her time over it. There was a light knock on the door and Vivienne came in, looking lovely in a scoop-necked dress of hazy blue with an overskirt of embroidered net.

'Hiding?' There was a twinkle in Vivienne's eyes.

'Getting dressed,' Prudence replied in a prim voice.

'Shall I help?'

'Go and make a fuss of Patience. This is her day.'

Vivienne sat on the bed. 'It's a big day for you too, in a completely different way.'

A sigh built up inside Prudence. It seemed to start in the floorboards beneath her feet and work its way up until it reached her lungs. She took a deep breath and slowly released it. That wasn't like her. She wasn't given to sighing. Sighing looked like self-pity.

'Once Patience has left,' she said, 'Lawrence will be champing at the bit, wanting to move in. I'm surprised he hasn't been round here on a regular basis, demanding to know how soon the house will be available.'

'I was preoccupied with my interview at St Nicholas's before,' said Vivienne, 'but now that I know I'm staying in Chorlton indefinitely, you and I must find somewhere else to live.'

A blockage appeared in Prudence's throat and she couldn't answer. In any case, what was there to say?

'We'll manage everything together,' said Vivienne.

Prudence made an effort. 'Yes, we'll face it together.' She had to hang onto that thought. How much worse it would be if she had to face it alone. She forced herself to brighten. 'Enough of that. Today we must concentrate on Patience.'

Vivienne stood and hugged her. 'We'll give her the best send-off we can.'

Prudence arrived at St Clement's to find that Evelyn had bagged the front row on the bride's side. Peering up the aisle from the church door, Prudence could see that on one side of Evelyn was Felicity and on the other was a space for Lawrence.

'Flaming cheek,' Vivienne murmured in Prudence's ear. 'It should be you at the front. You're Miss Patience's nearest relation and the two of you have always lived together.'

'Shall we wrench Mrs Hesketh out of the pew?' Jess whispered, her cheeky suggestion defusing the situation.

'Leave her be,' said Prudence. 'She and Lawrence would probably melt away and disappear if they couldn't have pride of place.'

From outside church came a squeal.

'Aunt Prudence!'

'Lucy!' Prudence exclaimed, smiling at the sight of her

pretty dark-haired niece and her husband. 'My dear girl, how are you?'

'All the better for being here to see Auntie Patience getting married,' said Lucy, letting go of Dickie's arm so she could kiss Prudence's cheek. 'After today I won't be the new bride of the family.'

'This is Jess Mason,' said Prudence. 'She's our pupil-lodger and she has the boxroom.' She turned to Jess. 'May I introduce Dickie and Lucy Bambrook. Lucy is my niece. She lived with us in Wilton Close for a while last year.'

'And I had the boxroom,' said Lucy. 'How do you do?'

Jess shook hands.

Vivienne kissed Lucy. 'Who's looking after Charlie? Did you bring him with you from Italy?'

'We're staying with Dickie's parents,' said Lucy. 'The doting grandmother has got him for the day.'

'Lucy,' said Prudence, 'your mother is sitting in the front pew, if you want to join her.'

'Trust her,' said Lucy cheerfully. 'We'll sit behind with you, Aunt Prudence.'

'You two go and take your places,' said Prudence. 'I'll join you in a minute.'

She watched Lucy and Dickie head up the aisle, then turned towards the church path, where Molly, Aaron and Danny had come through the gates. After greetings had been exchanged all round, Prudence said quietly to Molly and Aaron, 'Lucy's inside.'

Molly nodded. 'We knew she was coming.'

'I don't want things to be awkward,' said Prudence. 'Do you think you should say hello in church or save it for the reception?'

'We'll wait for the reception,' said Aaron. 'We don't want anything to distract from the pleasure of the wedding.'

'Here's Miss Kirby,' said Vivienne.

Prudence went down the path to meet her long-time friend. 'Good morning, Miss Kirby. Isn't it a beautiful day? You'll sit with Vivienne and Jess in the church, won't you?'

'Yes, please do.' Vivienne linked arms with her. 'Oh – do you mind waiting one moment, Miss Kirby? Here are Belinda and Gabriel.'

Miss Kirby smiled. 'I'm always happy to see Belinda. She's rather a favourite of mine.'

Almost immediately after Belinda and Gabriel joined them, Niall's daughters and their families arrived and the girls all greeted Prudence. There were introductions all round. Prudence couldn't help watching, though she tried not to be obvious about it, as Vivienne met her cousins for the first time. It brought home the deception they lived with. For the sake of Prudence's reputation as a respectable lady, Niall would never tell his family how his late brother had abandoned her and how she had subsequently had Vivienne.

Was this difficult for Vivienne? Did she wish she could be an acknowledged part of the Henderson family at this wedding? Certainly, seeing all the Henderson girls made Prudence long to give public recognition to her dear daughter, but she knew it was impossible. For her, a spinster, to announce such a thing to the world was unthinkable. Both she and Vivienne would be made to suffer as a result.

Niall arrived and laughed at finding so many of them outside. That was the signal for everyone to go into church and take their places. Prudence sat beside Lucy, feeling proud of the girl for having the gumption to come home for the wedding even though the original plan had been for her and Dickie to remain in Italy for a year so as to blur everyone's memories regarding the dates of their wedding and their son's birthday.

The organ, which had been playing softly in the

background, stopped and the guests ceased their chatting. At the opening strains of 'Here Comes the Bride', everyone rose to their feet. Prudence found her heart beating quickly. She watched as, with a faint flush in her cheeks, Patience walked up the aisle on Lawrence's arm, followed by the bridesmaids.

The vicar bade the congregation be seated and the service began. As it proceeded, Prudence felt deeply moved, touched by the sense of happiness that radiated from Patience and Niall and also by the looks of pleasure on the faces of the Henderson girls. Patience was undoubtedly going to find a warm welcome in her new family.

After the ceremony, Prudence followed the happy couple into the vestry to sign the register as Patience's witness. Then she and Vicky, who was her father's witness, returned to their places and everybody stood up ready for the new Mr and Mrs Henderson to walk down the aisle.

Outside, the photographer was waiting and then it was time to go to the reception, which was being held at the Lloyds Hotel, less than a five-minute walk away. A motor car took Niall and Patience while all the rest ambled up the road, chatting.

Inside the Lloyds, Patience and Niall stood at the door to their reception room to greet their guests.

'Come along, girls,' Evelyn said to her daughters. 'We should be first.'

'There's something Lucy has to do first,' Prudence said firmly, ignoring her sister-in-law's outraged expression. She drew Lucy and Dickie over to Molly and Aaron. 'I want everyone to be happy today. I'd hate for past experiences to cast a cloud.'

'There's no awkwardness as far as I'm concerned,' Molly said, smiling at Lucy. 'As much as it hurt at the time that you didn't let us adopt Charlie, I'm the last person to criticise a girl for not giving up her baby. I'm glad for you, Lucy – truly. And…' She laid a hand on her stomach.

Lucy's face lit up. 'Congratulations. I'm so pleased. When?'

Prudence left them to it and went to join the reception line. When Niall and Patience greeted her, they both kissed her.

'When we've welcomed everyone,' said Niall, 'we'd like a word with you and Vivienne. Left to my own devices, I would have saved it until later on, but after I told Patience on our way here in the motor, she said we must tell you as soon as possible.'

What could it be? If nothing else, it gave Prudence something to think about as she went through the uncomfortable business of making small talk with her fellow guests. 'Doing the polite', as Mother used to call it, had never been one of her strong points.

Presently Niall and Patience appeared by her side, with Vivienne in tow.

'Let's go somewhere private,' said Niall. 'I've arranged for us to use an office for a few minutes.'

He held open the door for them and they entered a small room containing a desk and chairs and filing cabinets. A large noticeboard was attached to one wall, with various lists pinned to it.

'What's this about?' Prudence asked as she, Patience and Vivienne all sat down.

Niall remained standing. There was a big smile on his face. 'Patience and I have got some news for you to do with the house in Wilton Close.'

Prudence suppressed a groan of pain. 'I was hoping very much not to be reminded of that today.'

Patience leaned towards her and touched her hand. 'Just wait. It's good news, I promise.'

'After your brother announced his intention of moving into the house after the wedding,' said Niall, 'I got in touch with him and – well, to cut out all the unnecessary details, I've bought the house from him.'

Prudence's hand flew to her chest. There was a dazed look on Vivienne's face.

'You've done what?' whispered Vivienne.

'I've purchased the house in Wilton Close, which means that Lawrence and Evelyn can look around for a property to buy, as befits Lawrence's exalted status as an alderman, and you – you can stay put.'

Prudence couldn't speak. She struggled to take it in. After all the worry and the fear since the reading of Pa's will, Niall had restored her to her proper place. She would be able to feel safe again. No wonder Lawrence hadn't been hounding her for a moving out date. He had known he would be able to choose a place to buy.

'You have always looked after me, Prudence,' said Patience. 'You shouldered the responsibility and made the decisions. Now I feel happy and proud that Niall can do something for you in return.'

'Not just Niall,' said her husband. 'This is from both of us.'

Patience smiled up at him, her love for him making her pale-blue eyes shine.

'You've bought the house so that we can stay there,' said Vivienne.

'There's more to it than that,' said Niall. 'The house will be mine for only as long as it takes to have ownership transferred to the two of you jointly.'

'To…?' breathed Vivienne.

'Yes, to both of you,' Niall confirmed. 'Prudence, you are my wife's sister and you are the daughter of the lady who used to own the house. It is right and proper that the house should belong to you now. Vivienne, you are my late brother's daughter. Before you were born, I offered to make provision for you and now I have the opportunity to do so. Please don't refuse, either of you. It is my privilege to do this for you.'

Standing up, Vivienne moved into his arms. Prudence didn't get up. She wasn't sure if her legs would have supported her.

Niall released Vivienne. 'We'll leave you to talk it over.'

As the door closed behind him and Patience, Vivienne turned to Prudence with shining eyes.

'We can stay,' said Vivienne. 'We can *stay*.'

'It's ours,' said Prudence. 'I can scarcely believe it.' Tears sprang into her eyes. 'It's *ours*. Yours and mine.'

'Not that we can ever announce it to the world,' said Vivienne, 'but it's a legal acknowledgement of a link between you and me.'

'The house originally belonged to my mother,' Prudence said wonderingly, 'and she was your grandmother.'

'Now Jess can stay on if she needs to.'

'And we can invite Miss Kirby to lodge with us, and she can become a tutor in the business school.'

'Since she's retired and is at home during the day,' said Vivienne, 'the school could offer some daytime lessons and that would mean you wouldn't have to teach five evenings a week.'

Prudence nodded. That would be a relief. 'Miss Kirby can have Patience's old room.'

'No, we'll offer her my room, the biggest room, and I'll move into Miss Patience's room. That way, Miss Kirby will have plenty of space for her things and she'll feel welcome.'

Prudence surprised herself by laughing. She didn't laugh as freely as other people. 'Perhaps we should invite her before we make any more plans involving her.' She stood up. Strength poured through her. 'Oh, Vivienne.'

'Yes?' Vivienne asked.

'Nothing,' said Prudence. 'Just – oh, Vivienne.'

Chapter Thirty-Nine

J ESS HAD TO leave the wedding reception early because of
going to Oak Lodge to see Mr Peters. She said her goodbyes and thanked the happy couple for their hospitality and
wished them well. As she walked across the foyer and out of
the front doors, she felt an unpleasant fluttering in the pit of
her stomach, but her nerves vanished like morning mist in the
sunshine at the sight of Tom waiting for her outside.

'I thought I'd escort you,' he said.

'I'm glad to see you,' said Jess.

They linked arms and set off for the bus stop.

'How was the wedding?' Tom asked.

Jess told him about it, happy to re-live the occasion.

'Molly has always said what a lovely lady Miss Patience
is,' said Tom.

They caught the bus to Seymour Grove and walked along
Whalley Road past the large houses behind their garden
walls nearly to the far end, where Oak Lodge stood. The
front garden, which Jess had first seen in winter-time, now
presented a gentler appearance, with pretty primulas and,
over to one side, a carpet of anemones in white and lilac.

Jess paused in the gateway, about to say goodbye to Tom,
but he forestalled her.

'I'm coming in with you. I'll chat with the old boys while
you see Mr Peters.'

They walked past a flourishing viburnum with fragrant pompoms of palest pink and made for the steps up to the front door. Tom rang the bell. Rose answered it, looking surprised to see Jess with a man.

'This is Mr Watson of Perkins and Watson, the builders,' said Jess. 'He's come to meet the old soldiers.'

'Good afternoon,' said Tom.

'Are you expected, sir?' asked Rose.

'I'm afraid not,' said Tom, 'but I hope no one will mind.'

He smiled at the maid and Jess saw the moment when Rose softened. She stood aside to let them in.

'Mr Peters is occupied at present, Miss Mason. He asked if you would wait in the residents' sitting room.'

'Of course,' said Jess.

It was always a pleasure to be with the old soldiers and it would give her the chance to introduce Tom. She led him into the room, with its sturdy chairs that were easy to get up from. Over to one side was a table with today's newspapers on it as well as a couple of magnifying glasses.

'Well, well, look who's come to see us, gentlemen,' said Captain Styles. 'Good afternoon, Miss Mason. It looks like you've brought a friend with you. We're doing well for company today, aren't we, chaps?'

To her dismay, Jess saw Mr Thorpe, looking quite at home, chatting to a couple of old soldiers. Then she realised Zachary Milner, the fire extinguisher man, and his fiancée, Nurse Nancy from the orphanage, were there too.

'Milner!' said Tom. As Zachary came across to shake hands, Tom explained to Jess, 'Milner's shop is just along the road from where Molly lives.'

'Small world,' said Jess, smiling at Nancy.

'You're the lady from Holly Lodge,' said Nancy.

'This is my fiancée, Miss Nancy Pike,' Zachary said proudly.

'I know,' said Jess, smiling at Nancy as the two girls shook hands. 'Mr Milner pointed you out to me through a window when he came to Holly Lodge.'

'Now then, what's all this?' cried one of the old men. 'You haven't come here to hobnob with one another. You're meant to be visiting us old 'uns.'

There was some laughter and Zachary bore Tom away to introduce him round. That was a relief in a way. It saved Jess from having to parry arch questions. Tom soon settled in for a good chinwag with a couple of old boys. It did Jess's heart good to see it and an idea popped into her head. If Tom could build a relationship with these dear old soldiers, might there one day be a friendship with one of them that was solid enough and went deep enough for him to confide his wartime experiences and receive understanding and support in return? No matter how much Tom was loved by Jess and his family, they could never truly comprehend what he had gone through. But the understanding of another soldier…

Maybe one day.

Captain Wingate and some of his cronies quizzed Jess about the progress that was being made at Holly Lodge. She smiled and told them all about it, but inside she felt jumpy. Was she telling them about something that would shortly turn out to be nothing to do with her any longer? Would she still be the manager of Holly Lodge when she left this building? Was that why Mr Thorpe was here? Because she had been such a trial to him and Mr Peters thought he was entitled to see her receive her marching orders? Even if Mr Peters wanted to keep her on, how long would it last? He wouldn't want a married manager. Not that Tom had proposed, but Jess didn't kid herself about the strength of the feeling between them. Much as she loved and valued Tom and looked forward to their future together, it would hurt dreadfully to have to give up her beloved job. She so wanted to welcome the new residents to Holly Lodge and be responsible for their welfare.

Presently Mr Peters entered the room, holding the door for Mrs Peters, who pushed in a wheeled tea-trolley. A quiet rumble of pleasure greeted its arrival. Nancy, who was obviously an old hand at this, immediately went to help Mrs Peters. Jess too helped serve the tea and cake, sharing a secret glance with Tom as she brought him a cup of tea.

'There's cherry cake and shortbread,' she told him.

'Shortbread for me, please. It's my favourite.'

'I'll remember that,' Jess murmured, feeling a little thrill of delight.

When most people had finished their first cup, Mrs Peters looked round the room. 'There's more in the pot if anybody would care for another.'

Mr Peters caught Jess's eye. 'Shall we leave everyone to finish their tea? I'll see you in my office now.'

Nerves churned in Jess's tummy as she stood up. In the next five minutes, she would know whether Mr Peters thought her worth keeping on. She followed him to the office and took a seat in front of his desk. He sat down and straightened a few things in front of him, although the desk looked perfectly tidy to Jess. Was he putting off giving her the bad news?

He looked up. 'Well, here we are. I said I'd give you until Easter to prove yourself.'

'Yes, sir.'

'It won't be much longer before Holly Lodge is ready to open. Knowing you, I imagine you have plans in mind.'

So this was how it was to be. Mr Peters was treating it more or less as an interview. How formal. Why couldn't he just tell her?

'For an official opening, yes,' said Jess, 'but not until the early summer. I thought it would be kinder to let the residents settle in first. Some of them will be elderly and the move will take it out of them, and the younger soldiers might have other reasons to feel fragile. But once they are settled and happy, I'd like to – that is,' she added, not wanting to seem to take anything for granted, 'I believe that a little garden party would be a good idea. The Oak Lodge men could come and we could – that is, the neighbours could be invited as well as relatives.'

Mr Peters nodded. Was he storing her ideas to hand over to the new male manager? Oh well, in for a penny.

'There's one more thing, sir.' Even if her own job was in jeopardy, she could still pave the way for Abigail. 'Abigail Hunter.'

Mr Peters frowned. 'Oh yes, the orphan you took on.'

'Yes, sir. She's very capable and willing. She's not afraid to get her hands dirty. I wondered whether there might be a place for her on the staff.'

'A capable and willing girl, eh? We'll see. It will, of course, be the duty of the manager to assist me in appointing members of staff.'

'Abigail would need to have a live-in post. All the orphans have to have live-in jobs.'

'I see.'

'There are the servants' old rooms in the attic.'

'Thank you, Miss Mason. I don't need reminding.'

'No, sir. I hope you'll keep Abigail in mind.'

'Well, I did ask whether you had any plans for Holly Lodge, didn't I?' Mr Peters remarked. 'I received criticism from all sides for taking you on. Some men laughed at me.' He paused. He didn't exactly smile, but his features softened. 'I am pleased to inform you, Miss Mason, that you have proved them wrong and I am formally confirming you in the post of manager of Holly Lodge.'

Jess let go a breath of pure relief. 'Thank you, Mr Peters. I thought Mr Thorpe was here because you were going to sack me.'

'On the contrary, I invited him so he could see you have my full backing. I take it you are happy to accept the post.' Now Mr Peters did smile.

Jess laughed. 'Yes – please.'

'Subject to the usual restrictions placed upon women,' added Mr Peters, 'but that goes without saying.'

Jess's spirits dropped like a stone. The usual restrictions. That meant no married women. She was about to start walking out with Tom... and she was in no doubt as to where it would lead. Was it wrong of her – was it selfish, unwomanly even, to want both?

Mr Peters stood up. 'Shall we go and spread the good news?'

Jess felt overwhelmed. Should she come clean right now? She ought to. It was the honest thing to do. But she would lose her wonderful job on the spot. The very best she could hope for would be to be allowed to stay on while Mr Peters found a replacement – a male replacement – for her. She couldn't bear the thought of that.

'Come along, Miss Mason.' Mr Peters was holding open the door.

Jess stood up, walking past him back to the sitting room, her mind whirling. Mr Peters shut the sitting room door and clapped his hands.

'Your attention, please, ladies and gentlemen. I have an announcement to make. Miss Mason has been on probation as the manager at Holly Lodge and today I have the pleasure of making her position permanent.'

Subject to the usual restrictions placed upon women. He didn't say that, but the words reverberated in Jess's mind. There was scattered clapping and the old boys called out their congratulations. Jess remembered how they had stood up for her and made sure she kept her job. Now their delight at her permanent appointment was there for all to see.

'I have to say she doesn't look all that thrilled about it,' said Captain Styles. 'What did you say to her, Mr Peters? Are you sure she knows she's got the job?'

'Of course she does,' said Mr Peters. 'I made myself perfectly clear. I always do.'

Jess stood where she was. Her shoulders had curved beneath the weight of her disappointment and she forced them to straighten. She made herself smile, but had to blink away tears.

Tom stood up and came over to where Jess and Mr Peters were standing. Was he about to congratulate her? Instead he sank onto one knee and a soft gasp travelled all round the room as everyone sat up straighter. Jess's heart sank. This was what she wanted, but not here, not now, not in these circumstances.

'I think you all know what I'm going to do,' Tom said clearly. 'I'm going to propose. No – don't step aside, Mr Peters. The proposal I have to make is directed at you.'

'At me?' Mr Peters sounded flummoxed.

'Yes, sir,' said Tom, looking at him. 'And it is a proposal; hence the bended knee. My proposal is this. I love Jess Mason and she loves me, but if I marry her, you'll throw her out of her job – the job she loves and urgently wants to continue in.'

'Married women—' Mr Peters began.

'Please,' said Tom. 'Hear me out. What I propose is this. You want Jess as the manager of Holly Lodge and I want her as my wife. Therefore I'll gladly move into the basement flat in Holly Lodge and that will be our matrimonial home. I think you'll find there are far worse people to have living on the premises than a builder. You can be sure that all repairs and so forth will be taken care of without delay. And you'll also have the peace of mind that will come with knowing that Holly Lodge couldn't possibly have a more caring or more committed manager to watch over the residents and ensure they are well cared for. That's my proposal to you, Mr Peters. What do you say?'

'I say, get to your feet, sir,' said Mr Peters, but Tom stayed put. 'I say that what you suggest flies in the face of tradition and common sense.'

'It is unusual, I agree,' said Tom, 'but that doesn't make it wrong or inappropriate. You'll never find a better manager than Jess and you know it; and I'll never find a better wife.'

'I'm sorry,' Mr Peters said gruffly. 'It isn't possible. The place of married women is in the home, not at work.'

'Excuse me,' said Mrs Peters in a crisper voice than Jess had previously heard from her, 'but what does that make me? The cat's mother? I've worked in Oak Lodge ever since the day it opened. In fact, I worked here before that, because I helped to get it ready, so don't tell me that a woman's place is in the home or I'll jolly well go straight upstairs to our flat and put my feet up.'

'My dear—' Mr Peters began.

'I mean it,' she retorted. 'Miss Mason – or may I call you Jess, dear? Only you are young enough to be my daughter. Jess has worked jolly hard in Holly Lodge and she's full of ideas for its future. I think she'll make a splendid manager and she'll make a splendid wife too. She's perfectly capable of doing both – just like I have all these years.'

Mr Peters opened and closed his mouth a few times. 'You aren't the manager here, my dear.'

'No, I'm just the cook and the housekeeper. I'm just the person who makes sure there are meals on the table and the house is spick and span. I'm the person who talks to the gardener about growing flowers for the dining table and keeps the household accounts. Have you ever had cause to question my ability to add up what we owe the butcher and the coal merchant? I might not be the manager, but I'd like to see how you'd get on without me. I mean it, Arthur. I've done everything I can to support you and keep our lovely old men happy, well fed and comfortable, and because I'm a woman and I don't have a fancy job title, nobody notices. I'm just part of the furniture.'

'My dear Rosalind, I'm sure your efforts are deeply appreciated,' said Mr Peters and there were murmurs around the sitting room as the old men agreed.

'Nonsense!' exclaimed Mrs Peters. 'The thing about being a woman is that when you do things right and make things run smoothly, everyone takes it for granted. Well, it's time I had some recognition. This is the twentieth century, not the Victorian age. I want to be the deputy manager here and I want Jess to be the manager over at Holly Lodge, and whether she chooses to get married is her business and nobody else's.'

'Well,' said Mr Peters. There was a pause and he said again, 'Well.'

His wife took his arm. 'It could be worse, Arthur,' she said with a smile. 'I could ask to be joint manager.'

Mr Peters placed a hand over his wife's. 'I never meant you to feel unappreciated.'

'I know. All I'm saying is, it's time for a change. You've already decided to have a lady manager at Holly Lodge in spite of what everyone will say. Why not have a married lady manager? That'll really give your cronies something to talk about! You and I both know that Jess will prove them wrong.'

At last Mr Peters nodded. 'Very well. I agree.'

'Don't say it like that, Arthur, as if it's against your better judgement. Say it kindly and generously. Say it the way you're going to say it to all the local businessmen and hoteliers.

You can't have them thinking you have doubts. Say it with conviction.'

Mr Peters stood taller. 'Very well. Miss Mason, my wife has been a great support to me for many years and I have decided to heed her advice. I am pleased to repeat my offer to keep you on as manager of Holly Lodge and if you... that is to say...'

Still on one knee, Tom grinned from ear to ear. 'You and Mrs Peters are talking very freely about Jess being married, so I think I ought to make another proposal.' He took Jess's hand and looked up into her eyes. 'Jess Mason, you are the most wonderful girl I've ever met. I enjoy your company; I admire your devotion to your work; and more than anything, I feel as if I have met the other half of myself. I love you and I promise to take care of you for the rest of our lives. Please will you marry me?'

A feeling of warmth and excitement expanded inside Jess's chest and tears sprang into her eyes as she said, 'Yes.'

The room erupted into a burst of applause. Jess tugged at Tom's hand, wanting him to stand up so she could move into his arms, but he stayed where he was, using his other hand to delve in his pocket. Jess uttered a small gasp, lifting her hands to cover her mouth as he produced a ring box. When he opened it and held it up to her, Jess's hands dropped to her sides and her heart melted at the sight of a darkly glowing ruby with a diamond on either side of it.

Even though they were in a room filled with people, it was as if the two of them were alone. Although she could hear the clapping that surrounded them, all Jess cared about was that Tom came to his feet to slip the ring on her finger, then he held her in a warm embrace.

'Will you marry me, lovely Jess?' Tom whispered in a moment that felt utterly private.

'Yes, my darling Tom,' she whispered back and he lifted her chin and kissed her softly on the mouth, a gentle kiss full of promise.

Then eager hands drew them apart and they were passed around the room to be congratulated. Everyone shook Tom's hand and all the old soldiers kissed Jess on the cheek.

'Congratulations, my dear,' said Captain Wingate. 'This is the most exciting thing to happen here in a long time.'

'Congratulations,' Nancy whispered to her. 'Everyone says what a lovely man Tom Watson is. I've never heard a bad word about him.'

Even Mr Thorpe cleared his throat and offered congratulations.

When Tom and Jess were reunited, Tom took her hands and smiled at her.

'Thank you, Tom,' said Jess. 'Thank you for all of this. I wanted to marry you, but I wanted to keep my job as well, and you've made it possible.'

'Well, me and Mrs Peters. She came up trumps, didn't she? I never expected that.'

Jess gazed lovingly into the face of the man she adored. 'Life can't be better than this.'

Tom lowered his head so he was speaking into her ear, the words for her alone. 'Yes, it can. When you're Mrs Tom Watson, it'll be even better – for always.'

Acknowledgements

I loved telling Jess and Tom's story and I'd like to thank everyone who made it possible, starting with my agent, Laura Longrigg; my editor, Hanna Kenne, whose thoughtful and perceptive comments made this a better book and who was a delight to work with; and the whole team at Corvus.

If you fell in love with this book's beautiful cover the moment you saw it, that's because Justinia Baird-Murray is a hugely talented designer; and if you felt a glow of satisfaction at what becomes of the house in Wilton Close at the end of this story, that's because Susannah Hamilton's idea of what to do with it was far better than mine.

Many thanks to Nicky Lovick, my copy-editor. Nicky, I still have no idea what 'invisibles' are, but thank goodness you solved the problem!

Thank you also to Jen Gilroy, Christina Banach, Jane Cable and Beverley Hopper, who all make the world of writing a good place to be.